STORM SURGE

DESTROYERMEN

DESTROYERMEN

STORM SURGE

TAYLOR ANDERSON

A ROC BOOK

ROC
Published by the Penguin Group
Penguin Group (USA) Inc., 375 Hudson Street,
New York, New York 10014, USA

USA | Canada | UK | Ireland | Australia | New Zealand | India | South Africa | China

Penguin Books Ltd., Registered Offices: 80 Strand, London WC2R 0RL, England
For more information about the Penguin Group visit penguin.com.

First published by Roc, an imprint of New American Library,
a division of Penguin Group (USA) Inc.

First Printing, July 2013
10 9 8 7 6 5 4 3 2

RoC REGISTERED TRADEMARK—MARCA REGISTRADA

LIBRARY OF CONGRESS CATALOGING-IN-PUBLICATION DATA:

Anderson, Taylor.
  Storm surge/Taylor Anderson.
    p. cm.—(Destroyermen)
  ISBN 978-0-451-46513-9
  1. Imaginary wars and battles—Fiction. 2. Destroyers (Warships)—Fiction. 3. Alternative
histories (Fiction) 4. Science fiction. I. Title.
  PS3601.N5475S76   2013
  813'.6—dc23   2012050859

Set in Minion
Designed by Alissa Amell

Printed in the United States of America

To:

My mother, Jeanette Anderson

A swell dame

ACKNOWLEDGMENTS

Again, I must thank my friend and agent, Russell Galen, as well as the utterly delightful Ginjer Buchanan and all the great folks at Roc. Otherwise, I'll keep this one short since all the "usual suspects" know who they are—as do all those who have joined us on this adventure by now, for better or worse! Ha! I *would* like to throw out a very special thank-you to those who were so steadfast and supportive during a really tough time. They know who they are as well. Adversity does tend to put things in perspective, but it also often reveals the many blessings we take for granted. Since I count my true friends and family among my very greatest blessings, I am a fortunate man indeed. Oh, and for those who crave the usual hint regarding the latest ridiculous thing to "happen" to Jim, propriety must prevail this time. All I can say is that it was, again, wildly—painfully—amusing for most concerned.

CAST OF CHARACTERS

(The following does not necessarily reflect initial or even final deployments, but only those most pertinent to the events described.)

See the back of the book for a list of ships and specifications.

Note:

(L)—*Lemurians, or Mi-Anaaka, are bipedal, somewhat felinoid creatures with large eyes, fur, and expressive but nonprehensile tails. They are highly intelligent, social, and dexterous, and inhabit a variety of regions, but are concentrated in and around the Malay Barrier. It has been proposed that they are descended from the giant lemurs of Madagascar.*

(G)—*Grik, or Ghaarrichk'k, are bipedal reptilians reminiscent of various Mesozoic dromaeosaurids. Covered with fine downy fur, the males develop bristly crests and tail plumage, and retain formidable teeth and claws. Grik society consists of two distinct classes: the ruling, or industrious, Hij, and the worker-warrior Uul. The basic Grik-like form is ubiquitous, and serves as a foundation for numerous unassociated races and species.*

x

Members of the Grand Alliance

USS *Walker* (DD-163)

Lt. Cmdr. Matthew Patrick Reddy, USNR—Commanding. CINCAF—(Commander in Chief of All Allied Forces).

Cmdr. Brad "Spanky" McFarlane—Exec. Minister of Naval Engineering.

Lt. Tab-At (L)—Engineering Officer.

Courtney Bradford—Australian "naturalist" and engineer; "Minister of Science" for the Grand Alliance and Plenipotentiary at Large.

Chief Quartermaster Patrick "Paddy" Rosen—Acting First Officer.

Lt. Sonny Campeti—Gunnery Officer.

Cmdr. Bernard Sandison—Torpedo Officer and Minister of Experimental Ordnance.

Lt. Ed Palmer—Signals.

Chief Bosun Fitzhugh Gray—Chief Bosun of the Navy and Damage Control Officer. Highest ranking NCO in the Alliance and commander of the Captain's Guard.

Gunner's Mate Pak-Ras-Ar, "Pack Rat" (L)

Jeek (L)—Flight Crew Chief, Special Air Division.

Earl Lanier—Cook.

Johnny Parks—Machinist's Mate.

Juan Marcos—Officers' Steward.

Wallace Fairchild—Sonarman, Anti-Mountain Fish Countermeasures (AMF-DIC).

Min-Sakir, "Minnie" (L)—Bridge Talker.

Chief Engineer Isak Rueben—One of the "original" Mice.

Cmdr. Simon Herring—Chief of Strategic Intelligence.

Lance Corporal Ian Miles—Formerly in Second of the Fourth Marines; assigned to Bernard Sandison.

USS *Mahan* (as rebuilt)

Cmdr. Perry Brister—Commanding; Minister of Defensive and Industrial Works.

Lt. (jg) Jeff Brooks—Sonarman, Anti-Mountain Fish Counter-measures (AMF-DIC).

Lt. (jg) Rolando "Ronson" Rodriguez—Chief Electrician.

Taarba-Kar, "Tabasco" (L)—Cook.

Chief Bosun's Mate Carl Bashear

Ensign Johnny Parks—Engineering Officer.

Ensign Paul Stites—Gunnery Officer.

USS *Respite Island* (SPD-1)—Self-Propelled Dry Dock #1.

MTB-Ron-1 (Motor Torpedo Boat Squadron #1) 10xMTB's (#s 4-14).

Lt. (jg) Winston "Winny" Rominger—Former carpenter's mate 3rd; head of the PT project; 1st Allied Raider Brigade.

Chack-Sab-At (L)—Commanding; Bosun's Mate (Lt. Colonel).

Major Alistair Jindal—Imperial Marine and Chack's exec.

Captain Risa Sab-At (L)—Chack's sister.

First Fleet

Admiral Keje-Fris-Ar (L)—(CINCWEST).

Indiaa

Allied Expeditionary Force (North)—Within "Alden's Perimeter" around Lake Flynn and in the Rocky Gap.

General of the Army and Marines Pete Alden—Commanding; former sergeant in USS *Houston* Marine contingent.

I Corps

General Lord Muln-Rolak (L)—Commanding.

Hij-Geerki—Rolak's "pet" Grik, captured at Rangoon.

1st (Galla) Division

General Taa-leen (L)—Commanding.

Colonel Enaak (L) (5th Maa-ni-la Cavalry)—Exec.

1st Marines, 5th, 6th, 7th, 10th Baalkpan

2nd Division

General Rin-Taaka-Ar (L)—Commanding.

Major Simon (Simy) Gutfeld (3rd Marines)—Exec.

1st, 2nd Maa-ni-la, 4th, 6th, 7th Aryaal

II Corps

General Queen Safir Maraan (L)—Commanding.

3RD DIVISION

General Daanis (L)—Commanding.

Colonel Mersaak (L)—"The 600" (B'mbaado regiment composed of Silver and Black Battalions)—Exec 3rd Baalkpan, 3rd, 10th B'mbaado, 5th Sular.

5TH DIVISION

Captain Saachic (L)—Commanding.

Includes remnants of First Amalgamated (Flynn's Rangers), 1st Battalion, 2nd Marines, 6th Maa-ni-la Cavalry, 1st Sular (about 140 total effectives).

6TH DIVISION

General Grisa—Commanding.

5th, 6th B'mbaado, 1st, 2nd, 9th Aryaal, 3rd Sular*, 3rd Maa-ni-la Cavalry

III Corps

General Faan-Ma-Mar (L)—Commanding.

9TH & 11TH DIVISIONS COMPOSED OF THE 2ND, 3RD MAA-NI-LA, 8TH BAALKPAN, 7TH & 8TH MAA-NI-LA, 10TH ARYAAL

Lt. Mark Leedom—COFO, 5th & 8th Bomb Squadrons and 6th Pursuit Squadron from *Humfra-Dar* (remains of Second Naval Air Wing) attached; also 1st and 3rd Bomb Squadrons and 2nd Pursuit Squadron from *Salissa* (CV-1).

Ceylon

Mackey Field—Near Trin-con-lee. 3rd Pursuit Squadron (P-40E's) Army Air Corps.

Colonel Ben Mallory—Commanding.

Lt. (jg) Suaak-Pas-Ra "Soupy" (L)

Lt. Conrad Diebel

2nd Lt. Niaa-Saa "Shirley" (L)

Staff Sergeant Cecil Dixon

Off Madras

Salissa Battlegroup

USNRS *Salissa* "Big Sal" (CV-1)

Admiral Keje-Fris-Ar (L)—(CINCWEST)

Adar (L)—COTGA (Chairman of the Grand Alliance) and High Chief and Sky Priest of Baalkpan.

Atlaan-Fas (L)—Commanding.

Lt. Sandy Newman—Exec.

Nurse Lt. Sandra Tucker Reddy—Minister of Medicine and wife of Captain Reddy.

Diania—Steward's Assistant.

General Linnaa-Fas-Ra—12th Division.

First Naval Air Wing

Captain Jis-Tikkar "Tikker" (L)—COFO (Commander of Flight Operations); 2nd Bomb Squadron and 1st Pursuit Squadron remain on *Salissa* (CV-1) after damage.

Arracca Battlegroup

USNRS *Arracca* (CV-3)

Captain Tassana-Ay-Arracca (L)—Commanding; High Chief.

Fifth Naval Air Wing

Frigates (DDs) attached: *(Des-Ron 9)*

USS *Kas-Ra-Ar***

Captain Mescus Ricum (L)—Commanding.

USS *Ramic-Sa-Ar**

USS *Felts***

USS *Naga****

USS *Bowles****

USS *Saak-Fas****

USS *Clark***

TF (Task Force) Ellis

Commodore Jim Ellis

USS *Santa Catalina* (CAP-1)

Lt. Cmdr. Russ Chapelle—Commanding.

Lt. Michael "Mikey" Monk—Exec.

Lt. (jg) Dean Laney—Engineering Officer.

Surgeon Cmdr. Kathy McCoy

Stanley "Dobbin" Dobson—Chief Bosun's Mate.

S-19

Lt. Irvin Laumer—Commanding.

Midshipman Nathaniel Hardee

Danny Porter—Chief of the Boat.

Motor Machinist's Mate Sandy Whitcomb

Frigates (DDs) attached: *(Des-Ron 6)*

USS *Haakar-Faask***

Lt. Cmdr. Niaal-Ras-Kavaat (L)—Commanding.

USS *Nakja-Mur**

Captain Jarrik-Fas (L)—Commanding.

USS *Tassat***

Cmdr. Muraak-Saanga (L)—Commanding; former *Donaghey*
exec. and sailing master.

USS *Scott****

Cmdr. Cablaas-Rag-Lan (L)—Commanding.

TFG-2

TF (Task Force) Garrett-2

(Long Range Reconnaissance and Exploration)

USS *Donaghey* (DD-2)

Cmdr. Greg Garrett—Commanding.

Lt. Saama-Kera "Sammy" (L)—Exec.

Lt. (jg) Wendel "Smitty" Smith—Gunnery Officer.

Captain Bekiaa-Sab-At—Commanding Marines.

Baalkpan

Cmdr. Alan Letts—Chief of Staff, Minister of Industry and the Division of Strategic Logistics; acting Chairman of the Grand Alliance.

Cmdr. Steve "Sparks" Riggs—Minister of Communications and Electrical Contrivances.

Lord Bolton Forester—Imperial Ambassador.

Lt. Bachman—Forester's aide.

Surgeon Cmdr. Karen Theimer Letts—Assistant Minister of Medicine.

Pepper (L)—Black-and-white Lemurian keeper of the Castaway Cook (Busted Screw).

Leading Seaman Henry Stokes, HMAS *Perth*—Assistant Director of Office of Strategic Intelligence.

Army and Naval Air Corps Training Center (Kaufman Field) Baalkpan

Lt. Walt "Jumbo" Fisher—Commanding.

4th & 7th Bomb Squadrons, and 4th & 5th Pursuit in extra training

Corps of Discovery

Ensign Abel Cook—Commanding.

Chief Gunner's Mate Dennis Silva

Lawrence "Larry the Lizard"—Orange-and-brown tiger-striped Grik-like ex-Tagranesi (Sa'aaran).

Surgeon Lt. Pam Cross

Imperial Midshipman Stuart Brassey

Gunnery Sgt. Arnold Horn—USMC; formerly of the 4th Marines (US).

Moe the Hunter

Pokey—"Pet" Grik brass-picker.

Also 6 Lemurian Marines and 2 more "tame" Grik.

Fil-pin Lands

Saan-Kakja (L)—High Chief of Maa-ni-la and all the Fil-pin Lands.

Meksnaak (L)—High Sky Priest of Maa-ni-la.

Chinakru—Ex-Tagranesi, now colonial governor of Samaar.

General Ansik-Talaa (L)—Fil-pin Scouts.

Colonel Busaa (L)—Coastal artillery; commanding Advanced Training Center (ATC).

Respite Island

Governor Radcliff

Emelia Radcliff

Lt. Busbee—Cutter pilot.

Bishop Akin Todd

New Britain Isles

Governor-Empress Rebecca Anne McDonald

Sean "O'Casey" Bates—Prime Factor and Chief of Staff for G-E.

Lt. Ezekial Krish—Assistant to Mr. Bates.

Lord High Admiral James Silas McLain III (relieved)

HIMS *Ulysses, Euripides, Tacitus*—Completing repairs.

Allied Assets/New Britain Isles

Sister Audry—Benedictine nun, and new Allied Ambassador.

"Lord" Sgt. Koratin (L)—Marine protector and advisor to Sister Audry.

USS *Simms****—Fil-pin-built; under repair.

Lt. Ruik-Sor-Raa (L)—Commanding.

USS *Pinaa-Tubo*—Ammunition ship.

Lt. Radaa-Nin (L)—Commanding.

Eastern Sea Campaign

High Admiral Harvey Jenks—(CINCEAST)

Enchanted Isles:

Sir Thomas Humphries—Imperial Governor of Albermarl.

Colonel Alexander—Garrison commander.

Second Fleet

USS *Maaka-Kakja* (CV-4)

Admiral Lelaa-Tal-Cleraan (L)—Commanding.

Lt. Tex "Sparks" Sheider—Exec.

Gilbert Yeager—Engineer (one of the original Mice).

3rd Naval Air Wing

(9th, 11th, 12th Bomb Squadrons, and 7th, 10th Pursuit Squadrons (30 planes assembled, 30 unassembled).

2nd Lt. Orrin Reddy—COFO.

Sgt. Kuaar-Ran-Taak "Seepy" (L)—Reddy's backseater.

2nd Fleet DDs (of note)

USS *Mertz****

USS *Tindal****

USS *Finir-Pel****

Lt. Haan-Sor-Plaar (L)—Commanding.

HIMS *Achilles*

Lt. Grimsley—Commanding.

HIMS *Icarus*

Lt. Parr—Commanding.

USS *Pecos*—Fleet oiler.

USS *Pucot*—Fleet oiler.

2nd Fleet Expeditionary Force: (X Corps) 4 regiments Lemurian Army and Marines, 2 regiments Frontier troops, 5 regiments Imperial Marines (3 Divisions) w/artillery train.

General Tamatsu Shinya—Commanding.

Colonel James Blair

Major Dao Iverson—Commanding Second Battalion, 6th Imperial Marines.

Nurse Cmdr. Selass-Fris-Ar (L)—"Doc'Selass"; daughter of Keje-Fris-Ar.

Captain Blas-Ma-Ar "Blossom" (L)—Commanding 2nd Battalion, 2nd Marines.

Spon-Ar-Aak "Spook" (L)—Gunner's Mate, and 1st Sergeant of A Company, 2nd Battalion, 2nd Marines.

Lt. Staas-Fin "Finny" (L)—C Company, 2nd Battalion, 8th Maa-ni-la.

Lt. Faal-Pel "Stumpy" (L)—A Company, 1st Battalion, 8th Maa-ni-la; former ordnance striker.

Allied Fugitives in the Dominion

Lt. (jg) Fred Reynolds—Special Air Division, USS *Walker*.

Ensign Kari-Faask (L)—Reynolds's friend and backseater.

Characters in and from the Republic of Real People

Emperor (Kaiser) Nig-Taak

Kapitan Adler Von Melhausen—Commanding SMS *Amerika*.

General Marcus Kim—Military High Command.

Inquisitor Kon-Choon—Director of Spies.

Kapitan Leutnant Becker Lange—Von Melhausen's exec.

Leutnant Doocy Meek—British sailor and former POW (WWI).

Lt. Toryu Miyata—Defected ambassador from Kurokawa and the Grik.

Enemies

General of the Sea Hisashi Kurokawa—Formerly of Japanese Imperial Navy battle cruiser *Amagi*; self-proclaimed regent and "sire" of all India.

General Orochi Niwa—Advising Grik.

"General of the Sky" Hideki Muriname

"Lieutenant of the Sky" Iguri—Muriname's exec.

Signals Lt. Fukui

Cmdr. Riku—Ordnance.

Captain Kurita—Commanding *Hidoiame*.

Grik (Ghaarrichk'k)

Celestial Mother—Absolute, godlike ruler of all the Grik, regardless of the relationships between the various Regencies.

Tsalka—Imperial Regent-Consort and Sire of all India.

N'galsh—Viceroy of India and Ceylon.

The Chooser—Highest member of his order at the Court of the Celestial Mother; prior to current policy, "choosers" selected those destined for life—or the cook pots—as well as those eligible for elevation to Hij status.

General Esshk—First General of all the Grik.

General Halik—Elevated Uul sport fighter.

General Ugla, General Shlook—Promising Grik leaders under Halik's command.

Holy Dominion

His Supreme Holiness, the Messiah of Mexico, and, by the Grace of God, Emperor of the World—"Dom Pope" and absolute ruler.

Don Hernan DeDivino Dicha—Blood Cardinal and former Dominion ambassador to the Empire of the New Britain Isles.

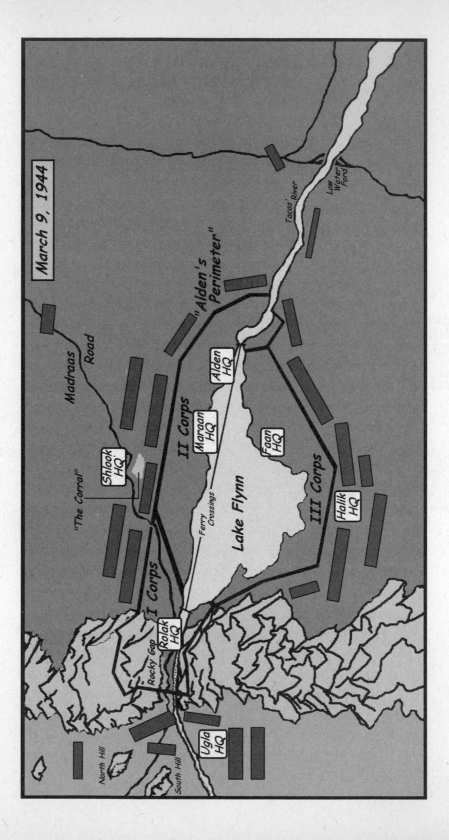

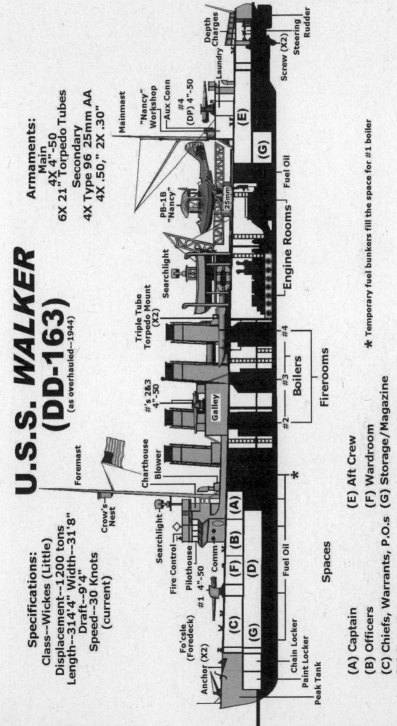

U.S.S. WALKER (DD-163)
(as overhauled--1944)

Specifications:
Class--Wickes (Little)
Displacement--1200 tons
Length--314'4" Width--31'8"
Draft--9'4"
Speed--30 Knots
(current)

Armaments:
Main
4X 4"-50
6X 21" Torpedo Tubes
Secondary
4X Type 96 25mm AA
4X .50," 2X .30"

* Temporary fuel bunkers fill the space for #1 boiler

Spaces

(A) Captain
(B) Officers
(C) Chiefs, Warrants, P.O.s
(D) Fore Crew
(E) Aft Crew
(F) Wardroom
(G) Storage/Magazine

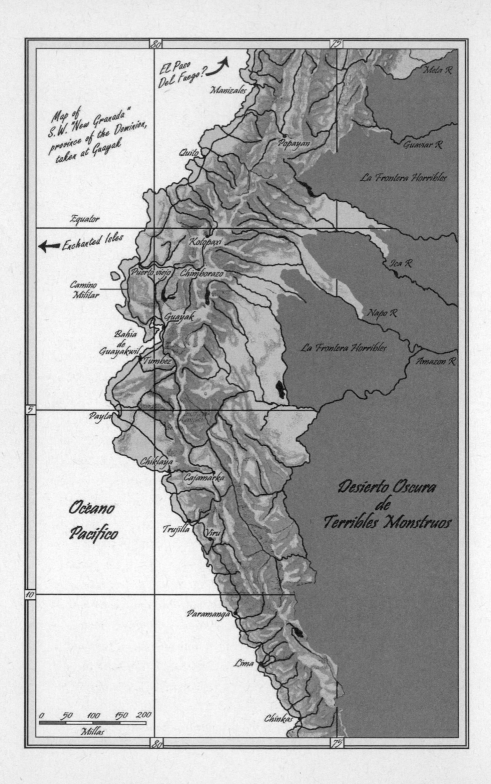

Map of
S.W. "New Granada"
province of the Dominion,
taken at Guayak

El Paso
Del Fuego? ↗

Manizales

Popayan

Quito

La Frontera Horribles

Meta R

Guaviar R

Equator

← Enchanted Isles

Kotopaxi

Ica R

Puerto viejo   Chimborazo

Camino
Mililar

Guayak

Napo R

Bahia
de
Guayakwil

Tumbez

La Frontera Horribles

Amazon R

5

Payta

Chiklaya

Cajamarka

Desierto Oscura
de
Terribles Monstruos

Océano

Pacifico

Trujilla   Viru

10

Paramanga

Lima

Chinkas

0   50   100   150   200
Millas

Species mimicking the physiology and behavior of flatworms are abundant on this world, as are leeches, mosquitoes, etc., so the familiar can certainly be found. Other creatures defy comparisons through relentless evasion or self-indulgent aggression. I'm struck, however, by how some apparently related species can exhibit such profound elemental similarities yet share so few behavioral or even physical characteristics. The Grik, or Grik-like beings, are prominent examples.

The Sa'aaran Lawrence, was our first confirmation that the Grik-like form is the dominant advanced physiology on this world, yet we subsequently learned the form lent itself to the most amazing variety and adaptation—or environmental evolution, if you will. We now know there are land Grik, flying Grik, amphibious Grik, and every other kind of Grik in between. Just as astonishing was our discovery that the Grik form is by no means culturally—or intellectually—monolithic. This created considerable confusion at the time, but also gifted me with a vast new sphere of speculation.

Given the multiplicity of adjustments the Grik form has achieved, is it possible that some levels of intelligence are more favorable to physical evolution than others? I'm convinced that humans and Lemurians attained technological sentience, for lack of a better term, far earlier than any Grik-like species yet encountered. Both adapted to environmental survival imperatives by employing intellectually devised tools. But the Grik-like forms apparently lingered at what I consider a "wolf-pack" level of sentience far longer, due to a superior, if more specialized, physiology. Sentient in the sense that they had some concept of self, social graduation, and perhaps "us versus them," they exploded in all directions and swiftly, physically changed to fill a variety of ecological niches.

Ridiculous? Perhaps, but such precipitous transformations are not unique. It is theorized that viruses spontaneously mutate in such a way. I remember the dreadful influenza outbreak at the end of the Great War all too well. It had to come from somewhere, and unless it simply popped into existence, it must have quickly changed from a relatively benign form into perhaps the most universally virulent disease of modern times. Pray God nothing like it ever appears here.

I shouldn't compare Grik-like forms to viruses, though some seem just as deadly. I certainly mean no offense to my dear friend Lawrence. I only mean to illustrate the possibility of dramatic, stunningly rapid change, in the grand scheme of things. I know little of microbiology and nothing of what mechanisms influence viral mutations, but I doubt they can transform more advanced forms so readily. I am compelled to speculate.

Minor physical adaptations occur in complex species all the time. Feral pigs quickly dominate lands that cannot cope with them, and grow indistinguishable from their wild ancestors over very few generations. (The "Holy" Dominion could serve as a human analogy to this from a societal perspective. Even technologically, they remained stagnant at best. Only their numbers and competition with the Empire of the New Britain Isles left them military parity. Otherwise, the sum of their culture had become more primitive and barbarous than any contributing component part.) In both instances, Doms and feral pigs, this is not evolution, but reversion to a previously realized form—if the pigs of this world and the last will forgive the comparison.

Imagine, however, the influence an insistent environmental imperative might have on a midrange intellect that perceives a requirement for profound adaptation on a subconscious level but cannot make the essential intellectual leap to achieve it by intuitive creativity. In other words, is it possible for a species to wish strongly enough that it can fly, for example, while lacking the intellect to recognize a fully formed desire to do so, that it might accelerate a physical adaptation? A less intelligent creature might plod along to eventual extinction. Greater intelligence might find a way around the need to fly—or construct an artificial means of doing so. But what of the species that wants to fly so badly, to escape danger or reach inaccessible food sources, that it tries for generations in spite of a physical inability? Might not an ineffectual leap eventually be combined with flapping arms? Might not, let us say, already somewhat feathery Grik-like creatures with superior plumage gain more height and duration of suspension, thereby achieving social acclaim, and be rewarded with breeding opportunities? Would not such societal encouragement result in more rapid, physical evolution than is possible for species without similar intelligence or incentive?

Warfare accelerates technological development. This is a fact observed even in the Dominion, where literacy was repressed to an almost Grik-like extent. The instinct to survive stimulates creativity like no other force. Might this not be seen as artificially accelerated intellectual evolution?

Once, in a moment of despair, I proclaimed the Grik the logical evolutionary masters of this world. That analysis was based on their physical perfection; hyperspecialized to kill, and what I imagined then as their almost antlike discipline and disregard of self. I was wrong. I now believe the Lemurians, with no assistance from us at all, should have eventually prevailed. It might have taken a thousand years, but their creative lethality would have surpassed the physical lethality of the Grik, whose very specialized physiology would have become a disadvantage.

All Grik-like forms evolved as apex physical predators, but the very attributes that make them so deadly with tooth and claw make it difficult for them to use, build, or even imagine the increasingly sophisticated weapons Lemurians could have made—eventually—to kill them. Sadly, however, just as the destroyermen of USS Walker and others came to aid the Lemurians, some Japanese survivors of Amagi aided the Grik. Not only did this accelerate the confrontation, but it created a technological parity that would never have existed otherwise, in my opinion. Perhaps I am mistaken again. The Grik are obviously capable of intellectual evolution, and if my notion of societally accelerated physical evolution has any merit at all, I suppose they could have found a way.

Ultimately however, technology can take you only so far—at least until your ability to apply it catches up. I'm often reminded of the battle at Isandlwana during the late Zulu wars—where all the bravery and technological advantage in the world could not prevail over sheer numbers, determination . . . and sharp objects.

—Courtney Bradford, *The Worlds I've Wondered*
University of New Glasgow Press, 1956

////// *Maa-ni-la Navy Yard*
Fil-pin Lands
March 9, 1944

L ieutenant Commander Matthew Reddy, High Chief of the Amer-i-caan Clan, Supreme Commander (by acclamation) of All Forces United Beneath (or Be-side) the Banner of the Trees, and Captain of the old Asiatic Fleet four-stacker destroyer USS *Walker* (DD-163), loved baseball. He loved football too, and just about any team sport, as a matter of fact, but unlike many of the dwindling survivors of *Walker*, *Mahan*, and the old subma-rine S-19 on this world, he'd never closely followed the professional va-riety. He couldn't recite team rosters or quote stats. He didn't much care about all that and never had. He *did* care about the ball games between the various ships' teams, however, and today his *Walker*s were playing the "Eastern League" champs from the Fil-pin shipyards: the Inaa Araang, or, roughly, "Rivet Drivers."

For just a while, Matt's anxious mind could concentrate on something besides the vast war raging across the known reaches of this "other" earth. He could suppress his revulsion over the treachery and barbarism on the eastern front across the broad Pacific, or Eastern Sea. He could worry about something less tragic than the dreadful losses and strategic setbacks plaguing the war in the west. He could let his own plans—and painful wounds—sink back away from his foremost consciousness, if only for a brief rejuvenating spell. For a few hours, he could enjoy himself and all the people around him, human or Lemurian, who took the same pleasure and comfort from an admittedly serious contest, but one not designed to end in slaughter.

The big game was underway in the main Maa-ni-la ballpark (one of three), in what had become the heart of the city. Once the area had been a kind of buffer between the city and its already impressive shipyards, almost a Central Park like Matt remembered in Manhattan. It was unlike the similar zone in Baalkpan, though, that pulsed with a never-ending bazaar. The closest thing in that distant city was the Parade Ground around Baalkpan's Great Hall, which had become a peaceful refuge for those come to visit the war dead buried there. Again like Central Park, this had been a common area anyone could visit and use. The same still applied, but now there was a dirt diamond and impressive bleachers. The seats were protected by a backstop of woven wire from the new barbed-wire works—minus the barbs—and there was no wall on the far end of the field, just a chalky line no one dared cross on pain of eviction. Still, just as many Lemurians clambered for good spots beyond the outfield, hoping to catch one of the still-rare balls, as did those who packed the bleachers.

It was a full house, and even the area around the ballpark was packed. Matt had grown accustomed to surrealistic scenes on this earth, but this was really weird. He was watching a genuine *baseball game*, played mostly by very feline-looking creatures covered with fur of every color or combination of colors imaginable. The sea of spectators reacted as any baseball crowd would, even if they were just as wildly colored and the sounds weren't exactly right. Beyond the crowd, the shipyard had grown to a sprawling, all-encompassing thing no buffer zone could

ever tame again. Masts of ships and coiling smoke and steam from
mighty engines practically blotted out any view of Maa-ni-la Bay or distant Corregidor, and the Maara-vella Advanced Training Center, or
ATC, couldn't be seen at all.

Matt knew the city behind him had expanded just as much. Already
bigger and more populous than Baalkpan, Maa-ni-la had exploded. Initially flooded with "runaways"—people from other lands and seagoing
Homes threatened by the ravening Ancient Enemy (the furry/feathery,
reptilian Grik) who only wanted to escape the war—there'd been some . . .
difficulty when Maa-ni-la joined the Grand Alliance. Most eventually
realized they'd have to fight sooner or later, because after the Fil-pin
Lands there was nowhere else to flee. This grew even more apparent
when they discovered new allies across the great Eastern Sea—but more
enemies as well. There were few "runaways" left, and, bolstered by its
industry and broader resource and population base, all the Fil-pin
Lands, and Maa-ni-la in particular, became a powerhouse. Baalkpan,
where Balikpapan, Borneo, should have been, had done very well for itself as well and remained the "first city" of the Grand Alliance. But there
could be no *offensives* without Maa-ni-la—and its high chief, Saan-
Kakja.

Saan-Kakja was a remarkable Lemurian. Her black-and-gold stri-
ated eyes were utterly mesmerizing, and though still young for her job,
she'd taken hold with an iron hand of the chaotic mess the Fil-pin Lands
had been. Actually considered somewhat authoritarian for the tastes of
some Lemurians, she'd united and directed her Home toward member-
ship in the Grand Alliance. She'd done it without any personal ambition. She had no desire to lead anything but her own Home, and wanted
equality, not dominance, for her people—and, ultimately, for all people
everywhere. Given that ideal, Matt recognized she was worldly enough
to have ambition for her people. She wanted all who opposed the evil
Grik, and now the Dominion, to live free and prosper—but if her people
were a little more prosperous than others, that was okay by her.

Matt smiled at the Lemurian leader seated on the other side of Sandra. Sandra was his wife, doctor, primary advisor, and the Minister of
Medicine for the whole Alliance. Saan-Kakja grinned back, her perfect

young teeth sharp and white. She was *really* enjoying the game, Matt realized. Well, so was he. It had somewhat unexpectedly become a nail-biter.

Lemurians had taken to baseball like ducks to water. The game was superficially similar to an ancient 'Cat (Lemurian) game in which contestants whacked a lobbed coconutlike object with a long, flat bat, the object being to attain the greatest distance. That translated easily enough to baseball, but the added complexity, strategy, and teamwork appealed to them as well. Initially dismissed by humans—and themselves—as somewhat unimaginative (except when it came to architecture!), Lemurians discovered a love for strategy that rivaled their blossoming interest in gizmos. They related structured strategy with rigid rules—like chess, which was also catching on—to complicated machines, and they loved it. Lemurians universally excelled when all the parts were there or all the pieces were on the table, but some—like Lt. Colonel Chack-Sab-At, his beloved General Queen Safir Maraan, General Lord Muln-Rolak, and even CINCWEST Keje-Fris-Ar, to some degree, were learning to use initiative and imagination.

Chack's plan for the reconquest of New Ireland had been good, but the way he'd reacted when it fell apart was actually rather brilliant, in Matt's opinion. With the exception of Safir and Rolak, there hadn't been any experienced Lemurian war leaders before the war, and there'd been an adjustment period while they had to shift mental gears as a people. Now quite a few 'Cats were starting to shine on the battlefield, quickly adjusting to unexpected situations and generally doing at least as well as any human commander might in the same situation. That was good, because their enemies were getting uncomfortably better too. Matt was proud, but still a little sad that it took this damn war to show the Lemurians their true potential.

A bat cracked and the crowd roared around him. Matt and Sandra had some of the best seats in the house, there with Saan-Kakja and her advisors. Still, as the others jumped up, Matt lost sight of the ball and tried to rise as well. A stabbing pain in his right thigh and lower abdomen put a stop to that—as did Sandra's restraining hand. *She knows me so well,* he thought, his inner smile masked by the grimace on his face.

"It's a line drive, right over the shortstop's head!" she said. "Yes! Pack Rat snagged it! She's out!"

Gunner's Mate Pak-Ras-Ar, or "Pack Rat," played left field and had a hell of an arm. He used it then, winging the ball home. The bloated catcher and ship's cook, Earl Lanier, took it on the bounce and only had to glare at the runner a step beyond third base before the 'Cat dove back at it. The stocky female Rivet Driver batter flipped her bat to the ground in disgust and strode sullenly to the dugout. Jeek, *Walker*'s small air division chief, was the 'Cat pitching for *Walker* that day. Her starting pitcher had been killed in action against the rogue Japanese destroyer *Hidoiame*, and Jeek had been designated his relief when they formed the team in the New Britain Isles. He was older and his fastball wasn't as strong, but with age came guile, and he might've been the first 'Cat in the Navy to master a curveball that struck like lightning. He grinned and waited for the next batter to approach the plate.

Understanding things like curveballs was one of the few things that kept humans competitive in the game they'd brought to this world. Lemurians generally had greater upper-body strength, particularly the former wing runners who came from the great seagoing Homes. They could throw and hit harder and farther. Humans were better sprinters, though, and their slightly quicker reflexes let them hit more of the high-velocity fastballs they always expected—even if they couldn't hit them as far. Far enough was good enough when the ball landed on the other side of the chalky line, however, and not every 'Cat who'd grown up with his or her own game thought that was quite fair. Human destroyermen were better at turning singles into doubles and triples too.

Right now, after a somewhat bitter game, the *Walker*s were magically only three runs down at the top of the ninth. That this seemed magical was because they'd had only a few days to prepare—and their most recent practice had been weeks before on Respite Island. The *Walker*s were also a "mixed" team, while the Rivet Drivers were all 'Cats, and that alone gave them an edge. They'd also had a *lot* of practice and were very, very good. The bitterness came from the age-old rivalry between "real" sailors and "yard apes" that was quickly transplanted here. Add the fact that USS *Walker* had been given priority over every ship in the yard, and her crew—particularly Tabby (Engineering Officer Lieutenant Tab-at), and *Walker*'s exec, Spanky McFarlane—had lorded it over everyone in the yard and criticized half the rivets they drove. That got *very* old, because in addition to repairing battle damage, they were basically reriveting the entire hull. The rivets used rebuilding *Walker* after the Battle of Baalkpan hadn't been satisfactory at all, and Spanky felt responsible. That made him short-tempered with himself and everyone else.

Despite the abuse, most of the yard apes thought *Spanky* had the right to be critical. He was Minister of Naval Engineering, and revered as a font of almost mystical wisdom. But Tabby had made quite the ranting pest of herself, and the yard apes had grown to resent her in spite of her obvious competence (and equally obvious beauty). Her fur had mostly covered the old steam scars, and those still visible to the crusty yard apes added an exotic dash to her appearance. Her appearance only went so far, however, and she wouldn't be satisfied with anything less than what she considered perfection. Even worse than Tabby, the weird little human Chief Isak Rueben had made everyone miserable with his shrill insistence that *Walker*'s ancient boilers come out of the yard even better than new. It was too much.

Adding insult to injury, even though the Rivet Drivers were the home team, the crowd's clear favorite was the team from USS *Walker*. Sure, they were heroes and they'd just been in *another* terrible fight, but that stung and made them want to punish the *Walkers*—only it wasn't working out that way. They led 9 to 6, but it should've been a blowout.

"It's all up to Jeek," Matt said. "If he can pick off this last batter, we might have a chance. Uh-oh."

Striding to the plate, his tail held high, a heavy bat twirling in his hand, was the Rivet Drivers' "cleanup" batter. He was the best they had, and with runners on first and third, all he needed was a hit to widen the gap.

Jeek watched him come and take his stance. He knew he'd allowed too many runs, but he'd had to pace himself. He *hoped* he'd saved his very best, sneakiest pitches for last. He blinked at Earl Lanier, and caught a nod in return. Even if Earl had ever taken time to learn 'Cat blinking, Jeek couldn't have seen his reply through the mask and helmet he wore. Finger signals hadn't been used before because all the pitchers were 'Cats, and so far all they knew to do was throw the ball like hell and hit the catcher's glove. Any finger signal then might've tipped off the batter that something new was on the way. Besides, they'd planned for this. Jeek's pair of blinks meant only "Okay," but they also told Earl to be ready.

Jeek wound up and launched. The ball looked way outside—until it veered right into Earl's waiting glove.

"Strike one!" cried Meksnaak. Saan-Kakja's High Sky Priest might not be as popular with his flock as those of other Lemurian leaders, but his impartiality in this new game he adored was beyond question. The batter blinked, trying to reconcile what he'd seen with the crack of the ball slapping the glove right in the center of the strike zone. He shook his head.

The next pitch came, and looked just like the first. For an instant, the Rivet Driver considered reaching for it, but let it pass.

"Strike two!"

The crowd was on its feet again, wondering what they were seeing. How could Jeek do such a thing?

"Help me up, wilya, honey?" Matt asked Sandra, and reluctantly his wife helped him to his feet.

"Lean on your cane, Matthew," she cautioned.

Jeek was staring hard at Lanier now, ball behind his back. To Matt it looked like he was wondering whether he could get away with the same pitch one more time. Finally, he wound up and let fly. With an audible *whoosh*, the Rivet Driver practically whirled out of the batter's box. Strike three! Now *Walker* was up!

The Rivet Drivers' pitcher was deadly accurate and as fast as a cannon shot. He also threw a little inside; his own "new" tactic he thought no one had noticed. Taarba-Kar (Tabasco), *Walker*'s assistant officer's steward, managed a single, but Chief Quartermaster Paddy Rosen and Chief Bosun's Mate Carl Bashear both struck out. Tabby got a pop-up single that the right fielder took on the bounce. Min-Sakir (Minnie), *Walker*'s diminutive (even for a 'Cat) bridge talker, almost had her head knocked off by a wild pitch; only her helmet saved her life. Due to the speed of the pitches and some of the hits, all batters and every infielder but the pitcher wore a combat helmet to play baseball on this world.

With a dazed Minnie making her way to first, the bases were loaded when Earl Lanier waddled to the plate.

"Oh no," Sandra muttered, and there was a collective groan. Earl was a good catcher and surprisingly quick, but his enormous gut was kind of in the way when it came to batting. "He shouldn't even be out there," Sandra said, a little hot. Earl's belly had been laid open pretty badly a few weeks before.

"He's okay," muttered Chief Bosun Fitzhugh Gray on the other side of Matt. Gray was past sixty and now officially Chief Bosun of the Navy. He was often referred to as Super Bosun, or just SB, but was even more than that to Matt and Sandra. He was their friend, and commanded the Captain's Guard. He took Matt's orders and served as chief damage control officer aboard ship, but was no longer confined to any normal chain of command. To Matt, he was just "Boats."

"He might split a seam, but it'll be worth it. Watch," Gray said.

"Well . . . but he's still on report for taking a swing at Campeti, isn't he?" Sandra demanded.

Matt shifted uncomfortably. "Uh, Campeti said it wasn't a swing after all. Lanier was just grabbing for something as he fell. The sea was pretty heavy."

Sandra glared at him, and he felt like squirming. "Campeti took it back!" he insisted. "What can I do? I didn't see what happened!"

"You're *in* on this! If he gets hurt . . ."

"Oh, he's *gonna* get hurt," Gray interrupted, rubbing his hands together in anticipation. "Think of it as takin' one for the team—for his sins," he added.

Earl suddenly struck a comically heroic pose by the plate and pointed upward at an angle of about 45 degrees past center field. The crowd roared and the bleachers thundered with stamping feet.

"Oh, my God," Sandra said, raking away a few sandy brown strands that had escaped her ponytail. "I can't watch!"

She watched.

Earl stepped into the box and pointed his bat at the pitcher. Then took a couple of grim practice swings before bringing the bat back, high, his fists behind his right ear.

The first pitch sizzled past and Meksnaak called it a strike. Earl stepped back, stunned.

"Scoot back up there an' take yer dose, you big, fat, turd!" came a nasally shout that reached them even over the thunder of the crowd. Isak Rueben was on deck, shaking his bat at the cook. Isak was one of the "original" Mice, two extraordinarily squirrely firemen who'd finally been forced to accept a wider—and different—world beyond their beloved fire rooms. The other original, Gilbert Yeager, was chief engineer on USS *Maaka-Kakja* (CV-4), off with the Second Fleet supporting operations around the Enchanted Isles. Tabby herself had been a third "mouse" before her promotion. Isak and Gilbert were half brothers—less of a secret than they thought—and they'd never been on the ship's baseball team before the Squall that brought them here. It wasn't because they weren't any good; they just didn't like anybody. Things were different now, of course, and if Isak still didn't much like anyone, he loved his old *Walker*. He'd play for *her*.

Lanier glared at Isak and yelled something back that Matt couldn't hear, but moved back in position, waving at the crowd. Finally, he was ready: bat high, helmet low, staring intently at the 'Cat pitcher. Here it came. In the mere instant the ball was in the air, Earl seemed to like what he saw. He started to swing, his great, fat body gaining momentum as it turned. The bat came around farther, faster, then stopped short as he checked the swing—just as the speeding ball vanished into his prodigious midsection. There was a stunned hush, until the ball popped out on the ground.

"Aaggghhh!" roared Earl, slamming the plate with his bat. "*Goddamn*, that hurt!"

Meksnaak took off his own helmet and stared at Earl, blinking amazed consternation. Then he saw the blood beginning to stain the tight, grungy T-shirt. Finally, he snorted and waved Earl toward first base.

"I can't believe he *did* that!" Sandra shouted in Matt's ear when the bleachers shook.

"What? You think he took a hit like that on *purpose*?" Matt hollered back. Saan-Kakja caught his eye, and he saw her amused blinking.

Tabasco trotted home—without notice by Meksnaak or the Rivet Drivers's catcher, who were both watching Earl lumber to first.

Isak Rueben shuffled to the plate. He was a little guy, wiry, almost scrawny. Most of the Rivet Drivers knew him well. He'd been flown in from Baalkpan to oversee the first steps of a scheduled overhaul on *Walker* even before the old destroyer limped in after her fight with *Hidoiame*, and he'd been driving them hard on other projects. No one thought he was a weakling, but he obviously wasn't a power hitter. They suspected he knew what he was doing, though, and the outfield moved in to prevent another scoring single.

Matt looked nervously at Gray, who stood with his arms crossed, wearing an expression of supreme confidence. Bashear was team captain, but Gray was the manager and chief strategist. Matt knew he'd conceived all sorts of schemes for this game to deal with any number of variables. One such was clearly unfolding now . . . but pinning all their hopes on Isak Rueben seemed a little nuts.

The first pitch blew past Isak and he just watched it go, as if studying it. He did the same for the second, and another huge groan rumbled in the park. The third pitch was way inside and probably would've shattered Isak's bony elbow if he hadn't jerked back. *Okay,* Matt thought, *Isak can read a pitch. But they can't be counting on a walk—not with this pitcher!* The fourth pitch came, and with a fluid, almost nonchalant ease, Isak Rueben slammed it high in the air and deep into the crowd behind the center-field line.

Matt looked at Gray, stunned, as the whole city of Maa-ni-la seemed to erupt. Gray shrugged. "I seen the squirt bat before," he shouted. "Back on Tarakan, after the fight with those three Grik ships. He was showin' some of the 'Cat Marines." He grinned. "I ain't sure Isak Rueben didn't *invent* baseball on this world!"

*　　*　　*

"A great victory!" Saan-Kakja gushed as their palka-drawn carriage and its me-naak-mounted guards churned through the busy streets toward the new industrial complex east of the city. There were seven in the carriage, counting the driver. Matt, Sandra, and Gray sat beside each other, facing Saan-Kakja, General Busaa of the coastal artillery, who now commanded the ATC, and the somewhat sullen Meksnaak. The driver, busy controlling his animal, said nothing.

Palkas, dubbed "pack mooses," looked like a cross between an overblown moose and a Belgian draft horse. They weren't fast, but they were strong and fairly steady under fire—much steadier than brontasarries. That made them perfect for pulling artillery, caissons, and virtually any combat-supply vehicle. They'd also eat just about any kind of vegetation. Me-naaks, or "meanies," were the preferred Maa-ni-lo cavalry mount, and looked like long-legged crocodiles. A thick thoracic case made them almost bulletproof. They were obedient, even devoted to their riders, but dangerously prone to snatch "snacks" as they trotted along, so their jaws were kept firmly secured.

"I don't know about that . . ." Sandra began.

"Of course it was!" Saan-Kakja insisted. "It showed our people that *Waa-kur*'s crew remains undaunted despite her injuries and losses. I cannot stress the importance of that enough! Also, it may perhaps boost the morale of your crew, Cap-i-taan Reddy, after the . . . inconclusive encounter with *Hidoiame*?"

"Didn't seem inconclusive to me," Gray grumbled. "And Spanky's sure the damn thing's done for."

"Still," Matt said. "We never *saw* her sink, and I know it nags the fellas. It nags me too." He raised a hand at all of them, particularly Sandra. "Hey! I'm not complaining. Spanky made the right call!" He nodded down at the wound that nearly killed him. "I was out of it. Hell, *Walker* was finished! We were like an old, beat-up mutt tangling with a mountain lion, but I'm still as confident as Spanky that we kicked *Hidoiame*'s ass. Even if we only gave as good as we got"—he nodded at Saan-Kakja—"we had someplace to run, to lick our wounds. *Hidoiame* and her murdering crew have *no place* to go that they could hope to reach, even if they somehow knew about the Japs helping the Grik." He shook his head. "Scouts haven't seen her, and we haven't overheard any transmissions. My bet is she's sunk or on an island beach somewhere, shot up and out of fuel, and her crew's busy cracking open those poison coconut things and slowly . . ." he stopped.

"Slowly shittin' theirselves to death," Gray finished with obvious satisfaction, "if you ladies'll excuse me."

The driver halted the palka in front of one of the largest wooden structures Matt had ever seen on land. It looked like a hangar for one of the old Navy's dirigibles. Even Grik zeppelins wouldn't need anything as big, since they were less than half the size of the ill-fated *Akron* and *Macon*. Standing near the building was a battery of smaller structures protecting boilers and direct steam generators. Matt reflected that the arrangement was a far cry from their first efforts at making electricity in Baalkpan not so very long ago, and the Lemurians deserved most of the credit. *Walker*'s own 25-kilowatt generators were direct steam drive, so the example was there, but their first domestic machines had been far cruder, more complicated belt-drive generators powered by reciprocating engines. They were already building the engines and hadn't had the machining capacity to make even the relatively simple turbines for the better generators back then. The 'Cats themselves changed that, and real turbine *engines* were in the works in Baalkpan now.

High Sky Priest Meksnaak was obviously thinking about the generators too, and blinked disapproval at the buildings protecting them. "I confess . . . discomfort over this invisible force called eleks-tricky we grow so dependent upon," he muttered. "It powers nearly everything now, particularly at this facility. The Sacred Scrolls themselves warn against placing faith in unseen forces other than the Maker."

"You can't see the wind," Sandra countered reasonably, "but it moves the great Homes. There's not much wind today, but you can feel it."

"But the wind is a *natural* thing, given by the Maker," Meksnaak insisted. "You build this eleks-tricky with machines!"

"*Electricity* is also made by the Maker," Matt countered, stressing the proper, less-sinister pronunciation. "Lightning's a prime example; it zaps down from the heavens all the time."

"And represents the Maker's *anger*," Meksnaak persisted. "I can think of no better reason not to fool about with it! Yet everything you build either makes or uses it!"

"A hand fan makes a wind," said Sandra. "Is that cooling breeze somehow dangerous?"

"A high wind can be most dangerous!"

Matt sighed and looked at Saan-Kakja. "Electricity's vital to our industry, and ultimately the whole war effort. Sure, we generate it, harness it, and bend it to our will, but it's not magic. We make it in much the same way the Maker generates it in the sky, only we make controlled amounts—and put it to use." He shook his head. "How exactly that's done is a question for engineers like Spanky, or the EMs Riggs and Ronson trained." He chuckled. "We didn't have electricity on Dad's ranch when I was growing up. We used oil lamps just like you. We had batteries for the radio and the car and trucks, but that was it. Little generators in the vehicles kept the batteries charged. Anyway, though I understand the basics, I'm no expert. I do know we wouldn't've had trucks or tractors or any number of things Dad needed around the place—things that gave him an edge—if electricity hadn't helped make them. We need electricity to gain and keep an edge in this damn war."

"We built many things before eleks-tricky came to us," Meksnaak grumbled.

"Sure, and Dad had a ranch before we had trucks and tractors—but it took ten times the labor to grow fodder, transport stock, haul hay and fencing . . . the list is endless. And that was just a ranch, not a war. To win the war we need to free up as much of our labor force as we can to fight—while still producing more of the tools to do it."

"Mr. Riggs explained it to me when I was in Baalkpan," Saan-Kakja interjected. "He was . . . frustrated with me, I think, but he likened electricity to the gaas-o-leen fuel for the 'Naan-cee' engines—and others now. Generating it is like refining the gaas-o-leen, while the wires carry it to the lights and machines like fuel lines—somehow—even though there is no hole. Changing or regulating the . . ." She paused, remembering. "The vol-taage," she said triumphantly, "is like metering the fuel to a machine engine, so only just enough can reach it. This . . . comparison helped me understand, though I remain unsure why two wires are needed. This ground, or dead, wire still confuses me." She smiled. "We Mi-Anaaka—Lemurians—understand machines. We are good with machines. This machinelike explanation was good for me." She peered at Meksnaak. "And elec-*tricity* is *not* invisible when it gets loose—or touches the dead wire somehow! It is like the lightning in the sky when that happens, so it is clearly running in the wires!"

"Huh," Gray said, getting in the spirit of the analogy. "Think of the ground wire as the igniter that lights the fuel inside the electric motor—or in the lightbulb! It acts like the ground when lightning strikes!"

Saan-Kakja smiled at him. The expression didn't extend across her face—'Cats didn't have near the range of facial movement as humans, but her exotic eyes twinkled. "Thank you, Mr. Gray!"

A broad inlet of the bay snaked up past the building, and a variety of interesting boats floated beside a pier. The small, two-seat PB-1B "Nancy" flying boats of one of Maa-ni-la's several patrol wings rested on wheeled trucks on a broad ramp by the water. Nancys were good little planes and had become the backbone of the Allied air arm. They looked like miniature PBY Catalinas, since that's what inspired their lines, but they'd proven themselves effective at many roles, from reconnaissance to dive bombing.

"Building our own 'bony blimps' now?" Gray asked, looking up at the building as they exited the carriage.

Saan-Kakja sneeze-chuckled. "That would be nuts," she said. "I have not seen the Grik zeppel-ins, but individually they are no match for any of our flying machines—now we have learned they are armed, and how to avoid their weapons. Cap-i-taan Tikker's report was most informative."

"Trouble is, they apparently don't come individually, but in swarms," Gray countered, "and I don't like these suicide glider bombs they're usin' at all."

"True," Saan-Kakja agreed, turning more serious. "But the notion of two such massive machines bumping into each other high in the sky . . . it amused me. No, I would show you other things." She paused, looking at Matt, then glanced at his cane. "If you are sure you are up to it?"

"I'm fine," Matt replied. "Besides, I can't wait to greet our guests when they get here." He glanced at his watch—always vaguely surprised to find it still working after all it had been through. "They should be along pretty soon."

Busaa remained with Meksnaak at the carriage. Meksnaak complained he couldn't breathe in the great building, but was also making his point that he didn't intend to associate with electricity any more than he had to. Besides, even though he hadn't brought it up, he remained somewhat affronted by what he considered the uncivilized tactics used by *Walker*'s team to win the baseball game. The rest of them entered the massive structure through a small door beside a pair of huge ones designed to roll aside. Matt had some idea of what they were here to see. He'd been told of the project headed by a former POW who'd survived *Mizuki Maru*, before the hellish ship was altered into a Q ship and sent against her former escort; the destroyer *Hidoiame*. That mission, commanded by Sato Okada, had failed, resulting in the loss of *Mizuki Maru* with all hands. But it was likely she'd landed some licks first, which possibly saved *Walker* in the long run. In any event, the forty-odd survivors of the ship's original cargo of mistreated prisoners had joined the Allied cause in various capacities and were beginning to make their presence felt. Carpenter's Mate Third Class Winston "Winny" Rominger was one.

Winny hurried over himself as soon as they stepped into the giant building. He was tall, with jet-black hair and a big, bushy mustache. He was still thin, and bags showed under his eyes in the uneven electric lighting illuminating the cavernous structure. Matt realized there were a lot of electrical machines inside as well, more than he'd seen in one place on this world before. It was probably much the same in Baalkpan now. He'd been away a while. Motors whirred and rumbled, and sharp cutters and serrated blades blew wood chips all over the place. A fine haze of dust swirled in the shifting air, blown by big fans that roared like *Walker*'s blower. Hundreds of dusty 'Cats and ex-pat female "Impies" operated the machines, heaved taglines on prefabricated structures suspended from hoists like those on the hangar decks of the great carriers, or weaved their way purposefully from place to place.

Matt caught Gray staring at a particularly well-endowed woman pulling on a line, her perfect, naked breasts swaying mesmerizingly with the effort. She wore nothing but a skimpy breechcloth. Lemurians considered clothing ornamental or occupational and wore as little as they could when working. The formerly virtually enslaved human women felt the same. Matt doubted he'd ever grow comfortable with that, but he'd become somewhat desensitized. Of course, he was married now too. Gray wasn't—and the older man was currently considerably flustered by the attentions of an exotically beautiful young woman named Diania. Diania, now officially a steward's mate, was Sandra's friend and, increasingly, secretary. Gray had also been teaching her to fight, with and without weapons, and she was considered part of the Captain's Guard now as well. Young enough to be his *grand*daughter, Diania had a serious crush on the old Bosun and it was growing clear that Gray was . . . not entirely himself . . . around the girl either.

Matt coughed at him, and Gray blinked. The air smelled of wood, glue, and solvents, and Matt was glad to see more fans mounted high in the walls, providing ventilation. His gaze narrowed and focused on the purpose of the impressive facility. "There they are," he said, feeling almost surprised. Beyond the closest construction was a long, staggered, double row of amazingly familiar hulls in various stages of completion.

"Yes, sir," said Winny, his hand extended. Matt looked at it a moment before taking it. "I'm sorry, Mr. Rominger," he said, smiling. "I got distracted." They had to speak loudly over the racket.

"He might'a been expectin' a salute too," Gray jabbed.

Matt shook his head. "No, Boats, I wasn't. Mr. Rominger's elected not to join our Navy, and that's entirely up to him and everybody else who was in his . . . situation." He grinned. "Besides, we're indoors!"

"Uh, no offense, Captain Reddy," Winny interjected, "none meant at all . . . but I joined the old Navy, and that didn't turn out too well for me." His expression grew haunted. "We did our best, even after we ran out of boats. But the brass *made* us surrender to the Japs." He shook his head and stared at the floor. "They weren't even on Mindanao yet," he added harshly. "We should've kept fighting, even if they killed us in the end. It would've been better than what happened. And a lot of fellas died anyhow." He looked Matt in the eye. "No, sir. I know the score here and I support your Navy and what you're doing, but I'd just as soon fight this war as a civilian."

Matt nodded seriously. "That's your decision. But nobody'll ever get an order to surrender to the Grik or Doms, Mr. Rominger, not from me or anybody."

"Thank you, sir."

Matt gestured at the hulls with his cane and started forward. "You were in MTB Squadron Five, correct?"

"Ron-Five, yes, sir," answered Winny as the group moved toward the closest hull. This one wasn't planked yet and the framework was impressive in its simplicity.

"Well, you've certainly captured the lines of your old PT boats."

"Yes, sir," Winny agreed. "They're not as big; only fifty feet, but the planing-type hull design's essentially the same, with the same diagonally planked, layered construction—a lot like those giant 'Cat Homes and the new flattops."

Matt scratched his chin. "I thought PTs were made of plywood."

Winny chuckled. "So many folks always said that, putting them down, that everybody thought it was true." He shrugged. "We kind of took pride in it after a while, everybody thinking we fought in plywood boats. I guess there's really not much difference when you get down to it, but we did a lot of good with what we had."

"What are the specs?" Gray asked.

"Fifty feet, like I said, with a sixteen-foot beam. Not quite just a smaller-scale version. We still need the width for the torpedoes."

"Just two tubes?"

"Yes, sir. The whole reason for keeping them smaller and lighter is so they can be carried by a ship—a flattop, or maybe a dedicated tender. The internal combustion engine works, or ICE house, is building monster versions of Nancy engines—six cylinders instead of four; something they were fooling with for bigger planes, but they were too heavy for the horsepower. They'll work for us, though, and with a pair of 'em we ought to get twenty-five knots or better. Maybe thirty. You may have seen some of the small boats outside. Scale models. Anyway, even with only two engines and two torpedoes, they're going to suck gas. We'll have to take them where they're going to fight."

"Not to mention they'll be vulnerable to heavy seas and . . . well, sea monsters."

"Not to mention, sir."

Matt gazed at the line of boats. "How long until they're operational?"

"I'm hoping to have the first squadron ready in four months."

Matt shook his head. "Too long. I want a dozen ready to go in one month."

Winny gaped. "But . . . it'll take more than a week for the *paint* to cure!"

Matt looked at Saan-Kakja with a grin. "I want twelve of these PTs finished and ready for transshipment to Baalkpan in one month, Your Excellency."

Saan-Kakja blinked tentatively. She'd been a little afraid Matt would think she was wasting time and materials on the little boats—especially when their enemies were building such monsters now.

"You approve?" she asked.

"Absolutely."

"But . . ." Winny interjected, "even if we finish them, we'll have to train crews. Hell, we haven't even started building torpedo tubes yet!"

"They have in Baalkpan," Matt countered. "We'll mate them up there. Send Bernie Sandison any specific requirements you think they'll have. I *want* those boats, Mr. Rominger."

"For the operation you outlined for Adar?" Sandra asked.

"Yeah. If we can get these PTs Mr. Rominger's so kindly provided, all the heavy stuff building in Baalkpan can go to Keje—or Jim Ellis in First Fleet. Adar isn't sold on my little 'sideshow,' as Commander Herring calls it." He frowned.

Saan-Kakja snorted. "I do not like that man!"

"So you've said," Matt said wryly. "But Adar's in charge. He was right about that; *somebody's* got to be in charge of everything, and he's the guy." Matt admired Adar tremendously and considered him a truly remarkable Lemurian. Once a simple high sky priest on *Salissa* Home, Adar was now High Chief and Sky Priest of Baalkpan, and Chairman of the Grand Alliance. Matt knew real efforts were underway to transform at least part of the Grand Alliance into a united nation consisting of land settlements and even the massive seagoing Homes. If the Empire of the New Britain Isles and other allies were not yet interested in joining, quite a few were, and the result was something akin to the United States under the old Articles of Confederation, in which the member states were politically united but retained more independence than was probably ideal. At least as far as the war effort was concerned. Fortunately, the main members—Baalkpan and the Fil-pin Lands, represented by Adar and Saan-Kakja—shared the vision of a united nation, even if they didn't always agree on priorities, and most of the other allies were willing to follow their lead. "Letting First Fleet have all the heavy stuff should make it easier for Adar to swallow my sideshow," Matt continued, "and maybe let Keje bring *Big Sal* along. Keje wants to go, and we need *Salissa* for her aircraft." He pointed at the closest wooden hull. "Now we need her to carry them too."

Admiral Keje-Fris-Ar was Matt's oldest Lemurian friend, and resembled nothing more than a short, powerful, rust-colored bear. His *Salissa* Home had been an immense, sail-powered, seagoing city before the war, but had been converted to a steam-driven aircraft carrier. He was CINCWEST, but had been forced to retire to Andaman Island with a battered flagship and a fleet that couldn't, at present, challenge the monstrous new Grik warships. He didn't want to abandon First Fleet, but he loved the idea of Matt's current scheme and desperately wanted to participate.

"But . . ." Winny tried to protest again. "Who've you got with PT experience? Who'll command your squadron?"

Matt looked at him. "Are you volunteering for *my* Navy, Mr. Rominger?"

The carriage driver entered and stood before Saan-Kakja. "The great plane approaches. You instructed me to inform you."

Saan-Kakja looked at Sandra. "Our guest has arrived!"

*T*he mighty PB-5 Maa-ni-la "Clipper" circled above its new primary support facility half a mile down the long dock and began its lumbering descent. The aircraft looked a little bizarre. The hull lines of a PBY were still apparent, as was the wing shape, but the hull was deeper and the wing was attached directly to the top of the fuselage. Four Wright Gipsy–type motors were positioned in an even row on top of the wing, elevated by fragile-looking mounts. Five and even six engines had been attempted, but the increased thrust didn't justify the greater weight and fuel consumption. Air-cooled radials powered the new, dedicated pursuit ships, or P-1 Mosquito Hawks everybody was calling "Fleashooters," and were already being tried as well. It was hoped their greater power-to-weight ratio would make a good match for the larger planes. The color scheme was the same as the Nancys—blue and white—but this Clipper wasn't a Navy plane, so there were no "Amer-i-caan" roundels on the wings.

Matt, Sandra, Gray, Busaa, Meksnaak, and Saan-Kakja made the short trip in the carriage and joined the crowd that always gathered to watch the plane touch down on the water. It was a remarkably graceful maneuver for such a large, ungainly aircraft, particularly one whose pilots were doubtless very tired after their long flight. The plane looked tired too, and its wood and fabric wings seemed to sag with exhaustion as it rumbled to a stop on the calm inlet. Ponderously, it turned for the dock and motored toward a jutting pier where line handlers waited. Quickly and professionally, they secured the plane, and the engines muttered to a stop. A hatch opened on the side of the hull, and the passengers began disembarking.

"There he is!" Saan-Kakja said with undisguised glee as the Australian engineer and self-proclaimed "naturalist" Courtney Bradford stepped awkwardly on the dock. He looked unsteady, but quickly covered his balding red pate with a wide sombrero. It hadn't been long since Matt and Sandra saw him, but Saan-Kakja hadn't seen him in many months. Courtney was an . . . interesting man; a little odd and absentminded, but still the closest thing they had to a real scientist. His insatiable curiosity, wealth of knowledge, and unconventional approach to discovery had been the driving force behind many of their advances. He had a knack for looking at various sides of any issue, and though thoughtless at times, he was never deliberately offensive. This combination made him a good choice for Minister of Science, as well as the Alliance's Plenipotentiary at Large. He'd been in the Empire of the New Britain Isles since first contact was made there, and he'd negotiated important treaties and reforms. Most recently, he'd served as a critical advisor to the new Governor-Empress Rebecca Anne McDonald, after the despicable plot that murdered her parents and savaged the Imperial government. Matt was glad to have Courtney back, but things in the Empire remained less than perfectly stable, and he wasn't sure his return wasn't premature.

Seeing them standing there, Courtney visibly straightened and tromped up the dock. He had a lot of baggage—enough to reduce the plane's passenger capacity by half—but he carried only what looked like a cage draped with a bright cloth. The rest of his belongings, mostly odd specimens from the east, would be offloaded and sent to Saan-Kakja's Great Hall. Puffing up before them, Courtney swept off his strange hat, set his package down, and threw them all a sketchy salute. Then he grinned hugely and advanced to embrace the diminutive high chief.

"Hello, hello! I'm so glad to see you all!" He hugged Saan-Kakja tightly and winked over her head at Meksnaak's disapproving glare. "And how are you, my dear?" he asked, stepping back to gaze at Saan-Kakja. "I've missed you so!"

"I am well, and better now you are here!" Saan-Kakja replied happily. "How are you, and how is my sister Rebecca?" High chiefs on land or sea always referred to their peers as brother or sister—unless they were actual cousins, which wasn't unusual. In this case, Saan-Kakja actually felt sisterly affection for the Governor-Empress of the New Britain Isles.

Courtney's smile faded. "I'm fine, as you can see. And our dear Empress Becky has borne her sad burdens bravely, but I'm concerned for her." He embraced Sandra next, and gave her a hearty kiss. "That's for the blushing bride, of course—and my, haven't you turned a pretty shade?" He released her and shook Matt's hand. "Much improved, I see, Captain Reddy! I'm glad to see you standing on your own two feet! I say, my heart nearly stopped when I heard of your dreadful wound!"

"It wasn't that bad," Matt deflected. "Besides, I had the best doc in the world." He winked at Sandra. "Prettiest too."

"Of course, of course! But . . . you *are* better?"

"Sure," Matt said with a hint of suspicion. "I said so, didn't I?"

"Indeed. I merely asked because I wouldn't want anything to prevent the lovely mission you're planning! Things are somewhat at a standstill in the East, I'm afraid, at least until sufficient forces have gathered at the Enchanted Isles to mount a creditable invasion of the Doms."

"I thought you were set on going to the Enchanted Isles—the Galápagos," Matt said with a smile.

Courtney's bushy eyebrows approached one another. "As you once said, it's not the same place here. And by all accounts the bloody Doms haven't left much to explore. It will be hustle, bustle, hurry up and wait for some time while enough troops are sent to sink the isles. High Admiral Jenks and General Shinya are planning raids to gain intelligence, but they'd never let *me* tag along."

Matt shook his head. He'd been discussing those raids with Jenks via wireless.

"I've far better prospects for exploration and honest excitement if I accompany you," Courtney continued.

"And maybe better prospects of getting killed as well," Matt said with a wry grin. "But you're welcome—if my mission ever even happens."

"Nonsense," Courtney snorted. "And of course the mission will proceed. Adar is a most sensible creature, and anyone can see the advantages from a strategic point of view. Your mission would doubtless relieve some of the pressure on General Alden! He's in quite a desperate situation, I understand."

Matt nodded grimly.

"Well. If our dear Adar lacks certainty regarding your scheme, for some unfathomable reason, I shall speak to him myself!"

"Still the ambassador," Sandra chuckled.

Courtney frowned. "No, my dear, and no strategist either. But as empirical observer—oh! Please do pardon the pun—I'm as convinced as anyone that we can't simply react to the actions of our enemies. We must keep them off balance and force them to react to us!"

"Damn straight!" Gray agreed.

"In any event," Courtney continued, his expression still grave, "I've done my bit as ambassador and had quite enough of it, I assure you. I'm not cut out for politics. I was most hesitant to leave our dear Governor-Empress, of course, but Prime Factor Bates has everything well in hand. Besides, I'm confident that any remaining traitors in the Empire have far more reason to fear the Governor-Empress than the other way around." He paused thoughtfully. "In addition, I was not insensitive to the necessity that the reorganization and reforms underway in the Empire should have an entirely *Imperial* face. As it is, the vast majority of the people there have come to embrace them—particularly after all that has happened: the murders of Governor-Emperor Gerald McDonald and his sweet wife, not to mention most of the rest of the government that remained after the Dom-inspired coup attempt! Then there's this confounded *new* war with the Dominion, of course!"

He smiled sadly at Sandra. "*You* have quite an inquisitive mind, my dear. Do you not find it tiresome how these dreadful wars constantly prevent our uninhibited study of the wonders this world has laid before us?"

He stopped suddenly, blinking. "Oh! Where was I? Yes! As I was saying, I consider it essential that we, by which I mean the Western powers in the Grand Alliance, not appear to be propping up a weak Imperial government and taking advantage of the mere girl—as many there see her—who runs it. We're the steadfast allies, but beyond those articles we negotiated regarding the institution of indenture, we must not be seen as meddling in the domestic affairs of the Empire!"

"Were you meddling?" Matt asked.

"Perhaps just a bit—as you know. And for a tense time our Marines and naval personnel *did* prop her up, I suppose. But as the new Governor-Empress herself insisted to me, she must be allowed to spread her wings, as it were, and rule her empire in deed as well as name."

That phrase suddenly struck Matt as familiar; then he remembered Chairman Adar had said much the same thing in a message sent to all commanders—that he meant to be Chairman of the Grand Alliance in more than name, and from now on, he'd make all major strategic decisions and take the heat when things went wrong. It sounded like his intentions were noble, and after Matt had been out of pocket so long, he knew he couldn't make all the strategic decisions anymore. As he'd said many times, somebody had to be in charge all the time, somebody in a position to see the big picture. But could Adar really see it from Baalkpan? Matt just hoped it was truly Adar talking, and the Chairman hadn't been influenced to get just a little tactical by Commander Simon Herring.

In fact, Adar's new stance was the reason Matt's plan wasn't complete. He was preparing as if Adar would give him the go order and fully expected him to, but for the first time, the order hadn't come as a matter of course.

"So, Courtney," he said, "basically, Empress Becky threw you out."

"Not at all," Courtney denied. "But I was . . . somewhat prominent in the aftermath of the dreadful events that resulted in her rise to power." His expression grew troubled. "She has suffered terribly, and though I'm confident my assistance and personal regard afforded her some comfort, a coldness has settled within her, I fear. It's as though she's actually pushing away those who care most about her—Sean Bates made note of it as well—and doesn't want the love and comfort we tried to give." He stooped suddenly and raised the package he'd brought from the plane. "A case in point," he said, removing the bright cloth and displaying the contents of the cage.

"Petey!" Sandra gasped.

"Petey," a little voice tentatively confirmed. A small, brightly hued creature stirred and gazed at them. It looked like a lizard, and was a little bigger than a parrot, but colored like one. Also, instead of wings it had a finely furred membrane stretched from just behind its little hands back to its hindquarters. The then Princess Rebecca had adopted the little tree-gliding reptile while marooned on Yap Island, a place Dennis Silva still called Boogerland.

"I can't believe it!" Saan-Kakja exclaimed. "She *loves* that ridiculous creature!"

"Yes, she does," Courtney agreed grimly, "which makes my point. She said she must 'dispense with childish thoughts and attachments,' and in her position could no longer go about with a pet lizard draped around her neck. There may actually be something to that. She will *not* remain sequestered, as other female successors to the throne have done before, and Petey's constant presence—which he would insist on—would likely only aggravate certain . . . antebellum factions. She practically forced the little bugger on me, and asked if any of her friends would care to entertain the 'greedy little thing.' Greedy little thing indeed! She doted on him!" He looked at Saan-Kakja and Sandra. "I believe this act was a cry for help—a kind of help I cannot give, I'm sad to say." He held the cage out to Saan-Kakja, but the Lemurian high chief backed away.

"*I* cannot care for it!" she objected desperately. "I do not keep pets! I . . . I wouldn't know what to do with it!"

"Just feed it fairly often and it will be quite happy, I assure you!"

"Eat?" asked Petey, suddenly less despondent.

Chief Gray's eyes narrowed. "You don't keep pets. Few 'Cats do. But there's critters like him runnin' around Maa-ni-la now. Some common . . . well, housecats, we'd call 'em, have jumped ship from our Imperial visitors too. I've seen a couple."

"You've seen creatures like *Petey* . . . here?" Courtney demanded, suddenly intense.

"Well, yeah, I guess. I don't know about *exactly* like him, but close enough."

"Why?" Matt asked.

"Yes, why?" Meksnaak insisted in turn. He'd begun to interpret human "face moving" to some degree, but in this case he caught Bradford's tone of voice. "Why does this concern you so?"

Courtney looked coldly at Meksnaak. There was no love lost between the two. "I'm *always* concerned when an invasive, destructive species is introduced into an ecology that cannot defend against it." He scratched his nose. "I doubt that is the case here, however. Housecats are nowhere near the top of the local food chain! Tree-gliding creatures like Petey, however . . ." He paused. "Blast! I've been around the little devil for months, and it never occurred to me to name his species! Gluttonous *maximus . . . minimus* might not be inappropriate. The thing is, though, if there are more creatures from Yap running . . . or gliding about *here*, then it follows that there have been unauthorized voyages *there*!" He looked at Matt. "We declared that place off-limits for a very good reason, you'll recall!"

Matt scratched his chin. "Yeah. I take it you haven't sent anybody, Your Excellency?" he asked Saan-Kakja.

"Never!"

"I'll ask Chairman Adar if he did—without telling me." He shrugged. "Not that he has to . . ." *He doesn't* have *to,* he said to himself, *but why wouldn't he?* The thought was troubling.

Sandra reached over and took the cage from Bradford. "I'll take him," she said with a worried frown.

"Oh. Well, back to the empress," Courtney said. "I do hope Sister

Audry will be some comfort to her. She asked for her specifically, you see."

Sister Audry was a Dutch Benedictine nun originally stranded on Talaud Island with Irvin Laumer and the rest of the survivors of S-19. She'd been sent to escort the children of diplomats, senior officers, and other luminaries when the antiquated sub fled Surabaya in the Old War. The surviving children—Abel Cook was one—were almost all midshipmen or -women now. Despite some alarming allusions to Catholicism practiced by the Dominion, Rebecca had grown to like and respect Sister Audry and thought she might be the key to subverting the perversions of the Doms. Her first chore was to go among the Dom prisoners of war on New Ireland and discover if exposure to the True Faith might break their devotion to what it had been twisted to here.

"I hope so too," Matt agreed. "The good sister ought to be on Respite Island by now, as a matter of fact. She'll be in the New Britain Isles soon enough, and I'll ask her what she thinks about how Rebecca is . . . adapting."

"Come!" Saan-Kakja said. "We will go to the Great Hall. Though he won't admit it, I can see that Cap-i-taan Reddy is tiring. We will resume our discussion there."

"Eat?" Petey asked a little more forcefully.

"I'm sure we can find something for you soon," Sandra assured the creature.

Courtney gestured at it. "You know, for such an, um, aerialist, I was surprised to discover he is somewhat given to airsickness! I wasn't sure he'd survive the flight." Courtney's eyebrows rose. "He made a dreadful mess in the plane, and I was quite convinced he would die, until he seemed to grow accustomed." He lowered his voice. "In fact, I was rather looking forward to dissecting him—but only if he died naturally, of course! And I'd never have told young Rebecca."

"Eat! Goddam!" Petey suddenly shrieked.

"You may still get your chance at him," Sandra said with a smirk. "Maybe I understand a little better why Rebecca had to get rid of him!"

////// *Grik India*
General Halik's HQ

"Is that the new enemy weapon?" demanded General Halik, commander of all Grik land forces in the "officially" reconquered Regency of India. His yellow eyes and reptilian stance were intense. General Orochi Niwa, formerly a lieutenant of the Special Naval Landing Forces aboard the doomed Japanese Imperial Navy battle cruiser *Amagi*, had entered the strange ruins they'd commandeered as a command post south of the Great Lake. He was carrying a long, slender object of bright, slightly rusty steel and battered wood.

Niwa nodded. "One of them," he replied shortly, gazing about with curiosity as usual. The ruins were truly ancient, their once ornate nature blurred by uncounted centuries of neglect. He speculated again about whatever lost civilization once inhabited the place. But the Grik conquest of India occurred so long ago that the builders were not remembered and Niwa would likely never know any more about them.

Halik hissed ironic frustration and beckoned him near. The enemy had *many* new weapons, and only Grik numbers and Halik's and Niwa's strategies had created the recent victory—if it could be called that. "Stalemate" was perhaps a more appropriate word, and if that somehow satisfied the new Lord Regent-Consort and General of the Sea Hisashi Kurokawa, it couldn't satisfy General Halik.

A makeshift roof kept out most of the rain that never seemed to ease. Halik and his immediate staff were infinitely more comfortable than his Uul warriors besieging the army of the "prey," but he was heartily sick of his circumstances. He was immune to hardship but was a creature of action, and the weeks of delay since the great battles that established this current unsatisfactory situation made him short-tempered, even with Niwa.

General Niwa said no more, but raised the object in question and placed it atop the heavy-lined maps on the table Halik leaned against. He made no response to Halik's tone either; he'd grown to accept it. But Halik knew as he peered at the weapon that Niwa wouldn't speak again as long as he sounded like he was feeling sorry for himself. *It is odd,* Halik reflected, *that he and I have grown so close, learned each other so well, when our physical forms are so different that we can barely even speak each other's language.* They could *understand* each other, but could form the other's words only with extreme difficulty. The result wasn't worth the effort and left them both feeling foolish.

Halik had initially likened his attachment to the alien creature to those transient . . . fondnesses that occasionally occurred between warriors in the heat of battle, but he'd never felt it this strong before or had it remain so long. Niwa often called Halik "my friend," and Halik had parroted the term, but he'd begun to learn what the still ill-defined word truly implied. Niwa *was* Halik's friend! He'd never had anything like a friend before, and, despite their differences, their strange— perhaps even unnatural—kinship was quite real. He'd come to believe the equally real understanding they shared might well be unique. In addition, both of them had grown apart from their own people, their own *species* in many ways, and though the concept of friendship remained a complicated thing for Halik to grasp, he knew he felt more . . . comfortable with Niwa than with any other being of any form.

"This *is* the weapon you described!" Halik said, his tone less severe. He traced the long, wood-and-metal thing with a claw. He'd seen some of the enemy's weapons before; far more advanced than those entering service with his own army, particularly the more elite members of the Hatchling Host—Grik-designed from birth to understand the concept of defense and trained as an *army* instead of a mob of mindlessly attacking warriors. Elements of that new army had been deployed far earlier than intended, but even now held the enemy bottled up in the rocky gap that followed the flow of the river feeding the lake. They fought well despite their youth, and obeyed even complicated orders amazingly well, but their weapons, large-caliber—roughly four-fifth's of an inch—tanegashima-style matchlocks, were primitive and unreliable—particularly in the rain!—compared to the enemy weapons he'd seen.

"What makes this one different, better than the others?" Halik asked. "It looks the same as the rifle muskets we captured from the force we destroyed beyond the pass. And these were found there also?"

"Some few were found there as well," Niwa confirmed. "The enemy obviously tried to destroy as many as they could—at the end. And it is the same as the others in many ways. Most of the parts are identical. But though the rifle muskets you saw right after the fighting were formidable and advanced enough, compared to what . . . we have, these are even better." Niwa's brows knitted. "With all the other advances the enemy has made, I would not have been surprised to see them eventually, but that they have them so quickly is a dreadful surprise indeed." He paused. "The Americans and their . . . Lemurian friends"—even Halik couldn't really consider their enemies "prey" anymore—"had smoothbore muskets when we first engaged them on Ceylon. Even before that campaign ended, their marksmanship made me suspect they had rifled some of their arms—a technique I described that forces their projectiles to spin, like fletching does a crossbow bolt . . ."

"Which makes them more accurate," Halik finished for him.

"Indeed," Niwa agreed, then gestured at the rifle on the table. "But this is a step, simple on its face, that not only increases the effectiveness of rifled weapons manyfold, but deeply concerns me regarding the enemy's capabilities—and the level those capabilities are likely on the very brink of becoming."

"You can see the future by gazing at a single weapon?" Halik asked skeptically.

"In a sense," Niwa replied, and took a breath. "I was not here for the fighting beyond the pass, and did not even know these new weapons existed at first, since they were simply gathered with the others. They *do* look much the same. The supreme difference is not what they look like or what they do, but how *swiftly* they do it—and how quickly the enemy has put them in the field!" Niwa picked up the weapon and cocked the hammer back. "For the most part, this is exactly the same weapon the enemy has carried since Ceylon. It was probably even made from those"—suddenly, he raised a small lever and the top of the barrel at the breech flipped forward on a hinge—"only this one has been made to load self-contained ammunition from the *back*!" Fishing in his pocket, Niwa produced several shiny brass things and inserted one in the back of the weapon, closed the top of the barrel, and fired a thundering shot into the earth at his feet! Quickly, he recocked the hammer, flipped open the breech—which somehow launched a smoking brass cylinder over his shoulder—loaded again, and fired another shot. To emphasize his point, he did it a third time before laying the smoking rifle back on the table.

Grik dashed into the confined space, sickle-shaped swords in their hands, and rushed about amid the cloud of white smoke hanging in the humid air. Halik only stared at Niwa, his hearing stunned but his mind racing.

"Get out!" he roared at the guards and staff members still scrambling to enter the ruined room. "Get out, all of you!" He shouted at those already inside. He looked back at Niwa. "A most impressive display, and I appreciate the . . . exciting way you did it. It was . . . disconcerting and unexpected. Exactly as it would be for our warriors facing such a thing." He clenched his sharp rows of teeth and blew the smoke he'd breathed through them with a gust of air. "No wonder the battle for the hill was so costly and prolonged!"

"With respect, General Halik, perhaps only one in ten of the enemy there had weapons such as that." Niwa pointed. "Do not presume it alone made such a difference."

"I know. Their aircraft remain better than ours as well, their artillery is superior, their ability to defend still favors them . . ."

"Their tactics, discipline, and individual combat skills are better too," Niwa inserted pointedly.

"Granted," Halik reluctantly agreed. "On the whole." He gestured back at the breechloader. "But why do you . . ." He couldn't say "fear." The Grik word had only one very insulting application. "Then why do you think that weapon *can* make such a difference, then? The war will grow costlier in Uul, of course. It will take longer. But even now we build more armies in the Sacred Lands! We will reach a point where we can make warriors even faster than they slay them!"

"That is a very distasteful thought, General Halik."

Halik blinked his large reptilian eyes. "Perhaps . . . I even agree with you, General Niwa," he allowed, "but that is the Way. Regardless, because it *is* the Way, and particularly because these new Uul warriors will be better than any before them—a grand swarm of such as now comprise the Hatchling Host—victory may come later, but is assured in the end."

"My uneasiness stems from this," Niwa cautioned. "Look at the craftsmanship of that weapon. Look how well it fits together. Consider the skill, the industry required to make such things in large numbers! Consider the enemy aircraft—and the larger ones we've now seen that supply the force entrenched around the lake. Think of the better bombs, ships, guns—all these new things—then hear what I say." Niwa looked hard at his Grik friend. "The Americans—the Lemurians—are *better* at war than we! We improve, but not as fast as they improve their weapons to kill us." He pointed again at the rifle. "Weapons such as that, and what must quickly follow, mean they will likely change tactics—again!— very soon. Already they kill us from trenches we cannot approach. None of your . . . *our* warriors have trained for that! I submit, you cannot *imagine* how quickly our enemies will soon be killing us—far quicker than we can possibly replace the slain, I promise." He nodded once more at the weapon. "Please take no offense, my friend. But can you even operate that?"

Surprised, Halik looked at the captured rifle. Curious, he picked it up. He managed to cock the hammer and with a little fumbling got the breech to flip open. He looked at Niwa triumphantly.

"Now load it," Niwa said, holding out a cartridge.

Halik reached to take it—and dropped it on the mushy, earthen floor. With a snort, he tried to pick it up, but his claws would find no purchase. He finally managed to snag it and hold it up. But it was clear it would take some doing to insert it in the weapon. He glanced at Niwa, pupils narrowing.

"You can," Niwa said, "but not efficiently. Your lower-class Hij, the makers of delicate things, remove their claws to perform their tasks. *Remove* them. Just cutting them will not do—and still the best machines they make are crude, clunky things. Again, I mean no offense. Grik are born hunters; the finest predators in the world, no doubt. But to make anything like the weapons the Americans and their allies will soon bring to war will take a whole new level of understanding and craftsmanship." He pointed at the cartridge. "That can be made, but to even prepare to make them in numbers will take time—and then we will have to train troops to use them, find a way to shape their claws so they can handle them with ease. You can't just cut them off. How long would even the new army stand once they ran out of ammunition if they didn't even have *claws*? More time lost."

"We will make do!" Halik shot back. "Our weapons may be crude, but the projectiles are large enough for a proper warrior to hold—and they inflict terrific wounds! They work, and we will soon have them in countless numbers—along with warriors to wield them!"

"And they will die," Niwa said relentlessly, "in countless numbers."

Halik swished his plumed tail, and his crest stood up. "Are you saying . . . we will lose?" he asked softly.

"No. I'm saying only that time is not on our side. You, First General Esshk, even Regent-Consort"—he almost sneered—"General of the Sea

Kurokawa have believed all we need is time for the new army of better warriors to mature, and we'll sweep the enemy away. I believe the enemy will sweep those better warriors away with better weapons by the time they are ready." He scowled. "Kurokawa has not ordered the general assault on the perimeter you plead for simply because he does not think it necessary. He thinks he buys time. As long as this . . ." Niwa scowled deeper and sighed. "The few prisoners that survived long enough to be questioned called our opponent General Alden. . . ." He looked away from Halik, wishing again he could've saved at least a few of those prisoners, but the Grik had no concept of quarter. Saving any even long enough to question had been an achievement. It had been Niwa's first look at the enemy as people, as warriors, and he'd admired their courage. None had surrendered; they'd been overwhelmed. He'd been struck by the irony that he could not only talk with Lemurians in English, but there was also no doubt that he had far more in common with them than the Grik. They were making a monumental fight against a terrible enemy—an enemy that attacked *them* and that Niwa was aiding. . . . He slashed that thought from his head.

"As long as this General Alden's army is trapped, Kurokawa thinks the enemy will concentrate on rescuing it. I agree, but I also think they may succeed if we wait too long!"

"But our warships control the sea. The enemy has nothing to defeat Lord Kurokawa's iron monsters at Madras, particularly with the addition of the slower ships that have arrived. Only a trickle of supplies can possibly come."

"The enemy *had* nothing that could defeat Kurokawa's powerful fleet," Niwa agreed, "but they *will* come up with something, I assure you." He looked strangely at Halik. "Perhaps they already have. Why else have our own supplies become so dear . . . unless they are being intercepted?"

Halik grunted at the disconcerting possibility. The tricky trails they'd found through the mountains to the west were too treacherous for reliable, large-scale supply from that direction, and the enemy often bombed them in any case. If any supplies were making it through a possible Allied gauntlet around Ceylon, none were reaching Halik's army from Madras. They'd been reduced to eating their own. That was not unusual or distasteful to Grik; they did it all the time. But it was annoying and wasteful that so much of Halik's army that made the long trek up from the south, though growing in numbers, could not seem to grow *decisively* as long as it was forced to consume so much of itself. Halik believed that if only he had sufficient supplies, he could very quickly trample underfoot the all-too-competent enemy he faced.

Niwa sat on a bench beside the table and steepled his fingers. "Do not forget the *other* information we gleaned from the prisoners: our enemy has another enemy besides us! These 'Doms.' Their efforts have been divided between two distinct fronts. Just imagine what that means. Without that distraction, they might have sent *twice* what they did against us, and our war—in India at least—would already be lost. As it is, whoever or whatever these Doms are—sadly, I could learn little about them, particularly where they are beyond 'in the east'—they do us a great service whether they know it or not. Still, the fact that our enemies are fighting two wars at once says much about their industrial capacity and reserves. Unless that other enemy has recently beaten them more soundly than we have, I would expect an increased focus on *us*."

"And yet it may be the reverse," Halik speculated. "If these Doms even now drive our enemy on another front, he may be hard-pressed to make good his losses, much less intensify his efforts here."

"Perhaps," agreed Niwa, "but that is only a hope—and a double-edged hope at that."

"In what way?"

"Our current enemy is quite enough to satisfy me. I do not relish facing anyone who could defeat him."

Halik was silent, contemplative, and Niwa finally took a deep breath.

"Ultimately, my friend," Niwa said softly, "between us, whatever plans the enemy has may not be our greatest concern. Do not place too much faith in our new regent, General of the Sea Kurokawa. He has plans of his own that do not include you or me, the Grik, or anyone but himself." He paused. "He is mad, you know. Do you understand what that means?"

Halik looked troubled. "Not angry, in the context you use. He is . . . mind sick?"

"That is close. He should have followed his naval victory with an immediate advance on the enemy, as soon as more ships arrived. Complete victory might have been possible then, but I'm no longer sure that's what he wants—or that he wants it *yet*. I know he has a scheme, but I have no idea what it is or what he hopes to achieve."

"So . . . he is a traitor to the Celestial Mother?"

Niwa actually burst out laughing. He couldn't help it. He suddenly sobered when he saw Halik's crest rise in anger—and when he realized he couldn't remember the last time he'd laughed. "I don't know if he's a traitor," he said at last, "but I know the man, and he's truly *loyal* only to himself."

Halik considered. "We should have attacked this Alden immediately also, with everything, before he had a chance to improve his position. Still, without reinforcement and major supply, time is not on *his* side." He looked at the rifle once more. "I believe he has few more of *those*, and his ammunition will be short for everything. I think we will use this time of delay to make him use as much of it as we can." He looked at Niwa, and his crest flattened. "That, we are already doing, as you know. As you say, we have supply issues of our own and cannot keep an army this size in the field forever in a land so barren of food beasts . . . without feeding upon our own, and doing our enemy's work for him! General Ugla's Hatchling Host west of the gap has all the supplies it could want, carried overland from ports in the west. They also have the large creatures of the plains to consume at need. But the gap was to be the principal path of supply for *us*! Few of the food beasts we gathered in the lowlands remain, and the enemy is actually better off in that regard than we. They discovered many of the kraals and captured a considerable herd." Halik gazed out at the rain. "So you are right after all, in every way. We simply cannot wait much longer for whatever Regent General of the Sea Kurokawa has in mind." He paused, considering. "And regarding him, I will think on what you said. We must discuss it again—and discover how we can destroy the enemy entirely before he destroys us."

Niwa was silent.

"Come," Halik said in an ironic tone, ringing a bell for his attendants. "It is time to demonstrate against the enemy again, to provoke him to use more precious ammunition!" He snorted angrily. "And help us ease our own supply problems once more," he added with heavy sarcasm. His attendant appeared. "Fetch my armor!" he ordered. "And bring something for General Niwa as well!" He looked at Niwa. "I know we decided not to put ourselves together on the field of battle anymore. We are co-commanders, after all. But this will not be a *real* battle; merely a harvest of provisions. Still, you might observe something of interest. Would you care to join me?"

"Of course, General Halik."

////// *Alden's Perimeter*
Lake Flynn, West of Madras
Grik India

T hunder muttered in the thick night sky, and accompanying strobes of lightning competed with the desultory flashing pulse and rumble of artillery. Brief torrents of rain seemed physically shaken from the trembling, pregnant clouds of sodden air, to bulge the swollen lake and flood its muddy, miserable environs. Around Lake Flynn and the upper reaches of the river that fed it through the high, craggy, Rocky Gap, the remnants of Alden's Allied Expeditionary Force (AEF) had dug in tighter than a tick.

A network of defensive trenches, protected by a blanket of the new barbed wire, zigzagged around the perimeter several lines deep in places. The reliable and deadly twelve-pounder "Napoleons"—as General Alden called them—were placed in thoughtfully situated redoubts where they could lay heavy fire support down long sections of the line.

The lighter, more numerous six-pounders strengthened the line itself at frequent intervals. Alden's own beloved 1st Marines, of General Muln-Rolak's I Corps, formed a mobile reserve with their breech-loading Baalkpan Arsenal "Allin-Silva" conversion rifles that fired a potent .50-80 cartridge. The rest of Rolak's I Corps held the stopper in the Rocky Gap. Rolak remained a little exposed to a Grik thrust to cut him off from the rest of I Corps and the beefed-up, reinforced remnant of General Queen Safir Maraan's II Corps in the main west-east-south defensive line, but a grand battery placed in a veritable fortress had bloodily repulsed such attempts so far. True, many of II Corps's "reinforcements" were actually support troops, auxiliaries, and even sailors, but all were veterans now. The heaps of festering Grik corpses, packed so thick that even the rain couldn't subdue the stench, lapped against every part of the line and grimly testified to that. General Rolak felt secure.

Somehow, General Pete Alden, onetime Marine sergeant aboard the lost USS *Houston* on another, different earth, and now General of the Armies and Marines of the Grand Alliance, had managed to wring order from the chaos of disaster. He—and Keje, Alden supposed—had lost the port city of Madras, and his northern component of the Allied Expeditionary Force had been cut off from most lines of convenient support. In the confusion of that month-old battle, III Corps, under General Faan-Ma-Mar, had slashed its way up from the south against scattered, surprised resistance, and his force was much appreciated, but it had been a costly move. Now Alden's *three* savaged corps were as effectively surrounded as Colonel Billy Flynn's scratch division beyond the Rocky Gap had been, and Flynn's force had ultimately been all but annihilated. But Pete had more defensible terrain; secure internal lines of communication; and more troops, artillery, and mortars than Flynn enjoyed on his crummy, rocky hill. There was an elasticity of depth, and the Grik had difficulty moving through the dense forest to mass against the formidable defenses he'd established, defenses Flynn never had the time, troops, or equipment to emplace. The lake in the center of the perimeter also meant Pete had a ready "airfield" for almost seventy PB-1B Nancy floatplanes that could provide air support. Perhaps most important, he'd secured most of the baggage intended to support an extended campaign. The AEF was in . . . decent shape.

For now, Pete Alden reminded himself darkly, checking his water-beaded watch in the lamplight of the CP tent. He was amazed the thing still worked. The case was badly corroded and the wristband had been replaced twice now when the leather rotted off his wrist. *For now,* he almost sighed. Only forty of his plucky Nancys were actually airworthy, and all had seen a lot of action with limited maintenance. Most came from the shattered carrier *Salissa,* and had been through a lot before they ever arrived, unable to return to their badly damaged ship. Fuel, spare parts, bombs—everything heavy that took up space aboard the meager but gradually more frequent supply flights was in short supply. All fresh supplies came from Ceylon—still in Allied hands—or via TF *Arracca,* which lurked offshore, from Andaman Island. It was a vital but rickety logistics train, stretched to the absolute limit.

The planes and their pilots were just as exhausted as the rest of Pete's army after months of almost constant combat, and there was no end in sight. Still, in the Lemurians that made up his army, from such diverse places and even cultures, he had the best troops he could want, and a good position to defend. But the swarming—unnervingly more professional—Grik host he faced was too numerous, and frankly too damn good, for Pete to consider any unsupported offensive action, and it galled his soul. Worse, for right or wrong, Pete still thought the whole situation was mostly his fault.

"It's almost time," he told his staff, also waiting in the shelter of the tent. "Anything from the lookouts?"

"No Gen-er-aal Aal-den," replied a stocky 'Cat hunched over the wireless receiver, an assistant methodically turning a hand generator.

"If we can't fly in this muck, Grik zeppelins sure can't," the young, blond Lieutenant Mark Leedom said, nodding at the sky. Leedom had been a torpedoman, but had become one of the hottest pilots they had.

"But we *do* fly in it, Lieutenant," Pete disagreed. "We have to." He shrugged. "Maybe not combat missions, but without the supply runs, we won't last long—and we're losing a lot of planes and pilots just bringing in the beans and bullets."

"Stuff wears out," Leedom pointed out in a low tone. "So do people. At least we're starting to get stuff up the Tacos River from the coast," he added. The river had been named for Leedom's Lemurian backseater, who'd been killed in action.

"We are," Alden agreed, "but the Grik'll figure that out eventually and start sniping at the boats and barges all the way in and out. They'll line the river with heavy guns—or, God help us, put a floating battery in it."

"At least they can't get one of their baattle-ships upstream," said the Lemurian General Daanis of General Maraan's Silver Battalion of her famous "600." He was tall for a 'Cat and had the same black fur as his Aryaalan queen.

"The water is too shallow, even with this unending rain," agreed Captain Jis-Tikkar. The sable-furred Tikker, as he was better known, was COFO (Commander of Flight Operations) aboard *Salissa*, or *Big Sal*, before the Battle of Madras. He was Leedom's boss and had brought what remained of *Salissa*'s 1st Naval Air Wing to join Leedom's pickup squadrons of Nancys after his ship was badly damaged by suicide glider bombs dropped by zeppelins, of all things. Some of the weapons had even made attacks within the perimeter, but most crashed harmlessly in the lake or surrounding jungle, and their carrier zeps had been shot down. "And there is the ford just east of the lake. Even we must transfer supplies to other barges to bring them here. No baatle-ship can pass the ford."

"They might think of something," Leedom warned. "We can't ever take for granted just because we can't do something, they can't. Not again. If one of their battlewagons—or anything with big guns—ever *does* make it to the lake, we'll be in big trouble." Nobody replied. It was obvious such a thing could be catastrophic.

"There's way too many worst-case scenarios for me, the way things stand," Pete said at last. "We're holding our own, barely, but the Grik keep growing stronger. We're standing on the end of an awful thin twig, supply wise, and Keje's got to figure some way to retake Madras!"

"Keje will come," Tikker said with conviction. "*Salissa* is under repair, and newer, better ships swell his fleet. Colonel Maallory is on Ceylon with his P-Forties, and they await only more powerful weapons."

"I'm sure you're right," Pete said, wishing he was. The Grik fleet in Madras was also swelling. He looked at his watch again. "Come on. The Clipper'll be here shortly. I want to see what they brought."

General Alden ducked out into the slackening drizzle, followed by half a dozen men and 'Cats. The lake wasn't far, its banks bordering the navigable portion lit by fires. There were a lot of fires in the damp forest: watch fires, campfires, places where wet troops could gather and dry their feet for a while and also clear beacons for the planes that came by night. From the sky, the lake would appear as an inky darkness surrounded by bright dots. Then, of course, there were the flashes of lightning and the seemingly endless battle that flared periodically. Even as Pete watched, the rumbling flashes quickened in the south, across the water, and he tensed. *It's so strange,* he thought, *how I've learned to gain a feel for the "life" of the battle by the surrealistic display that pulses in the night.* "The Second and Ninth Aryaal are catching it," he observed.

"Yes, sir," Daanis agreed. "That's the second thrust there tonight. This Gener-aal Haalik tests us everywhere."

"Him or his pet Jap," Pete grumbled, referring to the general, Niwa, whom Rolak's personal Grik interpreter, Hij-Geerki, had identified for them. Pete wasn't sure how "Geeky" got his information, since few Grik prisoners could ever be secured and those that were usually just . . . died. It was possible he went among the wounded after a fight and spoke to them as one of their own, but Rolak wouldn't confirm that. Pete shook his head. It was hard to imagine that canny old warrior, Lord Muln-Rolak, trusting the weird little Grik so. "They're not content to just keep us cornered here; they want us gone—or that damn Kurokawa does." They'd also learned that General of the Sea Hisashi Kurokawa himself was in personal charge of this enemy campaign.

"We still block the Rocky Gap; the most direct route to Madraas," Major Daanis said. "His fleet is there, but he cannot feel secure as long as we are at his back. . . . There! I think I hear the large plane. It sounds different from the others."

Daanis was right. A crackling rumble of multiple engines throttling back reached their ears, and they saw the blue exhaust flares slide across the darkness, dropping toward the darker water. Torches flared to life in little boats on the lake so the pilot would have some reference for where the slick surface was, and the engines roared as the pilot advanced his throttles to check his descent. A moment later, a yellow-gray splash reflected the firelight and the glare of lightning and war as the big PB-5 "Clipper" slammed down on the lake. One of the powerboats raced to lead it in to the hasty docks. Pete and his companions strode out on the rough-hewn planks and edged away from the busy stevedores unloading a long train of barges recently arrived from the transfer point at the ford. Crates of ammunition, weapons, food, equipment, and medical supplies were piling high, waiting to be dispersed to the scattered, improvised supply sheds, or whisked away to needy troops.

"They're weird-lookin' ducks," Pete said as the shape of the PB-5 resolved itself, drawing near.

"I think they're swell," Leedom said. "They look kind of like a Sikorsky S-40—with a proper tail."

"I do not care what they look like, only what they can do," Tikker said. "They can carry a ton of supplies—or maybe bombs—and more people than anything else we have. Once they are equipped with Colonel Maallory's rad-iaals, we will have true, long-range reconnaissance such as we haven't enjoyed since we lost the old PBY."

"And a relatively heavy bomber," Pete added. "I sure would like a heavy bomber!" He paused, looking at Leedom. "Anything else on those . . . mounted folks you and Captain Saachic reported when you broke out of the trap west of the Rocky Gap?" Pete immediately regretted asking. Leedom or Tikker would've reported if their pilots saw anything. Besides, what happened to Colonel Flynn and several thousand troops was still a very sore subject, and Leedom, shot down in the action, and the few others who made it out were amazingly lucky. Still puzzling, however, was that the survivors reported meeting some very oddly mounted . . . strangers, apparently led by some Czech guy. The mystery was driving Pete nuts.

"Ah, no, sir," Leedom said. "The guys are keeping their eyes peeled."

The big seaplane approached the dock and was fended off and secured while Pete and his staff waited expectantly. Finally, a hatch opened in the wood-and-fabric fuselage aft of the port wing, and a Lemurian face appeared.

"Watcha got?" Pete cried out.

"Mortar bombs, mostly," the 'Cat replied. "An' dispatches for you, Gener-aal."

"How many wounded can you take out this time?" Daanis asked.

"Only ten, they say, which means I take fifteen, anyway," the pilot grinned. "'Cats don't weigh so much as hu-maans! I ordered to pick up passengers this time too. Don't know who. They names in the dispatch." He tossed a wrapped packet to Major Daanis, who'd jumped down on a floating gangway being pushed up to the hatch. Daanis nodded and blinked his thanks, then brought the packet to Pete.

"It says COTGA, Gener-aal," Daanis said. COTGA stood for "Chairman of the Grand Alliance," which meant the dispatch was from Adar himself. A dispatch from Adar was akin to receiving direct orders from President Roosevelt on another world.

Alden started to untie the string around the wrapping but hesitated. Despite weeks of assurances via wireless, he half expected the dispatch to carry orders for his relief, and he wasn't sure he didn't deserve it. He'd even offered to resign, but the wireless replies continued to express Adar's trust. *Of course, under the circumstances, he wouldn't just blow "You're fired" all over the sky, would he?* He untied the string and unwrapped the waxy paper around the pages. "Gimme a light, wilya?" he asked, and someone raised a lantern.

The rain had eased for the moment and just a few drops fell on the pages he quickly read. To his mixed relief, there was only a brief preface regarding his offer to step aside, consisting of a statement of full and unreserved confidence. The rest was mostly concerned with an appraisal of what was being done to sustain his position and the assets on their way to him or Keje. They were the commanders on the scene, and Adar wouldn't tell them their business. Pete smiled at that. He and Keje had already discussed some possibilities via coded wireless, and the assets Adar was committing would be a big help. Finally, the pages described the overall strategic stance of the Grand Alliance. Adar's careful scrawl confirmed that Second Fleet and their Imperial Allies had secured the Enchanted Isles as a base to prepare operations directly against the Dominion, and reiterated that Captain Reddy and USS *Walker* continued to recover in Maa-ni-la. Finally, he expressed his view that Alden's situation was a temporary setback that would soon be put to rights.

Pete caught himself nodding in agreement, pleased by the note and impressed by the resources being lavished on First Fleet. If he could hold out long enough, he was sure Keje would deal with Kurokawa and retake Madras. He sobered. But Keje would have to hurry.

The last three pages were not for him, but he was grateful for them regardless. They were written orders from Adar himself for three very stubborn Lemurians to get aboard the Clipper and proceed to other assignments. The first, he knew, was pointless. It ordered General Queen Safir Maraan to Ceylon, to take command of IV Corps and prepare for the arrival of additional forces. Pete would pass the orders along, but there was no chance they'd be obeyed. Safir would never leave the troops she led now while they were in such a fix—and as a head of state in her own right within the Alliance, she couldn't really be forced to. The second set of orders were for Captain Tikker, standing right beside Pete, to report in person to CINCWEST, to resume his duties as COFO aboard *Big Sal.* The veteran flyer with the polished 7.7-mm Japanese cartridge case thrust through a hole in his ear read the orders just as Pete did.

"With respect, Gen-er-aal," he said, "why don't I take the next flight of Naan-cees out to *Arracca*, then catch a flight from her to Andaman? We have few enough pilots, and some of our remaining machines need a . . . steady hand."

In addition to their combat duties—the few machine gun–armed Nancys were hell on Grik zeps, and the rest were decent little dive-bombers—the planes were also making supply runs out to the *Arracca* battle group beyond the eastern horizon. *Arracca* was another Home-turned carrier, and the flights then returned with the small loads they could carry and repaired or replaced aircraft.

"I guess I can let you do that," Pete allowed, "but I may need your or"—he glanced significantly at Lieutenant Leedom—"*his* help making sure this last set of orders is obeyed."

Leedom took the page Pete handed him and read it. He swore. "You know she hasn't even *spoken* to me since I carried her out of that mess on the other side of the gap? She blames me for her surviving when most everyone else didn't. Hell," he murmured, "I don't much care for the thought of that myself."

"You're her friend, though, and she'll listen to you—maybe just because you feel the same way she does," Pete said.

Leedom's shoulders slumped. "Okay, I'll tell her. But where is she?"

Pete gestured at the battle flaring on the other side of the lake. "Over there, most likely," he said sadly. "Find her quick and get her back here and aboard that plane." He paused. "And be careful! You're acting COFO again. I can't afford to lose you."

Captain Bekiaa-Sab-At limped through the sucking mud at the bottom of the trench, Colonel Billy Flynn's '03 Springfield slung over her right shoulder. In her mind, Flynn's confidence in her and his example of simple courage and self-sacrifice had been his greatest legacy to her, but the magnificent rifle from another world was his final, personal gift. Bekiaa meant to see that it was well employed in his honor. She wasn't supposed to be on the line; the wounds to her left arm and leg had only torn the flesh, but they'd been ugly and painful. They were on the mend, though, and medical release or not, the battle line was the only place she could get even for all the friends she'd lost. Her left arm was almost numb and the fingers tingled strangely, but the leg hurt. A lot. Bekiaa welcomed the pain. It kept her rage hot and sharp—and kept her motivated to kill as many Grik as she could. Flynn's old Springfield helped with that. There wasn't a more accurate rifle in the world, as far as she knew, and she'd become an unattached sniper, for all intents and purposes, killing Grik at ranges unimaginable even for the few troops armed with the Allin-Silva conversions.

Her delicate, feline features were hard set and no one, not even General Grisa, whom she trudged past without a word, dared question her right to be there. She was literally moving to the sound of the guns, as the fighting flared along a section of the line defended mostly by Aryaalans and B'mbaadans. Blinking troops watched her pass, and all knew who she was and what she'd been through. They even understood her urge to avenge her friends. Most knew she was an outstanding commander, however, and wished she had a regiment of her own instead of pursuing this single-minded, personal vendetta. She even agreed with some of the more reproachful blinking that reflected that opinion. She *was* shirking her duty to some extent. But the surgeons hadn't officially released her yet, and until they did, she'd fight however she could. *This* was her notion of healing.

The firing ahead grew more intense and a pair of guns snapped at the darkness, their tongues of flame and billowing smoke clawing at the forefront of a Grik charge boring in. She knew she wasn't ready for bayonet work, and if she got any closer she'd just be in the way. Moving up on a firing step, she peered out at the battlefield. The Grik were coming in the same old way, mostly mindless, obsessed only with coming to grips with their enemy. The brass had begun to realize they faced almost two distinct species of Grik now: one that fought in this old, haphazard, wasteful style, and another that was more thoughtful, more disciplined. She wasn't sure what to make of that, but the combination was both confusing and somewhat effective. The Grik that General Rolak faced at the far end of the rising gap would rarely attack like this, but they couldn't be shifted either. They were clearly protecting something—*defending* like no Grik they'd ever known. Bekiaa didn't know if they were protecting Grik generals or simply trying to keep the allies off the high plains where they might threaten Grik supplies, but the point was they'd never met Grik who could—or would—*defend* at all. Even Hij-Geerki considered it an alien concept and had no explanation. Bekiaa, like General Alden, she suspected, was sure this new General Halik had something to do with it, but what he'd done, she had no idea.

She shook her head. That was not her concern at present. Carefully, she eased farther up for a better view. Many Grik had muskets now; powerful, if ridiculously crude. They were also matchlocks and almost useless in this weather. Still, some few Grik had learned to use them effectively, even at relatively long ranges, so Bekiaa was careful as she exposed herself. She'd feel awfully stupid if she got her head blown off by some half-wit Grik and his stupid musket, particularly armed as she was. With her muddy, blood-blackened, rhino-pig armor and brindled fur, she was almost indistinguishable from the terrain and she made the most of it, sliding the Springfield up through a gap between a shattered tree stump and lump of mud. Nothing was coming directly at her, though a few musket balls fluttered overhead or spattered her with mud. She strained her eyes—much better in the dark than her enemies'— looking for a Grik leader of some kind. She dreamed of catching Halik himself in her sights, but knew there was no way she'd ever know if she did. Grik officers, even senior noncoms, she supposed—wore taller helmets to accommodate the crests they grew with maturity. Some even wore metal breastplates and capes, but they all looked the same to her. She scanned the press for the taller, metal helmets.

There! A Grik fitting her criteria had paused on the flank of the charge boring in to her right. For a moment it just stood there, waving its warriors on, sometimes whacking them with its sword. *Encouraging them.* That was new, disconcerting behavior they'd also seen more and more. Bekiaa flipped the safety from the right to the left side of the bolt and took aim. The range was about three hundred tails, she guessed, a convenient range for the sights—if somewhat difficult in the darkness. She squeezed the trigger, and the rifle bucked against her shoulder. The Grik dropped like a stone. Smoothly working the bolt, she spotted another target.

The defenders to her right fired a volley, and choking smoke blanketed her field of view, engulfing the Grik charge as it bored in. Another heavy volley stuttered, stabbing through the smoke with jets of fire as the second rank joined the fight. Firing came from the Grik too somehow, and Lemurian screams joined the shrieks of Grik before the charge ever went home. Some of the firing might be coming from rifled muskets captured from the First Sular and most of Flynn's Rangers. There'd been little ammunition left for anything, and practically none for the breechloaders carried by the 1st of the 2nd Marines, but the enemy had the design now. They'd have designs for lots of things. The Nancy that crashed on the field below the hill had burned completely, but they'd have its engine to look at. The far-superior carriage design of

Allied artillery would be theirs to study, as would the mortars, comm gear, and small arms, of course. Besides the loss of Colonel Flynn and so many brave Lemurians, the massacre was a disaster in terms of intelligence.

Bekiaa lost her target and had to give up looking for a while as mud-spattered troops streamed past in the trench, moving to reinforce the part of the line under attack. She didn't know where they came from and hoped there wouldn't now be an attack wherever they'd been. She shook her head. The war had been terrible, but almost simple, in a way, for a long time. The Grik had been fiercely lethal, almost numberless, but utterly predictable. Ever since the arrival of this new General Halik, however, that had changed. He was clearly still burdened with a lot of "ordinary" Grik, and likely ordinary Grik leaders, but he'd brought new thinking to the war, and a new kind of Grik as well. As General Muln-Rolak often said, this was not a "fun" war, but it was increasingly interesting—and dangerous.

The last reinforcements hurried past just as the Grik charge struck with a crashing metallic thunder, and Bekiaa started looking for targets again. *There, barely visible in the flash-lit gloom about four hundred tails distant, just at the limit of the killing field hacked out of the forest. If that's not a Grik general surrounded by his staff, I shall eat my helmet!* She flipped up the sight and raised the slide to the appropriate mark, then settled the rifle into a rigid rest. The curved steel trigger was cool against her finger pad as she took up the lash and held it near the breaking point. Just a gentle squeeze now, and the report and recoil of the rifle would come as a great surprise if all went well.

"Bekiaa!" came a voice. She didn't quite jerk the shot, but it didn't feel right. She was almost sure the bullet would go low left.

"What?" she barked harshly, still watching. There was a commotion among the "staff meeting," so she probably hit somebody, but she was furious at the interruption. Suddenly, she almost laughed. She was angry about being distracted in the middle of a battle!

"What?" she asked more softly, turning to look at Lieutenant Mark Leedom. "You spoiled my aim, Lieutenant," she continued, trying to decipher the human face moving in the dark. She gave up. "Why are you here? This is an infantry fight." She couldn't help blinking wry amusement then. "I thought you preferred to 'stay above such things.'"

Leedom's flight suit was nearly as filthy as her battle dress, and Bekiaa wondered what he'd been through to find her. Even so, the young lieutenant's face split in a wide grin.

"I still surely do, Captain, but if I gotta carry a rifle"—he sheepishly hoisted a musket—"I'd just as soon do it with you—or for you."

"Are things that desperate yet again?"

"Huh? Oh! No . . . not yet, anyway."

"Then why are you here?" she repeated.

Leedom shrugged. "Lookin' for you. General Alden thought you might just hide from anybody else he sent. I wasn't sure you wouldn't hide from me."

"So you sneaked up on me."

"No! Well . . . yeah." The battle still raged to their right while they stood looking at each other, but the firing grew more intense and mortars began erupting amid the Grik horde. Both had heard far more desperate fighting, had felt the sense of uncertainty around them as the line teetered on the brink of collapse. There was no such sense now. It was as if the rabid bloodletting, so close to where they stood, didn't really affect them.

"Why?"

Leedom fished in his pocket and brought out a folded sheet of coarse paper. "Orders, Captain. For you. Please," he said when Bekiaa hesitated, "at least take them. You can do what you want with them later, but at least I've done what I was told. General Alden can be sore at *you*."

"What do they say?" Bekiaa asked, finally relenting. She could read some now, but even her eyes might not be up to deciphering the little words on the dark page.

"Would I read your mail?"

"Yes," Bekiaa said with suddenly fond blinking. "What are the orders?"

"Well . . . there's a Clipper, one of those big flying boats, sitting in the lake waiting for you. Alden wants you on it."

"Destination?"

"Andaman—and USS *Donaghey*, under Captain Garrett, to command his Marines. He asked for you specifically, if you could be spared." Leedom looked toward the battle, then back at Bekiaa. "Or you can go all the way back to Baalkpan to help Risa train up her part of this new commando outfit she and Chack are putting together. I guess it's up to you."

Bekiaa looked toward the battle as well. Some Grik were starting to run, even as others slew them for it. The attack was on the brink of failure, and no reserves were coming up. Other Grik were withdrawing from the fight in good order—but they were dragging the corpses of the slain, and she wondered at that. The rest of the attack finally broke and ran in something reminiscent of Courtney Bradford's "Grik Rout," and the cheers almost drowned the continuing fire that chased the enemy all the way back to the forest's edge.

"So it is more a request or suggestion than orders," she said softly.

"I don't know if I'd put it like that," Leedom replied, scrutinizing the page. "Says 'orders' right here." He snorted. "Course, I'm sure they already know what General Maraan's gonna tell 'em to do with the orders they sent *her*."

They both chuckled at that, but Bekiaa's grin faded. Lemurians had few facial expressions. A grin was a grin, and anger was unmistakable on their faces if one knew them well, but otherwise they relied on blinking, ear and tail positions, and body language. To Leedom's still limited perception, Bekiaa had become unreadable. "*Can* I be spared?" she finally asked herself aloud. She'd stayed to fight this campaign out of loyalty to Colonel Flynn—but Flynn was dead, and all she was really doing was hunting individual Grik; not much of a contribution to the overall effort. Alden would probably give her a regiment, medical release or not, if she stopped playing hooky, as the Americans called it. . . . But was that what she wanted? Then again, as much as she loved Risa and Chack, they were building a force not too different from Flynn's Rangers, if she understood correctly. They'd kill Grik, she had no doubt, and that was a fine thing . . . but is that all she wanted to do? She'd always hoped to serve with Garrett—or her old skipper, Captain Chapelle, again—and Captain Garrett had certainly earned her loyalty on a sandy spit of land on the south Saa-lon coast. Besides, the assignment would take her away from this grimy, bloody hell and all the stark, bloody memories it held. She'd be back where she belonged, on the clean, clear sea, where the unburned ghosts of countless comrades didn't linger in the fetid fug above the battlefield.

"What is Captain Garrett's assignment? *Donaghey* is our oldest ship, besides *Walker* herself. She has only her sails and wooden sides and cannot survive in the line of battle—particularly against such iron monsters as the Grik now possess."

Leedom spread his hands. "I don't know. There's a lot more secrets now than there used to be. Maybe that's a good thing, but it takes getting used to."

Bekiaa considered. Garrett was too senior and too good to waste on *Donaghey* unless her assignment was an . . . interesting one.

"I will go to *Donaghey*," she said, decisive. "I will miss you and worry about you, Lieuten-aant Leedom. You and Gen-er-aal Queen Maraan, since she is the betrothed of my cousin Chack-Sab-At. You have become my brother, and she is as a sister—but you two are the only family I have left in this terrible place. I will go."

"Take him to my headquarters at once!" cried General Halik. "Fetch healers—anything you need! General Niwa must not die! I will be there as quickly as I can." Halik watched as General Orochi Niwa was carried from the damp, flashing field of battle. It should've been relatively safe to observe the attack from where they had. The enemy fire would've been directed more downward from the raised breastworks bordering his trench, and misses should have been caught by the sucking mud. Even ricochets should've been mostly spent. Niwa had persuaded Halik that the captured enemy breechloaders could make deliberate shots at such a range . . . but in the dark? Yet it could only be such a terrible device that shot the neat round hole completely through Niwa's lower abdomen while he stood commenting on the fight at Halik's side. Despite his duties, Halik had an almost desperate urge to go with Niwa now.

He paced back and forth in the trees they'd retreated to, watching the Uul draw back from the fight. The professional in him was annoyed that the attack didn't press the enemy harder, but the budding pragmatist accepted what he'd expected. The attack had served its purpose; it blooded a newly arrived draft of troops from the south, showed him which might benefit from further training and instruction in his new way of war, and provided rations for his army.

"Choosers, divide the warriors I want from the chaff that passes back to the woods," he instructed the keen-eyed observers he'd appointed the task. They weren't court-sanctioned Choosers but knew what they were looking for, knew what he wanted.

"And those that turned prey?" one asked. Halik shook his head. "They are fodder. We do not have the luxury now of further evaluations. I know many could be saved, if inspected closely. More waste!" He gurgled a sigh. "But the army must be fed. Choose carefully, but make no exceptions."

"Of course, Lord General."

Halik turned to another of his "disciples" who'd stood silent so far, watching.

"General Shlook, move a bit farther west and test the enemy near his anchor on the slope yonder." Halik pointed at the distant escarpment, invisible in the darkness. "Use another new draft. We will transform this rabble into a *real* army through attrition if we must, an army better than the Hatchling Host for defense, at need, and even better at attack—when finally we make our decisive blow."

Shlook hurled himself to the ground at Halik's feet. "As you command, Lord General!"

"Get up, Shlook!" Halik said patiently but firmly. "You have always been Hij, and I was once Uul—no better than those warriors we waste to sustain us."

Shlook rose, his crest low in submission. "Yes, Lord General."

Halik waved him away and turned before Shlook could see his sharp teeth bared in delight. He may be unsure exactly what inspired friendship, but he'd learned precisely what loyalty was and had discovered an amazing method of inspiring it. Some Hij might disdain his humble roots, but most knew only real ability could elevate Uul to Hij at the direct order of the Celestial Mother's own Chooser. His ability—imperfect as he saw it—was clear to those he commanded. By not disdaining *his* Hij, by treating them as near equals, he knew most would bare their throats to him. He was proud of this accomplishment, largely because he'd divined it himself. General Niwa had recognized his effort and applauded it, since it was one of the few innovations Niwa hadn't suggested. Briefly Halik pondered if loyalty wasn't a major component of friendship, and realized it must be so. Fondness, loyalty, admiration . . . He hurried to follow the warriors that had borne General Niwa away.

CHAPTER 5

///// *Baalkpan, Borno*

he War Room in Adar's Great Hall grew more crowded all the time. The small office where the military ministers once gathered to quietly discuss the conduct of the "Great War" had been abandoned, and the name War Room now described the greater part of the entire lower level of the hall. There were still offices for all the original ministers, of course—Defensive Works, Communications and Electrical Contrivances, Medicine, Naval Engineering, Science, Ordnance, and so forth—but now there were offices for Logistics and Planning, Personnel, Manufacture, Finance, and Strategic Intelligence as well. New offices were constantly required as the bureaucracy of war expanded, and Adar, High Chief and Sky Priest of Baalkpan and Chairman of the Grand Alliance, became increasingly confused and annoyed by it all. Yet as he'd recently, forcefully reminded everyone, he *was* Chairman, and would henceforth remain engaged in all things pertaining to the unimaginably vast war facing his people, of whatever race or clan. That meant he must not only be present but also decisive at all meetings—such as the one about to commence.

The Great Hall was once elevated, in the Lemurian way, and built to encompass the mighty Galla tree that symbolized the ancient Lemurian homeland on, it was now believed, Madagascar. The many branches of the tree represented the different directions the People fled to escape the ancient Grik enemy so long ago that few could even guess at the time that had passed. The tree was believed to be a legacy of the fabled land of their ancestors, planted by the first arrivals on southeastern Borno to establish this land Home in the first place. There were other . . . almost-Galla trees around Baalkpan, but they'd been crossbred by local flora to some degree. The only pure Gallas were in the Fil-pin Lands, aboard some of the seagoing Homes, or on Great South Island.

No longer elevated, the Hall had "grown" all the way to the ground. Expanding upward had been deemed structurally difficult, and it was impossible to build outward into the surrounding Parade Ground; that peaceful, shady expanse had become a cemetery for the growing number of war dead that preferred burial to cremation. Even if that number remained a minority, the Parade Ground would remain a memorial park to all those who'd given their lives, human and Lemurian. Building to the ground was contrary to custom and even the Sacred Scrolls, which strongly suggested structures be elevated to protect from predators and floods, but Baalkpan was so well fortified against both now as to virtually eliminate that concern. Besides, they needed more room.

Adar sat on his favorite stiffly stuffed cushion in the noisy War Room and looked about at the animated blinking of Mi-Anaaka, and the still-more-animated human faces. Many present were good friends, but others he hardly knew. Some were new enough to their posts that he didn't know them at all, and he felt a sudden longing for the old days, when Baalkpan was surrounded by Grik and faced extermination. Those were desperate times and he didn't long for the situation, but he missed the . . . intimacy of the smaller cadre that successfully defended the city. He sighed. So many of those heroes were lost to this life forever, and others were scattered across the known world, in terrible danger he couldn't share. Finally, when he could endure the time-wasting chatter no longer and was fairly sure all were present who needed to be, he touched the bronze gong for attention.

"My friends," he said in the sudden silence. "My friends," he repeated, "we have much to discuss. I shall begin by saying that things go well in the East. The Enchanted Isles are firmly in Allied hands, and the colonial possessions and resources of the Empire of the New Britain Isles are secure. The buildup for an invasion of the mainland and the final destruction of the evil Dominion has begun." This was already known, but there were cheers and stamping feet. "In addition, I am pleased to announce that our own dear Governor-Empress Rebecca Anne McDonald has consolidated her power under the guardianship of Mr. Sean Bates, whom most of you remember as 'O'Casey,' when he was among us." The cheers were more enthusiastic now. "Princess Becky," as she'd been known in Baalkpan, was much loved, and her parents' murder had shaken the Alliance with fury. "Our ambassador and Minister of Science, Courtney Braad-furd, has performed heroically, and secured the firmest friendship between our people and the Empire that we could desire. He is returning to Baalkpan for a time, and a diplomatic contingent including Sister Audry is on its way to replace him. I understand Mr. Braad-furd will collect the Imperial Ambassador in Maa-ni-la, a Lord Forester, and bring him here."

Adar took a breath. "That is the good news. Now, this is the first general meeting we have convened since the initial shock of our . . . setback in the West. Most of you now realize our early fears of total disaster were unfounded, and, in fact, Gen-er-aal Aalden has stabilized his perimeter quite successfully." Adar allowed his gaze to linger on Commander Simon Herring. Herring, a survivor of a Japanese prison ship that came through another evident "Squall" with the destroyer *Hidoiame* that *Walker* recently fought. The gaunt man was new to his Ministry of Strategic Intelligence, but even so, Adar thought he'd said some very unintelligent things at that last meeting. Herring nodded, apparently accepting the implied rebuke.

"That said, the situation there remains perilous, if not desperate. *I* do not consider it desperate, because we will do something about it very soon. The preparations have already begun. Before we discuss those and form a final plan of action, I must tell you"—he looked at Herring again—"that I have sent a personal message to Gen-er-aal Aalden assuring him of our undiminished, unanimous support. I also directed him to order General Queen Safir Maraan to Saa-lon. . . ." He sighed, then actually chuckled. "But the wireless office informs me that *Gen-er-aal* Maraan regrets that *Queen* Maraan must decline the, ah, request. She will not abandon her corps, and I cannot say I blame her."

"But who else can command the army in Saa-lon if it is to relieve Gen-er-aal Aalden?" a colonel in the B'mbaadan delegation cried. That strategy had been the most discussed so far, and Safir Maraan was the Queen Protector of B'mbaado. Adar held up a hand. "Whether *that* army moves or not has yet to be decided, and we do have other experienced gen-er-aals now, you know. Besides, I have not given up on her. You forget, we control the sky." He smiled at the irony of a Sky Priest saying such a sacrilegious thing, but it was true in this context. "We can fly people in and out of the perimeter at will. She or Gen-er-aal Rolak— perhaps even Gen-er-aal Aalden himself may accept another command when we are nearer ready to strike, although I would rather Gen-er-aal Aalden coordinate the entire campaign from *Salissa* when the time comes."

"Fat chance," Commander Alan Letts blurted, then blinked apology, his fair skin turning red with embarrassment. Letts was chief of staff to both Adar and Captain Reddy, in Matt Reddy's persona of Supreme Commander of all Allied Forces. He'd also evolved from an arguably lazy supply officer to become Minister of Logistics and Planning.

"My sentiments as well," Adar agreed, "but with the miracle of wireless and the new tee-bee-ess voice communications, I suppose he can coordinate the fight from wherever he prefers."

"Discussing commands and who should have them strikes me as premature when our armies have been savaged and our fleets blown from the sea!" shouted the Sularan representative.

The crowd erupted in protest. The outburst was absurd, particularly coming from someone who, like most landed families across the strait on Saa-leebs, fled the Grik when they came against Baalkpan. A regiment of Sularans *had* stayed and even fought in that terrible battle. Many more Sularans were in the Allied armies and Amer-i-caan Navy now. *But somehow,* Adar thought with an almost embarrassed flash, *the excrement always floats to the top.*

"Our armies suffered, true," he conceded. "But the Grik did not destroy them, despite a numerical advantage on a scale we have never faced before. The Navy was far from 'blown from the sea,' and we lost only three ships outright in the Battle of Ma-draas. Others were damaged, but counting the transports, the Navy destroyed perhaps a *hundred* enemy vessels! All our armies and the Amer-i-caan Navy and Maa-reens are already prepared to fight again—and we are sending them a great deal more with which to do it!" He gestured at Alan but continued. "Our shipbuilding continues to surge at a pace that frankly astonishes me," he confessed. "You all have seen it. The sheer scope of the new construction has taken on a life of its own, and I honestly concern myself most with how we shall ever *crew* the Navy!" He smiled, but blinked sadness, looking around the room. "The old world is entirely gone, I fear, and sometimes I feel I could hate our Amer-i-caan allies for what they have done—if I did not love them so for what they have done." There were murmurs, from both humans and Lemurians.

Alan Letts nodded silently. He hated that they'd had to subvert the fascinating . . . *fun* Lemurian culture to such a wild extent in order to save its people from extermination. Adar was right: the old ways were gone forever. All Alan could do was hope that someday the free, happy spirit of the Mi-Anaaka they first met might reemerge and thrive.

Adar continued. "Regarding small arms for our troops, the fastshooting Blitzer Bugs, similar to the Thompson of the Amer-i-caans, only lighter and simpler, will soon outpace the Allin-Silva breechloaders we are issuing to our armies. They cannot replace the longer weapons, because they are for short-range only, but they have their place. For now they have been issued to Cap-i-taan Risa-Sab-At's Maa-reen commaandos, and enough were sent to Maa-ni-la for Chack's commaandos there to become familiar with them. The new . . . pistols—again, copies of the Amer-i-caan Colt Forty-Five, have been perfected at last"—Adar glanced at Bernie Sandison, who nodded—"and will soon be issued as well."

"Can we feed 'em all?" Letts asked.

"Ammunition production's on target, if you'll pardon the expression," Bernie Sandison, the dark-haired former torpedo officer and acting Minister of Ordnance in Sonny Campeti's absence said with confident pride. "I'd still like the troops to make an effort to pick up their brass, though."

"I hope they're on target better than the torpedoes!" said Letts, and there were chuckles. The results of the torpedo tests Bernie performed in front of the whole city several weeks before had been mixed at best.

Bernie flushed. "We'll have torps by the time the skipper gets here and wants *Walker*'s tubes back. I think we've finally got the guidance issues on the MK-3 hot-air fish sorted out. It's the same as it was on the other two we tried, but the fish is so much faster, I think it tended to overcontrol."

"I'll say!" said Rolando "Ronson" Rodriguez, smiling archly beneath his Pancho Villa mustache and making a motion with his hand like a porpoise jumping out of the water.

"It was better than your dud electric job!" Bernie snapped, and Ronson cringed.

"We'll make better batteries," Commander Steve Riggs defended. They would too. Steve was Minister of Communications and Electrical Contrivances and he'd worked wonders. They all had. But, realistically, it would be a while before they had good enough batteries for electric torpedoes. "Besides," Riggs continued, "what about Laumer? He wants torpedoes too." No one answered, and Irvin Laumer wasn't there. He was still working night and day converting the old, virtually useless submarine S-19 into a surface ship. He envisioned her as a torpedo gunboat, and the jury was out whether he was wasting his time or not.

"I am sure Mr. Sandison will soon have enough torpedoes for everyone," Adar said, his voice more positive. "Enough torpedoes—and many other new contrivances that were not yet ready for the 'torpedo day' demonstration. But we must now discuss what we shall do with them—

and all the other wonders I spoke of. What will the Grik do now, and what shall we do about it?"

"Certainly we need to consider what the Grik will do." Simon Herring spoke for the first time. "But perhaps the better question should be, What are *we* going to do, and what can the Grik do about it?"

Adar nodded slowly. "I like that question better." He looked at Herring. "And if the question is not so different from the one you posed at the last meeting such as this, your emphasis on recrimination and withdrawal seems . . . changed."

"Thank you, sir," Herring replied, and it was his turn to blush as he looked at Alan Letts. "And as my understanding of the situation has improved, I hope my analysis has as well." He shook his head. "You were right. Based on the sheer numbers of Grik and their apparently improved capacity for innovation, we can't surrender the initiative. Not anywhere or in any respect." He paused, looking at the large gathering. "I still believe we must plan our strategies in greater secrecy, however. Not only because of the Grik, but because we must also consider the Dominion—an enemy with an even greater capacity to learn our secrets. With the influx of Imperial personnel, particularly the formerly indentured females with no reason to love the Empire, we can't assume the Dominion hasn't already infiltrated us to some degree."

"Do you propose there may be disloyal elements in this very room?" Adar asked with an incredulous edge. "People who would aid our enemies?"

Herring looked around at the suddenly hard stares, human and Lemurian. "Of course not, Mr. Chairman. But my post as minister of Strategic Intelligence is little different from my duties in the old world. It's my *job*—and nature, I suppose—to be suspicious. I can't imagine anyone here being disloyal, but the possibility exists that someone may come in contact with agents of the enemy. *Any* of our enemies, even the Grik. Baalkpan's a very open society, and, don't forget, both we and the Grik have Japs on our sides. . . ."

Alan Letts rolled his eyes. "I object, Mr. Chairman! First, Commander Herring wanted to pull General Alden out of the game for a goof-up anybody would've made. God knows how bad that would've been for the war effort! Now he's picking on our Japs!" Alan looked at Herring. If he'd ever been "brass blind" toward the man, as Silva once suggested, he wasn't anymore. "There are precisely *two* Japs in this city right now, both of whom we saved from the Grik at Singapore. They're delegates from our Allied Home of Yokohama and were led by a man who gave his life for the Alliance! The only other Jap we've got in the information loop is General Tamatsu Shinya, commanding all Allied land forces in the East . . . and I'll take Shinya over *you* any day, Commander!"

Adar touched his gong to silence the roar of approval. "Please, Mr. Letts. Consider Mr. Herring's own admission: it is his nature to be suspicious, and perhaps he is even right about the need for greater care— particularly as far as the Dominion is concerned. As you all know, the Empire of the New Britain Isles has had serious trouble from Dom informants, spies, and even assassins." Adar shook his head. "The Grik are a terrible enemy, the most ancient enemy of our people, but the . . . insidious capacity for treachery demonstrated by the Dominion—and even elements within the Empire itself—must never be discounted. In their own way, the Doms are just as fanatical as the Grik, and being humaan, they *can* infiltrate us more easily." He sighed and nodded. "Everyone here must have a care that nothing discussed in the War Room leaves its confines!"

Adar shifted uneasily on his cushion. "I have a night terror," he confessed softly, "that often disturbs my sleep. I do not expect the Grik and Dominion could ever actively cooperate. The Grik might be willing to consider the Doms 'other hunters,' and even join them against us, but the Doms could probably never accept the Grik as allies . . . from what I understand of them. Still, if the one enemy ever learns of the other—of how embroiled and far-flung our forces are—they might certainly take advantage, even independently. My most horrifying night terror is that they *could* combine against us, but just knowing of each other would be bad enough."

There were nods and thoughtful, blinking agreement.

"I guess that's a good enough reason in itself to maintain secrecy and be careful who we let come and go—from the East in particular," Letts agreed. "But it's possible the ship's already sailed on that."

"Whaat you mean?" asked General Linnaa-Fas-Ra, of the newly formed 12th Division, composed mostly of Baalkpan, Sularan, and Maa-ni-la regiments. The 12th was preparing to deploy west. Linnaa had been a promising lieutenant during the Battle of Baalkpan but had seen no action since.

"Only that the news may have slipped east, through Dom spies. It's believed that damn Blood Cardinal Don Hernan made it out of the Empire somehow, and nobody thinks he knew the real score—but it's no secret what we're up against in the Empire anymore. Others might've snuck out with the news. . . ." Alan grimaced. "And there's another possibility: prisoners. The Doms could've taken some during the fighting that chased them out of California—I mean, the Imperial colonies in the Americas. Chances are, anybody they took didn't know the score either, but . . . well, we never found Lieutenant Fred Reynolds or Ensign Kari-Faask, even though a search party found parts of their plane on a beach. They're presumed dead—almost certainly are. But what if the Doms got 'em somehow?" He rubbed his forehead. "Anyway, I guess I agree with Commander Herring on that, at least. We need to keep our lips zipped."

There seemed to be universal approval for this almost-unprecedented step.

"Good," Adar murmured. "Now let us get down to business. The war in the East will remain a largely Imperial operation for the time being, now that our Allies have sorted out many of their domestic problems. Saan-Kakja and the Fil-pin Lands will continue to materially support that, while most of her troops come west. We also have more troops arriving from Great South Island, and a formal alliance may soon exist between us!" As for the situation in Indi-aa, we will support Ahd-miraal Keje, Gen-er-aal Aalden, and Col-nol Maallory with everything in our power. The precise use to which those commanders put our support will be up to them, but I am confident they will use it wisely and successfully." He looked around. "Keje has his repairs well in hand, and with all we are sending him and Gen-er-aal Aalden, I am confident that not only will the situation in Indi-aa soon be reversed, but the entire resource-rich region will be denied the enemy, as originally planned."

"There is one detail," interjected the Sularan attaché. "We may control the sky, as you say, but the Grik control the sea with their monstrous iron ships! Our entire navy has been rendered impotent at a stroke!" Cries of concern and agreement echoed his words.

"Untrue." Adar said simply. "Mr. Letts?"

"Thanks, Mr. Chairman." Letts scratched the stubble on his chin. "Sure, the Grik have battleships. At last report, there's twelve of 'em stopping up Madras now, and we have to get rid of them. Keje knocked the first ones around pretty hard with *Big Sal*, but our DDs had a rough time and toe-to-toe isn't the way to do it. We've concentrated on a fleet of frigates—DDs—and I think that's still a sound policy. They don't belong in a stand-up fight with battleships, but they're a hell of a lot more practical in the grand scheme of things. They're faster, more fuel efficient—particularly since we've retained auxiliary sail—and our fire-control efforts, while still crude, did let us give the enemy a pounding. That speed and versatility will largely negate the greater size and protection of the enemy ships once we make further improvements—particularly in torpedoes." He looked at Bernie Sandison. "Besides, as has been mentioned, we have the air for now. The Grik suicider flying bombs came as a hell of a shock, but if we keep their zeppelins away, they can't drop the damn things. That's air again." He looked back at the Sularan. "Don't worry; our navy's far from impotent!"

"Actually," added Adar, "we have reason to believe Col-nol Maallory's P-Forties should be able to help in respect to the Grik baattleships. He has ten Warhawks on Saa-lon now, near Trin-con-lee. One of his planes and pilots went down in the sea, flying from Andamaan, and he remains . . . rather angrily unhappy about that. He also complains that only three of his 'ships' are currently airworthy, and cannot promise more until his ground support consists of more than, quote, 'five scruffy 'Cats with a hose, a gas can, and a screwdriver.' Sergeant Dixon and a full complement of mechanics and spares are on their way, as are special antiship bombs. The Third Pursuit Squadron should be ready by the time the new campaign is ready to proceed."

Alan nodded. "That's right. And, finally, on our old world, in our Old War . . . we'd already figured out that even battleships can't stand up to air power when it's got bombs designed to deal with 'em. All we had at the Battle of Madras was antipersonnel stuff . . . bombs we'd designed to kill Grik in the open. Well, they work swell for that, but they aren't much good against battleships. They surprised us. None of us ever dreamed they'd build giant ironclads, but we *will* sort them out!"

"That all sounds swell. . . . But when do we *go*?" asked Commander Russ Chapelle. Russ had started as a torpedoman aboard USS *Mahan* and had become a talented and aggressive naval officer. He'd been awaiting the completion of a new, armored steam frigate, or DD in Baalkpan, when the current emergency arose. As the most experienced combat skipper in the city, he'd immediately been given command of *Santa Catalina*. The ship was an old freighter Russ himself had rescued from the swamps near Tjilatjap (Chill-Chaap) on South Java, along with her cargo of Curtiss P-40E fighters that Ben Mallory now had. *Santa Catalina* had spent many months in dry dock and along the fitting-out pier becoming a powerful "protected cruiser." "You say we're gonna do something, Mr. Chairman," Russ continued. "So when?"

Adar recognized Russ's question had a double meaning. *Santa Catalina* had been ready for sea for several weeks. "Only the Heavens know for certain," Adar said. "Much preparation remains. As you know, Six Corps has already sailed for Andamaan. But you and your ship specifically are waiting for *Baalkpan Bay* to finish the alterations necessary to launch and recover the new pursuit planes—I think you call them Fleashooters? *Baalkpan Bay* will also carry the newly constituted Seven Corps, and its components must be finalized and embarked. You will escort her and her battle group to Andamaan."

Russ whistled. *Baalkpan Bay* was the newest purpose-built carrier in the Alliance, the first of a new, standardized class. And with the exception of *Maaka-Kakja* in Second Fleet, it had been decided to follow the American example of naming new carriers after battles. *Baalkpan Bay* wasn't as big as the converted Homes, but she incorporated all the latest refinements and safety measures, including electric lights! Her ship-to-ship armament was limited, but she could carry a lot of planes and had made sixteen knots on her trials. Russ knew they were rigging her for direct, on-deck recovery of the new little fighters—that *did* look a lot like P-26 Peashooters—and his feelings were a little mixed about that. It would be damn convenient, but he wasn't sure he'd want to fly anything that didn't float, if it was forced down on the predator-rich seas of this world. *He* wouldn't have to, thank God. Fleashooters were single-seat jobs, and he didn't know how to fly. That realization didn't keep him from worrying about the 'Cats who would have to fly them. By all accounts, the new five-cylinder radials powering the tiny craft were almost idiot-proof, but if he'd learned anything in his twenty-four years, relying on "reliable" things only made it more traumatic when they crapped out.

"Uh, any idea when *that* will that be, Mr. Chairman?" he asked, then paused. "Look, sir. Mikey Monk had *Santa Catalina*, and I superseded him because of the emergency. He was okay with it, but I felt like a jerk. He'd done all the work getting her ready. Anyway, the ship I was waiting for has not only been completed, but she steamed out o' here last night with the supply convoy."

"Soon," Adar said. "Mr. Monk may have another ship if he desires, but Commodore Ellis was insistent that you take *Saanta Caata-lina*, once he learned of her capabilities. It is a matter of combat experience, Commaander."

Russ said nothing more, and Adar addressed the gathering again. "Speaking of airplanes, even though all but five of the Warhawks have been deployed, production of Fleashooters has exceeded our expectations. The skies above Baalkpan are secure from further attacks by Grik zeppelins. Planes have been shipped to Aryaal and Sing-aa-pore, as well as the Fil-pin Lands, where Saan-Kakja's people will begin copying them. Nearly all our Naan-cees are now being made in Maa-ni-la, and production of the new 'Clippers,' or PB-Fives is improving here."

He stopped and sipped a mug of nectar that had been placed on a simple wooden table similar to the one he and Keje so often shared during their morning meals aboard *Salissa* long ago.

"Gen-er-aal Aalden and Col-nol Maallory consider the 'Clipper' project essential, not only because the planes can carry more passengers, larger cargoes, and eventually heavier bomb loads than anything yet devised, but they will give us a long-range reconnaissance capability we have not enjoyed since the loss of the noble PBY. We must not let the enemy surprise us again!"

"I guess that means you're still sending Garrett and *Donaghey* on their cruise?" Letts asked Adar, but it wasn't a question.

"Yes, and Cap-i-taan Reddy himself has agreed to the importance of the voyage, as well as the choice of Commaander Gaarr-ett to lead it. *Donaghey* is nearly ready to depart, and she and the raa-zeed Grik In-diaa-man, or DE, that will accompany her have received numerous updates to help them cope with the threats they will face." Adar sighed. "I hope they will fare well."

"Me too," agreed Letts. "God knows what they'll run into."

"Speaking of Cap-i-taan Reddy," General Linnaa said, "What exactly is *his* situation, and that of *Walker*?" Linnaa wasn't the only one still annoyed that the outcome of *Walker*'s fight with *Hidoiame* had been kept from them all for some time. Adar had decided, on the tail of the disaster in the West, that the news should be kept quiet until it was sure Captain Reddy would live.

"As you now know, both Cap-i-taan Reddy and *Walker* were sorely injured in their fight with *Hidoiame*. Both are recovering and will soon be back in action. I am assured that the one will likely heal just as quickly as the other. So quickly, in fact, that they may participate in the upcoming campaign . . . in some capacity." Adar blinked animated excitement. "Cap-i-taan Reddy has even shared a new, quite audacious plan with me that could shorten and perhaps ultimately win the war!"

There was an uproar in the chamber, and Linnaa spoke above it. "Tell us this plan!" he demanded.

Herring cleared his throat. "Sir," he said to Adar, "in light of all we've discussed, particularly about secrecy, I think Captain Reddy's plan should remain confidential for now."

Adar slowly nodded. "I am afraid I must agree," he said. "I apologize for the tantalizing hint. Please put it out of your minds."

There was muttering, but no one pressed for more . . . yet.

"Well," said Bernie, "back to 'explorers.' What do we know of Silva's—I mean, Mr. Cook's—expedition north of the city to contact the indigenous feral Grik on Borno itself?" he asked.

"Mr. Riggs?" Adar asked.

"Communications are sporadic," Riggs confessed. "It might be interference from the jungle or mountains, or deterioration of their comm gear. I understand they're moving through some really crappy country. They have orders to turn back if they lose contact completely, but you know how well Silva follows orders—and he'll likely get Cook to agree to push on regardless." He shrugged. "That said, I'm not too worried. Silva can take care of himself, and he's pretty good about including those around him in that blanket of . . ." He grinned. "Lethal defense."

"Why don't we send Nancys to fly around where we think they are?" Ronson asked.

"Mr. Cook suggested that aircraft buzzing about might incline the natives toward greater concern or even violence when or if they meet our friends," Adar replied. "Remembering the first time I ever saw the old PBY land on Baalkpan Bay, I tend to agree with him."

"But surely they've seen planes flying around before," Ronson persisted.

"Almost certainly. We have mapped the region as best we can from the air, but the flyers and their observers have never seen any of the . . . 'Injun Jungle Grik' Mr. Silva described. It follows that they *hide* from aircraft and may fear them."

"I guess that makes sense. Moe told Silva that jungle hunters from Baalkpan have killed them on sight for so long that few others even knew about them. They're liable to fear us—anybody from Baalkpan, flying or not."

"Indeed," agreed Adar. "I never knew the creatures existed, and am confident that if the great Nakja-Mur knew of them, he considered them an almost mythical remnant of earlier times. Jungle hunters such as . . . the one called Moe had become rare before the War, before so much meat was needed to supply our armies and Navy—not to mention the expanding population of Baalkpan itself. Many new hunters scour the jungles now, and there have been reports of . . . contact between our people and these Grik-like beings. Some of those contacts have been violent." Adar blinked regretfully. Then he blinked irony. "Ultimately, if not for the peaceful outcome of Mr. Silva's meeting with the creatures, I never would have agreed to the expedition in the first place."

The conference continued a while longer, but finally dispersed. Alan Letts had the sense that it was a dissatisfied group that left the War Room and was pretty sure it had most to do with this new policy of secrecy. The People were used to openness, and keeping secrets left them feeling slightly dishonest. More importantly, they wanted to know everything that was going on, and Letts could understand that. He did too—and wasn't sure why he felt a little weird leaving the Great Hall to join his wife and daughter for supper while Bernie Sandison remained behind with Adar and Commander Herring. Doubtless they had more questions about Bernie's new ordnance schemes, questions he and Bernie had already discussed at length. But Alan couldn't completely forget it.

A few things at Ordnance weren't adding up, like what exactly some of its people and equipment were doing. Logistics was Alan's job, and he *knew* Bernie had more people working for him than were ever at the shops and mills. The thing was, Bernie had a lot of shops and mills, and a lot of projects going on. Alan might be wrong, but he didn't think so. If he wasn't, what difference did it make? Bernie was doing good work, and if he had an extra project or two lying around that he hadn't reported—maybe out of fear of another very public failure—was it really Alan's concern? Yes. When Alan suddenly became responsible, a transition from his old self to the new, as clear as their passage to this earth from the old, he'd jumped in with both feet. If Bernie was up to something he didn't know about, he needed to find out what it was. *Tomorrow,* he decided. It had been a long day—they all were lately—and right now he was going home to his wife and daughter. Bernie would keep until tomorrow.

Alan walked along the bustling, muddy pathway leading down to the shipyard. The relatively elegant quarters he inhabited with his wife, Karen, former Navy nurse and acting Minister of Medicine in Sandra's absence, and daughter, Allison Verdia, no longer stood alone. There were other married officers now—mostly Lemurians, certainly, but a few of the first surviving destroyermen had gotten hitched to ex-pat

Impie gals that had streamed into the city for a while to escape the institution of indenture. The Impie gals were almost all lithe, dusky-skinned beauties, even if they had a tendency toward plumpness in later years, and there were more human infants in Baalkpan now. Almost all the married women, and quite a few unmarried ones, bulged with child, and Alan foresaw an explosion in the human population of Baalkpan. He chuckled. He was a lucky man to have caught Karen Theimer when there were only a few known women in the world, but with the "dame famine" broken, a little money in their pockets, and a real war to occupy their thoughts, many of his old comrades had quickly reverted to the lifestyle they'd loved and lost in the Philippines.

Alan decided to go down to the shipyard proper and have a look around. The shipyard was a mass of noise and motion. Smoke and steam streamed skyward from boilers that powered engines in the big cranes and heavy machinery. Masts and smokestacks jutted everywhere, and yelling 'Cats heaved on taglines as heavy timbers, steel plates, guns, deck machinery, even engines were shifted about, raised, lowered, or mounted in place. At the moment, he was most interested in the new construction or alterations underway, and he moved to a pair of floating dry docks that occupied a long stretch of the pier.

Yellow-hot rivets arced through the air from furnaces situated almost everywhere, to be expertly caught in tin scoops by 'Cats or Impie women high on scaffolds. Tongs fished the rivets out and drove them into holes, where 'Cats with heavy mauls waited to pound them home. It was a scene Alan had witnessed many times, wherever he'd been during his relatively short Navy career, but to see it here now gave him a proud, but almost wistful sense of nostalgic unreality. Industry—and life—had been so simple here just a few short years before, but he realized that had been an illusion as well. An inexorable force had been gathering in the West to exterminate all these people. *Walker*'s—and Letts's—arrival may have altered the culture, but the people still had a chance to be free—and survive. That would have to be enough, and Letts was proud he'd helped.

The first ship Alan focused on was Irvin Laumer's pet project: the conversion of S-19 into something "useful." Even he had finally agreed

there was no way the submarine could ever again be trusted to rise to
the surface once she went underwater. She was just too complex and too
badly damaged. Alan could still see the old boat beneath what she was
becoming, but an untrained eye would scarcely recognize the sub. Right
now Irvin was reconfiguring her hull to make a better, more stable sea
boat. The pressure hull remained the foundation of the new vessel, but
Irvin had raised her freeboard and increased her beam for a larger deck,
while keeping her center of gravity low. The . . . thing ought to be fairly
quick on its feet now they'd gutted all the stuff out of her that she didn't
need anymore, and both her diesels—and all four of her torpedo tubes—
were operational. Alan still wasn't sure how much good she'd be, and it
probably would've been easier and made more sense to scrap her and
start from scratch. But Irvin and some of his mixed human/'Cat crew
had gone through so much to save her, the skipper had given him his
head on the project. The trouble was, there was so much other construction underway that it was hard for Irvin to keep the workforce and materials he needed.

Irvin's most irritating rival for attention was the "wreck" of USS
Mahan, right beside S-19 in the floating dry dock, and more fiery rivets
arced in her direction. *Mahan* had been shattered during the Battle of
Baalkpan, but her stern section, from amidships aft, had been raised
relatively intact. The yard apes were almost finished building a new,
shorter bow for the ship, and adjoining a new pilothouse with her amidships deckhouse. She'd have only two boilers and two stacks, but lighter,
she might be just as fast. Her armament would remain essentially the
same as before, and it was hoped she too could soon deliver Bernard
Sandison's torpedoes.

What might have added insult to Laumer's injury was that in another floating dry dock alongside, the keels and skeletons of two new,
exact copies of *Walker* and *Mahan* had been laid. The Lemurian yard
workers were intimately familiar with both ships now, having already
rebuilt *Walker* almost from scratch. If anything, with their . . . different
notions of shipbuilding, the two new four-stackers might even be better
than the originals. There were still technical problems, like how to
achieve the precision necessary for steam turbines, but the new

destroyers would be cheap in materials while providing priceless ship-building experience—and, ultimately, powerful additions to the Allied fleet. There were even plans in the works to lay down an upsize version, like a four-stacker cruiser!

Irvin Laumer might've taken it worse than he did, Alan supposed, his attention returning to the fair-haired officer directing the work aboard his old sub. He and S-19 were heroes, after all. What seemed to motivate him most, however, was that despite his adventures and his service as *Maaka-Kakja*'s exec during the fighting for New Ireland, he hadn't really seen any action. Letts thought he knew how Laumer felt. Before he'd gone to the "pointy end" in the West for a while, he didn't feel he'd really contributed much to the war effort. In Laumer's case, though, Letts suspected the man still yearned to prove himself the equal of those who'd been in so many fights. Like them all, to an extent, Alan supposed, Irvin couldn't help but feel he'd wound up on this world for a reason, and was somehow destined to do great things. Alan got that, but he'd realized *his* destiny was to support those at the front. Organization was just as important as troops in the field. But Laumer apparently couldn't shake the sense that his destiny remained tied to S-19.

Alan saw Irvin looking at him and waved. Laumer waved back a little self-consciously. Maybe he was wondering if Alan was there in his official capacity, comparing the progress on the various projects—and considering which ones to cut. Alan shook his head and moved along. Irvin was a good guy and had a lot of potential. He hoped S-19 was "worth" him—and wouldn't get him killed for nothing.

"Speaking of secrets, what about the special weapons?" Adar asked almost hesitantly when he, Herring, Bernie, and Herring's chief of staff, Lieutenant Henry Stokes, were alone in the War Room. Stokes had been a leading seaman on HMAS *Perth* on another world, but had been with Herring and a couple of China Marines when they came here. One Marine was with Silva now, but the other worked for Bernie in Ordnance.

"The one is nearly ready to deploy," Bernie replied nervously, "but there're still major issues regarding delivery, and some really serious moral and practical implications to consider." He shook his head. "The more I work with the stuff, the scarier it gets." He looked accusingly at Adar. "Captain Reddy would *not* approve, and Mr. Bradford would go absolutely ape if he knew what we were cooking up."

"Cap-i-taan Reddy and Mr. Braad-furd are not here—and you work on this project in the capacity of Minister of Ordnance to the Grand Alliance, not a naval officer in the Amer-i-caan Clan. Besides, the weapon is not gaas, and that is what Cap-i-taan Reddy was specifically opposed to. Even then, he was not opposed to developing it, only using it—unless as a last resort."

"With respect, Mr. Chairman, this stuff's *worse* than gas! A lot worse. If we turn it loose . . ." Bernie shook his head. "There may be no stopping it."

"It was well enough contained before," Herring said dismissively.

Bernie looked at the former Navy snoop and wished Adar hadn't told the man. Bernie had sworn not to tell anyone, even Letts. Now Herring and this Stokes guy both knew. Bernie liked Stokes, but Herring bugged him. Maybe it was just his attitude?

"That's because it was isolated," Bernie insisted. "You turn it loose on a *continent* and God knows where it'll stop—if it ever does. Jeez." He shook his head.

"I understand how you feel, Mr. Saan-di-son," Adar said softly, "and it will remain a weapon of last resort. You also have my word that I will never order it used without consulting Cap-i-taan Reddy, and even Mr. Braad-furd if possible. Cap-i-taan Reddy or someone under his command, within his clan, would almost certainly have to be involved in deploying it, at any rate, so his agreement and equal appreciation of the necessity would likely be essential. Do not concern yourself, Mr. Saan-di-son. You may discuss the project freely with Cap-i-taan Reddy when you see him. I only desired your secrecy for the same reasons we discussed earlier."

"But even from Mr. Letts? Do you really want him thinking he's not trusted, Mr. Chairman? He knows *something*'s up; he's not stupid. . . . And others have figured out at least as much as he has."

"Who?" Herring demanded.

"Well, Silva for one. He smoked it out almost immediately. He was working with me in Ordnance before he left, and noticed some of our brighter bulbs wandering off in the woods toward the secure facility."

"Did he find out what you were doing there?"

Bernie frowned at Herring and answered sarcastically. "No, and he didn't much care. He asked if it was something he'd be interested in—and since he's only really interested in doing personal, hot-blooded, *honest* violence, not this cold-blooded, remote, insidious—"

"Mr. Saan-di-son," Adar chided gently.

"I told him no, and he believed me," Bernie finished.

Adar paused and looked at Herring. "We *should* have told Mr. Letts," he said, then spread his hands, looking back at Bernie. "But I knew he would feel as strongly as you, and his . . . good opinion has become important to me, personally. Once the weapon is more near complete, I will tell him myself." He bowed his head. "Mr. Letts is a young man, with a mate and new youngling. With his current duties and all he has seen, he has enough to trouble his sleep—if only for this short time longer."

"Besides," said Herring, "as has been stated, the fewer who know, the fewer who might inadvertently reveal anything."

Bernie didn't feel any better. *As if Alan Letts would blow! If Herring knows, why not Alan?* He was sharply tempted to tell Alan everything, and to hell with it—maybe just *because* Herring knew.

"But that is not all I wished to discuss," Adar continued. "What do you think of Cap-i-taan Reddy's plan?" Bernie's discomfort grew. Alan damn sure should've been here for this part.

"The main objective of forcing the enemy to redeploy and thereby take some pressure off India is likely to work, but it's risky," Herring said.

"He can't do it alone either," Bernie interjected. "He'll have all the commandos, but what ships can he have?"

"S-19 an' *Mahan* might be ready by the time Cap'n Reddy gets here," Stokes suggested in his Aussie twang, much more defined than Bradford's.

"Ahd-mi-raal Keje craves them for his operation against the Grik fleet at Maa-draas," Adar pointed out. "More specifically, he craves the torpedoes they will carry." He looked at Bernie's fixed expression, and the former torpedo officer nodded.

"They'll be ready."

"But will they be *needed* there?" Herring mused. "Colonel Mallory's plan might have the best, shorter-term chance of success." He suddenly stood from his stool and began to pace. "Besides, as CINCWEST, Keje certainly had the need to know of Captain Reddy's proposed expedition, and now he craves even more for *Salissa* to accompany *Walker* on what he considers a masterstroke!" Herring snorted. "I've made no secret—among us—that I consider Reddy's plan little more than a dangerous, possibly very wasteful stunt. The man is a gifted leader"—Herring almost sniffed—"and has been very lucky. But he is, after all, an amateur when it comes to strategic thinking."

Bernie's face clouded, but Herring resumed before he could speak. "That said, and as I've said before, the 'stunt' might very well have the desired effect. To succeed, Reddy will need sufficient forces to deal with whatever he may encounter. *Salissa* is now, frankly, our least capable carrier, particularly considering her projected state of repair. She's the best choice to provide Captain Reddy with the more limited air cover his task force should require."

Adar nodded thoughtfully. "The assignment would please Keje for a number of reasons, but who will then command First Fleet for the Indi-aa campaign?"

"James Ellis would seem the best choice, as Captain Reddy proposed," Herring said. "I'm sure his broken jaw is painful, but it doesn't seem to have slowed him down." He straightened. "And he's an Annapolis man."

"So's the Skipper," Bernie almost snapped. "So am I. What difference does that make here?"

"Maybe none," Herring said insincerely. He looked at Adar. "We really need a naval academy of our own, you know." He blinked humility, as he'd learned to do. "I'd be willing to organize it, somewhat along the lines of the Advanced Training Centers here and on Maara-vella."

"I'm sure you would," Bernie muttered under his breath, then raised his voice. "*Walker*'s served pretty well as an 'academy' so far. Many of our best skippers started as cadets aboard her or *Mahan*."

"Perhaps. But this recent episode has underlined the fact that she can't last forever."

"You may be right, Mr. Herring," Adar said a little impatiently, "but that is a subject you must discuss with Cap-i-taan Reddy. I may be Chairman of the Grand Alliance, but I am still High Chief and Sky Priest of Baalkpan first, just as Ahd-mi-raal Keje-Fris-Ar remains High Chief of *Salissa*, a sovereign Home." He looked at Herring. "Just as Cap-i-taan Reddy remains High Chief of the Navy, Maa-reens, and all the Amer-i-caan Clan to which they belong, human or Lemurian. You are a member of that clan, by oath, if you have not forgotten."

Herring's face turned red. "I haven't forgotten."

"Good. Then you understand that when it comes to clan matters, you must consult your High Chief. However"—Adar leaned back on his cushion—"just as Mr. Saan-di-son has done as Minister of Ordnance regarding special weapons, as a minister of the Grand Alliance, it is your duty to counsel me on straa-te-gic matters that affect all the Allied clans. It is then my duty to issue straa-te-gic commands that the clans are bound to obey as long as they remain in the Alliance. Perhaps that . . . dual allegiance still confuses you, Mr. Herring?"

"No, Mr. Chairman."

"Very well." Adar blinked determination. "As I said at our last meeting, I will be chairman in deed as well as name. No more will I let others suffer for decisions that should have been mine." He took a long breath. "Cap-i-taan Reddy remains supreme commander of all Allied forces, and if I decide his very dangerous—as you pointed out—plan should proceed, he will command every aspect of it. But before we risk him, *Walker*, and so many other ships and lives, I must make the final decision to do so, not him." Adar's voice dropped to a whisper. "Cap-i-taan Reddy carries a great enough burden as it is."

Bernie felt a sudden chill. *Would Adar really consult the Skipper before using the new weapon he'd cooked up? Would he really be willing to burden him with something like that?*

////// *Corps of Discovery and Diplomacy*
The Wilds of Borno

"This is a bunch of shit!" groused Gunnery Sergeant Arnold Horn, USMC, formerly of the 2nd Battalion, 4th Marines on another earth. Currently, he was laboring up a steep, tangled slope behind Chief Gunner's Mate Dennis Silva. His outburst, which sounded suitably disgusted but also oddly surprised, increased the disturbance of their passage. Lizard birds and other flying things, not to mention small ground and tree dwellers, made constant noise and motion as they moved, but now the cries and rustling briefly surged, making some in the party that followed stare nervously about. Silva stopped and looked back with his good eye at the black-bearded Horn. The other one was covered by a sweat-crusted patch, giving the big, powerful destroyerman a piratical flair that matched his personality.

"Quit whinin'!" Silva said, louder than many in their group would've preferred. The day's march had been particularly grueling and they'd been forced to cross two streams so far—something nobody liked. Now there was this damn rise. Unlike most, however, Silva was barely breathing hard. "Can't stand M'reens who whine!" He paused his advance, and after a swig from his canteen, he stuffed a wad of yellowish leaves in his cheek. "You're new here, Gunny," he chided, "but you been through worse, if I recall." The two men apparently had a . . . history in China, but no one knew the specifics of their relationship there. "'Sides, this ain't a patch to when me an' misters Cook, Brassey, an' even ol' Larry was marooned on Boogerland!"

The panting column behind ground to a halt and Silva looked down on it. Ensign Abel Cook, their nominal leader, looked okay, but the Imperial midshipman Stuart Brassey wasn't going to make it much farther that day. Some of the Lemurian Marines were lathered up pretty bad as well, and though the Grik-like Sa'aarans seemed pert enough, their three actual Grik "porters" were struggling to breathe in the sodden air, their long tongues lolling from toothy jaws. Old Moe, the grizzled Lemurian hunter bringing up the rear, blinked impatience back at Silva, and beside him, breathing just as hard as anyone, was Surgeon Lieutenant Pam Cross. Silva's eyes lingered a moment to take in the way her chest rose and fell beneath the sweat-soaked smock . . . but he quickly looked back at Horn when he caught Pam's searing glare.

"No, damn it," said Horn, raising his foot to display a Lemurian-made boondocker. "I mean, we been tromping *through* a bunch of shit!"

Silva shrugged. "So? We're on a trail, ain't we? Not many trails through this damn jungle." He waved around, his . . . unusual collection of weapons clanking against one another. Once again Horn wondered why Silva felt compelled to carry such a large and diverse arsenal, and how he could stand the weight of it all. Horn had a Baalkpan Arsenal 1911 pistol, and a local copy of the 1917 Navy cutlass like everyone else, but the BAR (Browning Automatic Rifle) that Silva said was his and Horn was only "borryin'" was as much as he wanted, or honestly thought he could manage, and still keep up. But Silva not only had his "real" cutlass and 1911, but his web belt was crowded with an '03 Springfield bayonet, and as many magazine pouches as he could cram on it. Slung over both shoulders like a Mexican bandit in the Western movies, were bandoliers of what looked like 10-gauge brass shotgun shells with great long *bullets* sticking out of them. Cradled in his arms was his Doom Stomper, a mammoth version of the standard Allin-Silva breech-loading rifle musket—only this one was built around a 25-millimeter Japanese *antiaircraft gun* barrel. Perhaps most bizarre, an ornate, long-barreled flintlock pistol was stuck in his belt. Horn hadn't even asked about that. Silva was just as sweat-soaked as anybody, but the weight of his weapons *and* his pack didn't seem to bother him. Horn shook his head, slinging sweat off his eyebrows.

"Lotsa critters use this trail," Silva continued, deliberately letting the others catch their breath, "all of 'em dribblin' shit up and down it as they go. This cow-floppy-lookin' stuff ain't nothin' to worry about. It don't even really stink. That means vegitician critters is mostly what's usin' it for now, like those big, stumpy-legged, dino-goat-lookin' things. Ain't that right, Moe?"

"That right," Moe answered, sniffing and peering into the gloom around them. "For now."

"See?" Silva demanded. "I'm learnin' stuff." He looked back at Horn, then the others. "You all seen rhino pigs. They're good eatin', but bad news on a trail this skinny. As liable to come at you like a Jap torpedo as haul ass the other way. They throw a bigger, lumpier turd that smells like hell." He paused. "Now, a *super-lizard* turd . . ."

"If takin' a break means we gotta listen to a turd talk about his relatives," Pam Cross snorted in her sharp, Brooklyn way, "then I'm for pushin' on!"

Silva grinned beatifically at her. "Ain't she sweet? What I was gettin' at, doll, is when you come across a trail like this, don't get to thinkin' somethin' else ain't noticed it first. Super lizards are *smart*. They'll find a wide spot an' back away from the trail just a tad an' wait for the shmorgishboard to commence. That's how ol' Tony Scott got it; ate by a super lizard while wanderin' up the old pipeline cut, prob'ly happy as a clam." He paused. "Tony was . . . a right guy. Just had a little trouble with the water, is all. Then he got ate on dry land, where he thought he was safe." He shook his head and blinked irony in the Lemurian way. "Anyhow, the moral to this story, as my sainted ma used to say, is that you ain't never safe around here—no matter what shit yer trompin' through."

Silva heard a soft scritching sound and turned. Suddenly, there was Lawrence standing before him in his mottled smock and rhino-pig armor. The rest of his very Grik-like body was covered with orange-and-black-striped feathery fur, and Dennis was always amazed by how well his friend blended with the jungle.

"Why, there you are, Larry! We was just talkin' about you!"

"You 'ere talking loud enough to hear in 'aalk'an!" Lawrence scolded with a hiss. Even though he was clearly related to their Grik enemy, physically distinguishable only by a smaller stature, slightly longer tail, and his coloring, Lawrence was of an entirely different race. Originally hailing from the distant Pacific island of Tagran, he'd become the friend and protector of Rebecca Anne McDonald while marooned with Sean Bates and the crew of S-19 on the volcanic island of Talaud. Talaud was gone now, as were most of Lawrence's people, lost in a volcanic cataclysm that had stunned the Alliance. Some of Tagran's survivors were subjects of Saan-Kakja now, given the Fil-pin island of Samaar. Lawrence was Sa'aaran now too, but he'd also become one of Silva's closest friends—even though Silva once shot him. In any event, he understood English and Lemurian perfectly and could speak either as well as his lipless mouth allowed. With his help, even some of the captured Grik were speaking a little, something no one ever considered possible before Hij-Geerki actually *surrendered* to Lord Rolak and began to communicate.

"I heard you doin' yer nails," Silva accused, nodding at the small rock Lawrence held in his right hand. "You'll be paintin' 'em next." Lawrence hissed at him. "See anything ahead?" Silva asked. Lawrence had been scouting the trail.

"Good area to stay the night on the rise not too distant. The trail's . . . 'ider there, and there's old su'er-lizard sign. Good trees, though. Us get high in the air." Lawrence subconsciously scratched the dark crest on top of his head. He'd been doing that a lot lately, ever since Silva told

him they'd have to burr it off—like his own bristly blond scalp—if it got
infested with cooties. "There's so'thing else there I think you'll . . . think
interesting," he added cryptically. "It . . . created the clearing."

"What's that?" Dennis demanded, removing his helmet and scratching his own head. He'd been reinforcing Lawrence's phobia so long, it
was starting to backfire. He realized what he was doing and casually
sopped at the leather sweatband with his bandanna. He liked the helmet, even in the muggy heat, because it was fairly well ventilated—and
let him lower his head and plow through brush.

"You'll see."

Dennis rolled his eye. "Well, Mr. Cook? It's about that time, I guess,
and maybe we can get high enough to get a good fix on our position.
Might even get a message out."

"Uh, yes, very well," Abel Cook said, removing his own helmet and
scratching his head as well. He had only four fingers on his hand. They'd
been forced to amputate his pinky when it got infected with . . . something on Yap island. They'd been in the brush for almost two weeks and
he still hadn't gotten used to the fact that he was supposed to be in
charge. How *could* he give orders to Dennis Silva? The man had saved
him more times than he could count. Yet Dennis always deferred to
him, even while essentially leading them. It might've been embarrass-
ing if he wasn't absolutely certain Silva's attempts to "prop him up" were
sincere. Pam Cross—who acted like she hated Silva—assured him of
that. "He's a bastid," she'd said, "but he's a *Navy* bastid, through an'
through. He don't follow ordas worth a damn, but he'll treat an offica
with respect if he likes 'im—an' he does like you, Mista Cook."

Abel looked at Lawrence. "This thing you found. It's not dangerous?"

"I don't think so. Just interesting. You'll see."

Abel shrugged. "Very well. It is about that time." They needed plenty
of daylight to make camp in this dangerous place.

"We never gonna find these damn Injun Grik, we keep stoppin' all
the time," Moe complained when the column pushed on. "I don't never
even see tracks of 'em since we leave Saanga River. We go wrong damn
way, I think." He raised his voice so someone besides Pam might hear

him. "Why I even come, you don't go the way I say? I wanna go home, kill rhino pigs, sleep safe. I old."

Silva fell back as the others passed him.

"Hey, Moe," he said when he was walking beside the old 'Cat. Pam threw him a sneer, but moved ahead to let them talk.

"She don't like you no more," Moe observed.

"Nah. 'Fraid she does. Why do you think she made us take her along? She don't like this little jaunt any more than you do." Dennis grimaced. "She's just sore at me—an' wants me to know it every damn day." He shrugged. "Listen. You really think you could track these Jungle Griks?"

"Sure. I do before, to catch 'em, run 'em off," Moe blinked disdain and flicked his tail. "Sometimes I kill 'em. You know dat."

"Yeah," Dennis agreed, nodding. "And so do they," he added significantly.

Moe stopped and blinked at him. "So?"

"So if we took to trackin' em, they're bound to know. Good as you are, we're in their front yard. They figger that out, what do you think *they'd* think?"

"Huh." Moe blinked thoughtfully, introspective. "Dat we chase 'em," he said at last. "Maybe we come to kill 'em."

"Right." Silva waved at the column. "We'd never catch 'em with a group this size, and if we did, it'd be because they wanted us to—to kill *us*, don't you figger? This way, we're just trompin' along—careful-like, so we don't get ate—but not trackin' nobody. Anybody that might be watchin' can tell that easy." He shrugged. "Maybe they'll attack us anyway. We do make a temptin' target. But we're a *weird* target too. Humans, 'Cats, funny-colored lizard folks that look like them—all runnin' along together, practically holdin' hands. Maybe they'll get more curious than scared."

Moe slowly nodded. "I just a hunter." He patted the painted stripes on his dingy leather armor with the smoothbore musket in his hand. "I saar-jint of hunters now, an' I got dis mus-ket 'sted of my old crossbow, but still just a hunter. You think-fight ways better than me. Good. Maybe we not all die."

Dennis chuckled. "Maybe."

They reached the top of the rise, an arduous trek along an increasingly convoluted rocky trail, and gazed upon a scene just as interesting as Lawrence promised. The wide part of the trail was bigger than Silva expected, practically a clearing, largely—obviously—made by fire. Unlike other burn clearings in the dense Borno jungle, however, this one hadn't been caused by lightning.

"By God," Horn said, "A *plane* crashed here!"

He was right, and all but perhaps the Grik porters knew it as soon as he spoke. The crash had occurred some time ago, judging by the height of the grass and renewed leaves on the flame-scarred trees. Some trees hadn't survived, though, sheared off or toppled by the falling plane, and bright sunshine slanted through the broken canopy—the first they'd seen in many days. They began to recognize bits of wreckage protruding from the knee-high grass.

"Maybe Colonel Mallory's missin' P-Forty?" Pam suggested, pushing through the group that blocked the path.

"Maybe," Silva said doubtfully, "but we're, what, eighty, a hundred miles in now? Countin' the distance we came upriver?" He paused. "And looky there. That's a hunk of a wing stickin' up. Way wrong color. It was some damn Jap, I bet."

They moved forward, the Lemurian Marines alertly flanking the advance, rifles ready.

"The paint might have faded, changed..." muttered Abel Cook, stooping to pick up a fragment of aluminum. The bright metal bore the spalled remains of dark, leafy green paint on one side. He turned it in his hand, then looked at the trees in the direction of the setting sun. "It came in from the west, clipped those trees there, and began coming apart. I believe it struck those other trees ahead much harder, perhaps shearing off the wings or parts of them. There would've been burning fuel..." He trotted ahead, and Silva, Horn, and Lawrence hurried after him. "Yes," he said, pointing down at a large piece of fire-blackened metal as he passed. "More wing!" He stopped in front of what looked like, at first glance, a giant ball of rusty string. "A twin-banked radial engine! It must've rolled and tumbled a bit.... And there's a section of a landing-gear strut, if I'm not mistaken! It's definitely not the missing

P-Forty. Not with that radial engine!" He rubbed his chin. "Judging by the oxidation of the metal and the regrowth around the crash site, it's been here as long as we have. That's unfortunate."

"Why?" Pam asked.

"Oh, no reason, really. Perhaps I hoped to prove there'd been other events, such as the Squall that brought us here."

"There *have* been," Silva pointed out, gesturing at Horn. "That awful ship that brung them prisoners—and murdered most of 'em, an' that damn tin can, *Hoo-dooy-yammy*, that *Walker* tangled with."

"Yes, but those ships originated . . . appeared on this world, in the Philippine Sea. I'd hoped there might have been other, separate events *here* so we could begin to understand if we're dealing with a geographically specific phenomenon. . . ."

"Careful what you wish for," Silva said, then stopped watching Cook and resumed scanning the denser trees looming around them, his monstrous rifle at the ready. Suddenly, he didn't like it here. They moved farther along, the Marines watchful, the rest of the party grouped together, coming up behind.

"If I was a super lizard," Moe began, and Silva nodded. "Me too. Lots o' grass-eatin' critters would love this place; pygmy brontasarries an' such, and you can see where rhino pigs been rootin' around. You 'Cats better stay on your toes," he cautioned the flanking Marines.

"We on it," one answered.

Dennis looked down to see Pam's diminutive form beside him. "Startin' to cozy back up to ol' Silva after all?"

Pam glared. "I'm cozyin' up to that big gun o' yers, that's all."

Dennis feigned a hurt expression. "So *that*'s all I ever was to you?"

Pam's face flushed with rage and she stormed off after Stuart Brassey, who was moving farther along.

"Goofy broad," Silva muttered.

"A woman scorned," Horn corrected loftily. "You're poking at a hornet's nest with that one. I thought she was going to take that Blitzer Bug off her shoulder and hose you down. How come you don't leave her be?"

"Why don't she leave *me* be?"

Horn shook his head. The whole group was moving forward now

that Cook was finished staring at the engine. "You might have every-body else fooled, but I know you're not really that stupid. I knew you back when." He studied Silva a moment. "You've changed, though, maybe a lot. I know most folks think well of you, and that's a far cry from the old days." He shifted his helmet back on his head and scratched a mosquito bite on his eyebrow. "I'm still not sure you've changed for the better, though. Sooner or later you're going to have to give in to that gal, or make a clean break with her."

"Hell, I don't know *how* to break it any cleaner!" Silva protested. "I left her in the lurch, practically pushed her on another fella. I been treatin' her like crap . . . what else can I do?"

"You idiot. You know that's just the exact opposite of making a clean break. Or have you really been here long enough to forget? 'Hard to get' just makes 'em try harder to get you."

"She ain't no Filipino gal," Dennis protested.

"No, but mean and ugly as you are, she's got her sights set, and that's all there is to it. The next-best way to get rid of her besides actually chasing *her* is polite indifference. Be nice to her; treat her like anybody else. They hate that . . . but it won't make her want to shoot you." Horn grinned. "Then who knows? Maybe I'll start treating her like you've been doing, and she'll chase after me!"

"You couldn't handle her," Silva warned. Gunny Horn started to reply, but Cook called out.

"Come look at this!"

They hurried to join the others at a large but badly battered cylinder that must've rolled away from the greater violence of the crash. Moe trotted up to the group as well. "All clear—for now. M'reens'll stay on alert, an' I got them damn Griks gatherin' wood for fires. Nothin' likes smoke." He looked at the roughly thirty-foot object. "What dat?"

"Jap bomber," Horn declared. "One of those cigar-looking jobs—a 'Betty,' they were calling them. I figured it was a Jap plane when I saw the color, and now you can see the meatball." He pointed. "That's the tail section with the stabilizers rolled or torn off. It probably broke off the rest of the thing when it wiped out and rolled over here."

"Dat's 'loom-num, right?" Moe asked.

"Yeah, mostly."

"We all rich!" he giggled. "Ever-body lookin' fer gold, now dat gold means money, but ever-body told to keep eyes open for crashed-plane 'loom-num just like dis! It worth twice its weight of gold!"

"Woop-te-do," Silva said. "It ain't like we're gonna wag it outa here on our backs."

"But . . . we come back for it, yes?" Moe demanded.

"Maybe. Not likely we'd find it again from a different direction, though."

"I find it!" Moe persisted.

"So? What're you gonna do with it? Be the richest hunter in the history of 'Cats?" Silva looked at the trees nearby, planning their camp. "If we get the word out, maybe Baalkpan'll send somebody to get it. We sure need the metal." He looked at Moe's crestfallen blinking. "Don't worry, we'll get a share for findin' it. More than you can spend. What would you blow it on? A new car?"

"Maybe I get a little hut closer to city," Moe muttered. "Up off ground, like other Baalkpan folks, where old bones sleep good at night. Maybe I take a mate."

Silva stared. Moe was probably the oldest 'Cat he'd ever seen, next to old Naga, Nakja-Mur's Sky Priest who died with his Chief at the Battle of Baalkpan. Moe looked at least eighty, even if he was strong as an ox.

"Well . . . sure. Why not? Bound to be some nice, young . . . blind 'Cat gal who'll take up with you—if you got enough dough." He looked at Lawrence and the Sa'aaran beside him. The other Sa'aaran was scouting deeper in the woods. "Get them Griks to dump the woodpiles around those trees yonder, the white-trunked ones with no bark. Look kinda like yooky . . . yucky . . ."

"Eucalyptus trees," Pam supplied sarcastically.

"Yeah. Them. I like those. There's good visibility around 'em for a change, and lots of little branches to squirm up through. We'll rig our hammocks up there for the night, with three fires a little ways off. How does that sound, Mr. Cook?"

"Excellent," Abel replied absently, peering inside the crumpled fuselage. "Mr. Brassey and I will explore the wreckage to see if there's anything of immediate use. Perhaps we'll even find clues regarding the fate of the flight crew."

Silva looked at Horn. "My money's on 'death by sudden, fiery, crunchy stop,'" he whispered. "Come on. Let's get settled for the night."

Dennis shinnied up the trunk of one of the strange trees, scrabbling for traction with his own already-battered Lemurian boondockers. Compared to a Lemurian, his ascent was ludicrous at best, but almost graceful compared to Horn's similar attempt on a neighboring tree. Pam and Lawrence started up a third tree, and the dark-haired woman didn't seem to need any help and didn't ask for any. The Grik porters remained below to pass up their burdens. They didn't much care for climbing trees, anyway.

Dennis suddenly stopped his ascent, staring straight into the dark crotch of the tree just a few inches from his face. He never said a word and his expression didn't even change as he pulled the 1911 Colt from his holster and fired two shots directly in front of him. Lizard birds squawked and beat their membranous wings as the near quiet shattered.

"What the hell?" Horn cried out.

"Pokey" the Grik, the slowest (in a variety of ways) of the former enemy beings accompanying the expedition, dove face-first into the moldy undergrowth at the base of the tree, sniffing for the freshly fallen .45 ACP cartridge cases. Around his neck was a clinking bag filled with every shell he'd managed to find since they started out. Lawrence considered Pokey retarded, compared to the other two Grik they'd brought, and had appointed him the official "brass picker"; the only job he thought him fit for. Pokey quickly got more than brass when a heavy, long-tailed creature landed on his head, and he yelped.

"What was it, Chief Silva?" Abel cried, sprinting from his inspection of the shattered plane.

"Dunno," Silva groused. He'd wedged himself into the tree and was shaking a bleeding hand. "Some nasty, lizard-coon-lookin' thing."

"How's this trip ever gonna work if you shoot everything we run into?" Pam called from her nearby tree.

That ain't fair, Silva thought. There were lots of critters he hadn't shot. "Damn thing bit me," he defended.

"He's all'ays shooting things," Lawrence sighed conversationally to one of the Sa'aaran scouts who also came running, and the two standing Grik with the shelter/hammock canvas. "He's shot 'ountain 'ishes, su'er lizards, too 'any Griks and Doms to count. . . . He even shot I once!"

"That was a accident—but maybe you had it comin'," Silva snapped. "Don't anybody care that it bit me? I might'a caught rabies—or the lizard pox!"

Pokey had picked up the dead creature and was clutching it close. "'or 'ee?" it asked, almost reverently.

"Sure," said Silva with a sigh. "If you want. Let Mr. Cook and Mr. Brassey oogle it first. I'm sure they'll let you eat it when they're done."

"I thought we were supposed to be quiet," Horn observed. "You *have* shot a bunch of things since we started."

"There's quiet; then there's quiet," Silva countered. "Anything bites *me* is gonna die for it." He looked at his wounded hand philosophically. "Course, that lizard-coon didn't exactly chase me down and bite me. Little fella was just defendin' what was his."

"Well, it's *your* tree now," Pam said sarcastically. "I'll look at that hand when we're done makin' camp."

Clouds billowed in the sky as the sun made its customary rapid plunge. They contacted Baalkpan via their man-portable version of the wireless sets installed in the PB-1B Nancys while Pokey happily turned the crank on their pack generator. They couldn't give an exact fix on the wrecked "Betty," but they gave the best directions they could and reported their progress. Not much progress to report, really, but making contact with the comm 'Cats back home was always reassuring.

Their roost was as secure as they could make it. The branches intertwined the higher they went, so it was actually possible to move from tree to tree if they wanted. It must've looked odd, Silva thought; all the hammocks strung like bagworms in a juniper, but everyone was fairly close to one another. The trees weren't much real protection from a major predator. A full-grown super lizard could knock them over if it wanted, but with most of them thirty feet or more in the air, even a super lizard couldn't just snatch them like low-hanging fruit. Most of them, anyway. The Grik didn't like being in trees, and even ordered to do like the rest, they'd slung their one hammock lower than the others ever since they started out—with all three clustered like chicks in a nest. In this one and only respect, their obedience wasn't entirely pure, but Cook didn't press it. He was actually encouraged that their "auxiliaries" seemed to be developing a trace of free will. And the arrangement served a purpose. Now and then, a Grik would slide down a rope to the ground and tend the fires that gave them some visibility.

As usual, Silva had arranged his weapons in the limbs around his hammock so he could get at them in a hurry; then he settled in, squirming and flouncing until he was comfortable. The jungle sounds in the wilds of Borno grew thunderous at night, filled with monotonous calls, squeaks, grunts, and the occasional roar. One could usually track the progress of a predator, no matter how stealthy, by the cries that accompanied it. Silva was used to the noises. They were the same ones heard in Baalkpan, even if they'd grown more distant and muted there. The sounds actually soothed him in a way, like crickets, frogs, and whippoor-wills of his native Alabama. And up above, through the broad leaves and fleeting gaps in the clouds made visible by the freak passage of a doomed Japanese plane to a world its crew would never know, were the brilliant, searing stars. They were the same he'd always known. A little skewed at this latitude from the view he'd had as a kid, but still the same. He'd always loved the stars. Even as the high, racing clouds blotted them out, his eye slowly drooped. He was almost asleep when he heard a creak on a branch nearby and the eye popped open.

"Evenin', doll," he said, recognizing Pam crouching there in the glow of the fires and a sudden flash of lightning. "Come to cut my rope—or my throat?"

"Let me see your hand," she demanded.

"Too dark. Have a look in the mornin'."

Pam lit a small, silver-backed candle lantern with a Zippo and shone the reflected light at him.

"I'll look at it now." She propped the little lantern in a nearby crook.

"Suit yerself," Silva grumped, displaying his wound. Gently Pam cleaned the bite with a damp cloth, then smeared some of the curative Lemurian polta paste on his hand, working it into the punctures with her thumbs. The paste felt cold, but the massage was . . . relaxing.

"So, how come you're bein' such a jerk?" Pam asked suddenly. Dennis snorted. It had taken her two weeks in the wilderness to cough up the question.

"You're one to talk," he replied. "I'm just respondin' in kind."

"You dumped me. I got a right to be sore."

Silva sat up in his hammock. When he spoke, his voice was almost gentle. "I didn't dump you. I just went on doin' what I do—somewhere else. Sorry I didn't get a chance to say 'So long,' but I got shanghaied, if you recall."

"You could've said 'So long' when you got my letter in Maa-ni-la."

"What? You mean that grabby letter sayin' I *b'longed* to you an', an' I *better* come on home?" He shook his head. "In case you ain't noticed, there's a war on. An' aside from this little campin' trip, I b'long where the war is more than I b'long to you—or me." He shrugged. "It's what I do. What I *am* now."

"Sister Audry talks like that. Says you're a 'weapon of the Lord.'"

Dennis actually giggled. "Yeah, I heard that too. I like the good sister, but she's crazier than a shithouse rat if she b'lieves that."

"I don't know . . ."

"You too? Look, doll," Silva's voice went cold. "I ain't a good man. I done some real bad things, as a matter o' fact, things the good Lord won't *never* forgive, and damn sure wouldn'ta set me to. I done 'em 'cause they needed doin'—and I'd do 'em again. *Will* do the same sort o' things again, most likely." The terrified face of a powder boy, maybe ten years old, reappeared in his mind, staring at him through the flames he'd set that would quickly doom the kid—and maybe three hundred other mostly innocent souls aboard a ship he'd had to destroy. He'd killed all those people to save a handful that mattered to him, and that wasn't the first time. Or the last, he was sure. He shook his head. "Now, you're liable to maunder on about lovin' me anyway an' all that silly crap . . ."

"I do . . . *did* love you, you big ape!" Pam hissed.

"See? I knew that—an' it ain't fair. This war, what I do—in spite of how I do it—is the best thing I ever did. I expect to burn in hell for *how*, but good folks, folks like you, will maybe have a chance. To make sure o' that, an' to make sure all the folks I care about have the same chance, I'm in this war to the bitter damn end, an' I don't see that comin' any-time soon."

"So you *did* cut me loose because you care, just like Sister Audry said!"

Dennis growled with frustration. "Damn it, I ain't doin' this right. Gunny Horn was right. Look, doll, there just ain't no future for you an' me, not while there's this war, see? I can't make it any plainer than that."

Pam put out the light and surprised Dennis by crawling in the ham-mock with him. "That's fine. An' I guess it's all I really needed to hear." She snuggled up against him. "Besides, the war might not last as long as you think. They're workin' on a secret weapon in Baalkpan that might wipe out the Grik for good."

"How do you know that?" Silva asked, remembering a conversation he'd had with Bernie Sandison. Pam shrugged. "Everybody knows about it. I bet Adar's the only one who doesn't *know* everybody knows!"

"Huh. What's this weapon do?"

Pam shrugged. "Nobody knows."

"Ever'body knows about it, but nobody knows what it does," Dennis muttered thoughtfully.

"Well . . . That doesn't hurt, does it?"

"Hard to say."

A short time later, Silva squirmed out of Pam's embrace, still consid-erably uncomfortable with her sudden, unexpected tenderness after such sustained and apparently sincere hostility. He was always amazed how women could keep so many different personalities wadded up in-side them all the time. *Must all be skitso-phobiacs, er whatever. Every damn one!* he decided. Carefully he moved onto a branch and looked back at the gently snoring woman. She was heartbreakingly pretty, par-ticularly when her face was relaxed in sleep. He shook his head. *That didn't go like I meant at all,* he thought. *I spent all this time tryin' to save her from me, just to let her snuggle back up like that.* He'd known for a

TAYLOR ANDERSON

while he had a soft spot. Chack's sister Risa found it first, then Princess Becky wormed her way deep inside it. Pam found it too eventually, but then tried to crack it wide-open—into a dangerous gap in his armor. That wouldn't do, he'd decided, for him—or her—in the long run. But all it took was a bite on the hand and a little kindness . . . and now it looked like he was back to square one with her. He snorted angrily at himself and descended slowly to the ground.

Urinating against the closest neighboring tree trunk, he saw a rope snaking up into the darkness toward Horn's hammock. *That's dumb,* he thought. *Leave a ladder for all sorts of nasty boogers to scamper straight up in bed with ya. Why, somethin' like me might wander by!* Any number of boogers might visit their hammocks from the trees, but the dangling rope struck Silva as sloppy. Suddenly inspired and somewhat annoyed at the China Marine, he took a piece of dried fish out of his pocket and tied it securely to the rope. Then, after checking the fires, he climbed back up to his hammock.

"HOLY MOTHER O' GOD! WHAT'S GOT AHOLD OF ME?!" came the sleep-muddled shriek of Gunnery Sergeant Arnold Horn.

Silva came awake quickly, as he'd learned to do, but was surprised to find Pam had returned to her own hammock. How did she do that without waking him? He looked down at the . . . really weird creature yanking violently on the rope. He blinked. "Honest ta' God, Arnie," he said just as everyone began to stir and shout questions, "I ain't got a clue!"

The thing was shorter than a man, and looked a little like a Menjangen lizard, like bit Leo Davis so long ago, but it had a little head—with a big conch shell–like thing on its forehead—on the end of a long, skinny neck. Large, luminous eyes glared yellow. Feathery membranes stretched from elbows to hips, and an extra-long tail flared into a flat, brightly colored leaf shape, like the Grikbirds in the East. The short legs were what gave the initial impression of a Menjangen lizard, Dennis decided. "I never seen one before," he shouted at Horn as the creature yanked on the rope. Horn had his BAR now and was trying to draw a bead on the thing below, but his hammock was bouncing too wildly to allow a shot. "I thought we were tryin' to keep things quiet around here," Silva mocked.

Suddenly, the creature's eyes went wider, if that was possible, and it lunged to the left with a violence that nearly dumped Horn. "Somebody shoot it, goddamn it, before it yanks me out of the tree!"

"I can't, Gunny!" Abel shouted, his pistol weaving. Moe was aiming his musket, and Lawrence was trying to bring his rifle to bear. Pam yanked back the bolt on her Blitzer Bug. Silva suspected she'd hit the thing, but it might take the whole twenty-round stick in the simple, almost uncontrollable weapon. Everyone was so focused on the strange creature and scary-humorous tug-of-war, so distracted by the bouncing limbs as they shifted in their own hammocks to see or draw a bead, they didn't feel or even see the approach of what had suddenly frightened the little monster. Their first warning was a chorus of shrieks of abject terror from the Grik hammock, suspended nearest the ground. Silva turned in time to see the biggest super lizard in the world crash directly through one of the guard fires, scattering clouds of sparks and burning wood as it accelerated to a speed few would've imagined such a large creature capable of. Even fewer had ever seen it—and lived to tell.

"Ever'body *shut up!*" Silva roared.

If the shout distracted the giant beast (an overgrown allosaur, Dennis remembered Courtney calling the things), it didn't show it. It was wholly focused on the smaller animal that started hooting desperately— even as it tugged maniacally at the morsel Silva had baited it with. It apparently never even considered just letting go and running away. With a satisfied gurgle, the super lizard snatched up the smaller creature in its terrible jaws and silenced a last, desolate howl with a mighty crunch. One of Horn's hammock lines parted and he fell, still clutching the BAR. He actually glanced off the monster's right flank before landing on the soft, mushy ground. Apparently unhurt, he bolted around to the other side of the thick trunk.

Several limbs were shaken loose and fell when Horn did, and the super lizard appeared not to notice as it chewed a few more times, then raised its head to let the morsel slide down its throat. All still might have been well if that motion hadn't brought the great predator's head frighteningly close to the Grik hammock.

It's like the worms in a apple screamin' bloody murder when the bird flies by, Dennis thought with a sinking feeling. Unlike the other hammocks, the super lizard could reach that one with only the slightest hop—which it suddenly showed it was capable of. The jaws closed on the canvas package of flesh, and Dennis heard the same shrieks he'd listened to with perverse pleasure on many battlefields. Only this time, they came from "friendly Grik" who'd trusted him to keep them safe— and this whole mess was maybe just a little bit his fault.

The hammock brought larger limbs down with it this time, and the whole cluster of trees shook violently. Pam was bounced from her bed and fell with a startled cry. Half of Stuart Brassey's support lines parted and he slid out as well. Moe, Lawrence, both his Sa'aarans, and the two 'Cat Marines were already out of their beds and scrambling down the tree trunks.

"Shit," muttered Silva. He slid his giant rifle to the ground by the same line he'd hoisted it with, slung his web belt and bandoliers around his neck, clutched his hammock to him with one powerful arm, and slashed the line at his feet with his cutlass. The line parted with a snap, and he swayed out over the super lizard just as it stooped to examine the unexpected prize it plucked. To his amazement, Dennis saw one Grik bolt from the hammock and vanish in the dark. Horrible cries still came from within the Grik hammock, keeping the super lizard distracted while Dennis swayed. He wanted to throw himself clear, or at least bounce off the beast as Horn had done, but there was no way. "Shit," he repeated. Sliding down as far as he could, he dropped on the monster's back. For just an instant he stood there, teetering—and saw Pam's terrified face reflected in the firelight. He flashed her a gap-toothed grin and was suddenly inspired to stab down as hard as he could with his trusty cutlass.

That was stupid, he realized when the super lizard reacted as quick as a rattlesnake and spun around with an ear-splitting, indignant screech. *Guess I missed anything important,* he thought analytically when he was tossed away like a biting fly. He had just enough time to curl into a ball before he hit the ground rolling. A stick—something—poked him in the ribs, but he jumped to his feet just as Horn's BAR shattered the night with its staccato roar. *Dumb-ass! I told him these big'uns'll soak up '06 like a sponge—an' this is the biggest bastard I ever saw!"*

The noisy, painful impacts did distract the monster, however, particularly when everyone else opened up as well. *Maybe it'll run away,* Silva hoped. *Didn't think so,* he thought when it immediately turned to face this latest nuisance. Moe had gathered the shooters behind the farthest of their trio of trees, and they were shooting through the branches. Clearly thinking the tree was its enemy, the monster proceeded to destroy it. Trying very hard not to draw its attention—which he probably couldn't do with a bugle now that it was so focused on the enemy tree— Silva scrambled for his rifle. *There! Still in one piece!* All it would've taken was a stray step by the five-ton lizard to ruin it.

The tree was almost done, and very quickly the super lizard would figure out that its real enemy was beyond it. The damn thing actually was pretty smart; smart enough to realize their little guard fires were no threat. Maybe it couldn't see that well at night and the gun flashes likely had it confused, but in just a few seconds it would be *chasing* his friends in the dark, away from the light Dennis needed to kill it. He pulled a couple of the massive shells from the bandolier and raised the big rifle. Thumbing back the hammer, he aimed for what he hoped was the hip. Having studied the anatomy of super lizards with some interest, he wasn't sure he could break its neck with one of the hard lead bullets he carried the most of—and he couldn't tell in the dark if he'd chosen one of his "specials" with the bronze core penetrator.

"Hey, you stupid, walkin' backhoe!" he bellowed. "Get a load o' *this*!" He fired. The recoil of the quarter-pound bullet atop nearly three hundred grains of first-class mil-spec black powder almost slammed him off his feet and actually left him a little dizzy for a moment. The super lizard staggered, its left leg trying to drop out from under it. With a mighty squeal of rage and agony that saturated the jungle around them and finally seemed to shake the rain from the heavy clouds above, the monster managed to straighten. Then it turned toward Dennis Silva.

"Jeez. I think this sucker kicks even worse than the old Doom

Whomper," Dennis muttered, thumbing back the hammer and slapping the trapdoor breechblock up and forward. The big, empty shell casing clanged away amid a wisp of smoke as the extractor slammed it against the raised ejector knob toward the rear of the receiver. Dennis shoved another cartridge in the chamber and clapped the breech closed. All this was done with muscle memory, before he was completely recovered from the first shot. He could hear yelling and shooting but it barely registered, didn't signify. He looked up.

"Goddam!" he squeaked. The super lizard was almost on him, its mouth wide to gulp him down, strands of bloody saliva glistening in the firelight. Dennis snatched the big rifle back to his shoulder and fired in the general direction of the upper back of the great mouth that had grown to encompass all things.

He was still standing there a few moments later, staring dumbly at the enormous dead head in front of him, when Pam Cross flung her arms around him, plastering herself to his side. "You're somethin' else," she cried tearfully.

"He's a whopper, ain't he?" Dennis finally managed. Then his voice grew hard. "Yeah, I *am* somethin' else: a jerk." He caught Abel's eye as their teenage leader approached. "This was my fault," he admitted.

"How on earth?"

"I tied a piece of fish to that line hangin' from Gunny Horn's hammock. I . . . sorta left the bait that lured this big bugger up. I only meant it as a gag."

"Why, you . . ." Horn began, but Moe stopped the Marine before he could take a swing.

"Some gag," Silva continued bitterly. "Almost got us all killed."

"*Good* gag," Moe countered unexpectedly. He poked at the super lizard with Silva's cutlass. He must've pulled it out. "Dat booger runnin' roun', he catch our smell, come for us. Him see dat little lizard hoppin roun' *save* us. Udderwise, first t'ing we know 'bout him when he eatin' dem damn Griks or somebody else."

Silva wasn't convinced. He didn't get introspective very often, but he still figured he'd screwed up. "How many o' those Grik fellas did we lose? Is everybody else okay?"

"Two of the Grik died of their wounds," Abel said stiffly. "Pokey escaped. Barely. No one else was seriously injured. A few bumps and bruises."

"I guess that's somethin.'" Silva looked at Cook. "I'll accept whatever punishment you choose to fling at me . . . sir."

"But it *good* gag!" Moe persisted. "Dem Griks gonna die, sleepin' dat low, no matter what." He shrugged. "You all miss bigger t'ing! Dat damn super lizard smell smoke way before he smell us." He gestured around. "Out here, back home . . . anywhere . . . smoke mean fire. Fire mean burn, choke, die. Even dat little rope tugger come troo smoke. How come *both* them boogers come rompin' up like expectin' somethin' ta eat?"

Stuart Brassey looked at Abel. "Because, around here at least, they're used to fires—cookfires, perhaps. Fires that often mean food, or at least scraps."

"Indeed," Abel said, sounding very much like Courtney Bradford when the man was deep in thought. He looked at Silva. "No punishment, but no more gags, if you please. At least not without discussing them first."

"So . . . what do we do now?" Horn asked. "Our camp's pretty well trashed. No telling what else'll come running up to that big pile of meat."

"I hate to add more bad news," Brassey said, "but the transmitter casing is shattered. I think our big visitor may have stepped on it when it fell from the tree. I don't know if I can salvage it or not." The Imperial midshipman had become an avid electronics student and was their de facto wireless operator.

"That don't matter," Silva said. "We was bound to lose contact sooner or later—an' it ain't like anybody can help us now, anyway." He looked at Horn. "No reason to get all worked up either. We ought'a be safe as can be for the night." He hesitated. "Look, I'm sorry about the gag, but maybe Moe's right. Super lizards are top dog wherever their territory is. Blood or not, nothin'll pester us here until *he* starts smellin' dead, instead of like a big-ass super lizard."

"So . . . what do we do? Use the big bastard for a pillow?"

"Can if you want, if you can stand the smell. He *is* a bit rank. Besides"—Dennis's expression lightened—"meat's meat, and we already got fires." He shrugged. "And who knows? Maybe a little smoke an' cookin' meat'll lure up whatever else is out here startin' fires that critters ain't afraid of."

CHAPTER 7

////// *The Enchanted Isles (Galápagos)*
Elizabeth Bay

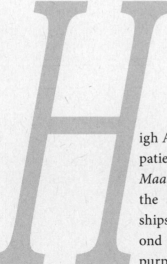igh Admiral Harvey Jenks, CINCEAST, impatiently paced the broad bridgewing of USS *Maaka-Kakja* (CV-4) while staring out at the already-impressive collection of warships anchored around the flagship of Second Fleet. *Maaka-Kakja* had been the first purpose-built aircraft carrier/tender in the Alliance, and currently, on paper, Second Fleet was the most powerful naval force in the Grand Alliance—particularly after the mauling First Fleet took at the hands of the Grik. In reality, though, the fleet's assets were still so strung out across the vast reaches of the Pacific—or Eastern Sea, as the Lemurians called it—that Harvey Jenks was confident only that he could hold the Enchanted Isles against any currently imaginable Dominion threat. But he chafed at the time it was

taking to consolidate sufficient forces to take the war to the bloody Doms.

He'd always known that would take time. The Empire of the New Britain Isles had absolutely no experience at projecting such power, particularly over such distances. And if his American-Lemurian allies had deployed comparably large fleets, even they'd never attempted it so incredibly far from their primary base of supply. Jenks had the colonial possessions in the northern Americas to draw from to some extent, but they were no closer. Besides, the shattered "Honorable" New Britain Company had jealously guarded against the rise of major industries in Saint Francis. The shipyards there were necessarily impressive by prewar standards, but the foundries were puny and the workforce sparse. It was never intended that the colonies *should* be able to sustain themselves without importing expensive manufactured goods—much less sustain a major fleet and thousands of troops so far from their shores.

That was changing. Even as the bulk of the Imperial Navy and most Allied assets in the theater moved to the Enchanted Isles, much of the Empire's extensive merchant marine was shipping the tools of industry to the colonies. Captain Reddy had even asked for and received permission to establish a Lemurian-American base as far south as (what they called) San Diego. The place had long been recognized as a potentially excellent port, but its proximity to the Dom frontier had made establishing one a dangerous, perhaps provocative act. Provocation was no longer a concern, and the new, slightly closer American port would help ease the strain—eventually. But that was all in the future. After what the Doms did to his country and to his people here in the Enchanted Isles, Harvey Jenks wanted to get at them as soon as possible.

He suddenly realized, not only was he pacing, but he'd begun twisting his braided mustaches again. Abruptly he dropped his hand and stopped to lean against the rail overhanging the flight deck below.

"Um. Any word from Admiral Monroe?" he asked Admiral Lelaa-Tal-Cleraan, who'd been—if not more patiently, at least more resignedly—pacing alongside him. Admiral Lelaa commanded *Maaka-Kakja*, and ultimately all Allied naval forces in the East. She wore the white kilt and neatly tailored blouse required of female Lemurian naval officers over her brindled fur, and she looked at him with her large, wide eyes.

"No, High Ahd-mi-raal. Not today—but I presume Monroe and his squadron of Imperial ships of the line is somewhat closer than when Lieutenant Haan-Sor-Plaar of the DD escort USS *Finir-Pel* sent their position report *yesterday*. Lieutenant Haan is a conscientious young officer, and I'm sure he would have sent a special report if, say, Ahd-mi-raal Monroe's squadron was suddenly destroyed by a herd of mountain fishes."

Jenks glanced sharply at Lelaa and caught her grin. He sighed. "I apologize, Admiral. It's just that those bloody things—the liners, you call them—are so damned slow!"

"But damned powerful, and I will be glad to have them when they arrive. And there is no need to apologize. I am as anxious as you."

"Am I that obvious?"

Lelaa blinked and swished her tail. "Yes, but I have learned a few things over the past few years. First, no matter how I may chafe against it, very few things can be made to happen *more* quickly than is possible. I am never satisfied by that, but I may have learned to accept it better than you." She flicked her ears. "Perhaps a lifetime under sail alone has prepared me for that revelation"—she gestured around at her massive ship and the planes on the flight deck and almost giggled—"despite what might seem somewhat significant evidence to the contrary!" She looked back at Jenks and blinked seriousness. "I have also come to know you well, I think." She pointed at the Imperial frigate *Achilles*, anchored nearby. *Maaka-Kakja*'s immediate battle group all rode at anchor within the confines of the port city and territorial capital of Elizabeth-town, on the main island of Albermarl. "I suspect you miss having your own deck beneath your feet. You commanded *Aa-chill-ees* a great while, and now, though you command our entire effort in the East, you have no ship of your own. *I* would miss that."

Jenks rubbed his chin. "That may be part of it," he conceded. "I had *Achilles* for almost five years. I commanded other ships for twelve years before that. I've *belonged* to one ship or another all my life, it seems. It does feel a bit, well, *unnatural* to step beyond that. I suppose I envy your

Captain Reddy in that respect. Militarily, he outranks us all, I suppose, yet he gets to keep *his* ship!" He smiled. "Not that he—or the entire Grand Alliance—would have it any other way!"

Tex Sheider, *Maaka-Kakja's* exec, stepped out on the bridgewing. "Admirals," he said, "it's fifteen hundred. You told me to remind you."

"Thank you," Lelaa said, looking at Jenks. "We will be along immediately." Sheider nodded and turned away. Lelaa blinked concern and lowered her voice so only Jenks could hear. "I do hope Governor Humphries is feeling better today. Such an interesting person, and such a waste if he should remain . . . as he has been . . . forever."

Maaka-Kakja's big steam launch plied back and forth between the ship and the government docks in Elizabeth Bay almost constantly. This time it carried Jenks and Lelaa, as well as General Tamatsu Shinya and Lieutenant Orrin Reddy. Shinya had been a lieutenant aboard a Japanese destroyer that *Walker* sank with a stray torpedo right before she steamed into the Squall that brought her to this world. Shinya had been torn by divided loyalties for a time, but was ultimately accepted by the vast majority of his former enemies. His strict sense of honor and devotion to the Allied cause helped bridge any remaining obstacles between him and Captain Reddy becoming close and trusted friends, and his talent as a field commander brought him his current appointment as commander of 2nd Fleet's Allied Expeditionary Force (AEF-2).

Orrin Reddy was COFO of *Maaka-Kakja's* 3rd Naval Air Wing—which was strange in itself, because he'd belonged to the 3rd Pursuit Squadron in the Philippines when the Japanese attacked. Additionally strange because even here he remained enough of an Army pilot that he'd refused the naval rank of commander. He'd been offered the army rank of captain, but declined that too on the grounds that one Captain Reddy, regardless of branch seniority, was enough for this screwed-up world. He meant no disrespect by that because, perhaps strangest of all, Captain Matthew Reddy was Orrin's much-admired first cousin. Whatever twisted fate had brought any of them to this world had been particularly cruel to the Reddy family back home.

The view from the launch was breathtaking. The sheer tonnage of shipping that choked the anchorage was impressive, but the sky was bright and the bay almost surreally clear. Most of the island itself was a dark, rocky heap of long-cold lava, but despite Orrin's initial description of the place from the air as hell, this part, at least, was lush with vegetation, and the saddles between the distant, craggy volcanoes were filled with tall trees and flurries of colorful flying creatures. Elizabethtown reflected the architecture that prevailed elsewhere in the Empire; an odd mixture of the classical with blocky stucco and wood. New London, on New Britain Isle (what should've been Honolulu) was reminiscent of "old" London in many ways, but here, as just about everywhere else except perhaps Respite City, simpler, more practical buildings sufficed. Still, the place had an odd, almost Mediterranean beauty to it—or would have before one noticed the virtual sea of tents that had sprouted on the broad plain south of the city, where the AEF was beginning to make its home.

"Fend off there, you lizard-faced buggers!" cried the Lemurian coxswain as the launch approached the dock and Imperial sailors jumped to comply. Orrin smiled. The humans and Lemurians in the U.S. Navy had developed a kind of mixed patois that incorporated many words from both languages. Those new to the Navy still butchered it with a kind of pidgin but could usually make themselves understood. This new association with Impies had begun to add even more terms and phrases to the odd, almost universal language that was developing.

Line handlers, bored with the routine visits of the launch, quickly straightened and creditably snatched the tossed lines when they saw who was aboard. A squad of Marines, 'Cat and Imperial, quickly gathered to receive the unexpected brass. Hopping ashore and exchanging salutes, Jenks dismissed the offer of an escort to Government House. He'd been there many times, and if there was anywhere on earth he and his companions should be perfectly safe from the enemy, it was within the military anthill Elizabethtown had become. They might get smushed by a toppling mountain of supply crates, trampled by hurrying troops, frightened horses, or mooing palkas, but those were hazards everyone had to guard against ashore these days, and an escort likely wouldn't save them.

"What a sight!" Orrin said, amazed. Even with the focus of the wider war inevitably shifting west, the city was a far cry from the half-starved ghost town it became at the tipping point of the Dom invasion, when the defenders were on their last legs. It was also clear that regardless of the shift in priorities, Allied industry and food production was starting to hit an impressive stride. Granted, a lot of what was arriving now had already been in the pipeline, before the Battle of Madras, but the Fil-pin Lands were still committed to sending nearly everything they produced—except more troops—and the Dom defeats had prevented them from strangling Imperial production.

"It *is* impressive," Shinya allowed, looking around as they hurried up the dark, gravelly street toward Governor Humphries's palace. Orrin didn't respond. He still disliked Shinya. Quite simply, the man was a Jap, and his experiences as a prisoner in the Philippines before his later arrival here had been much different from his cousin Matt's. He'd obey Shinya's orders—when his air wing was tasked to do so by Lelaa or Jenks—and he even kind of understood Matt's high opinion of the man, but he couldn't "forgive and forget" the treatment he and so many others received at the hands of other Japanese, not to mention the murderous hell they'd endured aboard *Mizuki Maru*. The hellish ship was gone now, along with some good men and 'Cats who'd fought her against still other Japanese, but deep down he was glad the damn ship no longer existed.

Imperial Marines stamped to attention as they mounted the steps of the palace, and the three men and one Lemurian returned the armed salutes before a small man in a civilian frock, tricorn, and gaudy cravat opened the tall entrance doors and bowed low. Inside it was dark and noticeably cooler, and the four visiting officers removed their hats and placed them under their left arms. Another, taller man they recognized as Governor Humphries's factor bowed as well.

"Good afternoon, gentlemen . . . and, uh, Lady Admiral Lelaa," he said a little awkwardly. "The Governor and Colonel Alexander are expecting you." He paused and lowered his voice. "I believe the Governor's feeling a bit better today," he added. "Perhaps the improved diet—and the discovery of some dozen tortoises that survived unmolested by the damned Doms on one of the neighboring isles has helped. He's quite devoted to our tortoises, as you know."

Jenks nodded diplomatically.

"Yes. Well, please follow me," the factor said.

"Governor Humphries," Jenks said when they entered the broad drawing room. "Colonel Alexander. How are you today?"

"Very well, thank you, High Admiral," Alexander replied, standing. Humphries remained seated behind a small table, the remains of a light meal strewn before him. He beamed. "Good afternoon, Harvey! I'm so glad to see you. I've had the most excellent news!"

"I heard, Your Excellency. Congratulations."

Humphries brushed it aside. "It was none of my doing. Your timely arrival"—he nodded at Lelaa—"with our Lemooan allies saved us all. Including the tortoises. None of us could have endured another week without you, I'm sure."

Jenks shifted uncomfortably. "That may be, Your Excellency, but now we must look to the future. Any advantage we currently enjoy will be fleeting if we give the bloody Doms a chance to recover. Obviously, they're much closer to their source of supply than we, and now they've experienced our technical advantages, they might quickly match them. That would have the same effect as surpassing them, with their numbers compared to ours."

"Indeed," Humphries fulminated. "We must drive them! How quickly can we take the war to them?"

"That's the problem, Your Excellency," Lelaa interjected. "We likely can't for a time. As you know, there have been setbacks in the West that will materially affect us here. Because of that, a grand, overwhelming invasion is out of the question for the foreseeable future." She looked sideways at Jenks, then Shinya. "I do believe we can—*must*—do *something*, however."

"But . . . what can we do?" Colonel Alexander asked. "If we cannot invade, what can we do to hurt them?"

"From a naval perspective, we can systematically hunt down and destroy what remains of their navy," Lelaa said confidently. "It is not inconsiderable, but for now, ours is overwhelmingly more capable. I suggest a combined air and sea campaign to destroy anything afloat that flies the Dom flag. Not only that, but with proper reconnaissance, we can destroy their shipyards and other coastal faa-cilities. We prevent them from building a new, better navy, even as we destroy the old one."

"That would afford us a number of advantages," Jenks agreed. "Combined with the captured maps and charts, we finally managed to take a few Dom officers on the other islands, who were willing to tell us what they could in exchange for honorable surrender." He glowered. "Not that they deserved it after what they did to our fishermen living there! Feeding them to their damned dragons . . ." He shook himself. "Well, I doubt they had much choice. None of the senior officers were taken, and at least the junior ones demonstrated some basic humanity for the men under their command. In any event, where before we knew only a few of their port cities and had only the most basic charts of their coast, we now have a greater grasp of the scope and geography of the Dominion than ever before. We even know approximately where their capital, this Templo de los Papas, lies." He frowned. "Nowhere near where we'd *thought* it was!"

He pointed to the new map Alexander had prepared and placed in the room. The Temple of the Popes, the holiest place in all the Dominion and seat of its wicked power, was not shown in the Valley of Mexico, as had been so long assumed, but in the vicinity of a much larger valley, or plain, in the north of the South American continent. Orrin and Shinya called it Venezuela, and the maps of Jenks's ancestors called the region the Viceroyalties of New Granada and Peru. The exact location of the capital city wasn't marked, apparently beyond the scope of the map, to the east.

"We always tried to be careful about revealing too much about the Empire to strangers," Jenks said ironically, "but then allowed a Dom presence there! The Company was largely behind that, as it turns out, for motives of its own, but the fact remains that we never learned much about the Dominion beyond the few ports they allowed us access to. Sadly, Company influence wasn't the only reason we failed in that respect; for far too long, we felt safe surrounded by our vast ocean, and frankly, simply didn't care. Without this latest intelligence, our disinterest would've returned to roost, as it were, and we still wouldn't know enough to launch a major operation, even if we already had the means. Now I think we do."

"Perhaps," Shinya said cautiously, gazing at the map of an empire extending from a strangely shaped Baja Peninsula in the north, as far south as Valparaiso. It hugged the Andes back northward until it sprawled eastward across Colombia and Venezuela. From there, it included all of Central America up to what was described as a terrible desert stretching as far north as where the mouth of the Rio Grande probably was—if the trend of major rivers being approximately where they were expected to be continued. For some reason, the Doms claimed the apparent desert sweeping west, northwest from there—all the way to the proposed American Navy base at San Diego. Beyond that, except for Imperial outposts in California, nothing was shown.

"But even with the captured maps and information we've gathered from prisoners, our map remains glaringly, apparently *deliberately* incomplete," Shinya continued. "Particularly regarding the region around Panama and Costa Rica. We have our own maps, from the old world, that might help in general ways, but we all know there are often significant differences." He shrugged. "*Why* does that place, of all others— even the general location of their *capital*—remain mysterious?"

"I don't know," Jenks confessed. He looked at Colonel Alexander, and the garrison commander shook his head.

"I believe the prisoners told us what they could," Alexander insisted. "Why not? They're dead to their country, by the act of surrender, and we secured no high-ranking officers. The junior officers, though intelligent and professional, are not well educated beyond their duties. Even the rank-and-file Dom is a good soldier, certainly, but has been deliberately kept ignorant of the most basic things. Much like the Grik, if I understand the latest theories," he added oddly.

"Well, I wish we had some of their *naval* officers to question," Governor Humphries brooded. "They'd *have* to know the coast of their own land, surely." He looked at Lelaa. "Please do try to acquire some of them for us. Won't you, Lady Admiral? That . . . mysterious region seems to beg our most ardent attention." There were nods. Lelaa looked at him and smiled, glad the man who reminded her so much of Courtney Bradford seemed to have recovered his wits.

"We know where most of their port cities are now," Jenks said. "And I rather doubt the ones we already knew are the most important, or they'd never have allowed us there in the first place." Absently, he twisted his mustaches. "As Admiral Lelaa suggests, all their ports, important or not, should be our focus now . . . for another reason beyond those she mentioned. One thing we're fairly sure of—and our new map confirms—is that the Doms have few roads beyond this coastal highway that stretches such a distance." He pointed. "Like the Grik in that respect, they rely tremendously on coastal shipping, not only for commerce, but apparently even communication. A campaign like Admiral Lelaa suggests would not only further secure us, as well as all Imperial holdings, here, but might also isolate large parts of the Dominion from itself."

"Exactly," Shinya suddenly enthused, "which might make it possible for us to stage smaller landings, to conquer the Dominion in detail!"

Jenks blinked. "That's . . . a very distinct possibility! Certainly, once we learn more about their strategic stance and what targets would most thoroughly disrupt it, quick, destructive raids at the very least—much like Captain Reddy has proposed in the West—would be valuable in terms of intelligence for us, and confusion to the enemy."

Orrin Reddy cleared his throat and everyone looked at him. "That's swell," he said, "and a good idea, but it's going to be dangerous as hell. We don't hold nearly as big an edge over the Doms on land as we do at sea and in the air. Our small arms are generally better, but not by a lot." He looked at Jenks. "Imperial Marines still have flintlocks, for God's sake, and none of the new breechloaders have made it out here yet. Who knows when—or if—we'll get any of the new repeating carbines, those Blitzer Bugs they're talking about. We're a long way from home, and the more advanced weapons have been going to fight the Grik." He paused, thoughtful, and everyone waited until he continued. "Captain Reddy's plan is kind of based on a similar operation I told him about on our old world, and I'm sure something similar would drive the Doms nuts. We need to improve our recon regardless—that's a fact. But they still have those damn Grikbird 'dragons'—that can tear hell out of my planes." He shrugged. "We're better against 'em now, and if we ever get some of the new pursuit ships out of Baalkpan, I bet we can eventually get complete control of the air. As it is, though, we go in there with nothing but Nancys, we're going to lose a lot of planes and pilots. The second time we go in, we'll lose more. Eventually, if they ever figure out what we're up to, they can throw a continent's worth of 'air' at us all at once—and there goes *all* our planes."

Shinya nodded solemnly. "Lieutenant Reddy is right. We must either plan a raid—a big one—that will destroy as much of the enemy's industrial and strategic infrastructure as possible, and then get out, or we must discover if we can sustain a continental foothold that can survive independently of air support, for a short time, at least. Properly supplied, such a thorn in its side might draw a disproportionate amount of attention from the enemy."

"You realize you're suggesting *placing yourself* in the same position General Alden is in?" Jenks asked.

"Not at all," Shinya denied. "We would have access to and control of the sea, for purposes of supply. And if we run into more than we can handle?" He shrugged. "We pull out under cover of darkness—and perhaps land again in a place the enemy has stripped of troops!"

Orrin nodded. "That could work. We'll still need recon either way."

"True," agreed Lelaa, looking at the flyer. "Your Nancys are faster than Grikbirds. If you are just looking about, they should not catch you."

"Yeah. And we can make it tough on the ones that try. We're still going to lose guys and machines, though. If only we had just a *few* of those Blitzer Bugs—or some honest Thompsons, it would save a lot of lives."

"What are the chances of that?" Jenks asked Lelaa. "Getting a rush shipment of those weapons for this operation?"

"Not good," Lelaa replied, blinking disappointment. "They are only now tooling up to make them in Maa-ni-la, so all would have to come from Baalkpan. Even if they have them to spare, it would take months for them to arrive, unless . . ."

"Unless what?"

"Unless we could talk them into using one of the big Clippers."

"Could one large plane carry enough of these Blitzer Bugs and the necessary ammunition to protect your aircraft?" Jenks asked Lieutenant Reddy.

Orrin considered again. "I honestly don't know. I haven't seen a Clipper before and don't know the specs. I doubt one of the old 'Buzzards' could do it."

"A Buzzard could not," Lelaa stated firmly. "And even a Clipper could not possibly make it all the way here unless it carried so much fuel that there would be no capacity for cargo. A pointless gesture. But with the new facilities Sor-Lomaak raised at the islands called Midway, one *can* bring the weapons as far as New Britain. I understand there is already passenger service that far." She looked at Jenks. "There are several islands between here and there that would have served us well just now."

Jenks nodded grimly. "Tiny, barren, remote little things that would've been useful for tending seaplanes, I believe, but of no use otherwise, I fear. Now that the notion has struck us, we should certainly emplace such outposts. But the cart must precede the horse in this instance—if you'll pardon the expression—and our tardy realization cannot benefit us in the very short term."

"We could send tenders—" Shinya began.

"We don't have any to spare." Orrin practically cut him off. "And even if we did, it would take the same weeks to get them to those little bumps in the water—I've seen 'em on the charts—that it would take a ship to get here from the New Britain Isles." He shook his head. "Then a Clipper pilot would have to find the damn things! That's asking too much. Most 'Cats didn't even *believe* in this part of the world not long ago!"

That wasn't exactly true. Lemurians always knew the world was round and must have a bottom. But based on their very literal concept of gravity—"Whatever it is, it always pulls down"—they'd believed you *could* fall off if you went too far from the "top," which was obviously centered somewhere between their ancestral home of Madagascar and the Fil-pin Lands. For that reason, and because the notion that you wouldn't fall off assailed some of their most closely held liturgy, many 'Cats back in Baalkpan, maybe even Adar himself, still had a hard time grasping the sheer distances involved in the conflict in the East. Most probably understood their teachings were a little off by now, but understanding and acceptance aren't exactly the same things, and one didn't inevitably lead to the other.

"Finding those little dots in so much empty sea is too damn much to ask of them," Orrin continued. "Chances are we'd lose them—and the cargo we'd been waiting for."

"Very possible," Jenks agreed. "Perhaps at another time an attempt can be made, with picket ships lining the route. The planes that fly as far as my homeland are often in range of vessels passing below—or any number of convenient islands. So. It will still take some weeks to ship the weapons here, in our fastest steamers," he calculated.

"Yes, but we will need to plan this operation well," Shinya advised. "Months give the enemy too much time to surprise *us*, I fear. But weeks is a realistic time frame for our own planning and preparations—if we *can* get the weapons."

"My boys'll fly with or without them, so I'm in either way," Orrin said softly, and Lelaa smiled to hear her COFO call *Maaka-Kakja*'s pilots "his" boys. Not too long ago he hadn't even been sure this was his war. "I'd rather have 'em, though."

Jenks looked at Governor Humphries. "It would seem, sir, we have the beginnings of a plan. I believe Admiral Lelaa can commence her part of it, the eradication of the Doms from the sea, almost immediately. General Shinya will plan various contingencies based on whatever reconnaissance Lieutenant Reddy can accomplish without unduly jeopardizing our air power. I will personally move heaven and earth to get these Blitzer Bugs here, and if—*when*—they arrive, the Third Air Wing should be able to provide more detailed information to General Shinya, and his operation will go forward as rapidly as possible after that, to maximize the element of surprise. Does that sound satisfactory to you, sir?"

"Most satisfactory!" Humphries beamed. "The sooner we strike those atrocious Doms, the happier I will be." Then he cleared his throat and looked away. "And may God protect and keep you all."

"Thank you, Your Excellency," Lelaa said with sudden hesitation. "But there is yet another thing we must consider."

Jenks raised his eyebrows at her.

"Chairman Adar may not release the weapons we desire for any number of excellent reasons, but he may also consider our strategy— and particularly General Shinya's part—too risky. General Aalden's setback in Indi-aa does not seem to have shaken Adar's resolve, but it does appear to have made him feel he needs to exert greater central control over the war effort."

"I understand that, but he's not here," Jenks replied.

"I don't know if that matters, High Admiral. His new attitude does not reflect on the competence of any leader so much as his desire to take the consequences of any mistakes they make upon himself to spare them the recriminations and, yes, pain, of those consequences."

"I don't know, Adar," Orrin injected darkly, "but that's bull . . . BS."

Jenks looked sharply at the Lieutenant. "I *do* know Chairman Adar, and he may be the most honorable being alive. He is misguided in this respect, however. If we, any of us, make poor decisions that cost lives, it is our duty to bear the burden for that. He cannot absolve us. He should *replace* us if our choices are bad enough, but just as Captain Reddy has said he cannot make all our decisions for us when he is so far away, neither can Chairman Adar. I repeat, he is not here." Jenks twisted his mustaches again. "I will draft a summary of our strategy to be sent with our request. With the ships en route to relay the signal, we should have fairly rapid communications all the way to Baalkpan. I will do my best to convince him that *this* is what we should do *here*, now. If he objects, perhaps Captain Reddy can speak to him when *Walker*'s refit is complete and he steams to Baalkpan himself."

"Time potentially lost," Shinya warned.

"We'll lose no time," Jenks insisted. "We will make our plans regardless. I've no doubt Captain Reddy and the Governor-Empress will support us."

"And if Adar doesn't?" Shinya persisted.

Admiral Lelaa-Tal-Cleraan took a deep breath and looked at Orrin. "Chairman Adar leads the Grand Alliance, but Cap-i-taan Reddy is my High Chief and supreme commander. I will consult him if I can, but, ultimately, I will do what I know he would in my place." She looked around at the others, her gaze steady, unblinking. "New weapons or not, we go."

////// *In the Wilderness of the Holy Dominion*
Province of New Granada

"Jeez! Would you look at that?" Lieutenant Fred Reynolds blurted, mesmerized, gazing down the long, sparsely wooded slope at the open valley beyond. He hadn't spoken much since his rescue. He remained worried about his friend Ensign Kari-Faask, and uncertainty about his own status usually kept him uncharacteristically mum. His borrowed horse started slightly at his sudden, unexpected outburst, and the silent, intimidating riders strung out along the soft, deep timber path glared at him. He barely noticed.

The heavier forest they remained within was impressive enough, and the closest thing he could compare it to was the redwood forests of his native California. If anything, these trees were even more massive in all respects, but the bark was wrong. They looked like gigantic pines, and even dropped pineapple-size cones and a carpet of very pinelike needles—even if the needles were arranged along a kind of spine, like a fern. Very little sunlight penetrated to the ground, and there was virtually no undergrowth in the vast, dark wood. It was a spooky place, and there was always the hint of nearby movement, odd rustling, and the occasional sharp squeal or bark to keep him on edge. Even if it weren't for his and Kari's situation, the forest alone would have kept him quietly tense.

But the creatures he'd glimpsed grazing at the edge of the forest and down the valley toward some unseen river left the word "gigantic" seeming ridiculously inadequate in his mind. The beasts looked something like the pygmy brontasarries often used for heavy hauling in Baalkpan, but where those creatures were the size of an Asian elephant, these monsters stood almost as tall as the shorter trees near the clearing— maybe a hundred feet—with their long, serpentine necks upraised, munching on the high, ferny needles. Their skin was rough and lumpy, blotched and smeared with an effective camouflage pattern, but what possible use camouflage would be to animals so massive was a mystery to Fred. Maybe it was handy when they were younger.

"*Silencio!*" hissed one of the nearest riders, menacing him with a Dom flintlock pistol. He didn't quite point it at him, but implied he'd conk him with it to make him shut up.

"Sorry," Fred whispered. He didn't understand his captor-rescuers' sudden insistence on silence. The horses made plenty of noise of their own on the forest trail skirting the valley clearing. He stared back at what he'd seen. "But jeez!" he murmured.

His companions were all dark, rough-looking men, thin but powerfully built. They all dressed much the same as well, in animal skins and worn, threadbare cloth. There were a few profound differences. Some wore strange cat-shaped icons on thongs around their necks—much like the revelers had worn that day he'd gone with the sadistic "Blood Cardinal" Don Hernan DeDevino Dicha to view Ensign Kari-Faask in her cage in the courtyard of the Temple of the Popes. A flash of heat seared his spine. He'd had to pretend he didn't care what happened to her then, and regardless of the circumstances, the memory filled him with shame. He'd become good at pretending, or Don Hernan wouldn't have believed his "conversion" was genuine. The scam saved his and Kari's lives, but also hurt Kari badly, and nearly broke her when nothing the Doms had done to her could.

Other members of their band wore what he considered "honest" crosses, however—as opposed to the garishly warped version he'd grown accustomed to as an initiate in Don Hernan's sick church. He didn't know what to think of that, and since none of them could—or would—understand him, he hadn't been enlightened. He *did* now know without any doubt what most in the Grand Alliance had long suspected: the approved faith practiced in the Holy Dominion bore no closer similarity to actual Catholicism than a dung beetle to a deer. Both creatures walked on the ground, but that was as close as it got. Any superficial resemblance was a deliberate disguise, an attempt to subjugate the largest number of people by using accepted, and, yes, respected ancient symbols of religious power. But the mixture of crosses and other newly familiar pagan symbols among his companions left him very confused.

"They might still kill you, you know," came a quiet whisper beside him, and Fred realized his enigmatic "savior" had moved his horse alongside his. "If you make too much of a nuisance of yourself," the man explained. For some reason, he seemed amused.

"Why don't they kill *you*, then?" Fred hissed. He didn't know much about Captain Samuel Anson other than his name, and in the weeks he'd been on the run with this outlaw band, he still hadn't learned what Anson was captain of, or hardly anything else. The guy didn't answer many questions. He *had* to be a spy or agent of some sort, judging by the way he'd gotten Fred and Kari out of the city, and considering his perfect, if strangely accented English, he had to be an Imperial . . . didn't he? He looked much like the others: his skin dark, hair and mustaches black, but that was common in the Empire—and understandable that an Imperial spy in this country would be suspicious of him. He'd have little or no independent confirmation of events in the West, and couldn't know his people had allied with the only vaguely remembered Lemurians, not to mention the American destroyermen he'd never even heard of. What didn't make sense to Fred, however, no matter how he added it up, was if the Empire had spies in the Dominion, beyond the port cities where traders had been allowed, why didn't they know more about it? The question gnawed at him.

Anson smiled crookedly. "They won't kill me, because I help them kill Doms. They like to do that. Maybe they even like me. I suppose they think I'm somewhat mad, to be honest, but I've contacts among the filthy Doms—and others—and that's useful to them." He peered at Reynolds, weighing his response. He'd essentially confirmed he was a spy, which was more than he'd done since they met. "And what is useful to them is sometimes useful to me," he finished, shrugging, then pointed at Fred's filthy, travel-worn robes. "You, however, are their enemy! A priest of the Dominion! A lowly initiate, by your once white, unadorned robes, but a Blood Priest nevertheless."

"I explained all that!" Fred snapped hotly but still quietly. "I'm no more a Dom priest than a Chinese cowboy!" He paused. "Hell, I'm *closer* to a Chinese cowboy!"

Anson smiled. "I'm not sure what that is"—he gestured around—"and neither are they, I assure you. It has sufficed thus far that you're a friend of Ensign Faask—and that you helped rescue *her*. It helps also that as she grows stronger, she's ever more insistent that they let her see you. Even they can see that you're genuinely important to her."

Fred grimaced, and twisted to look behind them, where the somewhat elaborate, covered travois was towed. Kari was alive, but still sick and weak after months of abuse and malnutrition. He'd spoken to her only a few times, first when she briefly awoke shortly after their escape. She'd been near delirious, but overjoyed he hadn't really turned after all. The second time he snuck close enough to talk to her, after they joined this larger group, he'd been badly beaten. Only Kari's apparent willingness to hurl herself at his attackers, weak as she was, saved him then. Since that episode, he'd been allowed to visit her under guard every few days, but that was it. "They wouldn't want to distress her overmuch," Anson finished.

"I'd hope not!" Fred whispered fervently, both for her sake and his. "But, well, why's she such a big wheel to them, anyway?" he probed.

Anson regarded him intently. "She's *not* particularly important to the Christians in our little group, beyond what she may represent in terms of allies against the Doms."

"Christians? *Real* Christians?" Fred demanded, diverted by the term.

"Quite real," Anson said bemusedly, "if what constitutes a Christian to them means the same as to us. I'll assume, based on your recognition that the Doms *aren't* Christians, that it does." He cocked an eyebrow. "And those around here have grown quite pragmatic and amazingly tolerant of other beliefs. Very interesting, as a matter of fact—and convenient."

"Convenient how?"

"For resistance to the Doms, of course! You've only seen a city where the Doms rule uncontested. I understand how you might think their perversions are universal and monolithic, but I assure you they're not." He gestured around at their companions. "These men are poorly armed and poorly led. They have few firearms, most of which they took from Doms. Their leaders are fractious and rarely agree—except in their shared hatred toward the Templo de los Papas. Hopeless as their situation may seem at a glance, however, opposition to the Doms is a very strong inducement for them to get along. No doubt you've seen the fate of those who don't submit to conversion?"

Fred nodded grimly.

"Of course you have," Anson continued. Fred's vestments and slow-healing scars bore eloquent testimony to his own ordeal. "But the good thing is, in addition to that powerful incentive, these ragged fellows we've fallen in with represent a sizable percentage of the population. They're a minority, to be sure, but just think how hopeless their position would be if they were constantly fighting among themselves." He quietly chuckled. "Which brings us back to you, I suppose. Another reason you're still alive and riding so comfortably along with people who will happily cut the throat of anyone dressed as you are is that they're fairly satisfied you're part of, allied with, or in some way associated with the Empire of the New Britain Isles—which is known to be at war with the Holy Dominion. Most thought the Empire had been swiftly conquered, by surprise. I did," Anson admitted, "at first. That was the story around the Temple, anyway. Now I'm not so sure."

"No way," Fred growled. "The Empire . . . and my people—Kari's too—continue to resist. I *told* you that! And we'll kick their asses too! I picked up quite a bit while I was pretending to be Don Hernan's stooge. Kari and I were captured right before the Allied fleet hammered the Doms making for Saint Francis, and the Imperial Garrison at the Enchanted Isles was still holding out. Don Hernan was afraid it would be reinforced before they could take it, and that's one of the reasons he wanted me to design his airplanes—flying machines."

"Did you?"

"Yeah. Kind of," Fred admitted, miserably. "I kind of *had* to, to make him believe I was a convert. It was the only way to save Kari. They already had most of my plane to look at anyway, and I don't think I gave them anything they couldn't have figured out on their own eventually."

"You might be surprised," Anson said grimly. "Just your existence was proof that powered flight is possible, but they had that before they caught you. Having you show them how all the bits fit together no doubt gave them insights whether you volunteered them or not."

"Maybe," Fred agreed, "but maybe I gave them a few *wrong* insights too. That was my plan, anyway."

"Good." Anson paused. "So, Don Hernan's worried about the Galápagos," he mused. "With good reason," he whispered more forcefully. "With the Enchanted Isles still controlled by the Grand Alliance you speak of, the Doms should be more focused there than against our insignificant little insurgency. That will make everyone happy—but Don Hernan!" Anson chuckled at his own little joke—a play on the rest of Don Hernan's name: DeDevino Dicha, which basically meant "divine happiness."

Fred glanced up and down the line of riders. "Okay," he whispered. "You've told me about some of our 'friends,' but what about the others? The ones with the Felix the Cat necklaces?"

Anson had no idea what Felix the Cat was, but understood Fred's question. "The cat figure represents a jaguar, a creature from their most ancient mythology."

"I know what a jaguar is," Fred said.

"Really?" Anson shook it off. "Amazing that any of *them* should after so long. Particularly since, to the best of my knowledge, there's nothing remotely like a jaguar around here." He stopped suddenly and gestured back toward the travois. "Not until now, of course."

"But Kari's no jaguar! She's a Lemurian, a 'Cat . . ." Fred stopped. "Oh, shit." He rode in silence a while, his mind racing. "Captain Anson," he finally asked, almost pleading, "is Kari being a jaguar a good thing or bad?"

"That's an excellent question. I haven't paid as much attention to the ancient religions among my various friends as I should have, to be sure. By the way they treat her, I'm encouraged. I've also learned that people here, even the Christians, can be a bit capricious and fickle at times, however. Honestly, there's no telling what their ultimate intentions are regarding her. She *is* important to them, and I gather they've been "waiting" for her, or something like her, for a very long time. It also seems significant that she arrived 'from the heavens' in a vehicle—your flying machine—with stars stenciled upon it."

Fred blinked surprise.

"Yes, they know about that," Anson confirmed, "just as well as I. I have been spying for them, after all." He smiled. "They also know— now—that you were with her at the time, so I really doubt they mean to kill you. I admit to practicing upon you in that regard, at least. That said, though I've never seen our non-Christian companions engage in the more barbaric rituals common to the Doms, those rituals did originate with their ancestors." He made a face. "So, ultimately, what they mean to *do* with your Ensign Kari-Faask is another question entirely— and I don't know if it would hurt or help if they discovered she is not a jaguar!"

Fred rode in silence again, wondering if he should just shut up or try to worm more information out of Anson while he was so talkative. He finally decided. "So?" he asked. "What's all this to you? You're a spy, but that doesn't make sense. If the Imperials had decent spies, they'd know more about the Doms than they do, and they should've known what was coming at them too. Maybe you're just a smuggler."

"I've been a smuggler," the man answered thoughtfully. "And maybe I'm an Imperial spy, and just wasn't able to get my information out." He looked closely at Fred. "Or maybe I'm something else entirely." He smiled again. "But whatever else I am, I *am* a spy right now, and spies don't last long by talking overmuch about themselves. Do they?"

Fred shut his mouth, but opened it again. "Maybe not, but the whole point of spying is to get information out, right? I've got a bunch of it, and I need to get it to the Allied fleet, or they—my *friends*, and the most powerful enemies of the Doms—could be in for a helluva surprise."

Anson looked at him. "Such as?"

"Well, for one thing, the Dom fleet's bigger than they have any way of knowing it is!"

"Ah! So you *did* learn a few things at the Temple! Don Hernan must've really believed he'd succeeded with you!"

Fred frowned and scratched the scruffy young beard on his chin. "I guess. I saw maps, heard discussions—I had to know *some* stuff to build his stupid airplanes." He blinked. "Wait a minute! *You* know about the rest of the Dom fleet?"

"Of course. I assume you mean the eastern squadrons beyond El Paso del Fuego?" He paused when he saw Fred's blank stare. "Hmm. Perhaps you aren't as smart as I thought."

"I'm smart," Fred defended. "I've heard of this El Paso, and I know they've got more ships. That's enough to make me want to tell my friends. You obviously know a heck of a lot more. . . . But if you do—if you have . . . why haven't you told anybody? That information would have to be worth taking it out yourself!"

Anson stared straight ahead, his features suddenly hard. "And just why would I do that?" he demanded almost harshly. "From what you say, this 'Second Fleet' should be more than capable of handling however many ships the Doms throw at it. And what if it's in my best interests that it do exactly that?"

"But the lives we could save—*you* could save!"

Anson rounded on him. "Clearly you've not yet learned that there are lives, and then there are *lives*. In war, some lives must be placed above others. The good above the bad is simple to justify; us over them is as old as time, no matter what world you're from. The helpless above the strong, can often be justified, as can the few above the many, if that few is precious enough. Sometimes the equation can be as brutal as those I know above those I don't, and perhaps that is what drives me now. Think on it, Lieutenant Reynolds, and be glad I 'know' you, and have such curiosity, and, yes, admiration for your most interesting Lemurian friend!"

"*Silencio!*" hissed another rider. This one didn't brandish a weapon, but seemed even more intent. Fred gulped and shut his mouth.

"As for El Paso del Fuego, you will see it yourself soon enough," Anson resumed, his voice quiet and conversational once more. "It's quite amazing, and surely one of the natural wonders of this world. That's where we're headed, in case you didn't know. We've been traveling generally west since escaping the Temple, and it's the intent of our comrades to get you and Kari to the other side—which is always exciting. Our pagan friends desire to take Ensign Faask to a certain place far beyond it, and I can't change that. Perhaps once at the pass, if we live that long, I can prevail on them to release you to try and make your way to the fleet. More than that, I can't promise."

Leave Kari? Fred thought. *No way. But if this weirdo's going to keep secrets from me and spout philosophy when my friends are in danger, I'm through telling* him *everything!*

The path remained far enough back, away from the clearing, that sometimes Fred lost sight of the massive creatures for a time, but his fascination was enough that other concerns began to fade. Suddenly, just as the valley became clear once more, displaying the broad panorama of wonders below, all the horses in the column abruptly halted and swung their heads to stare in the same direction.

"Wha—?" Fred began.

"Shush!" Anson hissed. "You know horses?" he asked, barely above a breath. Fred nodded. "Well, though I'm sure you understand they're not native to this land, whatever you've learned of them elsewhere, those that survive here have necessarily grown more attuned to their surroundings. We've been particularly careful about noise for the last while so *they* can hear better, not us. Be silent!"

Fred realized all the great beasts in the meadow below had stiffened, staring not far ahead of where the party had progressed. Based on the wind, he judged that their reaction had more to do with smell than what they might've heard. Then, to his complete amazement and, frankly, terror, something much like a Borno allosaurus, or "super lizard," burst from the forest a couple of hundred yards ahead. The thing was huge, and its massive feet and tall hind legs quickly accelerated it to a speed he wouldn't have believed possible for something its size. He'd never seen a live super lizard, though he'd gaped at the butchered portions of a young one Silva brought in to Baalkpan once, and he'd thought it was big—but this! It was a super-*duper*, super lizard!

The thing gave the impression it was mostly head and tail, and both remained amazingly parallel to the ground atop powerfully churning legs. That gave it an almost serpentlike fluidity of motion—like a monstrous torpedo flying fifteen or twenty feet off the ground. Its colors matched the dark woods and brown-gray bark of the trees very well, but in the meadow, it contrasted sharply with the bright flowers and golden-green grass. Unlike its apparent Borno cousin that had fairly long, powerful forelimbs, this creature had none at all—like the small, scavenging skuggiks Fred had seen in many lands. He fleetingly, irrelevantly wondered how *these* things picked their teeth.

The reaction of the giant—call them super brontasarries—was quick. They bugled panicked warnings probably audible for miles, and turned from the terrifying predator with admirable precision and began lumbering away. As one animal reached another, they joined ranks, thundering across the valley side by side, whiplike tails flailing madly behind them like enormous, serpentine pikes. Several, maybe a little smaller, younger, bolder than the rest, had strayed farther from the protection of numbers, and the meat-seeking missile subtly altered course to intercept one of those. Recognizing its peril, it squalled piteously, but its elders paid no heed, rumbling quickly through a wooded choke point to the broader valley beyond. Only there did the now largely consolidated herd pause and establish what looked like a defensive line, its flanks anchored by the forest. Maybe they knew their sudden wall of snapping tails would create an unbreakable defense—or maybe they just couldn't run very far and knew their attacker would be content with the laggardly offerings. Likely they didn't think about it at all, because their flanks were now exposed to the two *more* monstrous predators that suddenly exploded from the woods on either side of them.

The attackers could've hit those flanks and destroyed their prey entirely, but super brontasarries weren't their mortal enemies after all, just their prey. The two additions contented themselves with angling to stop the one or two tardiest animals, but then veered for the one the first attacker had focused on. Their approach slowed that one further as it recognized the new threat, and perhaps—even just for an instant—forgot what it was running from. An instant was all it took for the pursuing monster to snatch the suddenly motionless tail in its terrible jaws about twenty feet forward of the dangerous tip and begin wrenching its massive head from side to side. The super brontasarry squealed in agony, instinctively stopping and turning, perhaps to batter the attacker with its long, muscular neck. It never had a chance. A second bark-colored torpedo actually leaped slightly to catch the distracted head in crushing jaws—just as the third pounded home "amidships," its jaws impossibly wide.

The super brontasarry outmassed all three of its foes combined, but was suddenly utterly helpless. The "beater" had a death grip on its tail, the first "catcher" was rapidly chewing its head from its neck, and the apparent killer of the trio wrenched its own head and tore away a mouthful of skin, bloody white fat, and purple hawsers of intestines that stretched tight and snapped. Instead of swallowing the gory gobbet, the killer spat it out and dove in for more, tearing deep into the massive body cavity, gnawing forward, inside and around the heavy ribs and through the diaphragm, to withdraw a foamy orange wreckage of lung. The super brontasarry shuddered horribly, then collapsed in the colorful flowers, now bright with barrels of gushing blood. Only then did the killer leap upon the writhing corpse and emit a throbbing roar of triumph. Finally, with every indication of complete agreement among themselves, the three monsters began to feed.

"My God," Fred whispered.

"You haven't seen such things?" Anson probed.

"My friends have," Fred defended, "but not me. Not on such a scale. Jesus, those things are *big*!"

"The creatures on this continent have reached impressive proportions," Anson allowed, his tone a little condescending. "Now you can imagine why the Temple City—Granada—has such imposing walls and artillery facing all directions! Other cities have walls as well, if not so big and high."

"Oh, I've seen bigger," Fred stated, affecting nonchalance, "from the air. And the walls around Granada aren't half as high as those around Aryaal—on Java," he boasted. That wasn't true, of course. In fact it was just the reverse—but Captain Anson couldn't know that.

"*Vamanos!*" one of the riders hissed, pointing at the carnage in the meadow, then motioning forward.

"Yes, well. It's a most interesting world, to be sure. And if you want to see more of it, we should do what the man says—and always pay attention to your horse!"

Fred didn't move. "I want to see Kari—and I want to see her whenever I want, without one of these jug heads hanging around."

"I might help arrange something," Anson confessed as the riders started passing them. "Someone will have to be with you, but perhaps they will allow me to fill that role."

"They trust you that much?" Fred shook his head. "Then no dice. I won't see her at all if you're there—unless you figure out what they mean to do with her. You said they want her happy? We'll see how well that goes over."

Anson sighed. "All right. I'll see what I can discover. Now let's move along!"

"Okay," Fred said, nudging his mount with his heels. He reached down and patted the firm neck. "Good horse!" he whispered.

////// *Ben Mallory's P-40E*
Off the east coast of Saa-lon
April 9, 1944

"Flashy Leader, Flashy Leader, this is Flashy Two. Over." Amid the noise of the big Allison V-1710 engine, Colonel Ben Mallory wouldn't have recognized the Dutch pilot's voice over the SCR-284 radio, accent or not, without his flight number. But Lieutenant Conrad Diebel was Two, so he knew who was calling. He held the Squeeze to Talk switch on the throttle knob.

"This is Flashy Leader. Go, Two," he replied.

"Flashy Leader, I'm having engine trouble . . . again. Over."

Ben closed his eyes and cursed. "Same problem as before, Two?" he asked.

"Yes." Even over the noise, Diebel's single word dripped disgust.

"All right. Try to get your ship back to the strip. If you can't make it, set her down on the beach north of Trin-con-lee. Over." He didn't say what Diebel should do if he *couldn't* make the beach. He could bail out over land if he had to, but nobody would be nuts enough to do it over water. The 3rd Pursuit Squadron of the Allied Army Air Corps had taken flasher fish as their mascot, even painting the scary fish on the noses of their precious few P-40Es, resulting in a nostalgic similarity to the Flying Tigers of the AVG on another world. But the ferocious nature of real flashies, such as teemed in the shallows around Saa-lon, prevented any notion of winding up in the water alive.

"Wilco, Flashy Leader," Diebel said. "Flashy Two, out."

Ben smoldered. Diebel was a strange duck, but a damn good pilot. He needed him and his plane for this strike—not to mention operations to come—but the 3rd Pursuit had been out on a limb for weeks now, and still had no spare parts or real mechanics. They were getting desperately low on fuel and ordnance too. The fuel had always been a problem, but they were down to the nastiest dregs, and most of Mallory's nine P-40s were down because of it. Now Diebel's ship was down for the count, and that left Ben with a total of three airworthy planes. Soupy's ship had remained behind to guard against Grik zeppelins, but that left Ben's strike with only his and Shirley's planes.

He took a deep breath. *Well. We've done our best.* The 3rd had been tasked with slaughtering Grik ships coming to Kurokawa's aid at Madras, and to the best of his knowledge, nothing had gotten through in daylight except a few of the giant ironclads that his squadron had been specifically ordered to avoid. It wasn't believed he had anything that would hurt them—yet—and it was much preferred that nothing his advanced fighters attacked should survive to report to the enemy.

But this convoy, spotted by PatWing 4, and swift feluccas posted as pickets, was a big one, and that could mean bad news for General Alden. It had to be stopped. Nancys had pounded it for two days, but Ben was short of Nancys too, and the weary planes he had left at Trin-conlee were just as liable to fall out of the sky as his sick P-40s. Still, judging by the CW chatter he was picking up, the Nancys were doing a number on the wooden "Indiamen" transports of the enemy, with their simple incendiaries, although two had been shot down by what sounded like an improved shotgun-mortar device like they'd first seen in combat for Ceylon, and then behind protected ports on the battleships in the fighting for India. The simple weapons were short-ranged and had been fixed before, but now it appeared the enemy had developed some way of quickly aiming them.

Columns of smoke in the hazy distance marked the position of his targets, and a sudden meteor of fire indicated the "new" enemy weapons had struck yet another of the attacking two-seat floatplanes. Ben gritted his teeth. "Cat Lead, Cat Lead, this is Flashy Leader," he said. The Nancys' backseat OCs, or observer/copilot/wireless operators, could hear him, but could only transmit in Morse. The Allies had TBS (Talk between Ship) sets now, but they were too big for the planes. "Concentrate on the wooden ships!" A few moments later, he pieced together the CW response: WE DO X THEM HAVE MOST PLANE KILLING GUNS X THEY IS SIX ARMORED CRUISERS FOR YOU X WE DO OUR JOB XXX.

Ben grunted. Implied was "We'll do our job; you do yours." But now he had only two planes to destroy six tough targets. "Acknowledge, Cat Lead," he said. "Just try to stay out of range of the damn things! Out!" He looked at the P-40 off his port wing. "Did you get that, Flashy Three?"

"I hear," came Shirley's squeaky reply. Shirley was from B'mbaado, and her real name was Niaa-Saa. She was a tiny little thing and had to sit on two parachutes just to see through her gun sight, and had to have extensions attached to her rudder pedals so she could reach them, but of all his Lemurian P-40 pilots, only Soupy was maybe just a little better. She was already better than Ben had been when he shipped out for Java on the old *Langley* a long time ago and a world away.

"Then try to conserve ammo as best you can—and don't get too close!"

They approached the convoy out of the setting sun, and the panorama that gradually resolved itself was stunning. It *had* been a big convoy this time, and it stretched southward almost as far as he could see. Happily, most of the ships were marked by towers of gray smoke that added to the haze, but quite a few were still underway in little defensive clumps of three to six. A few Nancys still wheeled overhead, occasionally swooping to drop incendiary bombs, but most had already turned back for Trin-con-lee to refuel and rearm. They'd be lucky to get back in time for a final strike before the sun went down. With a sinking feeling, Ben knew there was no way they could stop the entire convoy. They'd get most of it, they already had, but some would get through this time. He shook his head. It couldn't be helped. His little "stepchild" air force had too few planes and pilots, and even if they'd already geared up to make some really neat flammable sap (or something) incendiaries for the Nancys locally, they were still short of gas, and the plucky little planes could only carry so much ordnance per sortie—and each sortie racked up time on overused engines and airframes. It was a harsh, unforgiving equation, and this time the Grik had simply sent more ships than they could kill.

With a sick feeling, he had to consider breaking off. Chances were, no matter how much damage they did, the two modern planes would be seen this time—and reported. But could the Grik report what they'd seen well enough that Kurokawa would understand the significance? Even if they did, would only two planes alarm him enough to alter or escalate whatever plans he might have? Maybe. The final question became was "maybe" big enough? Those armored, steam-powered cruisers had proven extremely vulnerable from the air, but they could match the Allied steam frigates, or DDs in a straight-up fight, despite the Allies' better gunnery and new fire control. He wished he had a better idea of the big plan to retake Madras so he could better evaluate the consequences of exposing his P-40s now—but he did know his planes would be a big part of that effort, and his orders to remain undiscovered implied that surprise would be a key element of the plan.

"Damn it!" he said aloud. He and Shirley would still be invisible in the sun, but he could see a couple of the cruisers now; steamers as long as *Walker*, with masts and sails. They were slow and beamy, but mounted heavy guns—and their ironclad hulls sported what looked like a formidable ram at the bow. They could be very bad news for his friends. But they *were* vulnerable from the air. . . .

"Shirley," he said at last, "we've got to let them go. We can't get them all, and they'll see us."

"But Col-nol! They right there! I get at least three!"

"You can't know that. Hell, your guns might jam and you might not get any. We can't risk it. Orders."

"But . . ."

"Lieutenant Niaa-Saa, we're breaking off to prevent observation of these aircraft," he said harshly. "That's an order from *me*. Over and out! Cat Lead, sorry to leave the party. Get as many as you can, but don't be heroes. We'll have new planes soon, and we need people who can fly 'em! Flashy Leader out."

The flight back to the coast of Saa-lon was longer than Ben remembered. He loved his P-40s, but not for the first time now, he cursed the day he'd ever heard of them, lying in crates aboard the beached *Santa Catalina* in a Tjilatjap swamp. What good were they if he couldn't use them? Adar had been right all along when he implied they'd be "hangar queens," and the effort it took to get them would be better spent building their own planes. His mood darkened further when they crossed the coast and he saw Conrad Diebel's plane standing on its nose on the sandy beach north of Trin-con-lee. Conrad waved at them as they passed, so they knew the Dutch flier was okay, but the plane would have a ruined prop, at least. He'd have to send palkas down to tow the ship all the way through the cruddy ex-Grik city and out to the grass strip they operated from. *Shit.*

He and Shirley lined up on the strip, and, with canopies open and gear and flaps down, their engines grumbled and blatted as they throttled back to land. Ben felt the jolt of touchdown, and heard the rumble of the landing gear as he quickly lost speed. Almost at a stop, he goosed the engine and worked the pedals to bring the nose around and head toward the revetments they'd built to protect the planes in case the Grik ever surprised them with a zeppelin raid. In front of his own revetment, he spun the plane around, facing away from it, then cut the engine. Even as the prop wound down, he stood in the cockpit, yanked his leather helmet and goggles off his head, and practically flung them at his approaching ground crew in frustration. Suddenly, he blinked when he saw who stooped to pick them up.

"Commander Greg Garrett?" he exclaimed, amazed. There'd been no warning that the man and his little task force (TFG-2) had arrived, only that he was on the way.

Garrett held out his arms and looked at himself. "Yep," he said in mock astonishment. "I guess it *is* me! Good to see you too, Colonel."

Ben hopped down and shook the man's hand. "Boy, are you a sight for sore eyes! We're down to exactly two ships, and little more than spitballs to throw at the Grik. I sure hope you brought some stuff along."

Greg nodded. "A little. We escorted a couple of freighters in with fuel, a few crated Nancys, and some of the ground crew kids from Kaufman Field. They brought you some ammo, and the most critical spares you asked for—a few weeks ago." He gestured vaguely east in the dwindling light. "Good thing we missed that swarm of ships you were after! We must've just squeaked past."

Ben frowned. "You'd have done more damage to 'em than I could, and as for the list, I need ten times that now."

Greg nodded. "Sorry. Things are a mess. Sergeant Dixon's en route to Andaman with every little thing your heart could desire, but it'll still take a while to reach you."

Ben shrugged. "Hey, I'm one to bitch. I've been on my own hook longer than I hoped, but my jam's not a patch to yours! Hell, do you even know where you're going?"

"Not really." Greg chuckled. "I've been admonished to 'go west, young man!' and that's about it."

"No shit?"

Greg laughed. "My instructions are a *little* more specific than that! I'm sorry to miss the show brewing here, but I've got an exciting mission, my pick of a crew, a sound DE consort—and my old *Donaghey*, of course! What more could I ask?"

"A lot," Ben grumbled, shrugging out of his parachute and looking around. "Hey, Soupy!"

"Sur?"

"Take this, wilya? You're in charge—of whatever there is to be in charge of. Commander Garrett and I are going down to Trin-con-lee to arrange transport for some supplies he brought us—and a certain stranded Dutchman." He looked at Greg. "When do you sail?"

"Hopefully, the day after tomorrow."

"Good," Ben grinned. "That means you don't have to wake up early! You got anything to drink on that tub of yours?"

"Why, Colonel! You know 'spirits other than medicinal or sufficient to decontaminate water' are against regulations on Navy ships!"

"That's okay, the Navy 'Cats and the guys from PatWing Six have raised a joint like the Busted Screw in town. The seep's no good, but the beer's drinkable." He looked back at Soupy. "You know where to find me, but I may not be back tonight. Commander Garrett and I are old friends, and we've got a lot of woes to compare!"

////// *The Wilds of Borno*

The misty jungle dawn had barely reached them when Gunny Horn kicked Silva in his sore ribs. "Wake up, jerk. Looks like you might'a been right."

"Course I was! 'Bout what?" Dennis grumbled, sitting up and flipping the nasty patch back over his destroyed eye. He wouldn't holster the .45 he always held whenever they slept on the ground until he was fully alert. It was kind of strange that this little habit should be reassuring to those around him.

Horn glared at him, then flicked his eyes significantly at Pam Cross, still sleeping next to Silva. He shrugged, then pointed beyond the dead super lizard they'd slept beside.

"About the neighbors."

Silva rolled up on his knees, holstering his pistol, and slowly climbed the Doom Stomper like a pole. He'd left it leaning against the dead beast. "I can't see crap," he whispered, wiping goo out of his good eye with the back of his thumb. The three 'Cat Marines were already awake, as were Lawrence and his Sa'aarans. Moe was waking Abel Cook and Stuart Brassey. Pokey had returned during the night, but remained huddled at the base of one of their trees a short distance away. He was awake, trying to be still, since he had to be in view of their "guests," but he seemed to be shivering in terror. Dennis tapped Pam's shoe with his own.

"Wake up, doll. We got comp'ny."

Pam's eyes flickered open, and, noticing the stealthy preparations around her, she nodded and eased back the bolt on the Blitzer Bug. There was a muffled *click* when the sear caught. Dennis frowned. He wasn't keen on the little submachine guns. The first batch were full auto only, which made them wasteful of ammo and nearly impossible to control, and therefore wildly inaccurate. They *were* smaller and much lighter than the Thompson they were meant to emulate, and were utterly idiot-proof. The commandos were training with them and might make good use of them, but Dennis preferred heavier, more accurate weapons. Pam was the only human to "come across" on *Walker* who was smaller than the average Lemurian, however. Even one of the precious Springfields would've worn her out, and she didn't have the training to make it shine. Dennis cursed himself for not taking the time to teach her—but he'd never figured she'd really need a weapon. She was a nurse—and a dame. Until recently, both were ridiculously rare. He looked critically at the Blitzer. Maybe something like a Cutts compensator would tame the thing.

Lawrence and his countrymen practically slithered up beside him, and Moe joined them with the two teenage officers.

"You see them yet?" Horn asked.

Silva rubbed his eye again. "Yeah. It's kinda foggy, but there's movement in the tree line yonder, where it gets thick." He glanced at Moe. "Rust-colored critters, like before."

"Dey check us out," Moe agreed quietly. "Prob'ly hear ruckus, smell smoke an' meat like you figger, come see who in der territory."

"You think they seen us?"

Moe blinked and swished his tail. "Dey workin' der way round us now, but first t'ings dey see is dead super lizard an' dat damn chikkin Grik over der. Dey know he ain't one o' dem, so prob'ly a enemy, but dey maybe be careful—wonder how he kill super lizard by hisself, with so much noise."

"Huh. 'Magine their surprise when I . . ." He paused and looked at Cook. "You mind if I rear up on this big lizard an' p'rade myself in all my glory, wavin' my rifle? If the same fellas we met before is amongst 'em, they might recognize me."

"I'm not sure . . ."

"Ensign Cook," said Lawrence, his eyes flitting nervously, "they are . . . 'orking around us. Soon they'll know 'ore o' us than us know o' they—"

"I think what Larry's tryin' to say with his polite, lipless gibberish is if these particular jungle Griks is hostile, keepin' em off balance and a little shook up might be the best way to keep 'em from jumpin' us. Right, Larry?"

Lawrence hissed sullenly. "Right," he admitted.

"But . . . such an act might frighten them, precipitate an attack!" Abel objected.

"Could be. Not if these are the exact Injun lizards we come lookin' for, I bet. Either way, though, I'd rather precipitate an attack before they're ready—and maybe have us plumb surrounded."

Cook finally nodded. "But why you?"

"They got no reason to like Lemurians, an' they'll likely see Larry and his guys as a trespassin' tribe. They shouldn't know squat about humans—an' I saved one of 'em once. Maybe that'll count."

"Oh, very well." Cook looked around. "Everyone stand ready—for anything. Just in case. But hold your fire unless I give the order!"

Dennis nodded approval and immediately scrambled atop the dead allosaur. He moved to the bloody hip area, as high as he could get, and stood as straight and tall as possible.

"Hey, fellas!" he shouted, his loud voice shattering the morning quiet. Lizard birds protested the noise, and a flock of batlike creatures with long tails stirred from the tops of what remained of the trees they'd started the night in. "Hey, there!" he continued, waving his big rifle over his head. "It's *me*, ol' Silva! Come ta visit them three of you guys I saved from bein' ate!"

Almost immediately, a harsh yelp answered from the jungle, taken up and repeated many times. Directly opposite Dennis, maybe seventy yards away, a rust-colored Grik emerged, pointing a fire-hardened spear in their direction. He had to be some kind of chief or leader. His tall black crest was festooned with colorful feathers and the furry tails of small creatures. Some of the decorations looked like the tail feathers of the smaller but clearly dangerous creature that drew the super lizard. The chief also wore something shiny around his neck, but was otherwise naked—as were the hundred or so similar creatures that emerged from the trees to join him, forming a semicircle before them.

"They *were* moving to encircle us!" Brassey gasped, his voice a little higher than normal because the creatures didn't seem friendly at all.

"Hey, guys!" Dennis shouted. "Any of you remember me? We came to say howdy. Don't mean no harm a'tall!"

The chief made thrusting motions with his spear and voiced a loud, shrill croak. Again, his warriors followed suit.

"You want this dead lizard?" Dennis jumped up and down on the corpse. "Pull up a chair, fix yerselfs a plate! Hell, we can't eat it all."

The chief roared again. This time the answering roar and militant demonstration was too much for Pokey, and he bolted to join his protectors from the base of the tree. An incredulous, furious roar ensued, and with a distinct pointing gesture, the chief urged his warriors forward.

"Shit," Dennis mumbled.

"Maybe it's a bluff," Abel cried.

"No bluff," Moe shouted with certainty.

"It's a hundred to twelve," Pam almost snarled, "not countin' Pokey. If we're gonna shoot, we only got a few seconds to do it!"

"Oh! Yes, certainly. Ah, commence firing!"

Dennis fired first, but not without a twinge of regret. He didn't have a problem killing whatever needed killing, but it was kind of disappointing that nearly everything they met seemed to fall in that category.

And, besides, after their last encounter with these creatures, he'd had high hopes. Oh, well. He quickly took a knee and literally spattered the chief like a ripe melon, just as Horn opened up with his BAR, using controlled bursts, and Pam tried to do the same with the Blitzer. Rust-colored forms began falling, screaming, crying out. Moe directed a volley of rifle fire from the Sa'aarans and 'Cat Marines, and the charging line staggered in the middle, some looking at their fallen comrades with astonishment. *Too bad they'd been too close and coming too fast for a few warning shots,* Dennis suddenly thought, but dismissed the notion. The survivors surged forward just like any Grik he'd ever fought. *Damn.* He fired again, bowling down at least two jungle Griks with one of his big bullets, but Pam's Blitzer stuttered empty just as Horn's BAR did. The Marines and Sa'aarans raced to the flanks, bayonets ready, just as a tide of lizards slammed into the super-lizard breastworks and started clawing their way up or throwing their spears at Dennis. The spears clearly weren't meant for throwing and most went wild, but a few came too close for comfort. Dennis fired again, then smashed a pair of jaws with his buttplate. He was done with his rifle. He let it drop behind him and out came his cutlass and .45.

The BAR opened up again on his left, the Blitzer on his right, but everyone seemed to have forgotten he was holding the "middle" by himself. He hacked with the cutlass, shearing flesh with the heavy blade, then took an ugly slash from Grik talons down his back. He whirled to fire his pistol—but the attacker fell away as Cook and Brassey joined him, firing their '03s and stabbing forward with their bayonets. He grinned. Both boys were young and unsure of themselves, but he'd never thought they were chickens. Pam joined them, then Larry, pushing her up from behind. Pam stabbed another Thompson magazine in the bottom of the Blitzer and sprayed around them, the little gun bucking like mad. Dennis hacked another attacker off their high point, then glimpsed *more* rust-colored creatures streaming from the trees! This group wasn't as big as the first, but it moved with far greater discipline, racing out in a column of twos, then *splitting* into what looked like a supporting line behind the first wave.

"Looks like the regulars is here," Silva grumped, shooting down another Grik with his .45. The slide locked back and he grabbed for another magazine. "Maybe they'll call this the 'Last Stand on Lizard Lump'!"

"Shut up," Pam snarled. Her dark hair was matted with blood. "I ain't gonna die here, an' you ain't gonna let me!"

"Just joshin', doll," Silva replied lightly, but he wasn't. Not this time. It may have started to settle in the night before, when he tacitly accepted that maybe he really did "belong" to Pam, but somewhere between then and now, he'd come to realize he probably wasn't going to live forever after all. That Jap, Shinya, had kind of warned him such a day might come, but he hadn't paid much attention at the time. To end like this, though, kind of . . . stupid, in the grand scheme of things, wounded his sensibilities. Why couldn't it at least have been aboard *Walker*, doing something important? Crap.

He mashed the slide release with his thumb and started firing again. Brassey was down, stunned, it looked like, but the kid was sliding off the super lizard into the grasping claws and teeth below! Silva grabbed an arm and heaved back—but he'd dropped the pistol to do it. He'd *never* drop his cutlass. It didn't run out of bullets. He stabbed a Grik going for Pam, but the thing shrieked and grabbed at him. Sharp claws sank into his right forearm, and he bellowed in rage and pain. He couldn't free the cutlass and couldn't drop Brassey. He was helpless to stop the rusty Grik lunging at him with a scorched spear tip.

He couldn't have been more surprised when a double-fletched crossbow bolt suddenly bloomed in the thing's neck and it dropped the spear and clutched the bolt. Silva finally wrenched his cutlass free and hacked down the other wounded creature. Slinging Brassey up behind him, he drew Linus Truelove's long-barreled flintlock pistol from his belt and stood for a moment, watching.

"I'll be damned!" He hooted. "I'm charmed after all!"

The second Grik force was attacking the first! Crossbow bolts thrummed through the press on shockingly flat trajectories, thumping into their attackers or festooning the dead super lizard. The first group, stunned, reacted in a fashion once predictable for all their enemies: faced with fierce, unwavering resistance and attacked without warning from the rear, it started to rout. These creatures didn't kill those that ran away, but they did catch the panic. Soon, more were trying to flee than fight. Dennis slid down from the massive carcass, followed by Lawrence. "Moe!" he called. "Moe! Are you still alive?"

"I still alive," came a pained voice, "but I lose half my guys down here! Bad fight!" Silva saw then that two Lemurian Marines and one of the Sa'aarans lay dead in the heap of corpses. They'd sold their lives dearly, but that was small consolation.

"Shit," Silva murmured. He looked at Moe. "You don't look so hot either."

"I had worse."

"I know."

All the attackers had vanished now, hounded by teams of their "rescuers." A small group of those now approached. Physically, they were identical to the others, covered in the same rusty brown, feathery fur—*Almost the same color as Keje's pelt,* Silva suddenly thought—but they were lightly striped with a darker shade of brown. They were a little taller than Lawrence, but that might have been because they stood straighter, with shorter tails. They were just as formidably armed as any Grik-like being they'd ever met, though, with wicked black claws on hands and feet, and mouths full of sharp, tearing teeth. Also unlike their attackers, these creatures wore pieces of copper jewelry—wristbands, neck rings, tiny cones that rustled and lightly clattered in their crests. They also carried crossbows, of course, amazingly similar to the ones Lemurians once used. Copper-tipped, broad fletched bolts protruded from quivers carried like shoulder bags. Most amazing, some of the creatures had bronze swords—shaped strikingly like the pattern of a 1917 Navy cutlass! The bronze, and particularly the weapons, were evidence of a far more advanced material culture than the creatures they'd just fought, or even the ones Silva, Lawrence, and Moe had seen before.

The small procession stopped near the tail of the dead super lizard, and a couple of its number gazed at the monster appraisingly. The rest stared expectantly at the survivors of the expedition.

"Well, these don't seem like the same lizard folks we was sent to meet," Dennis said softly, "but they did just save our asses, and that's a fact."

Abel nodded. "Sergeant Moe, Lawrence, please stay back with the other 'Cats and our . . . reptilian friends. Gunny Horn, Mr. Brassey, Lieutenant Cross, you stay back as well. Stand ready, but make no threatening moves." He looked at Dennis and blinked a little nervously. "Chief Silva? Would you accompany me? It appears they want to meet us."

Cook and Silva stepped forward until there were only a few yards between them and their visitors. Silva had left his big rifle behind, but his hand rested on the unsnapped flap of his holster. Pokey, who'd somehow survived the fight, had brought him the 1911, and the little Grik's cartridge bag now jingled with double the empty shells he'd carried before. More brass had surely fallen on the other side of the super lizard, but he'd get that later.

Not knowing what else to say or do, Abel chose the apparent leader of the group by its forward stance and a higher degree of ornamentation. Self-consciously, he saluted. "Ensign Abel Cook, United States Navy. At your service, sir." He was just thinking that he might as well have recited one of the bawdy limericks he'd learned from the destroyermen, when the creature looked at him, looked at Silva, then gave them the biggest surprise yet.

"You . . . Arricans?" he replied.

Abel was stunned speechless. In point of fact, the lad was British, but Silva decided now wasn't the time to confuse matters. "Yes, indeed," he answered quickly.

"All you?" it asked, looking at their companions. "E'en those that kill us? Those 'Cats?"

'Cats! English was weird enough, but where'd he learn that?

"Uh, we're all friends, if that's what you mean," Abel finally managed, "and would like to be friends with you. We appreciate your help against these others . . ."

"'Cats kill us! Not nice! Not . . . 'riends!"

"These won't hurt you. None will anymore. Things have changed a lot."

The creature looked unconvinced. "Us told look you, since us learn you look us. Others look too. Us go all."

"Well . . . May I have the pleasure of your name?" Abel asked.

"I Ca'tain I'joorka. Us," he gestured at his followers, "us Khonashi." He pointed at one of their dead enemies and hissed. "Those Akichi. Not nice. Us go all. Lots Akichi round here."

"Where're you takin' us?" Silva demanded, and I'joorka blinked at him. "To see king."

"Where's that?"

I'joorka pointed roughly north. "Long, long. Close to sea."

Dennis looked at Abel. "Hell, that could mean another two hundred miles across God knows what!"

Abel looked back almost challengingly and shrugged. "What if it does? We've got a job to do."

"We don't have enough seep to grog our water for a trip that far—an' back." Seep was an alcoholic drink, one of many useful things, including the curative paste, made from the ubiquitous polta fruit. Silva didn't miss the irony that he was the one urging caution for once.

"That may be," Abel countered, "but meeting these . . . people, whether they're the same you saw before or not, is what we were sent to do."

"Well . . . we met 'em. Let's talk to 'em here."

"No good here," I'joorka insisted. "Akichi here."

Silva looked at him. "How the hell do you know American?" he demanded.

"King talk Arrican," the creature replied. "I talk Arrican. Lots Khonashi talk Arrican now."

"How'd your king learn it?" Silva demanded.

"King all'ays talk Arrican. *Is* Arrican—like you."

Silva's eye went wide. "Zat so?" He looked at Abel. "I guess we *gotta* go. This just got way more interestin'. I hope we don't all die o' the screamers, though."

"We'll boil our water," Abel assured him.

////// *Madras*
Grik India

Lord Regent-Consort, Sire of All India, and General of the Sea Hisashi Kurokawa slashed his ornate riding crop across the back of the head of the Grik commander of ten hundreds, or colonel, who'd dared bring such annoying news. The colonel barely flinched, but writhed more desperately at Kurokawa's feet. Kurokawa struck him again and again, venting his rage, but finally stopped abruptly. The creature wore a leather helmet and cuirass, and all he was accomplishing was tiring himself. He had to admit the exertion was gratifying; he dared not treat his Japanese subjects so anymore. He needed them too much. But it satisfied his angry, frustrated soul that he now had the power to treat the hated Grik however he pleased—at least *some* of them.

"Get out!" he roared, releasing further tension. "Send me this pathetic General of the Sea who cannot protect his vital charges from the . . . insectile depredations of what remains of the enemy air on Ceylon, even with our most advanced protective weapons!"

"Of course, Lord Regent!" the creature murmured in the Grik tongue Kurokawa could understand, if not speak. It probably thought all that protected it from being ordered to destroy itself was that it could understand spoken English. It could even *speak* a few English words now, like a growing number of high-ranking Grik Hij, but its lord wouldn't allow any human tongue, even English, to be twisted by a Grik mouth in his presence. "At once, Lord Regent," it assured him again as it started to drag itself from the stone chamber.

"Oh, get up!" Kurokawa seethed impatiently, and the Grik colonel leaped to its feet and bolted down the passageway. After a moment to compose himself, Kurokawa sighed, glancing surreptitiously at the other men in the chamber. "I suppose it's no one's fault, really," he confessed in a much calmer tone, gesturing helplessly with the quirt. "But if I admit that to such loathsome creatures, they will not try hard enough."

General of the Sky Hideki Muriname eased forward on the bench he occupied in the dank chamber. Normally, in better weather, there'd be an opening in the ceiling to bathe the regent's throne with light, but since the weather remained so persistently wet, orange lamplight had to suffice. It was inconvenient and made the maps spread across the broad table difficult to see, but at least they weren't soaked to the bone like the rest of their army. He knew Kurokawa was arranging to move to an opulent palace away from the center of the city, one that once belonged to the former regent-consort, Tsalka, and he wondered if greater comfort would make his lord easier to appease. "Such treatment may induce them to try less hard to keep us properly informed, sir," he suggested tentatively. It was the closest he'd come to criticizing Kurokawa, and even that earned him a sharp glare.

"Brutality is what they expect. It's all they respond to!" Kurokawa fumed. "And it is all they deserve. The day is near when we will take our proper place as their direct, supreme leaders; their virtual gods. Then perhaps we might teach compassion, as we direct their energies toward more . . . comprehensive goals.

"More comprehensive than the utter annihilation of their foes?" Muriname ventured, unable to contain himself.

"Of course. It is easy enough to destroy. To *rule* is more difficult."

Muriname had nothing to say to that. Instead, he returned to the subject at hand. "At least we know what's been happening to our supplies and reinforcements. By sea, at any rate. The remnants of this convoy are the first to reach us since the Battle of Madras. Perhaps . . . we should have moved against the enemy on Ceylon already."

"With what?" Kurokawa demanded. "A few damaged battleships, and no transports for troops? We could have pounded their ports but not taken them—and I doubt they would have been so cooperative as to leave their aircraft bobbing in the harbor waters for us to destroy." He held Muriname's gaze. "And we know well enough how our zeppelins would fare against them."

"Numbers are the key," Muriname stated. "We get more airships all the time, as well as the special piloted bombs. Those *do* work. We just have to overwhelm their defenses."

"But we need those for when we meet the enemy fleet once more!" Kurokawa insisted. "It will come again—it must! Even now they build it back up, bent on rescuing this General Alden of theirs, and the troops he has allowed us to trap against the high escarpment. Why else has it made no appearance since the battle?" He paused. "As long as Alden holds, they *will* try to aid him. When they think they have the advantage, they will come with all they have—" His voice heated. "Perhaps they will even bring that damned American destroyer that has cost us so much!"

Only now, after Niwa interrogated the prisoners taken beyond the Rocky Gap—before they were eaten—had Kurokawa finally learned that his ultimate nemesis, USS *Walker*, the ship that destroyed his beloved *Amagi*, still existed. He'd been sure she was destroyed in the same battle that cost him his ship. But now he knew not only had she been repaired, she'd also been battling *other* enemies of the human/Lemurian alliance! He didn't know nearly as much about this "Dominion" as he would've liked, but just knowing it existed was very valuable information indeed.

"Destroying that particular ship would bring me great pleasure," he understated darkly.

"So we wait for the enemy to grow stronger before we fight him?" Muriname asked.

"Of course! We wait for the enemy to bring *all he can* to the slaughter! We may not have received all the supplies we desire, that Halik and Niwa's army on this side of the gap might need, but we are stronger than ever! The enemy has made no effort to stop our mightiest ships from joining us here. Why should they? They can't! We now have *fifteen* great battleships and dozens of armored cruisers assembled in this port; the most powerful force ever joined together on this world. When the enemy comes against us at last, we will meet him with that mighty fleet, and together with the hundreds of zeppelins you will have gathered by then, General Muriname, every ship the enemy has available on this, their western front, will be destroyed. Their aircraft on Ceylon and upon the highland lake will then wither from attrition and lack of fuel and be unable to prevent us from destroying General Alden and reconquering Ceylon." He shrugged with a smile. "After that, we will gather every transport we can and quickly conquer our way back to the place called Baalkpan and tear out the enemy's living heart! With those regencies added to this . . ." He paused, suddenly catching himself, as if unwilling to reveal more of his great plan. "Then, my friends, we will be ready for our next step."

"I would think," Muriname said slowly, "based on what we've seen of the enemy's *current* capabilities, your plan should work. We do seem to have the advantage. Remember how imaginative the enemy has been, however. We defeated them here and can do so again against what they had then, but we should not assume their imagination has not already given them better weapons, weapons not yet ready for deployment at the time. We have seen their new breech-loading rifles—we have nothing even close with which to arm our troops. I'm also disturbed by their apparent advances in fire control. You yourself said they inflicted much more damage than they should have been able to, given the relative weight of shot thrown by our fleet opposed to theirs. What if they have improved their aircraft, their bombs—particularly their bombs! Your mighty battleships might find themselves . . . inconvenienced. Our improved antiaircraft weapons should surprise them, but what might they surprise *us* with?"

"A good point, General Muriname. I don't think they could have a dramatic, widespread, qualitative advantage over what we've seen. Not yet. But the sprinkling of breechloaders our Grik captured proves they are advancing, and better weapons were already on their way when last we met. I will be vigilant for other examples of this—and I think it's time you returned to our private enclave at Zanzibar to oversee the completion of your secret"—he smiled—"*aeronautical* projects. Your executive officer, Lieutenant Iguri, can step in for you here. It is not as though your airships lend themselves to subtle tactical or strategic applications. You have my authority to strenuously encourage Commander Riku to complete his ordnance projects as well." He frowned. "I don't think they will be needed here, but regardless of our technical superiority over our Grik allies, we are very, very few. I do not trust First General Esshk in my absence from the court of the Celestial Mother." He smirked. "Esshk may decide to see for himself just how pastoral our retreat on Zanzibar has remained! No Grik may ever set foot there—or, having done so, depart alive."

Muriname stood. "With your permission then, sir, I will fly back to the aerodrome. I have much to prepare before I depart."

"You are dismissed, General Muriname. Do wait until dark before you ascend, however. The Americans' ape lackeys have quite exceptional eyesight and are disturbingly competent fliers. Even in the dark you must be cautious. They might not see your black-painted airship, but the exhaust flare of your engines could reveal you to their patrols." He looked away. "I cannot afford to lose you," he added in an uncharacteristically somber tone. "You and General Niwa have long been the only senior officers I entirely trust," he confessed, "and with Niwa wounded . . ." He stopped, as if suddenly aware he was speaking aloud. "Go!" he barked harshly.

Muriname hesitated, then saluted and left. Only after he was gone did Kurokawa's gaze turn to Signals Lieutenant Fukui. The boy had only recently arrived from Zanzibar and he'd been working to establish radio communications between the ships and Kurokawa's Madras headquarters. He was also still listening very hard to what floated about in the ether. That part of his job had been incredibly tedious—until recently—but he'd much preferred doing it at the Sovereign Nest of the Jaaph Hunters on Zanzibar to doing it here. Not only was Madras and its environs an active combat zone; it was full of Grik, which utterly terrified him. Also, his activities kept him in proximity to Hisashi Kurokawa, who scared him even more. At the moment, however, Kurokawa's expression had turned mild again as he looked at the young signals officer.

"There has still been no contact from Lieutenant Miyata, I assume?" he asked.

"No, Lord," Fuqui replied nervously. Miyata had been sent with two other Japanese to contact a group of—presumably human—"other hunters" in the far south of Africa. His orders had been to relay to them the offer to join the Great Hunt against the American-Lemurian Alliance. General Esshk had threatened to wipe them out if they refused, but doing so was not a looming priority. Everyone, Kurokawa included, assumed Miyata and his party had been killed by the elements or those they met. There *had* been strange radio signals from time to time, however, and for a while it was thought they were attempts by Miyata, perhaps with the aid of the "others" to contact them. Recent events proved otherwise.

"Then have there been more signals such as those you intercepted a few weeks ago?"

"N-not directed at *us*, Lord," Fuqui hedged. "Not like those we received in response to transmissions we made prior to and during the battle for this place." Those transmissions had been a calculated risk; necessary to coordinate the battle, but dangerous because of the possibility of discovery. The Americans and their lackeys gabbled away all the time—in code, of course—but they'd thoughtlessly advertised their presence. Kurokawa had kept the existence of radio secret from his Grik allies for many reasons, but one such had certainly been out of fear of what—or who—else might be out there. They knew so little about this world, and it was always possible that others, potentially more powerful than Kurokawa and the empire he'd not yet built, could inhabit it.

That fear had not been laid to rest, but the first and only word they'd received directly from the mysterious unknown source was a simple "Hello. Who are you?" Perhaps a friendly greeting, but most disconcerting. Kurokawa had authorized no reply.

"And you remain certain the message was not just the Americans toying with us?" Kurokawa demanded.

"Absolutely certain, Lord. We had enough listening posts even then, combined with our improved signal-direction-finding capability, to triangulate the source as emanating from a generally northwesterly direction; perhaps from North Africa or beyond. If the Americans had managed to reach such a point, I cannot imagine they would want us to know."

"Well," Kurokawa said, massaging his temples. "The Grik know nothing of what lies beyond the great desert in that direction. And whoever sent the message cannot be on this side of it, so I'm inclined not to worry overmuch about them now. Inform me immediately if you hear anything else at all, however."

"Of course, Lord."

"You are dismissed, Lieutenant."

"Yes, sir!" the boy said, and saluted.

"Wait. You have heard, no doubt, that General Niwa was wounded in the fighting some time ago?"

"Yes, Lord."

"I want to know exactly how he fares, if there is anything I can do to alleviate his suffering. Even if there is nothing, make sure he knows I tried. Go to him yourself."

"O-of course, Lord." Fuqui replied, then bolted from the chamber.

Alone, Kurokawa considered his position again, trying to find flaws in his strategy. He *should* have recaptured Ceylon, or at least parked a few heavy warships in the harbor at Trin-con-lee, but that time was past. Besides, that was the only avenue of supply for Alden, and if he allowed Halik to destroy the American-Lemurian "pocket," the enemy fleet would not rush to its aid—and he needed it *here*. Much as he loved his battleships, they were far too slow, their bunkers too modest, for him to chase the enemy. The enemy had to come to *him*. It would happen soon enough. Alden's position would make that essential, as the vise around his army tightened. The great battle he longed for was finally within reach, and after the Americans and their ape-man friends were finally, utterly destroyed, the Japanese of this world, *his* Japanese, would claim their lands as part of his regency. Then, with the Grik army he'd conceived, nurtured, and helped to build beholden to him above all others, he'd steam back and conquer the ancestral lands of the Grik and take his rightful place as their ruler at last! If he allowed the Celestial Mother to live at all, it would be as a figurehead only—much like his own Emperor Hirohito had become. Either way, Hisashi Kurokawa's shameful period of obeying, *subjugating* himself to, and, yes, fearing his vile Grik allies was rapidly drawing to an end.

O nce again, USS *Walker* looked almost new. Her fresh, light gray and glossy black paint was dazzling in the bright morning sun, and not a single streak of orange rust marred her tightly riveted sides. Her white number, 163, bordered in black, stood tall and bold at her bows, with smaller versions at the fantail behind her propeller guards. Her brass bell and whistle were polished to a painful glow, and she had a full complement of boats aboard. She had a full crew as well, eager replacements for the lost or reassigned, who couldn't believe their good fortune to be assigned to the legendary ship. They'd be up to speed fairly quickly. All were Navy, and though still technologically advanced in some respects—on this world, at least— *Walker* was no longer the almost magical marvel she'd been.

She might look new, but she's not, Matt thought somberly, striding up the long gangway from the dock where thousands of Maa-ni-los watched and cheered. He was still using his cane, but the sound of the crowd made him straighten and try not to lean on it much. The diminutive High Chief Saan-Kakja paced him on one side, and Sandra walked on the other. *The cheering's mostly for them,* he assured himself, and that made him feel better. Adulation made him feel uncomfortable and a little dishonest. He'd screwed up an awful lot and gotten a lot of good people killed. He didn't deserve acclaim. Besides, even if he'd always done everything exactly right, he was still just doing his job. *It's the ship and crew they're cheering, not me,* he finally decided. *If any of it's for me, it's only because I'm about to take her back to the fight. Walker* wasn't new, though. He couldn't fool himself over that. She was probably in better shape than she'd been when they came to this world, maybe even better than she'd been for a decade before the Old War even started, but despite all the new, there remained an awful lot of old—and it was so very tired. It was like they'd put a new roof and fresh paint on an old, rotten house. It might look swell, but the trembling bones could only barely stand the weight of it all.

He grimaced and scolded himself for his dark thoughts. It wasn't *that* bad! Somewhere on the world she came from, if the war they left still raged, some of her sisters doubtless still toiled without anything like the loving care that had been lavished on USS *Walker.* His eyes swept aft. *There's a prime example! Walker* had a Nancy scout plane once again, only now they didn't have to lower it into the sea to launch it. They didn't even have to stop! The ship had been equipped with the new catapult they'd been putting on almost everything with room for one. It was a little thing, sturdy and directional, and would kick the plane off the ship with an impulse charge, like a torpedo. They still had to stop to recover the plane, but that was okay. Of course, Matt's ship was supposed to get two of her triple torpedo mounts back when she made Baalkpan, and he was very excited about that.

Bosun's pipes twittered as he, his wife, Sandra, and Saan-Kakja reached the end of the gangplank to be met by many of his crew—his *friends,* damn it!—holding salutes. Matt saluted the Stars and Stripes, streaming from the short mainmast aft, then saluted the OOD, Sonny Campeti. "Request permission to come aboard."

"Permission granted." Campeti grinned. Saan-Kakja and Sandra came aboard in the same manner, and all were met with enthusiasm. It struck Matt that he'd seen many of these men and 'Cats, almost on a daily basis, but this was different. Their ship was ready for sea again, and with his official return, she was back in the war.

"Welcome home, Skipper," McFarlane said.

"Thanks, Spanky. Hello, Mr. Gray," he said to the Super Bosun, then grinned at his female Lemurian engineering officer. "Lieutenant Tabby." Unconsciously, he looked for Chack, who always reverted to what he considered his "permanent" status as bosun's mate aboard the ship he considered his Home. He quickly remembered with a pang that the re- markable young 'Cat had already sailed west with the Imperial Major Jindal and the transports carrying their mixed commandos. Chack was a fine bosun's mate, but a truly gifted Marine. He'd join the battalions they'd been training here with those his sister, Risa, had raised in Baalk- pan. Together they'd form the backbone of Matt's landing force—the 1st Raider Brigade—if his plan went forward. He looked at Bashear. "As- semble the divisions on the fo'c'sle, Chief."

"Aye, aye, Skipper."

A short time later, about two-thirds of the crew was gathered, port and starboard between the bow and pilothouse, flanking the glistening number one, four-inch gun.

"Good morning," Matt said, gazing down the lines. Most of those gathered were Lemurians now, but all wore the same white uniforms— except the 'Cats wore kilts instead of trousers. They'd revert to T-shirts (or no shirt at all) and dungaree kilts later, but right now they looked as sharp as any crew he'd ever seen, despite the fur. "Her Excellency Saan- Kakja would like to say a few words. Your Excellency?"

"Thank you, Cap-i-taan Reddy," Saan-Kakja said, looking down the same ranks with her mesmerizing eyes. "My friends," she said warmly, "this ship has suffered sorely in the course of this terrible war. My peo- ple have done their best to help you make her whole again. This was our pleasure and honor. Some of you have suffered sorely as well." She shook her head sadly. "Our dear Lady Sandra and the remarkable medical establishment she founded have done their best to heal you, but the rest of us can do little to make *you* whole beyond assuring you of the love, respect, and appreciation of all the Fil-pin Lands." She paused. "For some of your shipmates, no medicine, regardless how devoted, or repair, regardless how skilled, could suffice. They have gone to the Heavens to watch over us and await the happy day when we are reunited there. We will miss them, but their work here is done. You prepare now to continue that work, to rejoin the fight, and I am confident you will, as always, make a disproportionate contribution." She blinked a combination of admiration and sadness. "It always seems to fall to *Walker* and you to level the scales against our enemies, and this has been a terrible burden." Her tail swished restlessly. "I wish I could come with you. I meant to return to the war in the West long ago, but now the war in the East holds me here. But even if I cannot be with you myself, many of my people will join you soon. Even as we send ships east, we continue sending warriors west." She smiled at Captain Reddy. "And we already sent a dozen of the torpedo boats ahead, aboard our newest dry-dock Home, that should arrive at Baalkpan about the same time as you." Dry-dock Homes were the newest thing. Both steam powered and lightly armed for defense, they could move themselves where they were needed. They couldn't accommodate a Home or carrier, but could facilitate repairs to any two or more other ships in the Navy. "I hope this new 'mosquito fleet,' as I have heard it called, will complement *Walker*'s 'disproportionate' feats at her side!" Saan-Kakja added. She spread her arms wide, symbolically embracing them all. "May the Maker of All Things protect you, and accept you in His loving embrace when the time comes for you to join Him in the Heavens above!" She turned away, suddenly blinking rapidly.

Matt cleared his throat. "That's about it," he said. "We'll set course for Baalkpan, where we'll get our torpedo tubes back—and more important, torpedoes to stick in them! There'll be a lot of work, but many of you who hail from Baalkpan have been gone a very long time. There should be ample opportunity for liberty." He smiled at the excited blinking and tail swishing. "After that, I'm sure it comes as no surprise that we'll be steaming into action again. I can't tell you where, since we're still working that out, but I promise we'll be headed *west*, to kick the absolute hell out of the Grik!"

Cheers thundered on the ship and on the dock alongside. The war in the East, against the Dominion, was grimly necessary, but not necessarily popular. Most Lemurians couldn't grasp that humans could be just as bad and potentially even more dangerous than the Grik Ancient Enemy. *Walker*'s crew knew better, but were glad to rejoin the old fight. Everyone knew how dire the situation was in the West and ached to help. Even more than that, the war against the Grik—with all its rabid violence and barbarity—was so much simpler to understand. It was *cleaner* from a standpoint of definition, if not execution. Many sensed there were new, growing tensions over how best to proceed, but there was little chance the outright factionalism and treachery that plagued the effort against the Doms could ever take root and flourish.

Matt allowed the celebration to dwindle of its own accord, and shared the satisfaction around him. Finally, he turned to Chief Bashear. "Set the watch, if you please. Make all preparations for getting underway."

"I thought we agreed on the rules," Matt said a little sheepishly to Sandra that evening as they stood together on the starboard bridgewing. The sun was setting behind gold-red streaks of cloud off the starboard bow, and the pink-topped, purple sea folded neatly aside from *Walker*'s sleek hull. Maa-ni-la Bay was far astern, and the old destroyer was loping south-southwest on two boilers at twenty knots.

"They're not even rules; they're actual regulations!" Sandra said with a smile.

"Might as well be divine commandments," Matt agreed, but he wasn't smiling. "They're *my* regulations, Sandra. I can't just set them aside as I like. I have to follow them *more* closely than anyone else."

"It's a stupid rule," Sandra said.

"Regulation."

"Okay, it's a stupid regulation that married—'mated'—personnel can't serve on the same ship."

"Maybe. Maybe *here* it is." He sighed. "It's weird enough to me—still—just having women . . . *any* female aboard. But with a good third of the crew being female of one sort or another, I can't really complain, huh?"

"Especially when that third is a *good* third," Sandra said, reemphasizing Matt's words.

He nodded. "Still," he said, "we *are* married, yet here you are."

"I'm your doctor!" Sandra retorted. "And since I couldn't fly to Baalkpan, with the Clippers being diverted east with freight for Second Fleet, *Walker* was the 'fastest available' transport!"

Matt rolled his eyes. "Sure, and that's the angle we used. It's even a good angle, since you're still the ship's surgeon too. But this is *it*. You're off the ship when we get to Baalkpan, and no arguments."

Sandra's jaw tensed. "Okay. But I'll just hop another one going the same way. If you get to pull the stunt you want, you're going to need me." Her voice softened. "A lot of guys—'Cats—will."

"No! Don't you get it? I *love* you, and I don't want you there. It's going to be dangerous, damn it!"

Sandra actually burst out laughing. "God forbid I should expose myself to actual *danger*!" she managed, and Matt's face heated. He looked into the pilothouse and saw Chief Quartermaster Rosen, who had the deck and the conn, piously pretending he hadn't heard a word. *He's better at that than Norm was,* Matt thought with a stab of pain. Norman Kutas had survived many wounds, but his turn finally came. The Lemurian at the big brass wheel was new, but he was pretty good too—even if he was staring a little too studiously into the pelorus. The other watch standers were all Lemurians and kept their faces inscrutable—usually easy, since they could form few facial expressions.

"Okay, so you're a daredevil," he conceded. "That doesn't mean I have to like it."

Sandra reached up and cupped his cheek in her hand in the deepening gloom. "I'm not, though. A daredevil, I mean. I get scared. I'm scared for *you* all the time." She shrugged. "But it's war, and bad things happen. Bad things have happened to both of us and everyone we know. The only way to stop that is to win the war." She smiled ironically. "And, unfortunately, that's inherently dangerous." She looked at him. "I'll follow your silly regulations. I said I would, didn't I? And it was one of the rules we agreed on. But if Adar lets you do what you want, I'm going along. I'll be on another ship, but I'm going."

Spanky found Tabby sitting on a stool near the throttle station in the forward engine room. It was loud in there with the creaking hull; rumbling turbines; and deep, vibrant rush of steam through freshly painted pipes. There were other noises too. The whir of generators and pumps, the rattle of deckplates, a mumbling whine from the reduction-gear housing. Then there was the roar of the shaft itself. Over everything, Tabby didn't hear him cycle through from the aft fireroom, and didn't notice his arrival. It suddenly dawned on Spanky that he'd never seen Tabby like that before—just sitting there, not busily doing . . . anything. The sight disturbed him, not least because she hadn't been expecting him, and like days of old when she gloried in driving him nuts, she wasn't wearing a shirt in the sweltering heat.

He had two simultaneous reactions. The first came from the part of him that loved Tabby like a daughter—or something. He noticed that even slick with foamy sweat, Tabby's steam scars had almost vanished beneath her light gray fur. He was glad. Even by human standards, Tabby looked like a pinup in a cat suit, as had been remarked many times, and he was happy to see her blemishes fade. But even scarred, her shapely breasts and slim figure had always been far too—human—for comfort. This recognition led Spanky immediately to his second reaction, one he was all too familiar with from the old days when Tabby deliberately tried to get his goat: profound embarrassment. His secret physical attraction to the 'Cat mortified him, even at the height of the "dame famine," when so few human females were known to exist. And the fact that Tabby loved him in a much less complicated way than he'd come to care for her made it even worse. Spanky kind of had a girl in Maa-ni-la now, an ex-pat Impie who'd fled the onetime virtual enslavement of women in the Empire of the New Britain Isles, and he'd learned to disregard his deeper feelings for Tabby. But seeing her like this always made him very uncomfortable indeed.

Spanky wasn't easily embarrassed, but his normal reaction to the condition was a degree of irritation that could quickly build to a towering, legendary rage even more remarkable because of his slight frame. Chief Gray always said Spanky's rages could swell him up to twice, three times his real size, like a puffer fish, and that wasn't far off. Anybody who ever saw him mad would never recognize him otherwise—which had actually come in handy a time or two in old Subic before he jumped the rail into officer's country and had to become respectable. There was no telling how many bloody-nosed shore patrolmen looked right at him later . . . He shook his head. It was hot, and Tabby wasn't like that anymore. Besides, engineering was her division now. If she wanted to let female, even *human* female, snipes run around nude down here, that was her affair.

A throttle 'Cat noticed him and stiffened. Tabby turned and saw him, then quickly turned away, grabbing a T-shirt and pulling it over her head. "Decent" now, she turned and stood. "Comaander McFaarlane!" she said.

Spanky waved her back down, and everyone else in the compartment relaxed. "As you were," he said automatically. To Tabby's credit, she didn't pull her shirt back off, and he grinned. "How's the plant?" he asked.

"Swell," Tabby replied, looking at the maze of pipes. "Them Maa-nila yard apes—dogs, whatever—did good work, even if we beat 'em in the big game." She grinned back at him. "No leaks. Everything's tight."

Spanky grunted. "Did you report the problems with the gasket material?"

"Yep. The new stuff s'posed to be better." She shrugged. "We see."

"Yeah." He looked around. "Say, have you seen that creepy little twerp Isak back here? He wasn't in the firerooms. Maybe he fell overboard."

Tabby hesitated and her grin fled. "I seen him earlier, but it ain't his watch."

"So? Since when did that ever make a difference? Him and Gilbert, both of them Mice, which you were one yourself, if I recall, always hung around the engineering spaces on watch or not. What gives?"

Tabby looked down. "I don't think he likes me no more."

"What? Why? Because you're an officer now? He's the chief, and, squirrelly as he is, if there's justice in that, I'll eat my shoe."

"But *is* justice!" Tabby defended. "He still knows more than I ever will. He an' Gilbert taught *me*! Now I outrank him."

"Maybe he does know more," Spanky conceded. "Hell, maybe he knows more than I do, but what good is that if he can't teach worth a damn?"

"He teach me," Tabby repeated.

"I think you just picked up more than either of them told you. You didn't even speak English when you started, remember?" He simmered and put his hands on his skinny hips. "I'll sort him out. For him to get all puffed up just because you got promoted over him . . ."

Tabby shook her head. "No! No! That's not why he's mad at me! He don't care 'bout that, I think."

Spanky blinked surprise. "So? What's he sore about?"

"I . . . I tole him the firerooms stinked."

Spanky barked a laugh. "So? They do, by God."

"Yah, but he thowed a fit; said they was still too clean after the refit for him to settle in proper. Said they didn't look like any *workin'* firerooms he ever seen, an' they was prob'ly just as bad before the refit with a broad in charge." She shook her head.

"He can't be mad because you're a girl," Spanky muttered. "It's got to be something else."

"It *is* cleaner," Tabby allowed, "an' I like it that way."

"So do I," Spanky agreed, concentrating, "but I bet that's what did it. He finally got to come home after a long time away, and it wasn't like he remembered it. His comfortable, filthy firerooms weren't like he left them, and it doesn't feel like home anymore. I guess I get that. It's still no reason to blame you." Spanky nodded to himself. "I'll go talk to him, cheer him up—if he hasn't already poisoned himself by eating too much of Lanier's chow."

"What you say?" Tabby asked.

"That the firerooms'll be just as grungy as ever in a few weeks—if he doesn't do his damnedest to keep 'em clean."

"What good will that do?"

"Why, it'll make him mad at *me* instead of you, and he's used to that. And it's as big a taste of home as he's likely to get around here. Oh, the boilers'll get sooted up eventually, and the spaces'll be grimy and oily again no matter what he does, but by then he'll already love 'em again. He can't help it!"

With the possible exception of Isak Rueben, Earl Lanier was the only man aboard USS *Walker* dissatisfied with the recent overhaul, and for similar reasons. Lieutenant Palmer had lost his radios—the last of their kind they had from the old world—and nearly lost his life, but his replacement CW comm gear had close to the same range, and they'd get the new TBS gear when they reached Baalkpan. He was resigned to his loss. But Earl's beloved oven, encompassing the aft bulkhead of his semiexposed galley beneath the amidships gun platform, had been destroyed in action against *Hidoiame*. His even more beloved, if empty, Coke machine had miraculously survived, though utterly exposed to enemy fire. He took some consolation from that, but his new oven just wasn't right for various reasons. It was too big, too small, too hot, or too cold all at the same time. The racks inside weren't the same distance apart as they'd been, and that disrupted nearly a decade he'd spent learning every quirk required to produce bread and baked vittles for the crew with no more conscious thought than a mechanical phonograph. The oven had been damaged before, but always put to rights under his supervision. This time he'd been wounded seriously enough that he hadn't been able to help "shape and train" its replacement.

"Just look at that!" he rumbled from his creaking chair when Tabasco removed loaves of the strangely pumpkiny bread Lemurian flour produced, and slid them onto cooling racks. "Damn things are practically incinerated!" Tabasco looked at the loaves.

"They maybe a little darker on top," the 'Cat mess attendant allowed, "but they not bad. I think we gettin' the hand of it."

"*Hang* of it," Lanier corrected sharply. "I don't give a shit about that pidgin gibberish what's been spreadin' all over the goddamn ship, but *my* division's gonna talk proper American if you goddamn well die tryin'!" Tabasco blinked skeptically at the bloated cook. He wasn't convinced Lanier spoke proper Amer-i-caan, and, besides, he didn't consider himself part of his division anymore. Unofficially, he belonged to Juan Marcos's elite cadre of officers' stewards, and if Lanier didn't agree, at least he wasn't prepared for open warfare with the diminutive Filipino. That Juan wasn't far from his mind was confirmed with Lanier's next words:

"An' it *is* bad! Just look at it—with yer damn, bugged-out *eyes*!" Lanier heaved himself to his feet and waddled to the cooling racks. "Scorched, scorched, scorched—an' the ones from the middle look like dried-up, smoky turds. I don't give a damn what the crew thinks; they'll eat what we give 'em—and they'd bitch if we fed 'em ee-clairs, anyway. But we can't send that shit off to the *officers'* mess! That scrawny, peg-legged little Flip'd be rollin' his eyes and sighin' an' *apoligizin'* all the whole damn while 'bout how shitty the goddamn bread has got since 'poor' Earl Lanier got his hee-roic wound—an' it was too! But all the while he'll be stampin' his damn peg on the deck, like losin' one measly leg was a bigger deal somehow. Hell, he's got another one! But then he'll go on about what a beautiful new goddamn oven we got an' how sad it is 'poor' Earl Lanier can't do better with it than he does!" He shook his head. "No, sir! That won't wash, an' I'll never give him the satisfaction! I'll crawl in that shitty oven an' cook *myself* first!"

He fumed for several moments, staring at the broad, black iron object of his wrath. Even the color insulted him. As filthy as he kept himself, his stainless-steel galley had always been immaculate. He picked his nose vigorously and wiped his finger on his greasy apron. As if that led to some epiphany, he suddenly turned to Tabasco. "Now looky here! You run along and get your mates. I don't care if they're in their racks. Tell 'em to get their swishy tails in here and draw the fires. Then find

Johnny Parks an' tell him to grab every shipfitter he can lay his hands on—they'll come a-runnin' if they ever wanna eat again. I'm gonna shift these oven racks back where they belong—an' have a proper meal to send to the wardroom by suppertime—if it breaks the ship's god-damn back!"

////// *Empire of the New Britain Isles*
New Scotland

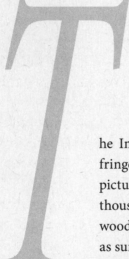

he Imperial Dueling Grounds stood at the forested
fringe of the naval port city of Scapa Flow. It was a
picturesque place, like a sports stadium designed for
thousands, bordered on three sides by the royal
woods. It had become a place to entertain the masses
as surely as the Colosseum of ancient Rome, but there
remained a significant difference. The Imperial Duel-
ing Grounds still represented the ideal that honor and valor might overcome injustice in the end, regardless of the odds and irrespective of
one's station in life. It was the place of ultimate adjudication for civil
and personal disputes that could be solved no other way. In reality, everyone knew that wasn't always the case. Professional duelists were
banned, but everyone knew they existed. Anyone with enough money
could always hire surrogates to offend or take offense in their stead. But

ultimately, for whatever reason, one had to *choose* to stand there, before God and the entire Empire, to defend his principles with his life.

Because it was considered a place of honor, the Dueling Grounds wasn't the customary place for executions, but an exception had been made in this case. It provided the most space for spectators, and repairs to the facility—so badly damaged in the opening battle of the war against the Dominion—had only recently been completed. The execution of one of the greatest traitors in Imperial history seemed an appropriate rededication.

A fine scaffold had been erected in the center of the arena, and the stands were filled to overflowing. Nearly everyone was in uniform, not only because the military had suffered greatly due to the actions of the condemned, but also because those very actions had helped ensure that virtually everyone *must* serve the war effort in some capacity if the Empire was to survive. Even Governor-Empress Rebecca Anne McDonald, seated in the royal box with members of her most trusted staff, wore a naval uniform of sorts. It was heavily braided blue wool, more ornate than that of the High Admiral of the Fleet, but void of any military decorations. In ordinary times, the formfitting tunic on any woman would've caused enough of a stir, and the spotless white knee breeches and polished boots would've been scandalous. But these weren't ordinary times. In fact, it was increasingly clear to the Empire at large that everything they'd considered ordinary for generations was rapidly slipping into history.

At the appointed hour, the crowd noises began to fade expectantly and the Governor-Empress stood, barely rising above the rail of her box. Her long hair was braided in the Navy way, but glowed like bright, burnished gunmetal around her expressionless, elfin face. With a curt nod, she signaled the tolling of a large bell that silenced further conversation. The bell sounded eight times, marking noon, and there was a hush as nine men started across the field below. Eight were Imperial Marines, in their red coats with yellow facings, bright against the dark volcanic sand. Their polished muskets and fixed bayonets glittered under the overhead sun. Between them strode another man, face drawn but defiant, wearing a rumpled, unadorned blue coat from which all decorations and braid had been stripped. He didn't shuffle or cause the Marines to prod or drag him, but kept step with them as they marched him to the scaffold and up the thirteen steps. At the top, he turned to face his Empress.

"Lord James McClain," Rebecca said harshly, "formerly High Admiral of the Imperial Navy, you have been judged guilty of high treason and despicable murder. Specifically, that while consorting with agents of the vile Dominion and other subversive elements, you did give aid and reassurance to our enemies. This aid included forsaking your duties as High Admiral while commanding a fleet sent to reinforce Imperial and Allied forces then engaged. The only reason you are not condemned for cowardice in the face of the enemy is that you never *faced* him! Instead, you deliberately abandoned your mission to pursue other aims! Specifically, and first of these, was to cause the treacherous murder of your sovereign, his wife, and two hundred and sixteen members of the Court of Directors. An additional fifty-seven persons in the vicinity of the court lost their lives when it was destroyed by the bomb you caused to be planted beneath it. There is also no doubt that you conspired with elements loyal to the Dominion to murder me—a scheme resulting in the deaths of three more loyal subjects of the Empire." Rebecca paused before remorselessly continuing. "For your treachery and murders, and the foul reward you gave your nation's trust, you are duly condemned to be hanged by your neck until you are dead." She stopped, visibly forcing her voice to remain level, calm. "Have you anything to say before the sentence is carried out?"

McClain took a step forward. His hands were tied behind his back, but he still managed to project a sense of dignity, even injury.

"I do," he paused. "Your *Majesty*," he added with scorn. When he spoke again, he slowly turned to address all those gathered there. "I *am* guilty of the crimes specified against me," he confessed. "But only because I am equally guilty of an overabundant love for my country! You've all seen the erosion of our precious institutions and traditions that began with the return of the Princess and the arrival of the American destroyermen and their . . . animalistic friends! It's *they* who subvert the natural order of the Empire! They infest our lands and demand that *we* conform to *their* barbaric sensibilities! The proof of that could not be better stressed by the appearance of Her Majesty here today, attired in the likeness of a man! They insist that we eliminate the age-old system of female indenture, a move that will morally and fiscally bankrupt our land. Already they use our women in *their* Navy, and God only knows what . . . perversions those unfortunates endure at the hands of their bestial lackeys aboard their ships! When will women join the ranks of our own beloved navy? Quite soon, no doubt, judging by Her Majesty's wardrobe! It's an abomination!

"I have no sympathy for the Doms, and am in no way in league with them, but I confess to using them to advance my efforts to stop the degradation and eventual destruction of the country I love. We would have survived their initial attempts against us, which I knew nothing about, without the Americans and their pets. Alone we would have prevailed against them, as we've done before. But Governor-Emperor McDonald embraced the unholy Alliance against my pleas. Gerald was like my brother, but *someone* had to act if the old order, our way of life, was to endure! I am sorry it came to what it did, but I saw no other option." He lowered his head. "I will die now, in defense of my principles, like so many have done before upon this hallowed ground. I will die without even the courtesy or comfort of a sword or pistol in my hand. But I will die knowing in my heart that I did my duty to God and the Empire of the New Britain Isles!"

Governor-Empress Rebecca Anne McDonald leaned forward in the rumbling mutters that followed. "Are you quite finished?" she demanded, her small voice carrying with the force of a trumpet. She looked around. "I am young," she admitted, "a child, most would say. I am also an orphan, thanks to that supposedly pious creature standing upon the scaffold! How many other children are orphans today because of his wicked treachery? How many more will there be because of the losses our forces suffered on New Ireland, at Saint Francis, the Enchanted Isles and elsewhere, all directly due to his *patriotic* acts? In addition to the murders he has confessed to, every battle death we've suffered in this war can be directly or indirectly attributed to his actions or inactions, and that was just to get us 'back' to where we were when the war began! The so-called Honorable New Britain Company played its part, as we now know, along with their puppets in the Court of Proprietors, but they've been dealt with. This *should* have been a time of union, when my father—" Her voice cracked. "When my father," she continued more firmly, "led us to final victory against the Dominion, which I fear has tainted even men such as Lord McClain in some insidious way. Instead, we've had nothing but strife among ourselves, while the true enemy of our land, our very existence, has been allowed to run amok. *Only* our friendship with the Western Allies has saved us!" She looked McClain straight in the eye when she resumed with a steely resolve. "Your pathetic appeal for a pistol or sword defiles the sanctity of this place. You are an admitted traitor and murderer. When, in the long history of our land, have such been afforded the right to defend their deeds? Not now, not ever. My father had prepared an address that he meant to give that fateful day when his voice, and that of so many others, was silenced forever. I will make that same address in his stead very soon. In the meantime, I want you to drop to the end of your well-earned rope with the following decree ringing in your ears: Henceforth, from the date of your execution—this Manumission Day forward—all indentures throughout the Empire without the legal protection of a true and voluntary contract will revert to the possession of the Crown. Any persons subject to those indentures, male or female, are, and shall be forevermore free of any obligation other than that they owe to the laws of the Empire of the New Britain Isles and myself, their Governor-Empress, as subjects and citizens. Likewise, they shall henceforth enjoy all the rights and benefits associated with complete citizenship, including the privilege of bearing arms in their country's defense!"

Her eyes lingered a long moment on the horrified expression spreading across Lord James McClain's face before she looked at the Marines standing beside him. "Do your duty," she commanded softly.

Sister Audry was disconcerted by the suspicious, almost hostile stares that followed her as she and the middle-aged Lemurian "Lord" Sergeant Koratin approached the broad porch of Government House in Scapa

Flow. She knew the stares weren't directed at Koratin; the 'Cat Marine had a checkered past in his homeland of Aryaal, but here he was a hero to Lemurians and humans alike. No, it was she who drew the stares, and she knew why. She was a Catholic nun, a "papist witch," as far as many in the Empire were concerned. They saw little distinction between what she was and represented, and the vile practices of the evil Dominion with which they were at war. She'd finally confirmed—to her relief— that there were quite dramatic, fundamental differences between her faith and the abomination of the Doms during the time she'd just spent on New Ireland. She'd stopped there to interview the Dom prisoners of war interred at the devastated town of Waterford, on the shore of Lake Shannon. The prisoners were engaged in cutting down the massive central forest that had burned in the fighting there, and preparing the timbers for transportation to Imperial shipyards. Audry had spoken to many New Ireland civilians as well. She knew it was up to her to teach them—and people across the Empire—just how profound the difference was between the truth and what they'd been taught. Maybe that would help, and she thought she'd made a start. She hoped so. In the meantime she'd endure the stares, and Sergeant Koratin was there in case anyone wanted to do more about her presence than glare at her.

She was anxious to see the Governor-Empress. She loved the child who'd been through such a terrible ordeal. The Dom attack that ravaged her homeland had been bad enough, but then to lose her parents, whom she'd been separated from for so long, to domestic treachery . . . It was almost more than Audry could bear. She'd yearned to comfort poor Rebecca ever since learning the news, and now that she was here, the yearning had become an almost desperate thing. She hoped Rebecca, who'd asked her to come, would feel the same way.

Sister Audry was disappointed when the Governor-Empress didn't meet the ferry that brought her over from New Ireland, but neither did the Prime Factor, the one-armed giant named Sean Bates, whom she also considered a friend. Concern began to blossom in Audry's heart. There was a small honor guard led by Koratin, so she hadn't been forgotten, but Koratin was tense as he led her through the city.

Since the attack that killed Rebecca's parents and virtually wiped out what remained of the Imperial government, Scapa Flow had become the de facto capital of the Empire. Even if the Court of Directors in New London hadn't been destroyed, Bates would've insisted that Empress Rebecca remain here in the heart of the Empire's most important military city. The populace, military and civilian, was uncomplicatedly devoted to her, and there was nowhere near the level of intrigue that thrived across the strait in New London. She was safe here, and *felt* safe, which was important. It was bad enough that she'd been forced into the role of war leader at such a tender age, without having to constantly worry that one faction or another would try to have her killed.

"Bear in mind that she has changed, Sister Audry," Koratin warned as they mounted the steps to the porch. "She remains a youngling, but must act the adult. That alone would not have changed her, I think; she has always been wise beyond her years, but on a personal . . . *feeling* way, she has gone to ground like a sorely wounded beast. She reminds me much of General Queen Protector Safir Maraan in that respect." He blinked sadness. "Our odd Alliance has *so many* orphan queens! Her will and mind are as strong as ever, but even as she knows she cannot retreat in war if she would win, her youngling's heart tries to retreat from anything that might scar it further." He paused. "And this is likely to be a most trying day, a day to rub her wounds quite raw." They stopped and he nodded at the red-coated sentries at the door.

"Her Excellency the Ambassador Sister Audry begs an audience with Her Majesty on behalf of the western members of the Grand Alliance."

"Afternoon, Sergeant Koratin," one of the men replied. "Afternoon, Yer Excellency," he added neutrally. "Her Majesty ain't got back yet. Ought'a be here d'rectly. I figger it's over by now."

"Where has she gone?" Sister Audry asked.

"To the hanging, Your Excellency," Koratin himself answered her. "The hanging of her parents' murderer, Lord High Admiral James Mc-Clain."

Their escort deposited Audry's things on the porch, and Koratin dismissed them. Then, for a while, he and Audry just sat there and waited. One of the guards summoned refreshments, and they drank chilled tea in silence. There was a commotion on the street beyond the lawn, and a squad of mounted guards clattered up, leading an ornate coach. Behind it were more armed riders, and they all drew to a halt opposite the porch. A footman leaped down from the back of the coach and opened the door, even as half the guard dismounted and formed a cordon around it. Other guardsmen tramped out from the house, across the porch, and assumed their place in ranks staring outward.

"My," Audry whispered.

"The precautions are necessary," Koratin insisted. "And Factor Bates—you remember him as Mr. O'Casey—is very serious about them, despite the young lady's protests."

"I see." Audry stood and moved forward to greet the approaching figures. She barely recognized Rebecca in her naval dress, but Sean looked much the same except for his fine clothes. There was a little gray in his magnificent mustache, but he hadn't changed otherwise. "My dear Rebecca!" Audry said, accelerating toward the girl, arms outstretched. A guard stepped in front of her, but Bates physically pushed him back in place.

"Och, let the lass through! She's a particular friend o' the Empress!"

Audry grabbed Rebecca's hands in hers and stood staring searchingly at the girl. "I have so ached for this meeting," she exclaimed.

Rebecca's features softened, but she didn't step into the embrace that Audry expected. "As have I," she said quietly, almost shyly. "I'm so glad you're here. Let us step inside, to my father's library. There is much to discuss."

In the library, the Governor-Empress invited them to sit and told yet another guard to pass the word for Mrs. Carr to bring more tea. Mrs. Carr had been a fixture at the New Scotland Government House as long as anyone could remember. In some ways, she was similar to Juan Marcos, the Filipino steward who'd carved out such an unassailable position of moral superiority aboard *Walker*. Utterly unlike Juan, however, she was large and matronly, and spoke very little. She was the household cook, maid to the Imperial family, and had been Rebecca's nanny when she was very young. She remained her body servant, and had very definite notions about propriety. Of all the inner circle Rebecca trusted completely, Mrs. Carr was likely the only one who disapproved of the reforms she'd enacted. There was no question of her loyalty, but despite her usual silence, she still managed to radiate her opinions quite effectively. She did so now when she entered the chamber and poured tea for Rebecca and her guests, lingering a moment longer than necessary at Audry's side. But her frowns and sighs were all apparently aimed at Sergeant Koratin and Factor Bates. Both were used to her and ignored the nonverbal admonishments.

"Thank you, Mrs. Carr. That will be all for now," Rebecca said quietly. Without actually huffing, the large woman stepped from the room and closed the door behind her. Bates rolled his eyes, and for the first time, Audry saw the faintest flicker of genuine amusement cross Rebecca's face. The girl turned to Audry. "To business. As I said, I'm happy you're here, and I do apologize for not meeting you myself." She grimaced. "It has been a most unpleasant day, in some respects."

"Damned pleasant for *me*, Your Majesty," Bates said. "I heartily enjoyed watchin' the traitorous b . . ." He cleared his throat. "*Divil's* face when ye made yer proclamation." He grinned. "An watchin' 'im drop through the trap shortly after was a relief as well. I feel much more comfortable with Lord McClain's dead corp molderin' in the sod, where he can cause no further mischief."

Rebecca took a long breath, her small nostrils flaring. "Quite," she agreed. "Now, Sister Audry, what news?"

Audry smiled tentatively at the child. "I'm sure you know more of the war than I, in the East and West, but I've brought some personal letters from your friends. I have them in my baggage. All but this one," she reached into her handbag and produced a folded, tied sheaf of papers, and handed them over. "Young Lieutenant Cook begged me to give you this the moment I saw you, and I promised. He was preparing for an expedition into the heart of Borno at the time." She saw concern flash across Rebecca's face. "Never fear. That monstrous brute Dennis Silva was to accompany him. He promised me that no harm would come to the lad! He also asked me to give you a, um, 'double-barreled squeeze' for him."

For just an instant, Rebecca's eyes seemed to mist over, but she dashed a hand across them and forced a brittle smile. "Thank you, Sister Audry." She laid the letter aside. "But now, what is the situation—as you see it—on New Ireland? What of the Dom prisoners? Can they ever be truly human? Can we even trust the populace there, particularly those that rose in support of the Doms?"

"I've learned much, Your Majesty, and confirmed much we already suspected. The Doms are not Catholic at all. They've embraced some of the trappings, but there is otherwise almost no similarity. The civilians of New Ireland, many of them, *are* rather Catholic, I believe, and did not embrace the Doms as much as they hoped to use them to further their own cause of independence." She shook her head. "Although I'm sure they didn't want independence nearly as much as they wanted religious equality. They were duped by the *appearance* of Catholicism the Doms project, and most fought alongside our troops to destroy them in the end. You've nothing to fear from them that you cannot cure with leniency. As for the Doms themselves," she sighed. "Some are not human. Many of their officers in particular can never be brought to see the light, nor can the few elite 'blood drinkers' that were captured alive. I've never seen such fanaticism before, except perhaps among the Grik, and I fear their sect, or whatever it is, will cause great suffering when our forces invade their homeland." She paused. "As for the rank-and-file Dom troops, I do hold out great hope. They are not as mad as the others, and the skillful and most imaginative way that Mr. Silva slew their leader was not supposed to be possible. That act in itself sowed fertile seeds among them that their faith might be misguided." She chuckled. "Once again, our inimitable and inestimable Mr. Silva may have found himself the coarsest of tools in the hand of God."

Even Rebecca laughed in delight, and Bates grinned at that. Koratin merely blinked sour amusement.

"In any event," Audry continued, "perhaps a thousand prisoners volunteered to hear the untainted word"—she glanced down shyly—"and I spoke a sermon as best I could. Several, in fact. I left chaplains among them, Lemurian, and those who preach the true Catholic and English faiths. As you know, a common thread binds all three, and I didn't see the harm."

"You did well," Rebecca assured her, "and I shall be more inclusive toward our Catholic subjects. After the decree I made today, how could I not?" She smiled at Audry's curious stare. "I will tell you all about it, but I suppose only time will tell what we must ultimately do with our prisoners."

"We may enlist a few, eventually," Bates said thoughtfully. He glanced around at the stunned expressions. "Aye. What'd *ye* do if ye discovered all the sufferin' in yer land, an' that which ye'd heaped on others was based on a horrible, nasty lie? Would ye nae try ta' put a end to it, as we ha' done ourselves?"

////// *USS* **Walker**
April 16, 1944

or five days, USS *Walker* had steamed carefully south, avoiding the numberless Fil-pin islands to the east, across the treacherous depths of the Sulu Sea, then west-southwest along the Sulu Archipelago. Finally, she turned south to cross the equally dangerous Saa-leebs Sea, pounding the depths with her sonar to discourage the monstrous but sound-sensitive denizens lurking there. By the time she steered southwest into the Makassar Strait, even Earl and Isak were more resigned to the superficial newness of their ship, and, weird as they were, they couldn't completely resist the sense of excitement animating the rest of the crew. At long last, after all they'd endured, through battles and storms across uncounted thousands of miles that many of *Walker*'s Lemurians once hadn't believed possible to cross or even exist upon, the old destroyer passed beneath the formidable defenses of Fort Atkinson and reentered her home port of Baalkpan Bay.

Matt was on the bridge with Sandra, Spanky, Gray, Courtney Bradford, and Tabby, and with the strangely more-than-essential watch standers present, the pilothouse was crowded. Both wings were packed, and most of *Walker*'s officers and new POs had found some vantage point from which to view the busy harbor so stunningly different from how they remembered it. The fire-control platform, amidships deckhouse, and aft deckhouse were packed with gawkers, and whatever crew could find a pretext to be on deck lined the rails.

Baalkpan Bay had always been a busy seaport, but the activity, structures, and sheer volume of shipping both moored and moving within its confines had increased exponentially. Matt was both elated and a little saddened by the sight. It clearly indicated that their adopted home was all in for the war effort, and the combat power, supporting infrastructure, and industrial might he saw encouraged him in the face of the increasingly global war forced upon them. At the same time, his mind's eye poignantly reminded him what Baalkpan looked like when his battered, war-weary ship arrived there the very first time, in company with a savagely mauled *Big Sal* just two short years before. The place had been busy then, but happily so, and there hadn't been the least warlike aspect to any endeavor in view. The innocent, inherent peacefulness of Baalkpan was gone, perhaps forever, and if Matt and his people weren't to blame for that, they'd certainly facilitated it.

"It ain't our fault, Skipper," Gray grumbled, as if reading his thoughts. "It's the Grik's. They were comin' if we were here or not. Nobody here would even be alive if we hadn't showed up."

"He's right, of course," Courtney said, his voice uncharacteristically subdued. "But it doesn't make the *sense* of it all any easier to swallow."

"I don't know what you all upset for," Tabby scoffed. "Baalkpan's different, sure. Not as pretty either. I always thought it was pretty here, when my Home come to visit. But it's *still* here, an' that's to be proud of, not so sad."

"Yep," agreed Spanky around a mouthful of the yellowish tobacco leaves. "Personally, I'm fairly proud to be alive instead of the swarms of

Grik we've shoveled into hell, and if Baalkpan had to quit bein' such a vacation retreat so we—and everybody here—can say that, I got no regrets." He glanced at Gray. "I don't know about Chief Bashear, but I know *your* notions of entering port were never so lax." He nodded meaningfully at the throng down on the fo'c'sle.

Gray grunted, but just then a bosun's pipe squealed and its call was taken up by whistles the 'Cats could manage. As usual, Petey was draped across the back of Sandra's neck, and he tensed at the commotion. "Goddam!" he practically mumbled, apparently aware that shrieks of any sort on the bridge drew more attention than he wanted. Almost reluctantly at first, but with increasing purpose as Chief Bosun Carl Bashear's nasal but forceful voice mounted, the crew of USS *Walker* scampered to line the rails more properly.

"The main battery will stand by to salute the flag of the Grand Alliance," Matt commanded. The newest "stainless banner" had changed a little, but only in ornamentation. It was a gold-edged field of white, with a circle of stylized gold and green trees representing its member Homes, or states. All surrounded a gold-edged blue star signifying the Amer-icaan Naa-vy clan that brought them all together. All clans were considered equal, but the Navy clan—Matt's (which included the Marines)—was the only one composed of *every* clan and that, despite its losses, continued to grow.

"All guns crews report maanned an' ready to fire salute," Minnie, the talker, announced a few minutes later.

"Very well. Stand by," Matt replied. He paused. "Have Mr. Campeti acknowledge that all guns will fire five salvos, except number one, which will fire six."

Spanky looked at him strangely. Twenty-one guns were usually reserved for entering a foreign port.

"What's that about?" Sandra asked.

"Just a subtle hint to Adar that even united, the Alliance still consists of sovereign clans—and the Navy's *mine*." He shrugged. "I doubt he'll even catch it, and, besides, it'll show we're glad to be home!"

"Oh, he'll catch it!" Gray murmured to Courtney, who glanced at Matt, concerned.

Walker had already steamed past the oldest, most prominent part of Fort Atkinson, but the fort had been enlarged all the way to the high, reinforced berm protecting the southern part of the city itself. Matt was waiting until the salute would carry to the greatest number of people ashore. "Commence firing," he said at last.

Five perfect salvos boomed out from *Walker*'s four main guns, then number one added a single shot. Almost immediately, every gun along the Baalkpan waterfront thundered out, one after the other, and the answering salute went on and on. Matt started to grin when the number passed their own, and didn't end until more than *seventy* great guns had choked the harbor with dense white smoke.

"Don't you feel just a bit petty now, Captain Reddy?" Courtney sniffed.

"No. Even if I wasn't making a point, seventy-odd rounds would have emptied our magazines." He chuckled. "Not much point in bringing a full load of the new shells back *here* from the Fil-pin Lands! I'm glad everybody seems happy to see us, though."

Walker slowed to a crawl as fishing feluccas jockeyed near, and every manner of small craft from steam barges to motor launches paced her progress. All were filled with excited 'Cats, ex-pat Impie women, and even a few teary-eyed members of her original crew who'd remained behind, running various industries and projects. They approached the same dock they'd tied up to after their first arrival in Baalkpan, the one that served the waterfront bazaar that remained the most familiar aspect of the city. It was bigger now, expanded to accommodate the growing population, but just as boisterous and colorful as the first time Matt laid eyes on it. The bazaar endured as an island of normalcy in the surrounding sea of change. And such change! The city had surely quadrupled in size, mostly with the addition of massive warehouses and factory buildings backing the expanded docks, repair slips, and fitting-out piers. Yet another mighty aircraft carrier was rising in the huge dry dock, and half a dozen floating dry docks, festooned with cranes, were building other ships. *Walker* had just missed the newest carrier, *Baalkpan Bay*, and her battle group including the rebuilt *Santa Catalina*. They'd sailed to join First Fleet just a few days before. Nancys from one of the patrol wings swooped and sported over the bay, joined by a few of the new P-1 Mosquito Hawks, or Fleashooters, that no one on *Walker* had ever seen.

Bashear's bosun's pipe twittered, calling the sea-and-anchor detail as the ship inched toward the dock. Lines were thrown to handlers, and the cheering throng redoubled their voices when *Walker*'s whistle sounded, deep and exuberant, amid a cloud of steam. Matt turned to Sandra and squeezed her hand. "Home, I guess," he said with a wry smile.

Sandra squeezed back. "Home," she agreed more forcefully.

"Captain Reddy," came Juan's voice from behind. "Your best uniform is ready." He looked at Sandra. "An' your Miss Diania has prepared yours as well." He sniffed. "I helped her, but she is learning."

"What about my fancy duds?" Gray demanded.

Juan looked at the Super Bosun down his long nose. "I believe that chore has been accomplished," he said a bit coldly. "Though I cannot say for certain." He waved a hand. "I passed the word that you desired it done." He smiled at Spanky. "Yours are ready as well, Mr. McFarlane, as are Mr. Campeti's." He looked back at Gray. "I saw to it myself."

There was good-natured laughing while Gray grumbled.

"And what of my things?" Courtney asked eagerly.

"I did my best to brush and press that bizarre . . . Imperial costume you presented to me," Juan replied in a long-suffering tone, "but I cannot answer for the results." He sighed dramatically. "Such oddly placed seams! And the shoulders are quite ridiculous." He paused, peering hard at Bradford. "Was that . . . thing . . . truly a *cravat*? Why can't you just wear a proper uniform like everyone else?"

"Because I'm not in the *Navy*, my dear Mr. Marcos!" Courtney replied cheerfully. "And that cravat, for indeed it is one, most likely saved my life. I will wear it—loosely in this climate—for no other reason than that." He looked down his own stubby nose. "And the ensemble you so haughtily term a costume is the height of fashion in New London. No doubt it will be all the rage here soon enough!"

////// *Baalkpan*

Traditionally, visiting High Chiefs went to the Great Hall to call on the High Chief of Baalkpan, but Adar and his personal staff were waiting on the dock when Matt, Sandra, Courtney, and Chief Gray came ashore.

"Cap-i-taan Reddy!" Adar greeted enthusiastically, moving through the happy crowd to stand before them. He embraced Matt and Sandra, then Courtney in turn. As usual, Gray backed away before he could be hugged, but Adar didn't mind. He stepped back to look at them. "I am joyful to see you!" Others followed Adar through the gap he'd made. Ambassador Forester was there, as was Major Jindal in his immaculate Imperial Marine dress. Chack and his sister, Captain Risa-Sab-At, were an even more impressive (and welcome) sight in their blue kilts and spotless white armor. Then there was Alan Letts with his peeling, boyish face; Perry Brister; Steve Riggs; Ronson Rodriguez with his bald scalp and Pancho Villa mustache; Bernie Sandison, dark haired, reticent. All were a sight for sore eyes, and all saluted crisply. Matt returned the salutes and happily shook hands all around. These people were like family to him now, and he'd missed them more than he'd realized.

He was quickly introduced to other people he'd never met. Adar's staff had grown dramatically and there were far too many new 'Cats to remember after only one meeting. There were new humans as well; half a dozen men who'd survived their ordeal aboard *Mizuki Maru* and actively joined the cause. One was a former Filipino scout who'd become a captain in Chack's commando outfit. Others had assignments reflecting past ratings, or preservice occupations. Another man Matt didn't know appeared behind the others.

"I must present Commander Simon Herring, Minister of Straa-tee-gic Intelligence!" Adar announced. "After a somewhat—you say 'bumpy,' I think? After a bumpy start, he has made great strides helping us . . . sort things out."

There was a briefly awkward moment while Matt and Herring looked one another over, clearly sizing each other up. They were of similar height and build—or would be once Herring completely filled out again. Matt got the distinct impression Herring expected him to salute *him*, but the man finally simply stuck out his hand. Matt took it, but noticed some disapproving stares.

"Mr. Herring," he said neutrally, "glad to have you aboard."

Herring smiled, but his eyes narrowed. Inwardly, Matt sighed. He'd hoped the reports were exaggerated, but Herring didn't make a good first impression. Still, he couldn't be quite the martinet he seemed. Could he? Adar was too good a judge of character. There was no question they'd all have a lot to say to each other when they got down to business.

Matt looked at Adar and waved at two very odd ships secured to the fitting-out pier a short distance away. He grinned hugely. "My God. I never expected to see *Mahan* again! And the other's obviously S-Nineteen—but Mr. Laumer's done a lot to her!"

Adar beamed. "*Mahan* is nearer ready for sea, but both will soon make great contributions, I believe . . . with their torpedoes!"

"So the torps really work?"

"They do! Mr. Saan-di-son can make you a better report, but I believe you will be pleased!"

"Bernie?" Matt asked.

"Yes, sir," Sandison answered. "They work. The range is pretty short, maybe a couple thousand yards before they get weird sometimes . . . but, they by God go off when they hit! Two of *Walker*'s triple mounts have been completely rebuilt and are ready to go back aboard as soon as you're ready for them."

"I'm ready now," Matt said eagerly. "We'll put them where numbers one and two used to be. We haven't, uh, added anything there." Not only were there armored tubs for twin 25-millimeter guns where the numbers three and four mounts had been, but the new Nancy catapult was nestled between them.

"We've also got the old number four gun ready to reinstall, if you want her," Riggs said.

Matt shook his head. "You know, this may sound weird, but I kind of like the dual-purpose nature of that four-seven Jap gun on the aft deckhouse. I think I'll keep it."

Bernie and Letts looked at each other. "Well, uh, maybe we forgot to mention we built a dual-purpose mount for old number four. It sits a little higher, so the CG does too, but it shoots the same four-inch-fifty as all your other guns, and you can tie her directly back into the gun director."

"Is that so?" Matt asked, impressed. "Well, unless you managed to bring the old three-incher back to life and want us to wag it around too, we should be okay, weight-wise. We've got the catapult to consider now, but Nancys aren't heavy—and the twenty-fives don't weigh near what the old torpedo mounts did."

"We fixed the three-incher," said Brister, "but we already put it on Laumer's boat, aft." He pointed.

"Well, there it is," Matt said, nodding. He was thrilled to see *Mahan* riding there, looking almost new, if a little weird, but he was frankly disappointed Laumer hadn't come up with something better for S-19 than a torpedo boat. He had other—better—torpedo boats from Maani-la now.

"I'll be derned," he finished. He gestured toward the two vessels. "Chairman Adar? Can we take a minute to have a look at them?"

"Of course!" Adar agreed. "The reception at the Great Hall cannot begin without us, after all. Besides, I spend so much time in the War Room. Outside air will do me good."

Matt asked Chief Gray and Bernie to go tell Spanky to move the ship where the torpedo tubes and new/old gun awaited her, then dismiss all but an anchor watch for a long-deserved liberty.

"Meet us back here when you're done, all of you."

"Aye, aye, *Skipper*," Gray said, stressing the word.

Together, the rest of them excused themselves from the understanding crowd and moved down the dock to stand alongside *Mahan*'s abbreviated form. Matt couldn't seem to take his eyes off her. The last time he'd seen *Walker*'s sister, she was charging *Amagi* through a hail of metal and towering splashes—before she blew herself up and sank to the bottom of Baalkpan Bay.

"A hell of a thing," he muttered, turning to Adar. "Where're you sending her?"

"I do not yet know."

"I want her," Matt said simply.

"You *want* her?" Herring suddenly blurted, incredulous. "Just like that?"

Matt turned to him. "Yeah, just like that. She's *mine*, and if I want her, I can damn well have her!"

"My friends!" Adar interceded. "We must certainly discuss warlike matters, but this is a day of joy. We will hash things out tomorrow. Today, tonight, let us celebrate—and be glad we are all together again."

The welcoming party was a splendid affair, much like the one thrown by the great Nakja-Mur when *Walker* first arrived with a damaged *Salissa* Home—back before the war. They enjoyed the traditional grand march up through the heart of the bazaar, where they were greeted by hearty cheering instead of the reserved curiosity that once prevailed. All the way to Adar's Great Hall, Matt, Sandra, Courtney, Gray, and most of *Walker*'s officers, and a little more than half her crew, smiled, waved, exchanged embraces, and accepted colorful bouquets pressed on them, until they couldn't hold any more. If anything, this party was even bigger than any Matt had seen, and since the populace suffered no anxiety over the arrival—or odd appearance—of the human visitors this time, the atmosphere of goodwill was universal. Baalkpan was very glad to see USS *Walker* again.

The reunion at the Great Hall was more complete than at the dock. There were many more familiar faces and people Matt was glad to see, and he was amazed by how big Alan and Karen Letts's daughter, Allison Verdia, had grown. He didn't see Herring again that night, and managed to forget all about him and enjoy himself and his wife at this, their first social event as a married couple at their adopted home. They danced to familiar but very strangely performed music, taken from sheet music or the many platters still with Marvaney's old phonograph at the Busted Screw. They even attempted some Lemurian tunes, amid a great deal of laughter. The merriment seemed universal, and at one point, Matt was stunned to see Gray dancing very stiffly and formally with Miss Diania! Courtney drank too much, and he and Ambassador Forester wound up in a very bizarre singing contest in which victory was apparently achieved by whoever could carry a tune the longest without stopping to breathe. Few of *Walker*'s crew stayed very long, preferring the company of mates and sweethearts they'd left behind or old shipmates down at the Screw. Some doubtless visited the newly established brothel nearby. Confident Spanky and the SPs would deal with things if their long-suffering crew got out of hand, Matt and Sandra left the Great Hall fairly early and were led to their house by one of Adar's youngling aides. They'd never laid eyes on the charming cottage, elevated in the Lemurian fashion, but were assured it *was* theirs. Inside there was little decoration. It had been left for them to make their own. There was furniture, though, and on the broad bed commissioned expressly for them, they spent their first night together at home.

CHAPTER 16

////// *Adar's Great Hall*
Baalkpan
April 17, 1944

att strode into the war room with Sandra, Spanky, Chief Gray, and Chack. Courtney followed along as well, but his heart—and head—weren't in it. Gone were the days when the war room consisted of a kind of desk in a small office. This chamber was nearly as big as Nakja-Mur's personal quarters had once been. There to meet them were Adar, of course, Alan Letts, Bernie Sandison, Steve Riggs, Ambassador Forester, a number of Lemurians, and an Aussie seaman named Henry Stokes whom they'd met the night before. Also there, on the other side of Adar from Letts, was Herring. It was a relatively small gathering—probably appropriate under the circumstances—since this wasn't a meeting for details but big ideas.

"Good morning Cap-i-taan Reddy!" Adar said pleasantly. "Minister Tucker—or I should say 'Reddy' now? I will never grow accustomed to that!" He grinned and nodded at the others. "Gentlemen! I am glad to see you all. I hope you enjoyed yourselves last night. I certainly did! Please make yourselves comfortable."

"Thank you, Chairman Adar. That was a swell shindig, and like I told you then, we're glad to be home."

"We are most glad to have you." Adar looked about, almost at a loss. "So very much has happened since you steamed away to rescue the hostages that terrible Billingsley person took! It is difficult to know where to begin."

"With respect, Mr. Chairman," Matt said, "it's not like we haven't been in nearly constant contact. I'm fully aware of the strategic situation. I may not be up on every detail in the works, but going over past events like we're all just hearing about them will only waste time, and that's always been a very precious commodity."

"Indeed," Adar nodded. "Well said."

"With that in mind," Matt persisted, "I'm not going to beat around the bush. I sent you my plan for a raid against the Grik, a raid I think will not only divert attention and resources from India, but might well shorten the war. I'm glad you've decided to take a more . . . proactive role in the command structure of the Alliance, but I'm not sure why you're dragging your feet on this." He took a breath. "In my capacity as Commander in Chief of All Allied Forces, by acclamation, I'm not even sure it's up to you."

"Of course it's up to us . . . to Chairman Adar!" Herring corrected sharply, discarding his genial mask. He paused and visibly collected himself. "I apologize for the outburst, Captain Reddy, but I've studied your actions as CINCAF quite extensively. I consider it part of my job. As a . . . relative newcomer here, I believe I'm able to look at your record more objectively than others, and form a perhaps more realistic assessment of that record than has been the case to date. The greater part of my job is to do everything in my power to pass advice to Chairman Adar that might help him, help us all, win this war as quickly possible. I try to do that with as much . . . disinterested professionalism as I can manage under the circumstances. From that perspective, I must first congratulate you on some impressive tactical successes. Extremely impressive, considering your limited resources—and the relative inexperience you arrived with."

Sandra almost seemed to coil to strike, but Matt placed a hand on her shoulder. She, in turn, reluctantly restrained the Bosun when he took a step forward.

"Strategically, however," Herring continued, as if oblivious to the sudden tension, "I cannot be so complimentary, and an accounting of the various strategies that have brought us to this point are entirely relevant, I believe."

Letts stared hard at the man around Adar, and though Adar didn't speak, he was blinking displeasure.

"I mean no disrespect," Herring quickly added, "but as we go forward, planning our next moves, it only stands to reason that we should objectively examine how successful certain previous strategies have been"—he leaned forward on his stool, regarding Matt—"particularly since they have all originated from the same source."

There was a collective gasp.

"Minister Herring," Adar said stiffly, "if it remains your intention, even after the assurances you gave, to turn this session into a *trial*, you may leave now and find other employment! This is the very reason I decreed that I would be the ultimate arbiter of strategic planning. If something goes wrong, *I* will take the blame. I will not allow you or anyone to insinuate that others—particularly *this* man—have done other than their absolute best when it comes to the prosecution of the war!"

"But that's not my intent at all!" Herring defended. "I have no doubt Captain Reddy, or, indeed, every commander currently in action against our enemies, have done the best they could. I merely think it's time to inquire whether their 'best' is indeed good enough!" Herring paused amid another roar of outrage, but didn't back down. "Please!" he said. "Let me explain!"

Oddly, almost every eye turned to Matt instead of Adar. He could feel Sandra quivering with rage beside him and suspected Gray was about to explode, but he'd been expecting this ever since he heard of Herring. He wasn't sure what motivated the man, and meant to find out—but he was very curious to see what, exactly, had become of the command staff since he'd been away. "Speak your piece, Herring," he said.

Simon Herring had been tenser than he seemed, and he gradually appeared to deflate. "I'm not good at this," he finally admitted, surprising everyone with the confession and his sudden change of tone. "When all is said, I'm really just an analyst and I've never been good with people." He looked at Matt. "I've never commanded a ship—much less an entire navy." He shook his head. "I've been to sea only once in my life as a free man. That was when we moved from Shanghai to the Philippines. I *flew* out from the States. I don't count my time aboard *Mizuki Maru*, as a prisoner of war, since I wasn't even in charge of myself at the time. I was nearly dead, and don't remember much. If not for those who helped me"—he nodded at Stokes—"I wouldn't be here." He turned to Adar. "Now that I *am* here, despite my initial restraint, I've made this cause my own with a conviction that I propose may be difficult for you to understand. I was a staff officer, protected and somewhat arrogant, no doubt, who was captured by the Japanese and made a *slave*. That was traumatic enough, I assure you, but then came the hellish fever-dream voyage of *Mizuki Maru* and our arrival in this world." He shook his head. "After all that, to be here, among friends, safe, well fed, *free* . . . Can you possibly imagine how precious this land and the Alliance that protects it have become to me?" He looked back at Matt.

"I admit my current happy condition is largely due to your efforts, and I can't imagine what it was like to be in your shoes. Nor do I think I could've done anything better, frankly." He frowned. "But might *you* have? Possibly, and that's what we must discuss."

Matt was taken aback. Herring had a point, and his perspective *was* much different than his own. Far more different and selfless than he'd suspected. What's more, he was right. Matt knew he'd made mistakes, lots of them. Most, he had to admit, were driven by the temper he'd nearly lost a few moments before; a temper that had doubtless caused him to make rash decisions on several occasions and might've cost more than a few lives. He'd had a hard time coming to terms with that once, and precious, lost faces still crowded his thoughts and often made sleep impossible. If not for Sandra, who understood and was the only one he dared talk to about it, he didn't know what he'd do. He'd learned to control his temper better, he thought, but he was conscious of the fact that it always lurked somewhere beneath the surface and could take control of *him*, if he wasn't very careful.

At the same time, he was perfectly aware that his temper wasn't the only cause of many of his mistakes. He had the same fundamental training required of any naval officer, but he'd never had the expanded training or experience to prepare him for the role he'd assumed here. He was a historian and that had helped, but otherwise, he'd been merely a junior skipper of an old and very obsolete destroyer. He'd been winging it since he got here, and knew it. Only luck and the outstanding people he'd had the good fortune to command had made much of what they'd accomplished together possible. And the Lemurians, of course. Without their amazing flexibility, courage, forbearance, and ultimately, trust, they'd never have survived long enough to learn, together, what it took to achieve what they had. Apparently, Herring had seen this right off, and in his awkward, brusque, impersonal way, he'd put his finger right on it.

"Go on," Matt said softly in the silence that had descended.

"Well," Herring continued, "when viewed objectively, one might gain from your strategic decisions that you don't really want this war to end at all."

Matt hadn't been prepared for that. "*What?*" he barked, his temper flaring anew, so surprised was he by Herring's sudden change of tack. "Are you nuts? *Jesus*, do I want this war over! I've lost so many . . ." he gestured at Adar, then all around. "*We've* lost thousands of fine people, people we care for deeply. How *dare* you say such a thing?"

"But the war drags on, and more die every day."

Matt blinked. "Yeah, and it's a hell of a thing, but we can't just snap our fingers and make it stop! Maybe you don't understand the Grik—or Doms—as well as you think. No matter how hard we hit them, if we let up, they *will* come for us again. Guaranteed. The only way to be free of them forever is absolute victory!"

"And yet you don't use every weapon at your disposal to ensure that victory—which prolongs the war."

"What the hell?" Realization struck and he glared at Adar. In the corner of his eye he saw Bernie squirm.

"Yes, we have developed this 'mus-taard gaas,' you call it," Adar confirmed, "but not in any great amount. You may remember agreeing to develop, if not deploy it yourself, some time ago."

"Yeah. I said it would probably be best to have it, but I and many others were against its use except as a last resort. Not so much because of the Grik, but because of the possibly unwilling nature of the Japanese aid they're receiving."

"It would seem that aid is not unwilling after all, or if it was, it is no longer," Herring stated. "We've learned to communicate with Grik prisoners to a degree, as you know. Their Hij military leaders, ship captains and the like, still destroy themselves rather than be taken alive, but some few um, 'civilians,' have told us quite a lot. Also, as you saw yourself before you began your adventures in the East . . ."

"Adventures?" Ambassador Forester exclaimed incredulously. "I must insist you rephrase that at once, Commander Herring! Captain Reddy saved my country and forged a strong alliance between us. I will hear those accomplishments made light of no longer, unless you are willing to meet me later!"

Herring blinked at Forester, suddenly remembering how common dueling was in the Empire of the New Britain Isles. "I do beg your pardon, Your Excellency. There are those who consider Captain Reddy's actions in the East, particularly those that involved us in yet another war on an entirely different and distant front, as . . . more premature than would be ideal from the perspective of prosecuting the war we already had."

"That may be from your very *immediate* perspective," Forester growled, "but then the Doms would have conquered us, and you would have only eventual certain enemies in the East, instead of an enemy and a very appreciative friend. I believe it is *your* strategic thinking that is in error here!"

"Perhaps, Your Excellency. And I apologize for any offense," Herring said. "I stipulated that I am not good with people." He looked back at Matt. "But even you saw that the Grik were changing. That change has accelerated, making them far more dangerous—but also more prone to consider their own survival at times. Statements from prisoners we took before the Battle of Madras have confirmed that not only has Kurokawa continued actively aiding the Grik, but he's also achieved a position of true power as their 'General of the Sea,' and perhaps more. Further, the rest of his surviving crew appears to support him."

"But *gas*," Matt said darkly. "If we can make it, there's no reason the enemy can't. And if we start throwing it around, they will too. And we can't protect our people from it! Even masks won't work. How the hell do you seal a furry face? If you come up with a hood or something, how will our people fight?"

"Basing our decision on whether to use a weapon such as gas on what *this* enemy may or may not do in response makes me wonder if *you* might not know him as well as you think," Herring accused. "Do you honestly believe the enemy, Kurokawa in particular, would even *care* if we gassed a bunch of Grik after they'd gassed our people first?"

Matt took a deep breath, stunned by his own stupidity. The no-gas policy had always been based on (or was it excused by?) a promise to Shinya—but if there *were* no noncombatant Japanese anymore, how would Shinya feel now? And Herring was right about another thing: if Kurokawa got gas, he'd use it. *But if we use it against the Grik, how long before we use it on the Doms—and why does the very thought of that make me want to puke?* he wondered. *Is it just because they're human? No. It's because even though some of them might be even more evil than the Grik, many aren't evil at all.* He wanted to pull his hair. Despite his near obsession with keeping things as black and white as he could, he knew, deep down, that he hated gas most of all because it made it impossible to pick and choose who he killed.

"All this is 'aac-aa-demic,' as you say," Adar said. "As I mentioned, we have created the capacity to manufacture gaas, but we have been working more on something else."

Matt's eyes jerked to Petey, draped around his wife's neck, and he remembered the other such creatures appearing in the Fil-pin Lands.

"Yap," he breathed. "My God, what've you done?"

"Nothing yet, Skipper," Bernie blurted, almost cringing.

"What are you talking about?" Alan Letts demanded.

"Well, you remember that kudzu stuff they ran into on Yap Island?" Bernie nodded at Sandra, whose face had paled. "It had thorns on it, like seeds, that when it stuck in something or somebody . . . Mr. Cook got a thorn in his finger—"

"And we had to cut it off to save his life!" Sandra shouted.

"Yeah," Bernie agreed weakly. "The thorns stick in you and immediately start shooting out roots through capillaries, veins . . . You're probably dead by the time they get in your arteries. But there's some kind of drug too, so even though it hurts, you don't really care what's happening. That's how the stuff spreads. The kudzu grows up out of the corpse it stuck with a thorn! It occurred to some of us that if you strung those thorns out over the enemy . . . Well, the Grik go barefoot. An awful lot of them'll get stuck, and they'll die within a few days." He took a breath. "Anyway, we got some—quite a bit—and Adar's had me stripping the thorns out past Experimental Ordnance."

Sandra gritted her teeth. "You're growing it here?"

"No, ma'am! We brought it in dried."

"And nobody told me about this?" Alan demanded. He looked at Matt. "Honest, Skipper, I didn't know!"

"Do you have any idea what you're doing?" Sandra ground out. "If just one thorn, *one* seed . . ."

"Yes, ma'am," Bernie assured her. "We've been careful as hell—uh, pardon the language. And all our tests show the dry thorns won't sprout in just water or soil." He shrugged. "I guess it takes blood. We brought it in aboard a captured Grik 'Indiaman'—which we burned in case any seeds got loose, even in the cracks. But that was before we knew for sure about the blood."

"That ship touched at Maa-ni-la!" Sandra accused.

"Yes," Herring stated, "but there was no way anything could have gotten off."

"Creatures like Petey did!" Sandra said, touching the furry lizard on the head.

"That's impossible," Herring replied, but his voice carried less conviction.

"We saw them there! You must warn Saan-Kakja at once that you might've contaminated her lands with the most pernicious, dangerous plant imaginable!"

"I doubt the contamination," Bradford said slowly, "if what you say is true. I imagine the creatures that went ashore are quite familiar with the threat posed by the thorns—but a warning must surely be sent so if anyone does become infected, it will be noticed." His voice turned angry. "But if you use this . . . weapon, the plant will sprout, and as soon as that happens, it will spread! Surely you've considered that? It could spread utterly unchecked in lands with no defense against it! You could ultimately make entire *continents* uninhabitable! My God, this is so much worse than gas that it buggers any comparison—or any understanding of the mind that could consider using it!"

"We have not *planned* using it yet," Adar stressed a little weakly. Bernie had made the same warnings as Courtney and he didn't *want* to use what they'd been calling the "kudzu bomb" for those very reasons. But he considered it his duty to seize any potential weapon he could, even if only to keep it as a last resort. He was confused, though. He'd thought, given Captain Reddy's stated aversion to gas, that the kudzu might be better received. But now, judging by his face moving, he seemed less opposed to using gas than he'd been, particularly compared to the kudzu! It was wildly frustrating. All Adar wanted was a weapon— *any* weapon—that would kill as many of the hated Grik as possible, while requiring fewer of his people to die while using it. He glanced at Letts, and the expression he saw on the Chief of Staff's face almost broke his heart. He *should* have told him!

"So," Matt said ironically. "I guess I'm not the only one who makes mistakes. We can keep raking mine up all day, if that's what you want, but I'd prefer to get down to business."

"Of course," Adar said softly, still looking at Alan, who refused to return his gaze. "Comm-aander Herring?"

"Very well," Herring said. "As you all doubtless know, the situation in the East is somewhat stable for now. Preparations for an offensive are underway, and as much as High Admiral Jenks would like to have better access to our newer weapons, he understands we must first stabilize the situation in the West."

"Nice of him," Matt mused, "but he doesn't really know what he's missing, does he?"

"He does," Herring countered. "He knows about the new weapons and would particularly like some of the new pursuit planes to protect his reconnaissance flights. He's planning a recon raid, in fact, to remedy his deficiencies regarding his understanding of the enemy's dispositions."

"Really?" Sandra blurted, suddenly glaring at Adar. "He's going to risk lives on the ground when sending him a few planes would make that unnecessary?"

"Sadly, it is not that simple," Adar replied. "We cannot fly the planes to him; they must be shipped. Some few are indeed on their way, but their arrival will take time, as will the modifications to *Maaka-Kakja* that will allow her to operate them. We are sending some of the automaatic weapons as far as we can by Clipper, and they should arrive more quickly. At least the planes Jenks has will be better protected. As to the rest, I am confident Ahd-mi-raal Keje will soon resecure Maa-draas, and we can resume our offensive there. Once we push the Grik out of Indiaa, we will have all the resources of that land and the Grik will never wrest it from us again."

"They will," Sandra insisted. "You're setting up a seesaw campaign there like we had in the last Great War on our Old World!"

"She's right," Matt agreed, a little surprised by her position. He knew that as much as he didn't want her to go on his raid, she'd secretly hoped Adar would nix it because she didn't want *him* to go either. "Even if we regain control of the sea, the Grik can keep pushing warriors in from the West. We know they have Arabia, at least along the coast. They don't have to use ships. It'll take a lot longer for troops to arrive, but we can't get there much faster—and time's the key. We can't let this war drag on for years and years, because sooner or later, as long as they've got Kuro-kawa and his Japs, they're liable to catch up with our slim technological advantage. They already have, in some respects. In the end, if we let this war turn into a slugging match that boils down to numbers, we've had it. Even if you could disregard the suffering, the math doesn't add up. They can crank out warriors a lot faster than we can."

"That is a dreadful thought," Adar murmured. "An endless war with no hope of victory, but every prospect of eventual defeat. I cannot bear it. I would use gas, kudzu—anything I could find—to avoid such a thing."

"So would I," Matt admitted grimly. "But why not make sure it doesn't come to that?"

"You really believe your little raid will make such a difference?" Herring scoffed.

"I do," Matt insisted. "We have to give the Grik something else to think about! Madagascar's become their capital, which means their 'Celestial Mother,' whatever the hell she—or it—is, is probably there. The Grik think she's *God*, but because of that, and how far she is from the front, Madagascar's probably the softest target in their whole damn empire. If we hit there—hell, if we just *threaten* to hit there—it'll blow their minds. More important, they'll have to keep troops and ships there, and lots of them, from now on."

"It is so distant, across such a deep and terrible ocean," Adar breathed, a strange, faraway look in his eyes. "No one has ever considered the crossing, even in a Home. And of course, we didn't know where it was before you came. And there were always the Grik. . . . But now that you have crossed the great Eastern Sea, I believe you can actually do it! But what then? What if the Grik are too many? What if they have a vast fleet? What if . . . there is nothing?" He looked at Matt, eyes aglow with intensity. "What if our ancestral home is as 'soft' a target as you hope? What if you could *take* it from the Grik? Would not that discomfit the enemy most of all?"

Matt held up his hands. "Whoa there, Adar! My plan calls for a hit-and-run. With *Walker*, *Mahan*, and the PTs Saan-Kakja sent, we should be able to kick the hell out of anything big they've got hanging around. If the coast is clear, we'll land the commandos"—he looked at Chack—"*raiders*," he corrected, "and let them raise hell on shore for a while. Give us *Big Sal*, like I asked, and we can really raise some hell. But keep it?" He shook his head. "We might do it with all of First Fleet—but First Fleet's got a job, and we don't even know what's *there*!"

"He's right, Mr. Chairman," Herring said, concerned by the dreamy look in Adar's eyes. "If he must go, asking more than a raid is madness!"

Adar blinked profound regret, then nodded. "Indeed. Ridiculous, youngling fantasies." He looked at Matt. "You shall have your raid, and *Salissa* as well. Keje could not live knowing you had done this thing and he was not there." He blinked. "But first, we must address the emergency in the West. I want you there with Ahd-mi-raal Keje, before he accompanies you. After we retake Maa-draas, Commodore Ellis can relieve Keje, as comm-aander of First Fleet." He paused and smiled slightly. "If that meets with your approval. It is *your* Naa-vy, after all."

"That's fine," Matt said. He was a little disappointed not to be starting his raid immediately, but knew its timing wasn't as important as his—and *Walker*'s—presence at Madras might be. "Madras is kind of on the way, after all," he said, stretching the truth, "and I would like to make the show."

"Let me get this straight," Sandra interrupted. "You, both of you, want *Walker* to participate in the upcoming campaign, *then* head for Madagascar?" She turned to Matt. "What if . . . your ship gets all shot up again?"

"Shot up!" Petey shrieked. Those who hadn't seen him before gave a start, but no one else seemed to notice.

"Then we fix her and continue with the mission," Matt said shortly. He looked at Adar. "May I recommend that General Alden take over as CINCWEST after Keje and I head south?" He glared challengingly at Herring. "Unless *you* want it?"

"Oh no. I agree General Alden should assume that post. But I must admit your suggestion that I don't know as much about the enemy as I could is well founded. Naval officer or not, I've been placed in charge of strategic intelligence, and I believe it's time I took a trip to the 'pointy end' myself. In fact, I'd like to come with *you*, Captain Reddy."

Matt was stunned, but not as much as he was a moment later when Alan Letts stood from his stool without a glance at Adar and stepped in front of him.

"Me too, sir."

///// *Templo de Los Papas*
Nuevo Granada, Capital of the Holy Dominion

on Hernan DeDevino Dicha, "Blood Cardi-
nal" to His Supreme Holiness, the Messiah
of Mexico, and, by the Grace of God, Emperor of the World, stepped through the ornate entrance to the Holy Sanctum at the
base of the great temple. He was well-
known by the many guards, and none even
dared meet his eyes as he passed, much less challenge him. Striding
softly down the long, dark corridor designed to resemble the living rock
of the sacred caves, he paused automatically at its end and smiled be-
nevolently at the pair of gold-painted but otherwise naked girls standing as attendants before the rich drapes at the entrance to the sanctum
itself. He didn't speak to them; there was no point. Both had been deaf-
ened with heated wires and had their tongues removed as soon as they

were old enough to understand their duties. Instead Don Hernan sat on a padded lounge, and one of the girls removed his slippers. Then both assisted him to his feet and took his robes, leaving him in only a sheer breechcloth; otherwise he was as naked as they except for the heavy, twisted gold cross around his neck. No one, not even he, could enter the Holy Sanctum wearing anything that might conceal a weapon. In this condition, he stepped through the drapes and beheld the scene within.

All was red and gold, flickering in the light of braziers lining the garishly columned walls. Like elsewhere throughout the Dominion, there were many crosses, and the columns themselves were formed to resemble the barbed, grotesque version Don Hernan wore. Masked statues of each great pope stood in relief between the columns, surrounded by paintings of scenes reminiscent of their rule. They represented the *true* servants of God in the Holy Dominion. He who was symbolized by the cross had been the holiest of men, God's own son, but even His understanding of the one True God had been imperfect. The lessons in his Bible had been greedily incorporated, and explained much about the nature of God previously unknown in this land. But like the first son, those who brought it had misunderstood the most significant lessons of all: God was all powerful, terrible, and jealous. His limitless power was founded on fear and reward, not love, and he required his servants to rule through fear, reward, and sacrifice, so much so that he'd required the sacrifice of his favorite son, who'd strayed from those fundamental principles. The cross was a constant reminder of the brutal sacrifice required of all mortals to find the path to salvation.

The popes—a relatively new title meant to placate the few obstinate and dangerously well-armed Spaniards of a few centuries past—were the true Messiahs, the living sons of God. They were chosen for elevation to the near divine, to replace the bizarre, inhuman monsters so many of the barbarians of this land still clung to against all reason. The twisted cross represented the power of God and inspired fear, as well as a fatalistic acceptance of the final trial of life. It was a symbol of unification that drew the masses from their pathetic, equally harsh but heretical traditions. In that sense, despite the suffering it represented, it was also an object of stability and comfort.

He continued gazing at the statues—the closest he would likely ever come to seeing any pope with his own eyes. Each held the painted and bejeweled skull of its inspiration in the left hand. One day, the present Messiah would be so honored, but even then his near-perfect likeness would remain behind a mask; the artist—and only person besides his successor to view him since his selection—would be slain in a joyful celebration. But for now, the Messiah was very much alive, and Don Hernan's gaze shifted to the silky red curtain he remained behind, and he knelt.

Fires flickered beyond the drape and Don Hernan *could* see silhouettes. From them he knew the Emperor of the World wore a large, elaborate headdress, but despite the effect of the shadows, he was clearly a small, spare man, with considerable nervous energy. His projected image was always moving, actually pacing, and was followed by more naked attendants like those at the entrance, except these had been blinded as well. They kept pace with him by clinging to his flowing robe. Their sacrifice was rewarded by his presence, and it was their privilege to anticipate his every desire and ensure he never touched anything but the ornate throne he sat upon, the goblets they brought to his lips, the food they placed in his mouth, or human flesh. They were his reward for service.

Don Hernan understood the principle; only constant contact with the living could keep their Messiah rooted in this life, and the sensuous nature of that contact represented a bribe of sorts. Without it, his spirit might quickly flee to the even greater pleasures awaiting him in the afterlife. Deep down, Don Hernan couldn't help it; he *so* wanted to be pope someday! Sadly, despite his obvious worth and almost unique relationship with the Messiah compared to other Blood Cardinals, his chance for that may have fled with the escape of Fred Reynolds and his pet . . . creature. He sighed, and spread his skinny arms wide in a pose of supplication.

"My dear Don Hernan!" the Messiah slurred. He was kept in a state of continuous inebriation with wine and drugs, but unlike some of his predecessors, he managed to maintain his energy and intellect in spite of that. Don Hernan had served four popes—the lure of the afterlife was great—but he admired and feared this one most for his ability to keep his mind in this world. "What news of your misguided protégé and his familiar?"

Instinctively, Don Hernan glanced at the entrance to ensure no guards had appeared there waiting for the command to take him away. "I was misled," he confessed humbly. "In my hubris, I did not imagine it possible for anyone to endure the High Cleansing and retain such impure, treacherous thoughts. I was wrong. Clearly, some are infused with such evil that even the High Cleansing is not sufficient to wash it away. I must reevaluate my procedures. Few are even allowed such an opportunity as I extended to my protégé—as I admit I hoped he was—but now I will be even more selective."

"You were deceived by the purest evil," agreed the slow voice, "but though I know you are crushed, not all was in vain. You learned much about our enemy."

"Indeed," Don Hernan agreed, brightening slightly. "Some information must now be suspect, of course, but not all. The 'American' enemy that joined the New Britain heretics against us are little different from them in some ways, and I spent enough time in the isles as our"—he smiled—"ambassador to know considerably more about them than they do about us. Their notions regarding the value of lesser lives still gives me pause." He shook his head. "It is so bizarre as to border on the insane. And their attachment to their animal allies . . ." He rolled his eyes. "Incomprehensible! Still, the fact remains that, deluded as they are, their beliefs are sincere and intractable. They *do* dislike heavy casualties, and they *do* apparently consider the lives of their animal helpers nearly as dear as their own. We can use that, I think."

"But we have lost the Galápagos to them, and your conquest of their continental colonies was thwarted," the pope said dreamily, swirling to continue pacing. It was not an accusation, just a statement of fact.

"True. They may even attack our own Holy Lands, but that may work to our advantage in the end, as long as none who witness such a desecration are allowed to tell of it. Our supply lines will be short, theirs impossibly long, and our troops and the Holy Land itself will swallow their armies like small morsels." He hesitated. "I would wish we could match their newer weapons, particularly their flying machines. The small dragons perform well to a point, but are difficult to train, and the enemy has devised defenses."

"You were confident before that your evil protégé would provide us with flying machines of our own. Did he not?"

"He did—to a point. I do not believe he was as good at building them as flying them. The examples he provided are different in subtle ways from the one he used, and I do not trust them. Even if the design is sound, he never finished training our warriors in their use. We have a start—he could not prevent that—but perfecting the machines and their use will take time. The project will continue, but we must redouble our efforts to train the small dragons, in the meantime."

His Supreme Holiness stopped moving and continued gravely. "Only two matters remain. First, there is this other enemy that plagues our foes—these Grik. What do you make of them?"

"Other animals, Holiness," Don Hernan replied. "More savage and numerous than our foes, but little more intelligent than dragons." He thought back. "Now I consider on it, the traitor revealed their existence during his initial cleansing, perhaps in a stupor. He likely didn't deny them later only because I already knew of them. In retrospect, he cannot have wanted me to know of them."

"But what do you *think* of them? Can we use them as we do the small dragons?"

"Perhaps," Don Hernan hedged. "According to the traitor, they are so far west that we can likely more easily find them, and perhaps catch some to evaluate, by sailing *east* across to Africa. Apparently, that is their home. But even Reynolds did not know if they extend as far as its western coast."

"Our expeditions there over the ages have not reported them," brooded the Pope.

"True, but such trips are costly and wasteful. Only a providential aspect of their nature protects us from the greatfish in our Pacific sea. They are not as . . . temperate in the seas to the east. It is difficult enough to maintain contact with our island possessions and keep a war fleet in the Atlantic, and we have not sent a mission to that dark land for nearly a hundred years."

The Emperor of the World was silent, considering. His thoughts often took time to form, but when they did they were usually astute. Astute or not, they carried the weight of a commandment from God, and that was another reason Don Hernan admired this pope.

"We must meet these creatures," the Pope said at last. "Use them if we can."

"I will commission an expedition at once, Holiness." Don Hernan paused. "It will be risky, as I said, and our colonies may be vulnerable for a time, particularly if we redeploy the greater part of our eastern fleet the enemy cannot even suspect exists. That fleet should overwhelm him, regardless of his tricks, but an expedition will strip our reserves."

"It cannot be helped, and should not be too risky. The eastern fleet protects only against Los Diablos del Norte, and they should never even know it is gone. Besides, *they* would never dare provoke us again. They know they exist only at our sufferance."

"As you command, Your Holiness."

"One thing more."

"Yes, Your Holiness?"

The Messiah's tone changed to one of outrage. "You *must* destroy the traitor, wherever he has gone. You brought him here, to this place, to meet *me!*" he sighed. "I understood your intention and blessed your plan for him, but even I could not divine his secret evil! How could anyone not be lured to the True Faith by my sublime presence? Such evil has never been known. In any event, he knows where I am and has learned of certain of the tools we use to control the people. He must be silenced."

"That is already being done," Don Hernan fervently assured. "I know who helped him; there can be no doubt it was a faction of the Jaguar Idolaters, and I know where they take him. He must cross El Paso del Fuego, and I have dispatched an entire regiment of Blood Drinker Cavalry to stop him. He will not escape."

"Very good, Don Hernan. You might yet succeed me one day, when

I am called to my reward. Perhaps you may even be chosen as the one to perform my elevation when the time comes."

"I am not worthy," Don Hernan protested, lowering his face to the stone floor.

"Of course not," agreed the Emperor of the World, "not yet. But your test is at hand."

///// *In the wilderness of the Holy Dominion,*
west of New Granada

s usual, a dense fog lay heavy in the wood as
the sun rose, unseen, above the forest. The
scent of invisible wood smoke was thick, and
Fred Reynolds blinked sticky eyelids and
rolled to a sitting position against a monolithic tree. He had a scratchy, burlaplike blanket now, in addition to his filthy robes, and it
helped a little in the predawn chill; enough that he'd even slept through
the swarms of mosquitoes that always came with the dawn. He yawned
and scratched new welts on his arms as he blinked again and looked
around. The soft sounds of the awakening camp were all around him:
chuffing horses, quiet voices that carried amazingly far, the snap of
twigs as other fires were made.

To his astonishment, he suddenly realized Kari-Faask was crouched before him near a small fire, roasting a pair of what resembled squirrels with long, meaty tails. She looked up at him and grinned, brandishing the steaming carcasses on the iron spit.

"If you slept much longer, I'd have ate both these myself," she chided quietly.

"Kari!" Fred exclaimed, louder than intended. He looked quickly around. "What're you doing here? If they catch you, we'll both be in for it!"

Kari shook her head. "Nah. They ain't worried 'bout me—or you— no more. I tole 'em we wouldn't run off. Besides"—she gestured around—"where'd we go? I also tole 'em you're my friend and I *will* run off, now I'm fit, first chance I get, if they keep keepin' us apart." She blinked curiosity. "They really don't want me to do that. Say they need me for somethin'." She shrugged. "I don't know what, but I promised I'd do it, long as they leave us alone."

"You shouldn't have promised that, Kari," Fred said lowly. "I don't know what they've got in mind, but they're weird, creepy ducks. For all I know, they might . . ." he stopped himself. "Maybe they're not as bad as Doms—I hope!—but if you'd seen what I've seen, you might not trust *anybody* anymore."

"I seen a lot, Fred. Maybe different from you, but probably just as bad," she answered quietly, swishing her tail. "I thought I'd lost you to the goddaamn Doms, an' I lost hope," she admitted. "But I *didn't* lose you! I was wrong to think so. Weak. I just didn't hold my hope long enough, an' I won't never do that again." She lowered the spit back toward the fire. "You saved me. Maybe these weirdos helped, but you was gonna do it sooner or later wifout them if you had to. I know that now. I trust *you*," Kari said firmly. "In the air, in the water, here—anywhere." She blinked thoughtfully. "An' I trust my promise to Cap-i-taan Reddy an' the Navy. Compared to that, any promise I made to these fellas is no stronger than them you had to make to that goddaamn Don Hernaan!" She gestured again with the spit. "I'll do what I can for these fellas if it makes sense. I don't think they wanna *eat* me or nothin'. But if it don't make sense, we'll haul our asses!"

Fred snorted. "Atta girl!" he murmured approvingly.

"Good morning!" said Captain Anson, approaching with a wooden bowl in his hand. He tossed Fred a skin that sloshed when he caught it. "Wine," he explained, "or what passes for such hereabouts. Vile stuff, but rather refreshing when you get used to it. Mind if I join you?"

"Suit yourself," Fred answered, uncorking the wineskin and taking a tentative sip. "Gha!" he said, but drank some more. Anson sat on a log beyond the little fire and turned his attention to the bowl, sipping the steaming broth between pauses to blow across it. Kari glanced at him occasionally, blinking wariness, and finally pulled one of the roasted creatures off the spit and handed it to Fred.

"Ow!" Fred chirped, handling his food gingerly. "Hot!" He blew on it and took a bite. "Pretty good, though. Tastes like chicken."

Kari giggled. She'd eaten chicken in Scapa Flow and thought it tasted like akka birds.

"We call those 'squeakies' where I come from," Anson said, then glanced up quickly.

"Squeakies, huh?" Fred pounced. "I don't remember any 'squeakies' in the Empire."

Anson waved it away. "I guess you didn't spend much time in the colonies, up north."

"No," Fred admitted, still suspicious. "No, we didn't. Never ate anything there." He nodded at Kari. "Our plane got knocked down and we got captured before we ever had a chance. Are you saying that's where you're from?"

Anson grinned. "No. But if that's what you want to think, it will suffice for now."

"Well . . . why the big mystery? You haven't told me squat. You've got to be convinced by now that we're allies! We're *helping* the damn Empire!"

"But does that truly make us allies?" Anson asked cryptically. "I wonder." He shook his head and looked at Kari. "I heard about your tantrum. Quite impressive. You must really like this young man. Are all your people so devoted to their human friends?"

"We are—if they really our friends," Kari replied defiantly.

"Well said," Anson granted. He emptied his bowl and looked back the way he'd come. "We'll be moving soon," he predicted. "We've far to go for many days yet, but there's a village on the coast where we should be welcome."

"The coast?" Fred asked.

"Yes—in a manner of speaking. You'll see when we get there. As I told you before, El Paso del Fuego is a most impressive sight, and one the Doms have fanatically guarded. When you gaze upon it, you'll have the sense of a coastline where there shouldn't be one! And the other aspects—the *fuego!*" He smiled.

"About that," Fred said, "I don't get that part. What's it mean?"

"You will . . ." Anson stopped, looked around. The horses, tied to a picket line between several trees, were staring intently into the misty woods.

"What?"

"Silence!"

Something about the size and shape of an emu suddenly bolted out of the mist. Reynolds had glimpsed the things several times and been assured they were timid, harmless creatures in spite of a formidable array of small, needle-sharp teeth. Apparently they subsisted on bugs and small animals. Their tails were long and whip-thin, and they were covered with a thick coat of colorful but otherwise very emulike feathers. Because they were so timid, however, they usually bolted from view, and he hadn't seen one up close before. This one was obviously running scared as well, but wasn't watching where it was going. Large eyes in a small head at the end of a long, skinny neck stared behind it as it ran and it collided with one of their escorts.

Man and animal tumbled to the damp, ferny needles. With a horrified squawk, the thing leaped to its feet and scampered on, perhaps a little drunkenly. The man gasped, recovering his breath, and started to rise. Another "emusaurus," as Fred spontaneously dubbed them, raced through the camp, then another. The horses squealed, rearing and tugging at the line. They weren't afraid of the things, but instinctively knew that if *anything* was running from something, they probably should as well. More emusauruses stampeded past, perhaps twenty in all, before a horseman galloped into view. He was one of theirs, probably a picket who'd been on watch.

"Doms!" he hissed, loud enough for all to hear, then carried on un-intelligibly as far as Fred was concerned, pointing urgently back the way he'd come and gesturing around as he spoke.

"What?" Fred demanded of Anson.

"Doms, as you heard. *Blood Drinkers!* Many of them. Closing in on three sides," Anson snapped grimly. "To the horses! No, leave the blanket. There's no time!"

A musket thumped dully in the humid air, then another. Two natives raced up and grabbed Kari, dragging her toward the horses.

"No, goddamn it!" Fred cried, knocking one man aside and pulling on Kari's arm. "She goes with me!"

Another musket popped and was answered by a ragged volley. The mist was thinning slightly and muzzle flashes could be seen. Balls *vrooped* past and bark exploded from trees. A man screamed. The other native snarled at Fred and pulled a dagger from a rope belt. Kari kicked him savagely in the crotch, and when he doubled over, slammed her foot hard against the side of his head. He went down like a stone, senseless or dead.

"Well," Anson said simply. Fred and Kari looked and saw him return a large pistol to a flap holster at his side, and at the same time it occurred to Fred that it was a *revolver* of some kind, he also had to wonder who he'd been prepared to shoot. "I suppose she does go with you, or rather, *us.*" Anson snapped at the other native, who'd also drawn a knife, and with a searching gaze, the man ran for a horse. "Quickly now, unless you wish to be guests of the Doms once more. I do assure you they'll be even less hospitable than before!"

Shouted commands echoed in the trees, and another volley crackled. A sound like hornets sped all around them, and horses and men screamed shrilly. Musket balls ricocheted or exited bodies with warbling moans. Fred, Kari, and Anson sprang to the backs of three nervous horses probably being held for Kari and the two natives sent to get her. It didn't matter to the holders who mounted now, as long as one was Kari, and they immediately raced away to fight or flee. Other muskets were firing now, from a slightly different direction, and one native stumbled and fell on his face.

"I've never ridden a horse!" Kari shouted uneasily, twisting her fingers in the thick mane. "I don't know how!"

"Learn quickly," Anson advised, spinning his mount around. "Grasp the mane farther up. Try to force the animal to look whichever direction I go. It will quickly get the idea and follow." He glanced around. Most of their companions had fled, but twenty or so had taken cover and were firing muskets, pistols, or arrows toward the gun flashes that were becoming harder to see as dense white smoke replaced the mist. What had been a peaceful morning camp just moments before had become a battlefield. "Hold on tight," he added, then drove his boot heels into his animal's flanks.

Kari's horse did get the idea, and soon they were loping away from the fight. The forest and poor visibility prevented them from moving as quickly as they'd like, but the moist air muffled their passage, and the sounds of battle quickly faded behind them. Sooner than Fred would've expected, Anson slowed their pace. "What now?" he demanded.

"This fog is heaven-sent." Anson pointed left, west, Fred thought, but he was disoriented and it was impossible to tell for sure. "We must work our way in that direction and try to slip past the enemy."

"Why don't we just keep moving away from them?"

"They're expecting that. This attack was well planned. For them to find us in this"—he waved around—"they had to know where we were headed. That's understandable, but they also had to know exactly where we would camp. That place, long considered safe, has been compromised. Obviously, there was a traitor among us." He grinned at Fred's belligerent frown. "No, I know it isn't you! Even if I hadn't been watching you, there's no way you could have known the location of that camp or told anyone about it. Personally, I suspect it may have been the man Ensign Faask disposed of so efficiently. Well done, that!"

"So that's who you were about to shoot?"

Anson shrugged. "I was prepared to shoot whoever required shooting, and moments like that often reveal who they are." He shook his head. "Let's discuss this later, once free of this box we're in. I did mention I suspect the attack was designed to drive us into the arms of another force. Kari was the priority of the people we were with, but you,

Lieutenant Reynolds, are the priority of our pursuers. They will want you very badly, no doubt."

Fred nodded. "Kari's just an animal to them, but I know too much," he agreed.

"Exactly."

"Fine, let's go. But when we're in the clear, I think it's time I knew more about *you*"—he looked pointedly at the flap holster at Anson's side—"and that interesting pistol of yours."

////// *Baalkpan ATC (Advanced Training Center)*
West Bank of Baalkpan Bay
April 22, 1944

att had never seen the Baalkpan ATC; it hadn't existed before he went east. Stepping ashore from the broad-beamed motor launch with his cane in his hand (he relied on it less and less), he saw that the facility was modeled after the Maara-vella ATC near the mouth of Maa-ni-la Bay. Much of the dense jungle along the shore had been cleared in places, but left in others so amphibious operations could be rehearsed against any kind of beach. Beyond that was a massive parade ground for assemblies and "traditional" linear drill, but the focus was on more open tactics the ever-improving weapons allowed them to employ. He'd come here today with Sandra, Chief Gray, Courtney Bradford, Alan Letts, and, to his continued consternation, Commander

Simon Herring, to review Chack's Raiders and see for themselves the new weapons they'd been issued.

Chack, Major Jindal, and several other Lemurian and Imperial officers met them on the quay, and they exchanged salutes.

"Hiya, Chackie," Gray said, and Chack looked at the SB. Only Dennis Silva had ever called him that. He wasn't offended. He recognized the term as an affectionate diminutive, but to hear it from the terrible Super Bosun was a shock. Then again, they weren't aboard ship, he realized, and he'd heard Chief Gray was—or could become—a different man ashore. He wondered if the human female Diania had anything to do with that?

"Hiya . . . ah, SB," Chack replied. He looked at the others. "Cap-i-taan Reddy, Minister . . ." He still found this assuming of married names confusing and fell back on the Imperial usage he'd heard. "Minister Lady Saandra." He greeted Bradford, Letts, and Herring as well, then turned back to Captain Reddy.

"Good morning, Chack," Matt said with a smile. "I hope we're not too early. I'm pretty eager to see what you've got."

"Not at all, sir. We are eager to show you!"

The "commandos," or 1st Raider Brigade, were composed of two newly formed regiments: the 7th commanded by Risa-Sab-At, and the 21st under Major Jindal. Both had a battalion of Imperial Marines, including one from the island of Respite (in the 7th). The Lemurian battalions came from Baalkpan (also in the 7th) and Maa-ni-la, (attached to the 21st). Chack was in overall command, and the force—which included light artillery and an impressive logistics train that Letts had helped create—totaled almost three thousand troops. The organization was impressive, as was the mix of weapons and capabilities. Chack, Risa, and Jindal had been given a free hand in the formation of the brigade, and what they'd come up with might not be ideal for a static defense like Alden was stuck in, but seemed perfect for Matt's raid. Each battalion had its own artillery, sappers, engineers, and cavalry company—though how the long-legged, crocodilian me-naaks would cope with such a long voyage was a mystery—and each company had mortar tubes and a squad of crude, crew-served *flamethrowers*, of all things, pressurized by a pump.

The devices were short-ranged and gave Matt the creeps, but seemed to work well enough when he saw them demonstrated. He wouldn't want to operate one. Otherwise, the weapons mix on the platoon level was intriguing and exciting. Riflemen carried a slightly shorter version of the newly standard, single-shot "Allin-Silva" breechloaders that fired the powerful .50-80 fixed, metallic cartridge. Those weapons were formidable enough, with their wicked bayonets and high rate of fire compared to muzzle loaders. Matt knew similar weapons (and ammunition) were being sent to Alden, but the supply effort there was slow. It would also be a long time before they could spare enough of the new rifles for Second Fleet—and even longer before they could get there. It bothered him that some of his troops had to risk their lives with outmoded weapons while others got the very best. There was little he could do about that. It was a matter of logistics and priorities, and a feature of the vast scope the war had assumed.

In addition, each commando squad had several troops armed with Blitzer Bug submachine guns. These newest versions were still basically a pipe with a barrel, shoulder stock, and Thompson-style magazine, and looked a lot like the bug sprayers they'd initially been called. But now they fired their .45 ACP cartridge either fully or semiautomatically. They were light and handy and easy to make compared to a Thompson, and could spray a lot of lead. Letts assured Matt they'd have light machine guns like the 1919 Browning very soon. The issues had been better barrel metal required by the necessarily jacketed bullets, as well as a better brass-drawing process for the higher-pressure, bottlenecked cartridges. The earlier methods worked well enough for the .50-80s and the .45s, but to Bernie Sandison's mortification, resulted in far too many case head and shoulder ruptures in the .30-06, .30-40, and particularly the .50 BMG. They could be used in the dwindling, scattered, '03 Springfields and Krags (preferably for slow, long-range work) but for now, the ship's machine guns and those mounted in Ben's P-40s—as well as some of the Nancys—still had to rely on the ammo they'd recovered aboard *Santa Catalina*.

There were other new weapons; copies of 1911 pistols Matt had already seen, better grenades, and breechloading 20-gauge "buckshot" carbines for some of the cavalry, converted from the earliest smooth-bores. Matt was pleased and impressed. Still, he didn't notice one of the most impressive innovations until they were actually reviewing the troops drawn up in ordered ranks for his inspection.

They all looked fine, Lemurians and Imperials, standing at ease in full combat kit. They still wore the rhino-pig leather cuirass over mottled, camouflage tunics and trousers (for humans) or long smocks (for 'Cats), but the armor had been stained dark. This was a departure for both races, who'd been accustomed to fighting in bright armor or uniforms. All had copies of the 1917 cutlass (nobody was ready to fight Grik without a sword of some kind to fall back on, and the cut-lasses really were the ultimate expression of edged weapon design), and their helmets were stamped and painted steel instead of polished bronze. Some of the troops wore large rectangular boxes strapped to their backs, however. At first, Matt assumed they were meant to transport ammo, but they were just too big; about two by three feet, and at least six inches deep. Nobody could carry as much ammo as one of those things would hold, not very far. Not even the strongest Lemurian.

"What are those leather boxes some of the guys have?"

Letts grinned. "Field telephones, Skipper," he said. "That Marine corporal—Miles—working for Bernie came up with the idea, and Riggs had Ronson draw one up. The 'Cats in his division built the first ones in their spare time!"

"*Lance* Corporal Miles," Herring corrected. "He came here with me. The design is based on the Double-E-Eight, and in this one instance, I'm surprised you didn't come up with the idea on your own."

Matt couldn't decide if that was another criticism or backhanded compliment. He let it slide.

"They're ridiculously simple," Herring continued, "and have been in service for nearly a decade." He shrugged. "At least in the Army and Marines."

"I've seen them before," Matt admitted, "but there's not much call for them aboard ship. Honestly, I never looked at one very closely. I fig-ured they'd be complicated."

"No more complicated than the field telegraph apparatus you've made such extensive use of here and on the battlefield," Herring said.

"Alan?"

"He's right, Skipper," Letts confirmed. "The only thing we couldn't've done until recently was the receive and transmit elements in the handset, but we'd already sorted that out for the TBS and other things before Miles came along. It just took somebody with a fresh eye."

"As I have said in many contexts," Herring prodded.

"But they still need wires?"

"Right," Letts confirmed. "But you can string them out like a party line or run them through a switchboard, and they take even less power than a telegraph."

"I'll be derned." Matt gestured at one of the boxes. "Can we get these to Alden? I take it you've looked into that?"

"Yes, sir. And I've discussed it with him via wireless, but since he already has secure internal telegraph and wireless comm, he told us to keep 'em for now. They're not as heavy as they look, but they're bulky, and he doesn't want so much as a toothbrush taking up room on a transport plane or barge if we can fit an extra bullet in the same space."

"Understandable," Matt muttered. "When the curtain goes up on the final act at Madras, he's going to need all the ammo he can get. What's the latest estimate?"

The Grik were still forcing Pete to burn ammunition at a prodigious rate, and supply wasn't keeping up, particularly with his artillery. Matt was only peripherally engaged in the planning for the upcoming combined offensive, but they'd been basing expectations for what Alden could do to help on projections regarding how long he, Rolak, and Safir Maraan could sustain full-blown assaults of their own against the forces surrounding them.

Alan looked grim. "Right now, it stands at about seven hours, give or take. That goes up and down every day, of course, but that's all the reserve he's got. If he has to keep up what he's doing now for the next three weeks, he has enough held back to unleash absolute, total hell on the Grik for about seven hours before running completely dry." Alan grimaced. "If the relief takes longer than three weeks, or if his own part of the plan doesn't work and he runs out of steam before he can break out . . ."

"He's finished," Sandra whispered. "And so are Rolak, Safir, Leedom, and maybe thirty-five thousand troops."

Matt looked stonily at the assembled brigade, then his gaze fell on Chack. General Queen Protector Safir Maraan was affianced to Chack, and they'd been separated for a very long time. Matt knew Chack had to be thinking how much his brigade could do to help the Allied Expeditionary Force—and the female he loved—but he blinked no indication of his inner turmoil, and his expressive tail remained rigidly still. Maybe they *should* use this force to help relieve Alden. Maybe the raid *was* a waste of time and resources after all. *No,* Matt thought. *Sandra's right.* The force assembling to break the enemy at Madras was far more impressive. It had been training for the operation and should be able to do the job. *But what then?* Even if First Fleet and all its troops accomplished its mission, the Grik *would* reinforce and the battle for India would degenerate into a war of attrition that the Grand Alliance simply couldn't win. Maybe they wouldn't *lose* it, but it could go on for years, and despite what Herring implied, Matt was sick to death of the war and all the suffering it caused.

Herring's comment made him think, though. What would he do if the war ever ended? In many ways, he'd *become* the war and his very identity was consumed by it. Yet . . . he had Sandra, and he had his ship. He—and *Walker*—would always be needed on this strange, strange world. *The raid's critical, and it* will *cause chaos among the Grik,* he determined. The little, almost insignificant raid his cousin Orrin told him Colonel Doolittle pulled on the Old World, the one his was loosely based on, may have even turned the tide by causing the Japanese to stop their steamroller advance, take a breath, and redeploy to protect their homeland. It had definitely compelled them to focus on eliminating the American carrier threat for good—which cost them their precious ass at Midway! This was about all Matt knew of that "other" war he and his people had escaped, but it was enough.

He turned to Letts. "We leave one week from today," he said, "except you, Alan. You've got to stay."

"But, Skipper!" Alan pleaded.

"No, you've got to stay. I need you here, the war needs you here, and Adar does too." Alan started to speak, but Matt stopped him. "I know you're pissed that he kept you in the dark. I am too. But he didn't do it because he doesn't trust you, he did it because he *loves* you, damn it! He's never taken a mate—how could he right now?—and you're like a son to him. Besides, I'm going to need a lot of the old fellas for this one. Brister has *Mahan*, and he needs some guys, probably Ronson and some of her old torpedomen and engineers, at least. I've got to have Bernie with his torpedoes. You and Riggs might be all that's left to keep the wheels from falling off."

"Most things run themselves now," Alan protested.

"Sure, but that's because of you. And who'll sort things out if things . . . go sour? Besides"—Matt's tone softened—"I'm not having that little girl of yours grow up without a dad, and that's final." He smiled a little sadly. "She was the first small trace of hope that we might leave some legacy here besides pain and suffering—and that somebody'll always remember our lost shipmates." He shrugged. "And us, I guess, in the end." He looked at the others and the assembled troops and raised his voice. "I wish you guys could be in on the show at Madras, but the raid you've been training for is important. Too important, I think, for you to get plugged in and *stuck* in someplace I might never get you out of, and we should already have sufficient forces to relieve General Alden. That said, our little raid may not be for all the marbles, but if we can take the Grik's best shooter out of the game, we'll have the ring— and the initiative—all to ourselves."

"At least for a while," Gray agreed, looking appraisingly at Chack. The 'Cat knew "marbles" now; this other game that came with the destroyermen had become even more universal than baseball, and glassmakers made crude marbles like mad in their off-duty hours to keep up with demand.

"No," Chack said grimly. "This game is for 'keeps,' and we're going to knock every one of the Grik's damn marbles out of the ring!"

///// *TFG-2*
USS Donaghey
Western Ocean
April 23, 1944

T he horizon was milky, but the sky above was a brilliant blue. A steady, easterly wind had prevailed for the better part of a week, and Commander Greg Garrett was pleased that his little squadron had logged more than one hundred twenty miles each day they'd been at sea since weighing anchor at Trin-con-lee. There was just the slightest pitch as the blue-green water foamed to white alongside USS *Donaghey*'s smooth, firm sides, and the rumbling rush was music to his ears. He leaned over the port, windward rail of the flush quarterdeck and watched the froth for a moment, then looked back at the big double wheel forward of the mizzenmast. His exec, Lieutenant Saama-Kera, Sammy, was standing beside the 'Cat at the helm, and grinned back at him, blinking delight. Sammy had been Chapelle's exec on *Tolson*, and if Greg's old executive officer, Lieutenant Saaran-

Gaani was unavailable, hurrying to Andaman with troops recruited in the Great South Isles, Greg was happy to have Sammy. He grinned back at the dark-striped 'Cat and looked to the horizon. The "milk" was turning darker, and there'd be squalls in the afternoon.

USS *Donaghey*, recently designated DDS-2 to signify she'd been the second of three sailing destroyers built on this world, was slanting southwest under a full press of canvas across the great Western or Indian Ocean. The designation seemed odd to Garrett, since *Donaghey* was the last of those first three ships. The others had been lost in combat—as had *Donaghey* for a time—but she'd been refloated and undergone a major refit that included a number of upgrades that made her perhaps uniquely qualified for her current mission. She and her consort, the "razeed" Grik "Indiaman" USS *Sineaa* (DE-48), keeping station several miles to leeward, constituted the second Task Force Garrett (TFG-2), and as dedicated sailors with no need to carry fuel for anything but auxiliary generators and the Nancy flying boats struck down in their holds, they could push back the mysterious boundary of the known world. Exploring the extent of the Grik Empire in the vicinity of Madagasgar was their primary goal, but other tasks had been added to that mission, and Garrett was excited by what they implied. Still, he was even more anxious to proceed with his secondary, lengthier, and perhaps most dangerous mission: to round the southern tip of Africa and see what lay beyond.

He hated sailing off on what he almost considered a personal lark right when the big show to clobber the Grik fleet at Madras and relieve General Alden seemed about to commence. He'd missed the greatest naval battle of the war while overseeing *Donaghey*'s refit at Andaman. But he was realistic enough to know the war had passed his ship by and she'd be hopelessly outclassed in the kind of battles it had spawned. His ship and crew were better armed than ever, but her main battery still consisted of 18-pounders. She had thirty now, and could easily smash any ordinary Grik ship she ran into, but was no match for the ironclad monsters now constituting the main Grik battle line. She'd have to be careful if her probing brought her in contact with those. But with any kind of wind, she could easily outrun anything the Grik were known to have. There lay her main advantage; with her extreme hull and a clean bottom, only *Walker* herself—and maybe the rebuilt *Mahan*—were faster. Greg had heard of the PTs of the new "Mosquito fleet," and they were supposed to be fast, but they'd never been intended to cross the broad, hostile seas on their own. He hoped they'd justify Captain Reddy's faith in them, but they'd have to be *brought* to the fight. There were things in this sea that could gulp them like top-water lures.

He snorted. *There's things out there that can eat* Donaghey! he thought, but one of his ship's upgrades had been a crude, active sonar, developed by Mr. Riggs, Ronson, and Fairchild. It ran off a wind generator that charged a high-yield capacitor and periodically sent a torturous bolt of sound into the depths ahead. This had been proven to discourage the largest, most dangerous sea creatures. It had no apparent effect on the giant sharks like the one that sank the second *Revenge*, but that fish had been drawn to the new ship's bright, spinning screw. *Donaghey* didn't have one of those, and all new ship's propellers were preoxidized now. That had been a bitter lesson.

Captain Bekiaa-Sab-At, commander of *Donaghey's* Marine contingent, which constituted a quarter of the crew, joined Greg by the rail. Tagging along was Lieutenant (jg) Wendel "Smitty" Smith, *Donaghey's* young but balding gunnery officer.

"Afternoon, Bekiaa, Smitty," Greg greeted them.

"Good afternoon, Cap-i-taan Gaarrett," Bekiaa replied, and saluted.

"You don't have to do that, you know," Garrett said with a smile. "And even if you did, once a day is enough!"

"But we're outside."

"Sure, but . . ." Garrett blinked consternation in the Lemurian way. "Skip it. Just once a day, though, okay?" Bekiaa nodded. Greg knew she was glad to be at sea after the hell she'd been through, but he also knew she'd brought more than a few ghosts aboard. She'd been wound pretty tight. He looked at Smitty. "How's gunnery shaping up?" *Donaghey* had a large number of veterans from herself, *Tolson*, and *Revenge*. Though originally from different ships, all had fought together at the Sand Spit and formed one crew almost seamlessly. The gun's crews were no exception.

"I like the new fire-control system. We still have to train the guns by eye, but with good ranges and electric primers, we'll get more rounds on target. Commodore Ellis was right; it works. I just wish we could do more live practice."

Greg nodded. "I know. Me too. We've got plenty of powder and shot now, but who knows when we'll get resupplied? We could be on our own a long, long time."

"Yes, sir. And I guess it shouldn't really matter that much. The range finder in the main top and the tables of elevation have taken a lot of the guesswork out of it."

"True."

Bekiaa was staring forward, squinting hard. "Those islands we're making for those 'Chaagos.' Do you really think they'll be there? We're a long way from nothing. I bet nobody's ever sailed these seas since the Mi-Anaaka got pushed off Madagaas-car before the beginning of time."

"They're not so much islands as an atoll," Greg corrected. "The biggest lump is Diego Garcia, though the chart just has a little D there. Used to be a French coconut plantation or something, and was barely big enough for a little Brit outpost on our world. As to whether they'll be where they were on *our* charts . . ." He shrugged. "Who knows. They could be bigger, smaller, or not there at all. I just know the Skipper asked us to find 'em if they're there. Any kind of waypoint between Ceylon and the heart of the Grik Empire, no matter how small, would be mighty handy for prepositioning fuel and supplies. As for us being the first to sail these seas since God knows when, you may be right," Greg agreed. "But that could be a good thing, because chances are if they *are* there, the Grik would've never found 'em. Why should they? Like you said, there's an awful lot of nothing out here."

"Deck there," came a cry from the masthead. "*Sineaa* signals 'sail' off her staar-board bow!"

"What the hell?" Greg muttered. "How far?" he demanded loudly, crossing to starboard and raising his Imperial telescope.

"Seven mile. Small sail."

Greg adjusted the telescope but saw nothing but the haze on the water.

"I go up?" Bekiaa asked. "See what I make of it?"

"Not yet. We'll wait a bit. A small sail way out here, I doubt *any* of us would know what to make of it."

Half an hour later, with signals flashing between the two ships and even Garrett able to see the sail from deck with his telescope, the consensus formed that it was a lateen-rigged fishing boat of some kind. That didn't make much sense either, until the masthead called down that he'd spied land.

"I'll be," Greg said. "An almost-perfect landfall on a place we weren't even sure was there! And that explains the fishing boat too. Must be natives." He frowned. "But what kind?" He paced back and forth, deep in thought. Sammy had joined the trio and seemed just as concerned.

"What if they is Grik?"

"Not much point in worrying about it. Lookout!" Greg shouted, "What's the boat doing now?"

"It seen us. It hightailing to land."

"Sing out the instant you see any other ships!"

"Ay, ay!" came the reply.

Greg looked at Sammy. "Make our course two one zero, and signal *Sineaa* to do the same. We'll come down on the north side of the atoll. We don't have any charts of the thing itself, and I doubt it would look the same if we did. Leadsmen to the bow. We'll take soundings."

More fishing boats were sighted as *Donaghey* and her consort drew closer, and the shout "No bottom with this line" came back periodically from the fo'c'sle. All the boats fled at the sight of them, making straight for the northwest edge of what was growing in view to become a much larger island than Greg had expected to find. It looked pretty flat, though, and was covered in a dense jungle of odd-looking trees.

"Have *Sineaa* take in her courses, and we'll adjust speed accordingly," Greg ordered, staring through his glass. "Looks like they've got some kind of anchorage those boats scampered to. Let's have a look at it."

Another hour crept by as Sammy shouted into the rigging to shorten or adjust the sails and slow their approach according to Greg's directions. As a precaution, Greg had his ship cleared for action. Rounding a small island lying off the coast of the larger one, they glimpsed a broad channel, maybe half a mile wide, that the little boats were still ducking into. Suddenly Bekiaa saw something else, just as the lookout reported it. "Cap-i-taan Gaarrett!" she cried.

"Holy moly," Smitty muttered, seeing it too. Everyone seemed to spot the stunning object at once, and it was no wonder; it was *huge*. The thing had been partially hidden even to the lookouts by the tall trees on the smaller island, but there, in the narrow gap between them, lay a very large iron-hulled ship with two tall funnels, leaning perhaps twenty degrees to starboard.

"Oh my God," Garrett murmured, and an unacceptable number of the crew surged to the port rail to gawk.

"Twenny faddoms," came the delayed report from forward, "an' comin' up!"

"Stand by the anchor!" Greg shouted distractedly, still staring at the big ship. The Lemurian bosun collected himself and roared at the crew to get back where they belonged.

"She been here a while," said Sammy when he found his voice. "She looks sunk, with that list, and she's low at the head too."

"A while," Greg agreed, "but not that long. She's rusty, but her paint isn't that old."

"Weird paint," Bekiaa observed. "That's a ship of human people," she said with certainty, "but I never seen one painted that colorful before."

Greg cocked his head to match the list. "It *is* pretty weird," he agreed. "She looks like a passenger liner—deserted too, thank God—you see she's got at least a couple of big deck guns? Anyway, I'd say she's about the same vintage as *Santa Catalina*, so she's old, but the last time I saw a paint job like that, it was on a Subic taxi!" He felt a chill. "Hey, it's hard to tell, but does that look like a dragon—or a big lizard—painted down her side?"

"Yeah," said Smitty. "I guess that leaves me wonderin' where she came from, how'd she get here, and did somebody paint all that shit on her before or after?"

"Where and how? Same as us, I guess. *Who* her final passengers were is the biggie."

Greg's two ships had crept far enough forward to pass beyond the hulk's leaning bow. "Yikes. Not *completely* abandoned, Cap-i-taan Gaarrett!" Bekiaa warned, pointing. A rough pier had been constructed along the big ship's port side, and it was packed with suddenly staring workers, apparently involved in removing cargo from large hatches in the sloping hull. More figures were in boats—some also standing and pointing now—that were rowing heavy cargoes through the mild, protected surf toward shore. Many tents and huts had been erected there, and a considerable heap of crates and other large objects had been gathered under protective coverings. Greg and everyone else who had them were staring intently through their glasses.

"Fi' faaddoms!" came the cry from forward. "Busted coral!"

"Well," Greg said at last, lowering his telescope and slamming it shut, "whoever they are, they're not Grik. Look like humans and 'Cats—like us! I wonder how the hell they got together way out here?" He snorted. "Guess we'll find out. Nobody's pointing guns at us, and I don't see any batteries at the mouth of that lagoon."

"What're we gonna do?" Sammy asked.

"Signal *Sineaa* to 'wear ship,' and stand off while we get to the bottom of this. We'll heave to, if you please. Stand by to drop the hook."

The afternoon was wearing on by the time someone "over there" apparently decided what to do. A boat that looked appropriate for the grounded steamer—aside from its own bizarre paint job—set off from shore with an equally bizarre collection of passengers. Some, both 'Cats and humans, wore coats and hats, and a couple had shiny breastplates and helmets. A couple of the 'Cats were entirely naked and, at a glance, looked even shorter than the norm. None appeared armed. The squalls that had loomed nearer all day took that opportunity to catch them at last, and long, dark tendrils of rain beat down on the open boat as it approached. Greg and those gathered with him to receive their guests got drenched as well, and it was amid this annoying but somewhat amusing circumstance that the momentous meeting occurred.

"I say," shouted a voice from below as the boat touched *Donaghey's* side, and an oarsman leaped up with a pike and hooked on. "Judging by your flag, you're the very bloody Americans we were off to meet! What luck, that?" The voice came from a grinning, bearded, light-haired man in one of the breastplates. "You *are* the ones fighting the . . . I guess you call 'em Grik, right?"

"We're at war with the Grik," Lieutenant Saama-Kera confirmed, but he was blinking annoyance at what he considered a scandalous breach of protocol.

"Bloody amazing!" the voice sounded back. "Our chap said he recognized your pretty ship . . . but ye do have more . . . an' some a bit bigger, I hope?"

"What chap?" Greg demanded suspiciously.

"Our Jappo there," he nodded at a dark-haired young man seated nearby. "His name's Leftenant Miyata, formerly of a monstrous great battle cruiser named *Amagi*. I understand you once made her acquaintance?"

. "We sank her, if that's what you mean," Greg replied, staring hard at Miyata. This was getting weirder and weirder.

"Aye! You're the right blokes, all right!"

A man in a dark coat and graying black beard snapped at the talker in what Greg thought was German, of all things!

"Right. Sorry. No sense yapping back an' forth in the rain like dogs across a fence. May we come aboard? You have my word we're friendly as can be, and, odd as it may sound, we're already on the same side!"

Greg blinked. "Then . . . by all means, come aboard," he replied.

One by one, the occupants hopped across and clambered up the side. All but the naked 'Cats gained the deck in the traditional way, saluting the flag and the officers they met. The two 'Cats, some kind of natives, Greg had to assume, stared around, amazed by the ship and the large number of taller but clearly related Lemurians aboard. Greg listened while the German introduced himself and the others.

"I am Kapitan Leutnant Becker Lange, executive officer of the armed auxiliary cruiser SMS *Amerika*, which you currently see so indisposed." He frowned. "Our real kapitan of over thirty years is equally indisposed at present, so I have temporarily assumed operational command of this expedition. The talkative fellow here is Leutnant Doocy Meek. Our his-

tory is . . . complex." He gestured at a Lemurian in a dark, sodden cloak
that covered ornate armor and a red leather kilt. "This is Inquisitor Kon-
Choon, chief intelligence officer to His Most Excellent Highness Nig-
Taak, Kaiser of the Republic of Real People. As Herr Meek said, our
Japanese friend is Leutnant Toryu Miyata. It was his arrival that has-
tened us in your direction, seeking alliance against our common enemy."

Garrett swallowed, but nodded at the two shorter 'Cats. "Who're
these guys?"

"We do not know their names," the Lemurian . . . snoop said with a
very strange accent. "They have been assigned to us by the other natives
of this island as observers, we think. They are not hostile, and though
curious about us, they are afraid as well. They have generally avoided us,
and we have tried not to inconvenience them, since we were forced to
seek refuge here."

"When your ship sank?"

"She ain't sunk," Doocy said in his clear British accent. "The bloody
tide's out, an' she's sittin' on her admittedly leaky bum. She floats after a
fashion at high tide. We're lucky we found this place, an' this is as far as
we dared bring her without attemptin' repairs. Her shaft alleys in particular have turned to sponges. The storms off the cape worked her
hard!"

Garrett held up his hand. "Wait! Storms at the cape, republics, Grik,
Japs, pygmy Lemurians . . ." He paused. "Look. I'm sorry. I'm Commander Greg Garrett, United States Navy, serving the Grand Alliance
of all the powers united beneath or beside the Banner of the Trees." He
quickly named his officers. "Welcome aboard USS *Donaghey*," he added,
then glanced at Sammy. "Signal *Sineaa* to join us and anchor. I'll want
her officers' thoughts." He turned his gaze back to their visitors. "In the
meantime, let's get out of the rain and see if we can sort this out."

They crowded down in the wardroom forward of the officers' quarters. Provided with cups of steaming monkey joe—the ersatz Lemurian
coffee—and towels to dry themselves, Greg Garrett began to piece together the story of the island, the Republic of Real People, and SMS
Amerika.

Probably like the island they'd found, the earliest inhabitants of the republic were Lemurians who'd wound up there after their ancient exodus from the Grik. They were later joined by Chinese explorers, Ptolemaic Egyptians, black Africans, and eventually Romans. All arrived from the sea, but it wasn't clear whether that was where their original crossover occurred, since some hadn't been sure themselves. The most jarring information Garrett learned was that the Romans appeared around the tenth century! He wasn't much of a historian, not even close to Captain Reddy, who claimed to only be an amateur despite his academy degree, but even he knew there was something very wrong with tenth-century Romans! He shook his head. *Let the Skipper and Mr. Bradford figure that out!* In any event, it was into this interesting mix of cultures that Becker Lange, Doocy Meek, and the mixed crew and prisoners of war aboard Seiner Majestät Schiff *Amerika* were adopted, apparently during the *last* war, before the United States got involved. That helped, since nobody but Miyata remembered Americans as enemies.

Garrett looked out the stern windows at the great ship and frowned, considering all her problems. She was certainly big, measuring nearly 670 feet and displacing about forty thousand tons. She was armed with two 4.1-inch rapid-firing guns and six Maxims, and had been designed to make twenty knots. She burned coal and that might be awkward, but she had plenty aboard to get her to Andaman if they could patch her leaks. She'd make a fine addition to the Allied fleet. Becker said she could carry three thousand passengers and crew—or a larger number of troops—and that could be handy too, but Greg wasn't sure if she'd fit in one of the floating dry docks at Andaman, and a dry dock was what she desperately needed.

"So you came looking for us, sight unseen, to join our alliance against the Grik. How'd you know we're not as bad as they are?"

"Do you eat your enemies?" Inquisitor Choon asked. "Do you have territorial ambitions beyond perhaps the lands you take from the Grik? Your own alliance is a collection of disparate races. Do you treat any as if they are inferior to you?"

"No!" Greg and Lieutenant Saama-Kera chorused.

"Then we are natural allies against a common, terrible enemy that threatens us both. My cea-saar, or kaiser, Nig-Taak, is a hereditary ruler, but like the ancient leaders of Rome, is bound by the will of the senate. He is not . . . emperaator. Not so much different from your own Chairman Adar, I gather."

Greg blinked. He'd mentioned Adar during the course of their discussion, but Choon was quick. He must've pieced the rest together from what he'd overheard, or what Miyata told him.

"Well, I've got *some* leeway for negotiations, considering my mission, and I guess we'd have found your republic eventually when we rounded the cape of Africa—which we still mean to do—so hopefully I'll talk to your Nig-Taak myself. I can't confirm any full-blown alliance here and now, but I'll send a message home and find out how much cooperation they'll allow."

"You can do that?" Choon asked.

"Sure. We send it in code."

"But won't the enemy hear? Might he not, uh, tri-aangulate our position? Fear of that has restrained us from transmitting in the past."

"I guess they might," Greg conceded. "We really don't know what the Japs or Grik can do in that respect."

"You say there is a great battle underway for India," Miyata asked, speaking for the first time, and everyone looked at him. "Kurokawa does have communications gear, though I doubt he has shared it with the Grik. He might hear, but I do not think he can judge distance or direction. Even if he can, there will be too much chatter for him to isolate us, I think. We have been listening."

"Really?"

"Of course," Choon confirmed. "We always listen, and we hear many things. We cannot decipher your code, but we know the difference between it and the one the Jaaps use." He nodded at Greg's questioning look. "Yes, the Jaaps communicate sometimes. We also hear . . . other things we cannot identify. But Lieutenant Miyata is probably right that your transmissions should not endanger us"—he looked at the two natives, still peering around, apparently oblivious to the conversation—"and, possibly more important, the people of this island. We must protect them at all costs. They are the oldest link to our heritage, and from what I gather of their . . . vaguely different language, they have remained the most unchanged from the days of the great exodus itself. We have much to learn from them."

"Okay, I'll compose a message and shoot it off," Garrett said. "See what we can come up with." He turned back to Miyata. "That leaves us with your Jap, I guess." He addressed Toryu directly. "I've heard your story and understand why you defected. Hell, the only thing I don't understand is why *all* your people haven't run. You've warned these folks about what the Grik mean to do, and that's swell. But what can you give me?"

Miyata bowed his head. "I have been to the Grik shipyards and know where they are. I have even been to Madagascar, to the palace of the great, fat Grik mother herself, though I have not seen the creature. I know the defenses and population centers there. Would that be of help?"

Garrett stared, then collected himself. "Why, it just might, as a matter of fact. I'll pass that along too, and see what Captain Reddy has to say."

////// *Adar's Great Hall*
Baalkpan
April 24, 1944

"A most interesting development," Adar observed, handing the message form to Commander Herring, who held it close to read. It wasn't lost on anyone that Steve Riggs had given it to Captain Reddy first, as soon as he, Sandra, Courtney, Chack, and Chief Gray arrived in the War Room. It was a small gesture and wouldn't have even been noticed before, but Matt didn't like the way "factions" seemed to be developing at the highest levels of the Alliance. He saw Alan Letts frown, probably for the same reason. Matt had finally talked Alan into returning to his duties, and Adar had been effusive in his apologies. The 'Cat really did think of Alan and his wife and daughter as the children he'd never had, and once Alan was convinced of that, he forgave Adar's attempt to protect his conscience. But as a condition for returning to the Great Hall, he'd demanded a promise that it would never happen again. Adar contritely agreed. "These inhabitants of the island, this 'Diego Gaar-cia,' or 'Laa-laanti,' as they apparently call it, are of particular interest," he continued. "That they survived, isolated, on that tiny speck of land so long, beyond reach of any of our kind, is astonishing."

"It is indeed, Mr. Chairman," Courtney Bradford gushed. "Why, just think of it! If they've preserved any rites and traditions of your ancient homeland, not to mention anything resembling a pre-exodus history of your people . . . I simply can't wait to meet them!"

"Nor can I," Adar agreed in a strange tone. "Nor can I wait to meet these representatives of this 'Republic' from southern Africaa." He blinked rapidly in a way reminiscent of the old, enthusiastic Adar Matt remembered. "They too may have preserved a chronicle older than ours." He looked at Matt. "Despite what you call the historicaal inconsistencies with your own past, that Cap-i-taan Gaarrett described."

"Those 'inconsistencies' may provide the ultimate clue to complete my theory regarding how we got here in the first place," Courtney enthused. "I may almost have an answer at last!"

Sandra looked at him curiously, but before Courtney could divert the meeting with a distracting, if likely fascinating, dissertation, Matt interrupted. "Maybe most important is that we have new allies we never knew about, and that this Miyata guy has intelligence on the target for our raid."

"*If* the Jap bastard can be trusted," Gray grumped.

Matt looked at him and nodded gravely. "If," he agreed.

"We'll have to evaluate that when we meet him," Herring said, "but the circumstances of his arrival among these . . . southern folk seem to weigh in his favor."

Matt raised his eyebrows. *Did Herring just give a Jap the benefit of the doubt?* He shook his head. "Yeah, well, when we meet him. First things first. When do we leave for Andaman? Time's running out for Pete. Spanky says *Walker* can be ready for sea in two days. It'll be a tighter squeeze for *Mahan* and S-Nineteen, but Laumer and Brister say they'll be ready one way or another. The torpedoes?" He shrugged.

"Bernie says they're as good as he can make 'em, and since we don't have time to test them properly from ships at speed, his word'll have to do. He and his whole torpedo division will be along, so if something occurs to him, he'll be there to sort it out."

"What does that leave?" Adar asked.

"The transports for Chack's Brigade and the PTs. The PTs arrived in a powered dry dock, *Respite Island*, just like Garrett says they need for this big steamer he found. We should send it and Chack to Diego immediately."

"But if they use the dry dock for the ship, how will we move the PTs, Skipper?" Gray asked.

"If they can patch her up quick enough, we won't have to worry about it. If they can't, we'll stow 'em on *Big Sal*, as originally planned." He looked at Adar. "If for some reason *Big Sal* can't come—after we sort out Madras—we might just have to do without them, unless we can tow a dry dock from Andaman."

Adar blinked concern. "With the offensive to recapture Maa-draas about to begin, we cannot count on having any spare dry docks in that theater. I am inclined to agree we should send what we can to the little island immediately, but I have been considering a fundamental alteration to your plan, Cap-i-taan Reddy."

Everyone was surprised by that. As much as Adar wanted to assume all strategic responsibility, it never occurred to anyone that he'd try, or even *want*, to meddle in an operation he'd already consented to.

"Mr. Chairman?"

"Yes. I have given this much thought, and believe I have devised a . . . compromise straa-ti-gee that will not only accomplish the ends you seek, but will *ensure* our victory at Maa-draas." He sighed. "It will also leave my own heart and soul at greater peace at last." He stared hard at Matt, his silvery eyes intense in the lamplight. "As Commander in Chief of all Allied Forces, *you*, Cap-i-taan Reddy, will not just 'pass by' Madras on your way to Mada-gaas-car, awaiting *Salissa*'s opportunity to accompany you. You will command the battle for Maa-draas, aboard your . . . singularly inspirational ship. With *Salissa, Arracca, Baalkpan Bay, Santa Catalina, Mahaan*, S-Nineteen, and all the

warships accompanying them, there can be no outcome but victory!"
He glanced at Herring. "According to all reports, in addition to our
common Grik enemy, we will face this vile Kurokawa, your own hated
foe. He is the root of all Grik initiative, all their advances that have cost
us so dear, and must be stopped. I would prefer that you should be there
for that." Adar blinked determination. "This is no great change from
what we have already decided, but now, after the battle—the *victory*—
we will take *Salissa* and any additional assets you might desire to participate in your raid." He blinked compassion at Chack. "Including
further infantry forces, perhaps commanded by our dear General
Queen Protector Safir Maraan?"

Chack reacted as if he'd been slapped, and his tail twitched excitedly, despite his obvious attempts to still it.

"With this augmented force," Adar continued, "we will proceed to join
those already sent to Diego Gaar-cia. From there, we will advance on our
ancient homeland in *strength*." He grinned with a savagery Matt had never
seen him use. "You will have your raid, Cap-i-taan Reddy, but I want no
pinprick there. I want to strike the Grik with a hideous dread that will
churn the marrow of their bones! Am I perfectly clear about that?"

Matt nodded, inspired by Adar's sudden passion. He smiled. "Absolutely, Mr. Chairman."

"I like it!" Gray said. "No more damn pussyfootin' around!" All
seemed satisfied, even Sandra. All except Commander Herring, who
was looking at Adar with a slight frown.

"'We,' Mr. Chairman?" he asked.

"Indeed," Adar said in a tone that brooked no argument. "We. As
Mr. Letts once argued for himself, it is high time that *I* should go to the
'pointy end' for a time. And if this campaign proceeds as I hope, the
Heavens above could not keep me away."

"But, Mr. Chairman!" Herring protested. "You *can't* leave! The Con-
stitutional Congress has finally convened, with representatives of all the
Western Homes, at least, to determine what, if any, united government
will rule this . . . well, *country* you've made! Ambassador Forester has
just agreed to represent the Empire of the New Britain Isles! He's only
committed to observe, but—"

Adar shook his head. "It has become my fondest dream that our Grand Alliance might one day be united into a great nation"—he looked at Matt—"perhaps like your own United States." He smiled. "United Homes?" He shook his head. "But it will not be a nation of Mi-Anaaka or hu-maans only, or even just folk like Lawrence and his Sa'aarans. It will be, if it comes to pass, a nation of 'People,' of every race. Commander Alan Letts is far more knowledgeable about building nations than I, and his organizational skills will be essential to control the chaos that is sure to engulf the Congress."

It was Alan's turn to stare, stunned. His mouth opened, but he couldn't speak.

Adar turned to the others. "I have already decided. This is a fight I must join, if only to beseech the Heavens to make it decisive. Mr. Letts will represent Baalkpan, his Home, at the Congress in my stead." He looked at Matt. "May he also speak as your representative? On behalf of the Amer-i-caan Navy clan?"

Matt looked at Letts, whose eyes were wide as he took a step back, shaking his head.

"You bet, Mr. Chairman," he said with a smile. "And I'll be happy to have you along when we stomp Kurokawa—and his damn Grik roaches. All the way to Madagascar."

////// *Wilds of Borno*

"Whatcha thinkin' about?" Dennis Silva asked, dropping to the damp mulch beside Ensign Abel Cook. Water dripped constantly from the dense canopy in the aftermath of the daily deluge, and Silva removed his helmet and slicked back his sodden hair. Nothing could repair the wild appearance his beard had achieved, and like them all, his clothing had begun to rot off. What remained of the "Corps of Discovery" and its native Khonashi guides had stopped for a brief, unusual rest, and the majority of Abel's command was making the most of it. Many were already asleep where they'd dropped their packs. The Khonashis themselves were suddenly very busy, however, grooming themselves and each other, and cleaning their weapons and gear. Abel nodded at them and snorted.

"I assume we must be near their home at last, and they want to look their best when we arrive."

Silva nodded, and Abel looked at him, surprised the big man didn't comment further. Maybe even Silva was finally worn out? *No*, Abel realized disgustedly, when Silva started *humming* to himself while he picked at something on his shoe with a stick! Abel groaned. It was impossible to say how far they'd come in a straight line, since no part of their journey hadn't gone up, down, or around innumerable obstacles. The confusing, convoluted track I'joorka and his band led them on constituted countless miles, and they'd taken them at a literally killing pace. Three of I'joorka's warriors had been slain by creatures they probably could've avoided or killed if they hadn't been so exhausted themselves, and a 'Cat Marine had fallen to his death crossing one of the mind-numbingly numerous gorges that snaked and squirmed through the darkest interior of the land. Everyone, even their Grik-like escort, had grown thin and haggard, subsisting largely off things Abel preferred not to contemplate. He still considered himself a naturalist in training, but their pace had made serious studies difficult, and honestly, his enthusiasm had waned. He was still fascinated by many of the creatures of Borno, but he'd developed an intense dislike for the large, frightening insects. There'd been little time for hunting, and I'joorka didn't allow cooking. As they'd suspected, cooking actually *drew* predators. As for the bugs, Abel's most intense scrutiny now involved breaking off the bits he simply wouldn't eat.

Most of Abel's party had been violently sick at some point. The pace they maintained and injunction against fires made it impossible to boil all the water they drank after all. The resulting "scramblin' screamers," as Silva dubbed the condition, hadn't killed anybody—yet. But only time would tell if they'd picked up any toxic parasites. Everyone had eventually recovered to various degrees, but the acute stage of the affliction had made it impossible to maintain one's dignity, and I'joorka's people had been amused by the discomfiture of their charges—until

Pam Cross silenced their hacking laughter at her expense and sent everyone pelting through the trees with an apparently indiscriminate fusillade from her Blitzer Bug. Abel was reasonably certain the shots had been aimed high. But Pam was treated with the most respectful care by the Khonashis after that.

It had been a grueling trek in every way, and only Silva and Moe seemed little affected by the water or exertion. Moe had lived in the wild all his life, and Cook suspected Silva had "inoculated" himself against the water at some time past, against standing orders, by drinking it without telling anyone. In any event, just then, Silva was far fitter—and even cheerful—than Abel Cook would've preferred.

"They do appear to be dandyin' theirselves up," Silva finally agreed, gazing about. "I'll be glad to get outa these sticks an' meet this English-speakin' honcho o' theirs." He chuckled. "At least that's made our chore o' gabbin' with the critters a touch easier."

"If all this isn't just some elaborate scheme to lure us to their home as hostages—or food," Abel grumped.

Silva laughed. "T'joorka ain't gonna *eat* us! Him and his pals are sociable as puppies! Larry's even glommed on to a little o' their lingo. He likes 'em. Ain't that right, Larry, you fuzzy little gecko?" he added as Lawrence approached.

"I think they're okay," Lawrence said seriously, crouching down. "They're less angry around the 'Cats, in general . . ." He nodded at Moe, who was gumming a piece of jerky. "They still don't like he, though. They know he's a hunter."

Silva grunted thoughtfully, then tossed his stick and fished out his tobacco pouch to stuff a wad of the yellowish leaves in his mouth. "Mmm." He looked back at Abel. "Well, anyway, I think they're square. Hell, one of 'em bought it savin' that silly damn Pokey, who was laggin' behind, pickin' up the brass you dropped shootin' at that thing that looked like a sport-model skuggik!" He saw Abel's expression. "Not your fault, Mr. Cook. I'da shot it too. Nothin' the size of a turkey deserves that many teeth. How was we s'posed to know they run in swarms like that?"

"I should've known," Abel said with a frown. "I believe they *are* skuggiks of a sort and they, like most scavengers, congregate together." He didn't mention he'd shot the thing because it just suddenly appeared in front of him and scared him very badly.

"Well, I'joorka wasn't pissed at you or us. Just warned us not to be shootin' at them things unless we was willin' to get 'em all. Took it pretty well, actually, an' even seemed pleased ol' Pokey was okay. Really, if it was anybody's fault, it was mine," Silva admitted, "for lettin' us get as strung out as we were at the time. If there's one thing I've learned since we got on this world, it's that lone wolfin' it ain't such a good idea. Folks have to stick together."

He chewed for a minute, looking around. Gunny Horn was asleep, and so was Stuart Brassey. Pam wasn't, but she was with one of the Lemurian Marines a short distance away, cleaning weapons. All were within a perimeter maintained by I'joorka's warriors. "Anyway, I was hopin', once you an' the rest are secure amongst the friendly aboriginites, maybe you'll cut me an' Moe, an' ol' Larry loose so we can scamper back ta Baalkpan. Somebody's gotta report, an' not only do us three have the best chance o' makin' the trip in one piece, but *Walker*'s refit's bound ta be finishin' up by now—an' honestly, Mr. Cook, I don't want to miss my boat."

Abel sighed. "I thought you just said we need to stick together?"

"Sure, an' you do. Me an' Larry an' Moe'll be stickin' together too, all the way home."

"What about Lieutenant Cross?" Abel asked, cutting his eyes at Pam.

"Well, she stays with you, o' course."

Abel shook his head. "We'll see, Chief Silva. Once we discover the situation at our destination." He glanced at the big, black-bearded Marine snoring against a tree. He was still skinny, but they all were, and he'd muscled back up amazingly. *That probably has a lot to do with the high-protein diet we've subsisted on,* Abel mused distastefully. "Gunny Horn should be sufficient to protect us, if intimidation is all that's required." He squared his jaw. "And the rest of us can take care of ourselves."

"No doubt o' that, Mister Cook!" Silva hastily added, sensitive to the boy's feelings. "An' like you said, we need to see the setup first. Just thought I'd plant the seed." He paused. "Now, what else have you been thinkin' about?"

Cook's face reddened. "That's none of your business, Chief Silva."

Dennis nodded. "That's what I figgered. You're worried about the munchkin princess. Me too. An' I'd be lyin' if I said another reason I'm anxious to get back ain't to get the latest news outa the Empire."

Abel formed a protest, but it never came. Instead he just looked away and repeated, "It's none of your business."

"I reckon it is," Silva countered. "I'm mighty partial to the Imperial scudder, as you know, and uncommon protective of her too." He took a breath and spat a yellowish stream. "That said, I know Princess Becky kinda likes you an' Mr. Brassey, and I sorta wish one er both of you was with her about now. She's bound to be havin' it rough."

"She does like you," Lawrence confirmed, his crest rising in what could have been amusement or protectiveness. He pointed his snout at Brassey. "He too."

The mating customs of Lawrence's people were very strange to, well, everyone else, and the idea of human or even Lemurian monogamy was just as alien to him. He did understand friendship, however, and had learned to equate human and Lemurian mating rituals to intense friendship with a procreative component. Sometimes he wondered how that would work among his people, but knew, with his own Sa'aaran race so reduced, such a thing couldn't happen for a long, long time. Customs change, however, and with his people's close association with the Maa-ni-los, who knew what Sa'aaran culture would become in the future?

"Why not you and he oth— each—'arry her?"

Silva laughed as Abel turned even redder; then he ruffled Lawrence's crest. "Don't work that way, little buddy! If it came down to it, much as they like each other, Mr. Cook an' Mr. Brassey'd face each other on the Imperial Duelin' Grounds before that ever happened!"

"They'd *kill* each other?" Lawrence demanded, eyes wide.

"No!" Abel finally managed, rising. "I've no reason to believe the princess—I mean Governor-Empress—Rebecca likes either of us in *that* way, at any rate. Even if she did—does—the choice is entirely hers, and she'll likely choose another long before either of us sees her again! And, like I said, it's no one's business! Look," he said, changing the subject. "I'joorka is coming. I suspect our short rest is at an end. Get everyone on their feet, Chief Silva!"

"Aye, aye, Mr. Cook."

They reached I'joorka's village within the hour, and even more surprises awaited them there. The first thing they noticed was sharp, animalistic cries from the trees that seemed to carry a great distance through the jungle, yet whoever—or whatever—made the sounds was extremely well camouflaged, and they couldn't pick them out amid the leaves and branches overhead.

"Perimeter guards," Gunny Horn said to Silva. "Good idea."

Silva was squinting above with his good eye. "Yeah. Enough scary boogers rompin' through the woods, even without enemy tribes."

"An' they don't eat bugs heah, thank God," Pam added, moving up alongside them. "I smell wood smoke."

"Me too," Silva confirmed, "but that don't mean anything except maybe they *cook* their bugs at home. Besides," he leered, "I figgered you was getting' partial to 'em, considerin' what they done for your figure."

"Shut up, creep."

The first sentries showed themselves soon after that, coming forward to greet I'joorka and his comrades and stare at the newcomers.

"Close ranks!" Horn barked at the straggling group. "Shoulder arms!" he added, hoisting his heavy BAR to lie against his collarbone. The 'Cat Marines quickly scurried into line, pushing Pokey along with his sack of brass. Moe, maybe a little chastened, put his musket on his shoulder and so did Lawrence. Even Silva raised his massive rifle from where he habitually kept it in the crook of his arm. Pam left her Blitzer Bug slung, but straightened. Abel looked back and smiled thankfully at Horn; then he and Brassey look their places at the front of the little column.

More of the rust-colored, striped, feathery/furry, reptilian . . . folk . . . appeared. Younglings, so much like the "Griklets" that plagued their armies in the West, scampered everywhere: up and down trees, across their path, even around their feet. They seemed just as curious and ill-behaved as their Sa'aaran cousins, but unlike Griklets, they weren't hostile, only rudely curious. The procession continued on.

"Hey . . ." said Horn, looking around, surprised, and the rest suddenly realized they were surrounded by permanent dwellings. They'd probably been moving among them for some time before they noticed. The structures were built high in the trees to avoid predators, in the Lemurian way, but were wildly organic, formed and shaped from the living jungle. They'd all heard tales of how the "swamp lizards" of *Chill-Chaap* had encouraged a similar warren to engulf the once-stranded *Santa Catalina*, but only Moe had actually seen it—and he wasn't the first to spy the related technique here. The dwellings weren't deliberately decorated, although colorful, flowering ivies covered them like spiderwebs—but that had grown increasingly common throughout the local jungle. If anything, great pains had apparently been taken to camouflage the structures and the ivies only added to that effect.

"Wow," Brassey said, "no wonder our aircraft have never seen anything from above! One has to look hard to distinguish the buildings from the *ground* right beside them!"

"Yes," Abel agreed. "And even the wood smoke from cookfires will dissipate before it filters through the trees and up as far as the sky! It might resemble the evaporative haze that is so prevalent. Amazing! They've obviously been building this way for a very long time, long before they could've seen aircraft. Does it help them hide from other tribes? Perhaps the dwellings are defensible from ground attack as well? Fire might be a concern . . . but the living foliage would be difficult to light. They could slay their enemies from above. . . ." He abruptly stopped speaking, stunned, because it was then that they saw the first *human* Khonashis.

"I'll swan," Silva muttered. "*Real* Injuns!"

Groups of humans dressed in leather breechcloths and little else intermingled among the Grik-like Khonashis in an everyday way that indicated they were perfectly comfortable with the association. Most had shaved heads and were daubed with paint that made their dark skins match the coloration of their friends', to a large degree. Some were garishly decorated with claws and teeth, feathers and furs, and most appeared to have filed their teeth to sharp points. Silva had seen that before and wondered if it was a tradition these people brought with them—from wherever they came from—or did it to simulate the sharp teeth of their Grik-like friends. All of them, males and females, carried longbows almost identical to those the Lemurian armies used to such good effect before they had firearms. Many wore what looked like bronze-bladed "Lemurian" short swords or cutlasses as well. Just as the travelers had suspected when they first saw the Khonashi crossbows, it appeared again that there had to have been some kind of contact between these people and Baalkpan around the time the destroyermen were first helping arm the Lemurians there against the Grik.

"You never tole me there was Injun jungle *humans* out here before!" Dennis accused Moe.

"I didn't know!" Moe replied with clear surprise. "I never catched one before! Never *heard* of any bein' catched!" Everyone knew, in this instance, "catched" was Moe's euphemism for "killed" while poaching in what he and others like him considered their private hunting grounds. "Maybe dey not go so far south as Baalkpan? Maybe dey new here?" He shrugged.

Word of their arrival had preceded them, and a delegation of both the Grik-like and human Khonashi greeted them at a jumbled rock-rimmed water well. Like everything else, an effort had been made to make it look like a random, natural formation, but at present, its purpose was obvious because villagers were drawing water from its depths. Brassey waved at the well. "I suspect we must be near the center of this, ah, town," he said.

One of the humans took a wooden bucket from a larger, crestless—and therefore probably female—"lizard" visitor to the well. Abel had seen female Sa'aarans before, and there was a distinct similarity in form, if not coloration. *We must come up with another description for all the various Grik-like species,* he thought once again. *"Lizards" is too ingrained as slang to change, but they're* not *really reptiles, despite appearances and certain characteristics. Like Mr. Bradford has said, they're actually more like birds,* he reflected. *Even the term "Grik-like" is problematic, because it insults those such as Lawrence, who know what Grik are!* He sighed and commanded himself to stay focused.

"Hi," the human said in a strange, warbly voice. "Heer's water! You dreenk! My keeng prays dat you reefesh yourseeves, den meet wit heem!"

"Ah . . . Sure. Swell. Whatever you say," Abel accomplished.

"Whatever will I wear?" Silva mused lightly, but one of their fuzzy hosts regarded him seriously. "You dress too lots already. Too hot, too sweat."

Dennis grunted. "Why, maybe so."

They didn't have long to wait before the delegation hurried them along to meet their "keeng." I'joorka had been whisked away with most of his warriors—for debriefing, Silva suspected. I'joorka's lone return seemed to indicate to their keepers that it was time, and Dennis wasn't the only one who sensed an air of urgency. His inquisitive, possibly cynical eye had noticed that a large percentage of the villagers were armed; more than he'd have expected. Part of that could be because the strangers were known to have fantastically deadly weapons, but that didn't explain the sheer number of combat-age warriors in the camp. "Somethin' simmerin' here, Mr. Cook," he warned as they walked, and Abel nodded.

"I think you're right. I don't believe it has to do with us, though. Even if I'joorka was specifically sent to get us, as he said, they couldn't have known exactly when we'd arrive. I see no sign of real agriculture, and a village this size couldn't support so many warriors for long."

"Something's up," Horn agreed.

They moved, en masse, back through the growing crowd of onlookers and approached a large structure similar in concept to the Great Hall in Baalkpan, except this building was very crude and erected with trees at each corner instead of around a single, great tree. It was made much like the other Khonashi houses, practically woven from the four trees supporting it, but it was bigger and far more obvious. Dennis suspected that meant it was more defensible as well. Maybe it served as a central fort that villagers caught in the open could retreat to? A kind of railed stairway was lowered to the ground as they approached, which struck Dennis as far more sensible than the rope-ladder arrangements he was used to, and I'joorka and several others scampered up ahead of them. When they reached the top, they motioned for Cook, Brassey, Dennis, Horn, Lawrence, and Pam to join them. The 'Cats and Pokey weren't restrained, but it was clear they were expected to wait below.

"It's all right, Sergeant Moe," Abel assured. "They've got a history with 'Cats. We'll sort that out. But they haven't tried to take any of our weapons. Keep our Marines together, and don't let Pokey wander off. By the looks of things, the brass he's carrying is worth more than gold."

"Ay, En-sin Cook," Moe agreed.

Abel looked at the others. "Shall we?"

The Great Hall of the Khonashi wasn't as large as Adar's, and though the thatched, broad-leafed roof looked tight enough, the sides were largely open. Silva had been right when he surmised it was designed with an eye toward defense, though. There was a high rail all around the structure, and the walls beneath it were thick enough to absorb arrows or spears from below. Otherwise, the interior was amazingly spartan. There was little decoration, and the only furniture consisted of rough-hewn, saddlelike stools similar to those they'd learned the Grik used. That made sense. Unlike chairs, which Grik couldn't use at all, anybody could sit on a stool. There were a couple more of the Grik-like Khonashi present, and to the visitors' surprise, several human females almost obliviously occupied by domestic chores. A raised brazier stood in the center of the room, and meat was cooking over a bed of coals.

For a moment, there was an awkward silence while the visitors finished filing in. The Khonashis were looking at them, but there was no sign of the king they'd been brought to meet. Then they heard muted voices from behind a woven partition; something that sounded like "Alright, damn it. I'm hurryin'!" And a moment later, a man limped into view, leaning on a carved and painted crutch that kept his weight off a withered right leg. A small, dark woman came behind him, almost pushing him along. The woman was dressed only in a short, gold-tanned skirt, but the Khonashi-style stripes were tattooed instead of daubed on her body, and the effect was striking. Her expression was hard, but severely beautiful in a strange, feral, Asiatic way. A tentative smile flashed when she saw the humans, and they noticed that her pearl-white teeth had been filed to sharp points, like many of the human warriors they'd passed coming in.

The man had some nasty scars around his bare midriff but appeared fit and strong—except for the leg, of course—and his white hair and beard looked out of place on a young, weathered face. The expression he wore, regarding them, was as unexpected as his appearance. It looked . . . sheepish, embarrassed.

"As I live an' breathe," Silva said in a subdued, fascinated tone. "You the 'king' ever-body's fawnin' over?" he asked.

With a largely invisible grin behind the long beard, the man nodded self-consciously. "I guess so. It's kind of a long story."

"I bet," Silva agreed. He turned to the others. "His Uppityness here may appear hard-used, but he looks a heap better than the last time I *thought* I seen him—as a super-lizard turd!"

"You *know* this guy?" Pam blurted.

"Sure I do. You might've even met him when you first came on *Walker* back at Surabaya." He cocked his head. "I don't reckon any o' you others could know, but this here 'king' of the Khonashis is Tony Scott, late cox'n of USS *Walker*! He disappeared and was presumed ate . . ." Dennis calculated. "Near two years ago, on the old pipeline cut."

"My God," Abel mumbled, then his expression turned indignant. "My God!" he exclaimed. "Mr. Scott, do you realize we've named a *whole class* of new DDs after you?"

"Yeah!" Dennis accused. "An' me an' Moe downstairs, Paul Stites, and ol' Courtney Bradford too, killed a purely innocent super lizard, plumb certain he was guilty o' gulpin' you down!"

"Lawsy," Scott said softly. "I never knew I was so well thought of!"

"That's changin' pretty fast!" Pam declared. "We've been fightin' for our lives in a damn big war while you've been takin' your ease with the friendly natives! I thought Dennis was bad at goin' AWOL, but you take the cake! Mr. Cook's in charge of this expedition, but I'm the senior officer. I'll have you on charges if you don't have a damn good reason for bein' gone!"

Because they understood a fair amount of English, the Khonashis were alarmed by the turn the conversation had taken, but Scott calmed them down—in their language!—then turned back to Pam and the others. "I guess I've got a pretty good reason. I'll leave it up to Cap'n Reddy to decide, if he's still livin'."

"He is."

"Thank God," Scott murmured sincerely. "Anyway, I knew sooner or later I'd turn myself in, but things ain't worked out exactly like I hoped." He looked at Silva. "Startin' with the day after that big Strakka, when I went to check the pipeline cut—and kinda *did* get ate."

Very quickly after USS *Walker* came to this world, Tony Scott had grown increasingly afraid of the water he'd always loved. More specifically, he was utterly terrified of the creatures *in* it. He still fought courageously, but Captain Reddy allowed him to remain in Baalkpan—ashore—when *Walker* and the first allied Homes went to raise the Grik siege at Aryaal. There'd been a terrible storm, and Tony went to check the pipeline carrying oil to the fueling pier from where they'd sunk their very first well. Away from the water, he'd been careless, and when he'd stopped along the path to relieve himself, he'd been snatched up in the jaws of a super lizard. Unknown to him, other creatures—a Khonashi scouting party—had been watching him too, wondering why someone who looked so much like their human tribesmen had been wandering around alone in lands controlled by their Mi-Anaaka enemies. I'joorka himself distracted the great monster into spitting Tony out, then lured it into chasing him and the rest of the party that split up and ran. Eventually, they shook the pursuit and returned for Tony Scott.

He'd been in bad shape. The great teeth had torn his flesh and he was unconscious. The Khonashi lived nearer to Baalkpan then. They carried him to their village, where they nursed him back to health and he'd learned, by necessity, to speak their tongue. The first thing he'd gotten them to understand was that he needed to go home, but he still wasn't fit to travel. By then the Grik had come to Baalkpan. Through a network of observers and allied tribes, the Khonashi knew much of what happened across Borno. They already feared the Grik were worse enemies than the 'Cats, from accounts of encounters with their strange ships in the north-west, and Tony convinced those who still doubted.

He tried to get them to join the Lemurians, but they fled the war in-stead. The problem was, the lands they found on the north coast of the island—as far as they could get from the invading Grik *and* the Lemurians—belonged to the Akashi, and the Akashi didn't want them there. A brutal, bloody war ensued. Having no choice but to help those who'd helped him, Tony taught them crossbows, and longbows for the humans, as well as the short swords his shipmates had been training the Lemurians to use. With those weapons and others, the Khonashi de-feated the Akashi.

Ironically, it was in that fighting, not the super-lizard attack, that Tony's leg was wrecked, and it became impossible for him to return to Baalkpan. Ultimately, one thing led to another, and he married a high-status human member of the tribe. Eventually, through no fault of his own (he swore), he "wound up" king. There was a lot more to it, of course, and it really was a long story, but those were the bare essentials, and sufficient to bring them up to speed on *his* situation, at least.

Abel was nodding. "I can see all that," he confessed. "Some of us have been marooned before—that's how I wound up here myself; stranded with S-Nineteen and a bunch of submariners." He looked at Silva. "Then we got marooned again . . ." He shook his head. "That's a long story too. But my question is, now that you mention a 'situation,' why did you send I'joorka to find us? I'm not complaining. We were sent to meet *your* people, and I'joorka's band probably saved us. Still, the coincidence is most interesting."

"Yeah," Tony replied. "About that: we knew when your group set out, and figured you were coming to find us at last. For one thing, I wanted to get you before the Akashis did." He shrugged. "They might not've killed you, but I couldn't take that chance. Besides . . . we got a problem I was hopin' for some help with."

Silva arched his brow over his eye patch. "A problem?" He rolled his eyes at Gunny Horn. "I knew it was more than just a reunion o' beloved shipmates!"

"Yeah, well, down the coast about fifteen miles is a little bay. Not much of one, but big enough for one of those big 'Cat Homes to anchor in. You remember that *Fristar* Home? Under a Lemurian called Anai-Sa?"

"Sure," Silva said. "Ungrateful bastards. Joined the Alliance to get cannons, and hung in long enough to get some muskets too, but then skedaddled. Buncha weenies. Didn't want in the fight. Last I heard, they was huntin' gri-kakka fish in the China Sea."

"They're in the fight now," Tony declared, "but on the wrong damn side."

"How do you know it's *Fristar*? Lemurian Homes look a lot alike," Brassey said.

Tony looked at the Imperial midshipman curiously. "'Cause it's got ten big bronze guns, and our scouts described Anai-Sa, with his dark fur and gold rings, pretty good." He frowned. "They ain't helpin' the enemy because they want to, and I been tryin' to keep everybody convinced of that, but a bunch of our folks around that village are dead now, and a lot of my people have blood in their eyes." He snorted. "Hell, I do too. But those *Fristar* 'Cats are doin' slave labor, it appears to me, and I don't want 'em hurt." He gestured around. "Considerin' my lizard folks' history with 'Cats on Borno, some ain't that particular. They're all invaders, far as they're concerned."

"Enemy? Slave labor! What are they doing?" Brassey asked.

"Drilling for oil. At least that's what they've got the 'Cats doin'. Workin' 'em to death too!"

"*What?*" Pam cried. "The Grik? What do they need *oil* for? It doesn't make any sense!"

Tony blinked. "No! Not the Grik. The goddamn Japs!"

In the stunned silence that followed, Abel looked hard at Scott, then leaned over and whispered something to Brassey. The Imperial nodded grimly.

"Perhaps we should let Mr. Scott explain from the beginning, Lieutenant Cross," Brassey said.

"Yeah." Scott looked back at Silva. The two had been friends, and he felt more comfortable talking to him. "Both ships showed up about two months ago; that big-ass Home, and a heavy Jap tin can. The can was all shot up, like, as bad or worse than *Walker* was when we first made it to Baalkpan. But they'd captured *Fristar* and had her under their guns. About two hundred Japs came ashore with rifles and machine guns and shit and just about wiped out the whole village I was talkin' about. Next they put most of the 'Cats, a couple thousand or so, ashore, and started 'em drilling for oil on half a dozen rigs not much different from the one those goofy Mice cooked up." He grinned at the memory, but the smile faded and his eyes turned grim.

"Have they struck oil yet?" Abel asked.

"I'm not sure. They might have." He paused. "Will they?"

"Good question," interjected Horn. "*Is* there oil around here? I mean, you guys found a bunch down south—and I guess that's why the Japs wanted the Dutch East Indies in the first place, you know, back home. But will they find any here?"

Abel jerked a nod. "I'm afraid so. Mr. Bradford's notes indicated significant local reserves discovered in the twenties. What's more, these . . . later-arriving Japanese are sure to be aware of them, since they conquered the region from my people—the British—before we even fled Surabaya." He sighed. "Barring a miracle or gross incompetence we can't count on, they probably will find oil, if they haven't already."

"Later arriving," Scott said, nodding. "I figured you knew about that Jap ship—or she knew about you. That explains why they keep her snugged up, close to shore, covered with trees and bushes and such. You guys have airplanes now—we've seen 'em a few times—so I thought the Japs might be hidin' from you."

"*Hidoiame*," Brassey said, his tone certain, and Abel nodded agreement. "It has to be, particularly based on the description."

Silva swore. "Bitch has more lives than a . . ." He shrugged. "Well, you know what I mean."

Abel frowned at Tony. "You're right, Mr. Scott. The Japanese destroyer *is* hiding from us, and USS *Walker* gave her many of the wounds you've seen. We thought she was doomed, but she clearly survived long enough to coerce *Fristar*'s aid. Even with her few cannons, *Fristar* would've been helpless against *Hidoiame*. Her people would've had no choice but to obey the Japanese. I'm glad you've restrained your people from attacking the workers, Mr. Scott. They're just as much victims as the Khonashi."

"That's what I thought, but it ain't been easy. Especially with them workin' for those murderin' Japs, willing or not. My people have suffered and they're mad. I can't make 'em love the 'Cats, but so far I've been able to keep my folks from killing them—on the condition that we *will* kill the Japs." He blew a frustrated breath. "The trouble is, as we taught the Grik, swords and crossbows ain't no match for modern weapons, and a straight-up fight'll be a bloodbath. We might win, but even if we do, we'll be easy pickings for our other enemies." He looked ruefully at Silva. "Bein' king ain't all fun and games." He turned back to Abel. "Maybe I'm AWOL, but these're my people now, just as much as my old shipmates and even the Baalkpan 'Cats. I know you won the fight at Baalkpan, but I also know the war ain't over. Too many ships keep building and sailing off, and too many troops too. I been doin' my best to get it where my people here, and my people down south can get along with each other, but it's to the point where I need some kind of *goddamn help up here!*"

"You could just wait them out, let them get their oil and leave," Abel said softly.

Scott turned back to Silva. "Who the hell *is* this kid, Dennis? I'll let my people kill every single worker on the rigs before I let those Japs just steam out of here! That's what I'm trying to *stop!*"

"Relax, Tony," Silva assured him. "He knows."

Abel nodded. "I was merely pointing out that despite your unusual circumstances, you've not forgotten your duty. Ultimately, it's in all our interests to capture or destroy *Hidoiame*. With fuel, she may well reach our other enemies and make them even more difficult to defeat."

He glanced at Silva and Horn, and suddenly looked very much the young teenager he actually was once more. "I . . . I didn't expect this sort of thing at all. I suppose our next move should be to see the situation for ourselves, then decide what to do about it."

"Yessir," Silva agreed. "That's exactly what we gotta do."

"I wish we could just whistle up some air from Baalkpan to take care of that Jap can," Horn grumped.

Stuart Brassey nodded helplessly. He'd long since discarded the damaged wireless equipment. He couldn't fix it, and not only was it heavy, but their relentless pace and the climate-induced corrosion had outdone his best efforts to maintain the salvageable components.

"We could cut a large clearing in the jungle and light a signal to 'atrol 'Nancys'!" Lawrence suggested, joining the conversation. He'd been conscious that he was the center of much curiosity from all the natives, as well as this Tony Scott.

"Jaaphs see s'oke, go search us!" I'joorka warned.

"Probably not from that far away," Tony speculated.

"Yeah," Horn agreed, "and we lay out a big arrow or message that says 'Japs are anchored to shoreward of *Fristar*.' "

"It's not a terrible idea," Silva grudged. "An' besides the usual patrol grids, our folks are prob'ly out lookin' for sign of us, anyway. But Borno's near as big as Texas. You might have to keep a smoke signal like that goin' for weeks before anybody sees it. If we *could* lay out a message they can read from the air, they'd likely spot *Hoo-dooy-yammy* once they're lookin' for her, though. Prob'ly use the P-Forties Ben Mallory left in Baalkpan to paste her. Ever'body's happy—if it goes down like that."

"P-Forties?" Tony asked, incredulously.

"Another long story."

"That may be the most sensible course of action," Abel said thoughtfully, "and we should certainly do it immediately. But I believe we need to consider it 'plan B,' as you say. Chief Silva has reminded us that there's no guarantee our planes will see a signal for some time, and *Hidoiame* may steam away"—he shrugged—"well, tomorrow." He set his jaw. "Under *no* circumstances can that ship be allowed to leave this place."

Silva grinned and thumped Abel on the shoulder, nearly knocking him over. "Then what are we waitin' for?" He glared at Tony's wasted leg. "You ain't good for much, so why don't you get the smoke signals started while we go have a look at this Jap?"

"I get around better than you might think," Tony snapped back, "but I'll have a detail get started on a clearing and a fire that'll draw attention for a hundred miles!"

"Excellent," Abel said, then paused. "I think we should begin as soon as possible, but I'd like to ask a few questions first."

"He's kinda Courtney Bradford's pro-to-jay," Dennis said, rolling his eye. Abel glared at him. "Quite so." He looked back at Scott. "But I simply must ask where all the humans came from, and how long they've been Khonashis!"

Scott blinked at him. "Hell, I don't know. I figure they're Malays or somethin'. Wound up here a hundred years or so ago on fishing boats. Least, that's their story. Joined up with the Khonashis against some other tribe in the southeast and been together ever since." He gestured at the woman who'd ushered him out. "She knows the whole story by heart, and you can nag her about it all you want when we ever get a chance to just sit around and swap yarns."

"I look forward to it," Abel said, looking at the woman.

"I got a question," Pam interjected when it seemed they were all about to just dash back off into the jungle. "I mean, I'm tired and starvin' and I just gotta know: you folks don't eat bugs all the time, do you?"

CHAPTER

23

////// *North Borno Coast*

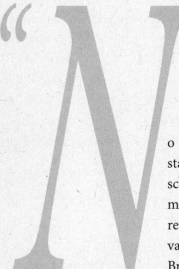

"No half measures," Dennis Silva muttered, staring through his small Imperial telescope. To all appearances, *Fristar* was moored in the narrow, deep-water cove to render oil from the huge gri-kakka fish— various types of plesiosaur, according to Bradford—which was the primary commercial occupation of all the great seagoing Homes. Her massive "wings" were stowed athwartships, and dark smoke streamed shoreward from multiple tryworks. Gri-kakka boats, lateen sails set, towed a near-continuous stream of the massive, lance-festooned fish into the cove. There they were hoisted onto wide, floating platforms away from the flasher fish feasting on them. Dennis had seen the operation only a few times, and he'd always wanted to go on a gri-kakka hunt. The idea of harpooning such a large animal, then riding the small boat like the whalermen of old—but on an even more hostile sea—absolutely thrilled him. He'd been *ordered* not to do it, of course, but that didn't matter as much to him as the fact there'd just never been the time. Also, like any hunt, chasing gri-kakka wasn't all adventure. Even here, more than a mile away, the fishy, fatty stink of boiling lard and rotting flesh was sharp.

At a more than casual glance, the hunt and subsequent rendering of oil and meat was all that was happening in the vicinity of the cove, and it took Silva some careful study to spot the Japanese destroyer. "They're bein' damn sneaky about it too," he murmured. "They've made their ship look like a beaver dam!" He closed the telescope. "That's her, though."

"How can you say so sure?" Lawrence hissed beside him. "You hadn't seen her afore now."

Dennis glared at his furry-feathery friend. "'Cause you can see her hull down by the waterline. That's how I spotted her. There's damage there, and believe me, if anybody can tell a hole made by a four-inch-fifty, it's me." Pam scrabbled up on her hands and knees to join them. "Well, why don't *ever'body* just come on up?" Dennis griped. "Hell, we can wave flags an' shoot rockets in the air!"

"If they haven't already seen your big, giant ass, they ain't gonna see me," Pam snapped. "Gimme that!" She motioned for the glass.

"Okay, doll, but shade the lens with your hand. There's 'Cats over there, remember? I doubt the Japs've made friends with 'em, but if they spot us, it might get others lookin'." He scratched his moldy eye patch. "They've got a fair number o' 'Cats doin' their usual thing, but I wonder where they're keepin' the rest when they're not workin' on the rigs." I'joorka had supplied them with the locations of all six oil wells, built very much like the Fort Worth Spudders the Allies used. Some of *Fristar*'s people had helped in the Baalkpan oilfields for a while and might've supplied the design, thinking the quicker they finished, the quicker they'd be free of their captors. Dennis had plotted the sites on a map he was making.

"Maybe we'll find out soon," Pam said, hopeful. Moe and his three remaining Marines had crept down to what Tony's scouts had reported seemed like a kind of prison camp in the jungle near the water, east of the slaughtered Khonashi village. Labor continued at the wells night and day, but only a few hundred workers could possibly fit in the protective perimeters around the rigs, so perhaps a thousand Lemurians remained at the camp. Gunny Horn, once a prisoner of these very Japanese himself, suggested they probably kept them there as hostages against the good behavior of those on the great ship, as well as the laborers in the jungle. Some of Tony's people had shown Moe's little squad the way, and their objective was to make contact if possible and not only tell *Fristar* that aid was at hand, but also that the Khonashi *weren't* Grik. No matter how well armed the Japanese were, Abel had theorized that only the fear of being overwhelmed by Grik could keep the 'Cats so docile under the Japanese. Dennis wasn't so sure. *Fristar* remained under *Hidoiame*'s guns and was a powerfully restrictive hostage herself. But he conceded that whatever they decided to do, they needed to ensure that the people of *Fristar* would cooperate with the Khonashis, not run away—or try to kill them.

"There's Japs," Pam reported. "Workin' on the ship. I see 'em movin' now and then through the bushes and brush draped across her. But they've put up shelters past her, over in the trees too. Damn, they've *moved* whole trees! You can tell because they don't look so good compared to the rest. Like they're dyin'. Maybe they're usin' 'em like little cranes?"

"Here, gimme that back," Dennis demanded. Pam handed the telescope over. "Huh. I think you're right! Pretty smart. They *have* built cranes an' scaffolds an' all sorts o' stuff outa livin' trees." He looked appraisingly at Pam. "Course, they ain't as livin' as the others. Good catch! For somebody whose eyes is so close together, yours seem to work okay!"

"Gee, thanks. Be still my flutterin' heart!"

"Don't mention it. Okay, Larry. Scoot on back an' send misters Cook an' Brassey up to have a look. We need ever'body with the same picture in their heads. When they shift back down, send I'joorka an' Gunny Horn up—but make sure I'joorka's pals keep an eye out behind us!"

Once everyone had observed the layout, they all pulled back to a well-hidden shelter in the jungle to await Moe's return. An army of nearly three hundred Khonashis, of both races, had been gathering all day and I'joorka had assured them that the meeting place should be secure. The enemy no longer patrolled, he said. There were plenty of terrifying predators in the coastal jungle, but the unknown—and the Khonashis themselves—were more likely reasons why the Japanese relied on a perimeter defense and heavily armed squads to escort and protect their Lemurian workers and their worksites.

"King" Tony Scott and maybe a hundred more warriors joined them as the sun plunged from the sky and the mosquitoes and night creatures inherited the earth. He limped rather badly, but did move better than Silva expected with the aid of a rigid, split-bamboo brace encompassing the outside of his leg from his hip to his foot and ending in a shelflike sole for his foot to rest upon. Otherwise, the brace was secured by straps, and the top was fastened to a belt around his waist. Dennis doubted he'd walked all the way from his village, but he was moving pretty briskly now.

"So? What do you think?" Tony asked when he joined them under the shelter.

Abel looked at Silva, then turned back to Tony when the big man didn't respond. "We're, ah, still waiting for Sergeant Moe to report, but with your people's description of the Jap perimeter, we're gaining a good idea of the tactical challenge." He motioned to Silva's map, laid out on the ground. It was crudely drawn with charcoal on the flesh side of an animal skin, but the cove and its environs were unmistakable. "I think we're agreed that our first priority is securing or destroying *Hidoiame*. Not only is she a threat to our Alliance, but she's the Japs' only hope. They can't sustain themselves in this country forever, and they have to know that. All they want is to fuel her and leave." Nearly everyone was nodding. "Take her away, and everything crashes down around them. Even if we can't defeat them outright and never get outside help, the Japs will eventually realize they have no choice but to surrender or die. Everything we do must be geared toward getting a defensible force aboard *Hidoiame*!"

The nodding continued, and Abel's voice firmed up. "At the same time, though, we have to rescue the Lemurians." He noted a few mutters, but continued. "Think of it. If we capture *Hidoiame*, the Japs will certainly use their hostages to try to get her back!" He swallowed and looked directly at Tony Scott. "No matter what they do to them, that will never happen, I swear. But our secondary objective must be the prevention of atrocities against the prisoners! Besides, if Sergeant Moe is successful, we'll be in a much better position to defeat the Japs completely if we add the Lemurian numbers to yours." He frowned. "I'm quite sure they'll be more than happy to kill their captors."

"Okay," Tony said. "But how do we *do* all that?"

Gunny Horn spoke up. "We know the Japs had a heavy crew to start with, after they abandoned the *Maru*. *Walker* probably killed some, but you said at least two hundred armed Japs killed the folks around here."

"Two hundred or *more*—and there had to be some still on the ship."

"At least an anchor watch," Horn conceded, "but with crews on all her guns trained ashore and on *Fristar*. Let's assume there's three hundred and fifty of 'em. But they're spread around. See? They've got this perimeter around their camp, guards at the well sites and the prison camp, and workers on the ship. Probably have at least a few guards on *Fristar*." He pointed at the map. "The weak link's the shore, right *at* the ship. They can't be thick everywhere, and they've got no reason to think we *want* their damn ship! Even if they're thicker close to her, they can't stop a determined wedge of warriors"—he hoisted his BAR—"with a few modern weapons they don't expect, runnin' straight down their scrawny damn throats!"

I'joorka's large eyes flicked back and forth at the map. "Yes, yes! Exce't Khonashis attack all round at start, draw their thoughts!"

Silva looked at I'joorka with genuine respect. "A big diversion would be my very favorite thing about then." He ruffled Lawrence's crest. "How come you didn't think of that? Are Tony's lizards smarter than you?"

"I thought it too!" Lawrence defended, and there was a bizarre mixture of laughter. Silva looked back at I'joorka with a serious expression. "You know we been fightin' Griks—folks that look a hell of a lot like some of you—for a long time." It wasn't a question, and I'joorka bowed his head. "Well, I just want to say that you Khonashis are right guys, in my book," Silva finished.

Tony was grinning. "They really are, you know."

There was a disturbance among the warriors gathered to hear, and Moe and one of his Marines stepped under the shelter. Both saluted, though Moe's was a little awkward. "Gotta report, Mr. Cook," Moe said.

"I'm glad you're here," Abel greeted him. "Was your mission successful?"

Moe blinked affirmative. "Aye. I sneaked into compound and talk to Anai-Sa hi'sef." He spat. "Chikkinshit. But his Sky Priest and some warriors dat trained wit our Marines once was der, an' dey listened up. I tole dem what was what an' dey said dey'd rise up whenever we attack the goddamn Jaaps." He paused. "Dey not in such good shape, though. Dey not been eatin' good for long time."

Horn swore. "Same ol' Japs!"

"Where are your other Marines?" Abel asked.

Moe shrugged and blinked uncertainty. "I send dem to check wells. We was too many together for sneakin.' I thought dey be here by now."

"If they got captured . . ." Tony began.

Moe shook his head. "Dem boys not be captured. Dey maybe dead, but not captured."

"Still," Brassey said, "Whether captured or killed, the enemy may be on to us."

"Jaaps not tell dey was *Marines*," Moe objected. "Dey taked der swords an' Khonashi spears, but leaved their rifles. Dey look jus like *Fristar*s."

"That may not matter," Horn said. "Even if the Japs think they were 'Cats escaping from the compound or one of the worksites, it might put 'em on their toes."

Silva was nodding. "Then we have to attack tonight. *Now*. Like I always say, when in doubt, don't just stand there; *do* somethin'. Let the bad guys worry what's comin' next. We better get to work."

"I agree, but one thing remains," Cook said, pointing at the map. "Here's *Fristar*, moored near the center of the cove. We can't signal her, since there're bound to be Japanese aboard. We must get word to her, though, just as Sergeant Moe did at the camp."

"How?" Scott demanded. "Why? The Japs ashore and their damn destroyer are our main concern. We take them out, and we're done."

"I think I see where Mr. Cook's headed with this," Pam said. "Whatever we do, most of our forces will look like *him*." She motioned at I'joorka. "How do you think the Japs *and* Lemurians on *Fristar*'ll react to what they'll think is a general Grik attack against everybody? *Fristar* has cannons. Remember?"

"Shit! Good point. But how can we get word to 'em?"

"Dennis can s'im out there!" Lawrence said enthusiastically.

"My ass! I ain't swimmin' out there! With all that gri-kakka cuttin' goin' on, that cove's prob'ly got the thickest pack o' flashies that ever was! Besides, I'm boardin' the Jap can!" The last was not a request, but a statement of fact.

"You s'im in 'lashy 'ater once," Lawrence persisted.

"Yeah!" Pam agreed. "When you jumped ship outa that 'Buzzard' that was supposed to bring you back to Baalkpan! What did you do?"

"I smeared grease on myself," Silva answered reluctantly, "like ol' Moe suggested once."

"Dat worked?" Moe asked, amazed.

"You mean . . . Why, you fuzzy old bastard!"

"It doesn't matter if it worked or not," Abel interrupted. "We don't have any grease."

Tony Scott shifted. "Ah, yeah we do. Maybe. Sorta. There's places around here where tar oozes up out of the ground. Always has, here and back home, both. You think smearin' that on will keep the flashies away?"

Abel considered. "It might. It should. How far is it? We do need to get moving."

"I ain't swimmin' out there!" Silva repeated defiantly.

"I'll do it," Stuart Brassey said, his voice a little uncertain but his expression set.

"I," Abel started, then stopped when he saw Brassey's face. He looked down. "Very well, Midshipman Brassey." He looked at Tony. "Mr. . . . King Scott, can Mr. Brassey ask your people for volunteers to accompany him?"

"Holy shit. Sure, I guess. Swimmin' with flashies? Goddamn!" Tony looked at Stuart. "You got more guts than I do, kid."

Pam Cross sighed, cutting her eyes at Dennis. "Well, I guess I do too, 'cause I'm goin' with ya, Mr. Brassey." She raised her Blitzer Bug. "This might come in handy, and it don't go nowhere without me." She returned Silva's sudden glare with equal intensity. "What? You can swim with flashies an' I can't? Think again, you big jerk!"

Dennis took a breath to argue, but one of Tony's human advisors spoke up. "You all swim if you want, but I ask why." He pointed at the sky. Those who'd been on the expedition from Baalkpan realized this was the first good look at it they'd had in weeks. The moon had horns, and Venus was near it, bright and sharp. "Why not take boats instead? There enough light to see, but not so much they see you comin' against dark water."

"Boats are better," Silva agreed, glaring at Lawrence. "Just because *somebody's* worked up an obsession for swimmin' with flashies don't mean it's a good idea."

Abel nodded at the man. "Of course boats would be better. It should've occurred to me to ask if any were available." He frowned at Dennis. "Perhaps it doesn't always hurt to stand about for a moment or two, to think things through."

Silva just shrugged and stifled a yawn, but Abel suddenly realized that the exchange had revealed something very profound. He was in command, but he'd always followed Silva's lead. Always. For as long as he could remember, Silva had always saved the day with his impulsive snap decisions, but Abel had just seen how those decisions could lead to rash, possibly unnecessary risks. Not only by Silva himself, but everyone around him. Lawrence's wild suggestion had been only that: a suggestion. But Abel was amazed how quickly everyone jumped at it as a viable option. Even Tony Scott, who clearly remained terrified of the water after all this time. That happened because Silva allowed a debate on the merits of the notion, instead of immediately proclaiming it a stupid idea. *He* obviously thought it was stupid and hadn't been willing to do what Lawrence suggested, but he hadn't seemed too concerned that someone else might try it—at least until Pam volunteered.

Abel still trusted Silva's instincts and believed he was right about it being time to act. If Moe's Marines had been discovered, it would heighten the enemy's readiness, and the longer they delayed, the more likely Tony's encircling Khonashis would be discovered and the readier each Japanese position would be. But Abel also recognized for the first time how narrow Silva's focus could be. Of course Dennis should lead the attack against *Hidoiame*. If anyone could get aboard her, he would. But the "Lady Sandra" had been right so long ago when she said Silva had no business being an officer or being in a position of authority over anyone beyond his own, immediately personal objective. Abel would have to remember to bear that in mind.

He studied the map a moment longer, then glanced up at Tony. "With your permission, King Scott, may I suggest a plan?"

Tony waved a hand. "Sure, kid. I'm a coxswain who got elected king because I knew about a few weapons and married well." Abel knew there had to be more to it than that and was anxious to hear the story, but now wasn't the time.

"Okay. I suggest we gather as many small boats as necessary to move Mr. Brassey, Lieutenant Cross, and twenty or thirty volunteers out to *Fristar* without delay." He looked at Brassey and the small woman. "Take the ship as quietly as possible, but if you draw attention, the rest of us will consider that our signal to begin the general attack. If you manage to take her quietly, wait for the fighting ashore to begin, then cut *Fristar*'s cables and get her underway. Hopefully there are enough 'Cats aboard to do the job. I'm betting nobody'll think much about her once we get their attention. Regardless, I want you to move her out of the cove and *Hidoiame*'s line of fire. That'll be one less thing to worry about."

"I guess you've seen those cables before, Abel?" Brassey asked. "Cutting them won't be a thirty-second job."

Abel nodded. "Right. Leave a detail in the boats to cut them from the water as you board. The idea is to get her moving as fast as you can. . . . And if things don't go well for us, make for Baalkpan. Bring help." Pam shot a neutral glance at Dennis but nodded. "You got it, Mr. Cook."

"That'll take weeks!" Silva objected. "Damn thing's slow as hell."

"So? Our only do-or-die mission is *Hidoiame*. If we take her, we'll *have* weeks to wait for relief! All our shore-bound forces will have to do is contain the remaining Japanese."

Dennis scratched his eye patch, nodding.

Abel looked at Tony. "Regarding the shore action, you and I should take your warriors and encircle the enemy perimeter. We'll be on the right, with Sergeant Moe and his Marine. There we'll be in a position to support the Lemurian breakout from their camp—if it comes. Mr. Silva, you, Gunny Horn, Lawrence, I'joorka, and one hundred Khonashis will attack from the left, along the beach on the west side." He pointed. "Your objective, obviously, is to break through and secure the ship. If the assault on *Fristar* raises no alarm, wait for our attack to distract the enemy before you go. Once you break through, we'll send more warriors from our left to widen the gap, hopefully rolling up the Japanese perimeter and reinforcing you." Abel paused, looking at the map, wondering what he'd forgotten.

"Looks okay," Horn said. "But what then?"

"With the enemy cut off from their ship and hopefully encircled by our forces and the Lemurians from the prison camp, the survivors will have no choice but to surrender."

"With respect, Mr. Cook, Japs ain't much for surrenderin'," Horn objected.

Abel held his hands out at his side.

"One more thing," Scott said. "What about the Japs at the well heads?"

"You'll have to send blocking forces to keep them contained," Abel replied, then realized what he'd said sounded like an order. "If you please," he amended. "Their forces can't be large enough to break back through to their perimeter—and maybe the Lemurians there will rise as well."

"Or join 'em, if they think their Home's at risk," Pam suggested darkly.

Abel frowned. "With luck, Moe's Marines contacted them and explained the situation before they were captured or killed."

"So, what do we do once we're on the tin can?" Gunny Horn asked.

"Simple," Silva answered flatly. "Kill ever'body." He looked at Moe and hesitantly handed the short Lemurian his giant rifle. "Thing's not much good for what we're up to tonight. You take care of it, wilya? Hide it someplace safe er somethin'. I'll take one of the rifles and bayonets your Marines left behind."

"Sure you don't want to use it for a preparatory bombardment of the Jap position?" Horn asked innocently, and Silva rolled his eye.

CHAPTER
24

////// *"Battle of the* Hoo-dooy-yammy*"*
May 6, 1944

"Plans are all just a stupid waste of time," Silva grumped softly. "Nobody ever uses the damn things when it gets down to it."

The boarding party assigned to break through the Japanese closest to the ship had been waiting in place for almost three hours, and the general attack on the perimeter should've begun more than an hour before. This was on top of all the time it took everyone to get in position, and it had to be close to 0300. "If we don't get on with it, we'll be at 'em in the daylight, because we can't just sit here and wait for 'em to see us. They'll pick us off like flies."

"Plans do seem highly overrated," Horn agreed.

"It take longer to get Jaaphs surrounded than exkected, I guess," I'joorka said. Silva looked at him in the gloom.

"Hey, do your fellas see pretty good in the dark? Larry sees better than me, but most folks do nowadays. Grik don't fight a lot in the dark, though, an' we always figgered it was because they got crummy night vision."

I'joorka cocked his head. "I don't see as good in night as day, 'ut I can still kill Jaaphs."

Dennis looked at Lawrence, who seemed utterly motionless, peering from behind a big, gnarled root at the edge of the trees. Only a meager, telltale scritching sound betrayed that any part of him was moving. "What're they doin'?"

"They changed their guards a little ago. I seen they clear. They got . . . phires in a circle around their shelters on the other side o' they. Stu'id!"

"Yeah, stupid. They're fine targets even for good crossbowmen. But what about that forted-up spot close the water? What do you think?"

"I think they got a light 'achine gun there, like you say."

Dennis scooted back and turned to sit in the sand. "Yeah. Figgers. They may be stupid, but we can't count on 'em bein' nuts. I would'a put machine guns all around the perimeter if I was them and had 'em—which I guess they do. Wish we had grenades!"

"Look at the bright side," Horn urged absently, staring at Lawrence. "There shouldn't be many, if any, light machine guns left on the ship."

"I bet there'll be *one*," Silva predicted. "At least one. Right at the top of that brushy gangplank we gotta go up!"

"Hey!" Horn hissed. "Why so gloomy? I've never seen you like this." He took a breath, realization dawning. "It's that gal! You're worried about Lieutenant Cross!"

"Am not!" Dennis denied. "That's the stupidest thing you ever said. Besides, even if I was a little partial to her, she's probably got the easiest job tonight—and she can take care of herself."

"Sure. You always were a bad liar."

"That's a lie!" Silva denied, indignantly. "You'd be amazed what I've got away with lately!"

Horn chuckled quietly, but looked back at Lawrence. "Say, what the hell's he scritchin' on? He got a case of the jitters?"

"Not much gives my little lizard buddy pause," Silva stated. "He's just manicurin' his claws."

"Sharpening them?" Horn guessed.

"Nah. Dullin' a few of 'em up on a rock. He does that now and then to handle cartridges for his rifle better. His finger claws ain't as big as a Grik's, but they can make 'eem fumble a bit. He rakes 'em off to where his finger pads can get a grip. Not as likely to set his damn rifle off by accident either."

"Huh." Horn settled back. "A *real* bad liar, if I recall," he continued.

"Maybe I've took a stone to *that* skill," Silva defended.

"You didn't beat the rap at the Fourth Marines Club in Shanghai," Horn reminded, and they both chuckled. "I think you broke every specification under Rule Nine: intoxication, misconduct, destruction of club property, *skylarking*! What the hell's that?"

"I think it's aimed mostly at Navy men," Dennis snorted.

"Then they tacked on 'objectionable conduct'! I figured misconduct would've covered that."

"They just threw that in because somebody objected extra loud to my misconduct."

Horn looked at I'joorka, who was staring at them. "Got us both thrown out of the club for good!" he explained. "Not that it mattered. Lotsa better places to kick up your heels in Shanghai." I'joorka nodded politely, but had no clue what they were talking about. Horn frowned. "Not counting the fight with the super lizard and the Akashis, since those just fell on us, this'll be the first fight we've been in together since that goose pull-down on Soochow Creek."

"We got a *medal* for that," Dennis practically giggled.

"Shoosh!" Lawrence hissed.

"Shoosh yerself!" Dennis whispered back. "We can hear you preenin' yer nails from here!" He eyed Horn. "Course, that one wasn't real."

"They might've given us *real* medals if it wouldn't've pissed off half the world," Horn reminded.

Silva's smile faded. "Yeah."

They both sat silent after that, contemplating an anecdotal episode that they alone in all the world—except Dean Laney, whom neither liked—remembered, and the only sounds were buzzing, rattling insects, punctuated by the harsh shrieks of night creatures. Then, suddenly, from half a mile out over the water came the muffled but distinctive clattering *burrrrup!* of Pam's Blitzer Bug. Lawrence tensed, but it didn't look like any of the Japanese paid much attention until it came again, and heads began to bob behind the perimeter breastworks.

Silva shifted back to look for himself. "Damn it, I hope Cook heard that!"

He must have, because just then, whether he was ready to attack or not, a terrible ululating screech arose, gathering voices until it thundered all around the enemy camp. More heads bobbed, but then, with a muffled, whickering hiss, hundreds of crossbow bolts and arrows streaked through the dark, slashing across the firelight. Some must've found a mark, because terrified, agonized shrieks and cries erupted here and there. A machine gun stuttered. Then another.

Gunny Horn hefted his BAR in his left hand and absently patted the belt of magazine pouches encircling his torso. Dennis nodded to himself and slid the triangular bayonet out of the scabbard he'd added to his pistol belt and quietly affixed it to the muzzle of his borrowed rifle, twisting it until it latched on the front sight lug, then turning the locking ring. Lawrence had already fixed his bayonet, and his yellowish eyes glowed in the light of the fires and sudden, flashing shots as he stared back at Dennis. I'joorka had a crossbow, like most of his warriors, and he edged forward. The woods behind him were filled with shifting, jostling, whispering Khonashis as they prepared for their part in the attack.

The Japanese perimeter was becoming a place of nervous chaos. Sailors awakened by the growing fight on the south breastworks dashed out of shelters, carrying Arisaka rifles and even a few spears. An officer hurried them along, waving a sword. Several men snatched up a light machine gun at the foot of the gangplank and awkwardly carried it and two crates of ammunition toward the sound of battle.

"That's handy," Silva murmured. "Didn't even suspect that one." He frowned. "How many of the damn things do they have?"

"Figure one on the other side of the perimeter, like the one in front of us. That one . . . and it sounds like maybe three more already shooting. Six, at least. I guess that's about right, but they may still have some mounted on the ship." He looked at I'joorka. "Remember what to do?"

The Khonashi jerked his head in agreement.

"Then good luck."

"No such t'ing as yuck," I'joorka said. He grasped a handful of leafy, moldy turf. "This is the skin o' our God," he said, then gestured around. "The trees is his crest. He is *ours*. Jaaphs is like nasty ticks, an' us gotta yank they out!"

"Okay. Well . . . happy yankin'," Dennis said dubiously, and looked at Horn. "I thought I was gettin' used to runnin' into crackpot religions, but *dirt worshippers*?" he said when I'joorka moved down to the very edge of the trees.

"Who cares, as long as they're on our side?" Horn replied. "I figure a fella can pray to a toad as long as he doesn't try to make me do it."

"But that's always the itch, ain't it?"

Before Silva or Horn could continue their theological discussion, something neither was particularly comfortable with, I'joorka trilled a distinctive, hair-raising cry unlike anything they'd heard before. It was like a Grik war cry in a way, but it was a singular thing, unaccompanied by thousands of voices, like Dennis had always heard before. He stood, along with Horn and Lawrence, and most of I'joorka's force burst from the trees and down to the beach, where they quickly formed a ragged line. At another shrill cry, every crossbow and longbow was raised and pointed at the Japanese machine-gun position about seventy yards away. Without any further command, the missiles were released in a whickering wave of twanging strings or clacking rollers, and a hundred bolts and arrows converged on the suddenly terrified, staring Japanese machine gunners. The sharp projectiles festooned the area around the weapon—and the half dozen men within. Only one even managed a scream.

"Let's go!" Silva roared, and he, Horn, Lawrence, and ten human Khonashis armed with longbows and swords charged through I'joorka's troops toward the Japanese perimeter. Other longbowmen joined them as they passed, and Silva shouted, "Even better than a grenade!" as he ran by I'joorka. The Khonashi war leader was already trilling for his warriors to launch another flight of bolts beyond their initial aiming point.

Lawrence reached the gun pit first but saw nothing alive. He immediately detailed several men to turn the weapon south. Horn's BAR hammered up the line at Japanese firing down the breastworks. A Khonashi man screamed and fell, then another. Dennis jumped down beside the machine gun and looked at it for a second. He snatched a pair of paint-daubed men to help him. "One o' those Type Eleven heaps," he declared. "Okay, I'm a little rusty on these, but here goes!" He felt in the hopper mounted on the side of the weapon to ensure it was loaded, then racked the bolt back. Settling down behind the butt-stock, he aimed up the perimeter as best he could and squeezed the trigger. The thing didn't kick at all, with its bipod and relatively light 6.5-millimeter cartridges, but the report of his three- and four-round bursts echoed back from the trees with a harsh, crackling rush. "Crap! No tracers!" he complained, but he hadn't really expected them. The Type 11 was designed to be loaded with standard five-round stripper clips, the same that Japanese rifles used, fed in the hopper. The incoming fire tapered off, and Dennis stood and flung one of the men he'd grabbed behind the gun.

"You speakee English?" he demanded.

"Some . . . little . . ."

"Good enough. You're a machine gunner now. No! Put the butt *to* your shoulder, not under your damn arm! There! Keep that knob up there in the notch, if you can see it, and put it on the Japs! Short bursts—just squeeze the trigger and let it go. It's up to you to keep those bastards back." He grabbed the other man. "See these clips?" he demanded, snatching one from the metal crate. "Keep stackin' 'em in the hopper here, like this." He demonstrated. He got the gunner's attention again. "When it jams or quits shootin'—an' it will—just yank this bolt back and try again." He looked around at the Khonashis Lawrence had detailed to assist. "You keep the Japs off 'em with your bows." He waved at a couple of rifles lying in the pit. "Don't fool with those. You'll get killed while you're trying to figure 'em out." He pointed at the Type 11. "But if that thing quits and you can't get it goin' again, throw it in the water, if it's the last thing you ever do!" With that, he raced after Lawrence and Gunny Horn, who'd already charged forward with I'joorka's advancing ranks. I'joorka was shouting something that must've meant "Here, here," as he placed Khonashis in a skirmish line in the brush along the shore. They were nearly invisible against the dark water and should be able to discourage any enemies that got past the machine gun and tried to come around behind them.

Silva moved among the trees alongside the big Japanese destroyer, which was snugged to a makeshift timber dock. Horn's BAR hammered up ahead in the tangle of wooden cranes and camouflage, and Lawrence's rifle boomed and flashed. Other muzzle flashes sparkled in the dark amid a swirl of foreign, alien shouts and screams, and the clash of steel as swords met rifle barrels and bayonets. Wood shattered, and blizzards of splinters flew as a heavy automatic weapon on the ship joined the fight with pounding, thunderous reports, but its crew had to be careful because the melee had become so mixed. Dennis saw a Japanese sailor right in front of him, aiming his rifle at somebody, and he slammed his bayonet into the exposed chest behind the man's elbow. There was a scream, and Silva twisted his rifle away and thrust again, even as the man crumpled to the ground. Another man ran at him and nearly got shot before they both realized they were on the same side. The dark man made a strange, apologetic gesture, then turned and vanished in the night.

"Dennis! Dennis!" Lawrence was shouting, and Silva hurried to catch his friend. The lizard was panting, his tongue lolling, bayonet black with blood. Horn's BAR slashed at a stuttering gun through the tree cranes, and Dennis realized it must be the one they'd seen carried away. "Quit skylarking," Lawrence admonished. He must've been listening earlier. "Us gotta get on the shi' afore the Jaaphs get their shit in their socks!" he shouted over the noise.

"What's up the ramp?"

"There's no 'achine gun!"

"How 'bout that? Where's I'joorka? I'joorka!" he yelled.

"Here!"

Small exploding shells erupted among them, shattering trees and bodies and throwing clouds of sand in the air. Dennis spat bloody grit and dragged Lawrence from the dubious protection of a teetering tree he'd ducked behind. "We gotta silence that big boy up there, that twenty-five millimeter, or it'll chew us up on the gangplank!" A bullet splintered the butt of Silva's rifle and snatched it out of his hand.

"Goddammit, Gunny. Can't you shut that machine gun up? We need you to put fire on that gun tub up there!" He pointed high amidships on the destroyer.

"I'm doing my best!" Horn yelled, dropping an empty magazine and fumbling for another.

"Then quit goofin' around an' do better! I'joorka," Dennis cried, "try and do what you done before! Get as many arrows as you can to fall in that tub up yonder!"

"I try. It hard to gather Khonashis! They get lost in dark an' killing!"

Silva thought there were forty or so warriors present. "Do it with these! As soon as you shoot, we go up! The arrows ought to at least keep their heads down long enough for us to board!" He pulled his precious .45 and placed it in his left hand, then drew his 1917 Navy cutlass. "Give the word or hoot or whatever you do!"

Another burst of 25-millimeter fire sprayed the trees, a little to the side, but I'joorka raised his odd cry again and added what must've been instructions. A final cry loosed the arrows, and Silva flipped his head so his helmet would lay farther back. "Let's go!" he roared. The long gangplank connected the dock to *Hidoiame* just forward of amidships on her starboard side, and it juddered and bounced under running feet. A Japanese sailor appeared at the top, rifle at port arms. His expression showed amazement, then terror that the attackers had already made it this far. He had no time to register another thought before Silva's first pistol shot struck him below his left eye. Another sailor was behind him, but the falling body kept him from raising his rifle in the confined space. Silva shot him too, then bolted left, toward the elevated gun platforms aft. A dozen yipping Khonashis followed. Lawrence turned right, leaping the bodies, and charged forward with his own squad, his bayonet leveled before him.

Gunny Horn's BAR pounded the night and finally silenced the Japanese machine gun, but the weapon they'd captured earlier went quiet as well. The sound of battle was still growing, however, and at least one more of the perimeter guns had gone down. Dennis resheathed his cutlass and scrambled up the damp iron rungs of a ladder. The arrows from below had stopped, and the surviving gunners on the .25 were starting to peer over the lip of the steel tub when Silva jumped in from behind, his 1911 Colt already barking. The gunners sprawled on the bloody deck, joining two others with arrows in their bodies.

"Quick!" Dennis roared at the Khonashis who'd followed his charge. "Check the other tubs!" He pointed in case they didn't understand. He stabbed the magazine release button with his thumb, and the empty magazine clattered on the deck. His left hand had already grabbed a full one from his pouch, and he slammed it in the well. Lawrence's .50-80 rifle boomed forward and smoke drifted aft in the dim light of an open porthole. Dennis quickly scanned his surroundings. There was a screech from a nearby gun tub, quickly silenced by ringing swords. More rifle fire erupted near the fantail, and small, high-velocity bullets crackled past. He couldn't worry about that. His squad of Khonashis would have to deal with it. He started to try to bring the 25mm up to support the attack in the woods, but realized he couldn't do that either! The jungle battle around and within the perimeter was a seething, chaotic mess. He was almost sure Abel's force, at least, had broken through on its right, but it had become impossible to differentiate targets. Even where he *knew* the Japanese were, he couldn't shoot the powerful weapon without risking friendlies beyond! He swore.

Horn's muzzle flashes were at the top of the ramp now, pulsing outward. He would've come up as a rear guard, Dennis was certain, which meant most of their boarding party had to be on the ship. He wondered if that meant there were seventy or eighty of them, or just ten or twelve by now. He snatched at a Khonashi lizard running aft. "I'joorka?" He shouted. The warrior waved behind him, and Silva saw the creature. At least he thought it was him. "I'joorka? Is that you?"

The warrior joined him, breathing hard. "It is I."

"Good." Silva waved at the cluster of gun tubs. "We can't use these—too dangerous to our folks—but you gotta keep the Japs from takin' 'em back!"

"I do it!"

"Swell! I'm goin' forward. You keep an eye on the companionways too. There's bound to be Japs below, tryin' to sneak up at us."

"Yes! Good!"

Dennis pushed his slide release, chambering another round in his Colt, then hopped the tub and ran back the way he'd come. Horn was lying prone on the deck beside the two sailors Dennis killed, but two more had been piled across the gangplank and Horn was using them for protection and a rest. Beside him, two men were trying to figure out the second Type 11 they must have captured, and several crossbowmen were covering them.

"Hey, Gunny," Silva called.

"Hey, yourself," Horn shouted between bursts. "This is the most goofed-up fight I've been in since I don't know when!"

"Yeah. Ain't a patch to some *I've* seen lately. Kind of a hoot, though, huh?"

"You always were nuts. Get down, wilya, before some Jap knocks your noodle off."

"I gotta check on Larry, forward," Silva replied. "I'joorka's gonna finish clearin' the topside, aft. You just keep any more Japs from gettin' aboard."

"You got it."

Silva trotted forward, his boondockers making remarkably little noise on the linoleum-covered deck. He'd seen *Amagi* while they were breaking her up, and the scorched-and-melted linoleum had been a surprise at the time, but he kind of expected it now. It was probably handy with the right shoes, he reflected, but slick under his leather soles. "Japs are so weird," he muttered, seeing another unidentifiable fixture attached to the deck. No doubt it did *something*, but why couldn't it look like anything it ought to do? At that moment he was all alone, though he could hear fighting ahead. He passed every hatch and port with care,

half expecting shots from within, but so far there didn't seem to be anyone belowdecks. There *had* to be Jap snipes aboard! At least one boiler
was lit to power the pumps and the few lights he'd seen. Maybe they'd
already come up and had their go?

He clambered up the stairs to the long, raised fo'c'sle, and almost
tripped over a pile of bodies lying in a twisted, bloody heap. There were
Japs and Khonashis there, but no Lawrence, he was glad to see. There
was another *boom* ahead, muffled, maybe inside the long, narrow bridge
structure, followed by the dull popping of a semiauto pistol. He darted
through a hatch—and right in the middle of a brawl. Two Khonashis lay
dead or hurt just inside the cramped space, but the rest, five or six, had
closed with their enemies before the pistols could overwhelm their
swords. The lizardlike Khonashis used their teeth and claws just like
Grik, and Silva couldn't help feeling an inner, visceral twinge. He saw
Larry then, pinning a man to a bulkhead with his bayonet, wailing with
a vocal savagery he'd never seen in the little guy. Larry was a killing
fiend when it came down to it, but he was usually quieter about it.

A sailor managed to work his pistol around to shoot the Khonashi
man he grappled with, and when the man fell, Dennis put two bullets in
the sailor. He got a quick opening and shot another man, but there was
just so little room and the desperate fight so fluid! He yanked out his
cutlass and dove in.

"More Nips comin' down the companionway from above!" he
shouted, seeing legs pumping down the stairs beside him. He stabbed at
one, tripping what looked like an officer, and the man tumbled headfirst
to the deck. He hopped the handrail and started up, but found himself
face-to-face with another officer, pointing one of the stumpy-looking
Nambu pistols right at Silva's good eye. Maybe it was the sudden appearance of the towering, one-eyed, blood-smeared apparition that gave
the Japanese officer pause, but Silva didn't hesitate, and stabbed forward
without thought. The pistol must've drawn his aim, because the clipped
point of the cutlass pierced the officer's hand and drove up through his
arm alongside the bone. The pistol clattered down the stairs, and the
man screamed shrilly. Dennis dragged his blade free with a savage
snarl.

"I surrender! Surrender!" the officer squalled. Dennis checked his killing blow and glanced at the braid on the bloody sleeve.

"Okay, Commander Nip. Up you go!" He motioned back up the companionway. "One wrong move, and I'll split your goddamn spine! Larry!" he yelled down. "Quit"—he grinned—"skylarkin' around with those Japs and get your stripey ass up here!"

There were several unarmed men waiting nervously on the bridge, and the remnants of Lawrence's squad took them prisoner. There was no discussion of terms and none officially surrendered, but the only choice was instant obedience or death. None courted the latter.

"Any o' you the captain o' this tub?" Dennis demanded. No one answered, but he knew Japanese rank insignia and he saw the furtive glances. He rested the tip of his cutlass against the chest of an officer who glared back at him, teeth grinding, eyes bulging. "You're the guy. Kurita, ain't it?" Silva's eye glittered with hate, and he smiled in that frightening way he sometimes did that left no doubt what he was capable of. "You're gonna wish my ol' *Walker* had sunk your murderin' ass!" He paused then and frowned. "But much as I'd enjoy skewerin' you right now, for what you done to prisoners an' civilians, there's a few folks who deserve to watch you die more than me." He pushed forward with the blade until the point drew blood. "You're gonna *hang*, mister!" He finally stepped back and waved the Khonashis forward. "Tie these bastards up good."

Dennis removed his helmet and slung the sweat from his brows with a finger. "Whoo," he said, looking out the high bridge windows at the darkness beyond; then he strode out on the starboard bridgewing. "Damn thing's big as a *cruiser*," he muttered, looking down. Little light from the moon could reach through all the trees and brush rigged to conceal the ship, but he finally got a decent feel for *Hidoiame*'s size. He almost snorted at the idea of poor little *Walker* going up against such a thing, but he'd seen clear evidence of damage here and there, and of course *Walker* had gone up against *Amagi*. Instead he gazed about. One machine gun still chattered to the south, but a roaring tide of what he distinctly recognized as Lemurian voices was surging in from the direction of the prison camp. Horn's BAR was silent at last, and he hoped it was because he had no targets.

All in all, a pretty happy fight, Dennis thought optimistically, *and all our immediate objectives met.* A pang rolled his stomach and he remembered *Fristar. I wonder how that went?* He walked through the bridge. "Tell your pals to get those Japs the hell outa here," he told Lawrence. "If they make a peep, they can eat 'em." Lawrence relayed the command, though some probably understood. More importantly, most of the Japanese surely did.

"Now?" Lawrence asked, joining Silva on the port bridgewing, squinting to pierce the brush and darkness.

"We'll have to chase the rats out from below," he patted the rail, "but I'm startin' to think we may have ourselves a brand-new, slightly used, Jap tin can to add to our humble fleet!" He grinned at his friend, but then turned back to stare at the gloom. "I wish we knew what the hell's goin' on out on *Fristar*, though. I don't see any muzzle flashes out there, so maybe the fightin's over, but I can't see the damn big-ass *ship* neither."

Lawrence squinted harder. "A 'Cat could see. Not I, though."

"C'mon," Silva said. "Let's get out on deck. We'll see how the fight's goin' ashore, but we need to post fellas at all the hatches we can find and make a sweep fore to aft."

They were about halfway down the switchback companionways when it started. There was a heavy, rending *crunch*, and the whole ship began to lean to starboard. Almost in slow motion, it kept rolling farther and farther onto its side. Silva and Lawrence grabbed the rail and hung on, utterly mystified, as the lights flickered off and the crunch became an all-consuming, ripping, grinding screech. Both fell against the bulkhead that was quickly becoming the deck, and then the entire ship seemed to surge sideways with a wrenching crack. Still they rolled, until the bridge structure slammed down against the dock itself and Silva was momentarily stunned.

"'At the *hell*?" Lawrence demanded, his voice high-pitched, as the light structure around them began to collapse.

"*Fristar* cut her cables," Silva explained simply, dizzily, "and the tide brought her ashore. That's why she wasn't where we was lookin'. She was already on *top* of us!"

The plates rumbled with the vibration of tons of water gushing into the hull, and the hot boiler exploded, jolting them even harder against sharp steel and fittings in the dark.

"We've just been sat on by a brontasarry!" Silva laughed bitterly. "C'mon. We better get the hell outa here!"

"Jesus Christ, Silva," Alan Letts groaned. "I've seen you make messes in the past, but this is . . . amazing." Letts was standing, hands on hips, staring at the aftermath of the battle—and the catastrophic . . . crushing of *Hidoiame* by *Fristar* Home.

"Yeah? Well, you missed some of my better ones, an' this ain't even my fault," Dennis griped. He was wiping sand from his monstrous rifle, laid across his lap, and sitting near the same overlook west of the cove where he and the others laid the plan that actually went amazingly well—with one glaring exception. Cutting *Fristar*'s cables had been a mistake. But they'd never imagined all those 'Cats they'd seen working on her or towing gri-kakka alongside during the day were being kept ashore with the rest of the prisoners, leaving nothing but a few Japanese caretakers aboard. Perhaps it made some kind of sense, but Dennis couldn't see it. Ultimately, Pam and Brassey's boarding party killed or captured all the Japanese quickly enough, but they didn't have the people to fully man even *two* of the great sweep oars needed to move *Fristar* out of the cove. Just ten of her hundred great sweeps might've kept her off the beach against the incoming tide, but two didn't even slow her down. They tried everything they could while the battle raged ashore. They tied cables to *Fristar*'s guns and tipped them over the side, but they dragged. They even tried to *sink* her, by opening the great seacocks used periodically to flood the ship down, but that was much too slow. *Fristar* took on enough water to make it easier to get her off the beach after they pumped her out, but nothing they'd done could save *Hidoiame* from being crushed like a beer can by a truck tire.

Fristar was moored in the middle of the cove again, her freed people working to repair the damage to her bow. But *Hidoiame* lay, her
forward half high on shore, nearly upside down. A crumpled funnel
and her highest 25-millimeter tub was all that remained visible of her
sunken stern section. Some of I'joorka's warriors were still on the bottom with it.

Also in the cove, however, five days after the battle, were half a dozen
PB-1B Nancys and two of the great four-engine "Clipper" flying boats,
all secured to a hastily rigged pier.

"It's a good thing we spotted your signal when we did," Letts said,
turning to look at him, "and the pilot decided to check it out, thinking it
was too tight a smoke column for a lightning fire." He chuckled. "Imagine his surprise when he saw a big arrow laid out in a clearing beside the
word 'Japs'! That was good thinking. That one word—and the signal
itself—told us an awful lot."

"I didn't do it," Silva said, opening the trapdoor breech of his weapon
to tease more sand out with a rag. *Damn Moe* buried *the thing to hide it,
then nearly couldn't find it in the daylight! Maybe he's hurtin' a little, an'
that's some excuse,* he conceded, *but I'd hate to've lost the Doom Stomper! Just as well I didn't have it with me, though,* he reflected. *It's really
not good for much other than killin' super lizards or blowin' up Blood
Cardinals at a distance. Not the best choice for close combat at all.* He
flapped sand off the rag and went back to work. There was a red-stained
bandage wrapped around his head where he'd conked it when *Hidoiame*
flipped, and he still felt a little woozy.

"I don't care who did it; it brought us here," Alan continued. "And
when we got our first report of what happened, we came as quick as we
could with medical supplies and corps 'Cats." He paused. "You did well,
Silva. The Skipper's happy. I sent word by wireless before I came."

"Mr. Cook was in command," Dennis insisted, looking at Alan intently. "He really was! He's a good kid, an' ready for more." He looked
down. "But I missed my boat."

"I wouldn't worry about that," Alan assured. "Seems I'm kind of in
charge while everybody's gone." He looked back at the cove. "You made
friendly contact with potential allies, and not just the jungle Grik we

were hoping for, but more humans!" he said at last. "Mr. Bradford's liable to hang himself for missing meeting them." He paused. "And how ever it happened, *Hidoiame*'s goose is cooked for good. You also helped shape what'll turn out to be a couple of damn good officers. I think that's earned you a seat on one of the supply flights west. You can catch *Walker* at Andaman Island."

"Thanks, Mr. Letts. Larry gets a seat too?"

Alan laughed. "I wouldn't think of splitting you two up!" He arched an ironic brow. "At least not now. I thought we'd need him to liaise with these Khonashi folks, but for some reason a lot of them speak at least a little English. Imagine that."

"Sure surprised me," Dennis admitted truthfully. So far, Tony Scott was keeping scarce. Dennis suspected *Walker*'s old coxswain would come forward eventually, but he had a lot of thinking to do—not just about himself—and Silva wouldn't blow. Nobody else would either. They'd discussed it as soon as they saw the first Nancy fly over. Tony Scott had earned the right to decide what was best for himself and his people.

Alan sighed. He knew something was up, but he also knew it was pointless to push Silva past what he'd already said. At least for now. "I'm going to leave Mr. Cook and Mr. Brassey here for now as our representatives to these folks. I'll probably send Moe back too, once he's better." Moe had been shot through the left bicep by a 6.5, and the little bullet blew out a pretty good chunk of meat. "He and his Marines are the only 'Cats they like around here right now." The lost Marines had returned during the fighting with 'Cats from the wellheads, and that had been a relief. "He'll have help," Alan went on, "a real diplomatic contingent eventually, and Adar already sent word that any hunters who summarily shoot anybody that looks like a loose Grik on Borno without being attacked will go on trial for murder."

"That's not a bad idea," Dennis judged, "but apparently there's some bad lizards runnin' around out there." He waved at the jungle to the south. "General orders can be just a tad general sometimes, if you get my meanin'. Have to sort that out." He stared down at *Hidoiame*'s corpse. "If you was askin' me, though, I wouldn't leave Mr. Cook here long. Think about sendin' him east. He's pinin' for Princess Becky—I mean the Governor-Empress—and I bet he'd be good for her too."

"Really?"

"Yep."

"I'll think about it."

Dennis nodded. "Let me take Gunny Horn with me too."

"He's hurt. Damn, Dennis, he practically had a ship fall on him!"

"He ain't hurt that bad. He'll want to go."

Alan shrugged. "Sure you don't want to take that weird little Grik brass picker with you too?"

"Nah. You can keep him."

"Okay. Well, I'm going back down there"—Alan waved—"and try to talk to I'joorka. See if I can get him to spare some of the Jap prisoners. Not all of them were bad men."

"What about the officers?"

"They'll hang for what they did at Okada's colony—not to mention what they did to their prisoners here and before."

Dennis frowned. "Good. That's what I told 'em, an' I wouldn't want to be made a liar. So long, Mr. Letts."

"So long, Chief Silva."

Dennis sat there for some time, just staring down at the cove, after Alan and his small escort left. A big copper-colored beetle landed noisily in front of him and marched purposefully toward his bare foot. He'd removed his half-rotten boondockers to let his pale, peeling feet breathe. "Purty bugs is always the most dangerous," he muttered to himself, paraphrasing or warping something Courtney Bradford told him once. "I guess the same goes for broads. Course, I think he was tellin' me not to *eat* the purty ones—like *he* ever ate a bug! Most bad, stingin' bugs I ever saw was ugly as hell." He picked up a stick and flicked the beetle away. "No sense takin' chances. Bugger had some ugly choppers!"

Suddenly, Pam Cross plopped down beside him on the sandy rise. He'd heard her approach.

"Who were you talking to?" she asked.

"Just a bug."

"What did he have to say for himself?"

"Not much."

Pam waited a few minutes, but when Silva said nothing more, she sighed. "So," she said expectantly.

"So what?"

"We gonna keep bein' mad at each other? I thought we got things sorted out that night in the tree, but we hardly even talked after that."

"I ain't mad."

Pam's face turned stormy. "Well *I* am, damn it!"

Dennis nodded. "I knew that. That's why I kept my distance."

"But . . ." Pam picked up her own stick and slapped the sand in frustration. "But I wasn't mad then! I got mad *again* because you froze me out!"

"What the hell was I s'posed to do?" Silva countered, exasperated. "This trip wasn't exactly a stroll down a nature trail, where we could cuddle up in our hammock bower ever' night after a ro-mantic hike!" He scratched his beard. "Cooties, I'll bet," he murmured, then continued. "Look, I'll admit I kinda hoped we'd patched things up, but I ain't much of a cuddler when I'm in a fight—an' we been in one ever since that super lizard nearly got us! That was my fault," he conceded, "but it sorted me out an' put me back in 'fight gear,' where I should'a been all along. You're always shiftin' me into neutral, doll, and we never would'a made it this far with me just revvin' my motor." He took a long breath. "I ain't never told you that I was anything but what I am. Not only is there nothin' I can do about it—there ain't nothin' I *want* to do about it! Even if I did, I can't—won't—right now. Don't you get it?" He avoided looking at her because he knew her big eyes would melt him if he did. Instead, he churned on, making his point while he could. "Maybe, just maybe, I'm tolerably sweet on ya. But the only way we'll ever get to keep anything goin' between us is if you know, *know*, deep down, that I been me so long you can't do anything about it. What's more, you really shouldn't even try. At least for a while. That's just the way it is, sweetie, and the harder you try to make me somethin' else, the more miserable you'll be."

Slowly, tentatively, Pam's small arm snaked around Silva's waist and she leaned against his shoulder. "I've been miserable ever since I met you," she said softly. "But I guess it's worse when I haven't got you, because I've never been happier either. Sometimes."

"You're gonna get my cooties," Silva warned. Pam held out a clump of her greasy, tangled hair and started laughing.

"Whut?"

"My lice can fight your lice. Winner take all."

CHAPTER

25

///// *Guayakwil Bay*
New Granada Province (Ecuador)
May 10, 1944

Second Fleet had been running wild along the west coast of the Holy Dominion, from what would have been San Salvador in the north, and south beyond where Lima, Peru, should have been. Ships were cut out of harbors at night or left burning in the daylight. Soon, virtually nothing moved by sea between Dominion ports within range of *Maaka-Kakja* or DD-escorted tenders carrying Nancy seaplanes to bomb and scout the enemy. Planes and pilots had been lost to malfunctions, weather, and simple inexperience, but Grikbirds had taken an increasing toll as well—particularly in certain areas—and that struck High Admiral Harvey Jenks and Admiral Lelaa-Tal-Cleraan as significant. Clearly there were places the Doms didn't want them to see, but that had been the case since the Empire of the New Britain Isles first knew them. Always a secretive society, described mostly by the illiterate slaves they sold or the company captains allowed only in certain ports, the nature of the Dominion remained amazingly vague. Its priests were twisted monsters, and its troops were competent and savage, but little was known of the country itself beyond those few ports. Regardless how costly, reconnaissance was essential.

One place no one had ever been allowed was the Sea of Bones, north, where the Gulf of California ought to be. No Imperial ship had ever returned from there, and Harvey and Gerald McDonald themselves, as young midshipmen, once attempted to reach it from Imperial holdings in the north by crossing the most horrible desert known. They failed, and were forced back by desiccating heat and terrible predators that took most of their expedition. That place was of little concern at present, however. The Dom capital was presumed to lie within the Valley of Mexico, based on the Dom pope's title and the apparent holiness his priests ascribed to the place, but Harvey wasn't interested in the enemy capital just yet either. He had nowhere near the forces for anything so ambitious. The presumably sparsely populated breadbasket of the Dominion in South America was his goal. Not even to take *it* yet, but to prick it, bleed it, force the enemy to protect it—and, incidentally, spread his forces across a continent.

Two other places had always been strictly protected by the Doms. The coast near Acapulco was one—which made sense, considering it gave access to the Valley of Mexico—and the other was the region surrounding what the American charts described as Costa Rica. No one knew why the Doms considered that such an important place, but the fact that it was suddenly so fiercely guarded by so many Grikbirds that none of Orrin Reddy's planes could approach it was sufficient reason to send a squadron of steam frigates to investigate. Ships were even now on their way—just as other elements of Second Fleet made their first landings on enemy soil.

There were three landings in all. One force of a thousand Imperial Marines went ashore at a sleepy fishing village called Quito. Another force of five hundred men and 'Cats landed at Chiklaya, in the south, but the largest incursion was at a respectable port city named Guayak, in a large bay called Guayakwil on Imperial charts. All three were just east of the Enchanted Isles and close enough together that they might support one another. Also, it seemed logical to occupy, long term or short, the most likely places a Dom attempt to retake the Isles might assemble. It was equally logical to take their first step on Dominion soil close enough to their base of operations that they could most easily support or relieve it, or, if necessary, evacuate. It was a tentative peek, to be sure, but it was also the first offensive act of the war in the East.

The first invasions of Dom America occurred without warning. There was no naval bombardment and there hadn't even been recon flights for several days before the landings, so they came as a complete surprise. Barges crunched ashore unopposed in various places along the coast, and columns quickly slogged through the darkness to converge on their objectives. With the dawn, Colonel Blair met Captain Blas-Ma-Ar along the Guayak harbor waterfront, where the battalions under their direct control completed lightning sweeps through the city. Few inhabitants had shown themselves at that early hour, other than to peer from doors or wood-shuttered windows before slamming them closed again. Occasional shots echoed as Marines encountered Dom soldiers. Maybe they were part of the sleepy garrison of the formidable fortress overlooking the town, but the fortress itself fired no shots at the DDs that crept ever closer or the barges that carried more and more troops ashore, virtually under its guns.

"I don't get it," Captain Blas told Blair, blinking and swishing her tail in agitation. "Where are all the daamn Doms?"

"I've no idea," Blair replied worriedly, staring at the fortress. He was relieved, of course, but nervous that they hadn't faced any real opposition. It didn't make sense. The sky was growing brighter, but the town still lay in shadows cast by the rugged mountains to the east. "The fabled Andes, I believe," he remarked, turning to look at the high, craggy range. "I never dared hope to stand beneath them!"

Blas blinked mild annoyance. "You think they seen us comin' and took to the hills?"

Blair shook his head, stirred from his reverie. "Why?" He gestured back at the fortress. "That wouldn't have stopped us, but it could've made things a bit tedious. I can only assume we did indeed achieve complete surprise."

"If it's aall right with you, sur, I'll keep assumin' they *let* us aashore, and still mean to take *us* completely by surprise!" Blas said darkly.

"Quite right you should, Captain," Blair agreed. He motioned for an orderly and consulted a map the man held before him. He pointed at it. "Take your battalion north along the waterfront to this shipbuilding district. That's where your Eighth Maa-ni-la is landing. Make sure there are no surprises waiting for *them*!"

"Ay, ay, Col-nol Blair!" She turned. "First Sergeant Spook!" she called to a pale-furred 'Cat named Spon-Ar-Aak, who still considered himself primarily a gunner's mate on *Walker*. Chack-Sab-At had set the precedent for such dual identities, and it stuck. Spook belonged to A Company, but he'd fought the Doms before, and Blas used him almost like an exec. The young replacement lieutenants in her 2nd Battalion, 2nd Marines didn't mind. They knew they had much to learn, and the 2nd of the 2nd remained one of the most prestigious outfits in the Alliance, even if its sister battalion had practically ceased to exist in the West.

"Ay, Caap'n?" Spook replied, hurrying up.

"Start 'em moving toward the shipyard. We'll push out as big a perimeter as we can and wait for the Eighth to fill it in behind us!"

"Ay, ay!" He turned to the Marines. "Aall right! "You heard the caap'n! Column o' fours, at the quick time—haarch!"

Blas saluted Blair and followed her Marines.

"Remarkable creatures," volunteered Major Dao Iverson, 2nd Battalion, 6th Imperial Marines. The man was Blair's exec. His tone wasn't exactly condescending, but didn't match the esteem Blair held for Lemurian troops.

Blair glared at him. "Quite remarkable *people*, Major Iverson, and staunch allies when we desperately need them."

"Of course. Forgive me, Colonel Blair. No slight intended, and I know our allies' worth. It remains odd to me to see *females* in their ranks, however."

Blair had to agree with that, and sighed. "They'll be in *our* ranks soon enough, I shouldn't wonder, if we don't quickly finish this war. They're already on our support ships—and the warships of our allies." He smiled at Iverson. "We must convince ourselves that we fight to make a better world, for we can't—mustn't—remake the old. The treachery and evil that lurked unseen, even at home, is sufficient reason why we should not even want to do such a thing."

"Of course," Iverson repeated noncommittally. "What are your orders for my battalion?"

"No change. Push toward the fortress and ensure it truly is undefended. If it awakes, hold back and let the Navy's guns do their work before you launch your assault. We'll lose no more men than we must. You understand?"

"Perfectly."

"Then good luck to you."

Blair remained there for some time, watching more troops come ashore and listening to reports relayed by runners from all over the city. Aircraft finally appeared over the bay, scouting inland and northward, but they attacked nothing and there was still no significant resistance from any quarter. He could hardly believe they'd accomplished such overwhelming surprise, and given its proximity to the Enchanted Isles, Guayak should've been packed with troops. It really made no sense.

The streets remained largely empty as the sun's rays finally washed across them, but some of the natives were venturing out at last, gawking at the newcomers. Squads swept in to search homes and shops, ensuring the enemy hadn't simply hidden, waiting to spring forth at a predetermined time, but so far there was no evidence of that. More Dom troops were found, but they'd been hiding in fear, not anticipation, and nearly all were old men and boys, not prime Dom infantry. Most surrendered easily enough.

Blair turned to watch the progress of Iverson's battalion scaling the slope beneath the fortress west of town. There'd still been no shots fired there. He was frowning when he heard his name called, and he saluted General Tamatsu Shinya as the former Japanese naval officer approached with his staff.

"Good morning, General," Blair said.

"It is good," Shinya replied wryly. "Perhaps too good for comfort?"

"Indeed."

"What news?"

Blair nodded at another runner, just trotting off. "The comm 'Cats, as you call them, are stringing telegraph lines as we speak, and installing their wireless gear and other equipment in that impressive building there." He pointed at an elegant but scantly adorned hall. "We won't have to rely on runners much longer. Perhaps a hundred Dom troops have been captured, and we're trying to determine whether we can communicate with them. As you know, most Imperial officers have a smattering of Spanish, but the dialect here seems inconvenient."

"What of the civilians? Have you spoken to any of them?"

"I haven't, General, not yet. I just learned that some civil officials are forming a delegation to speak to us, however. I instructed that they be escorted to that building as well. I'm told there's a chamber within that should be suitable for a conference."

Shinya was looking at the HQ Blair had chosen. "I wonder what manner of building it is? There is some interesting architecture here."

Blair nodded. "Yes. Quite interesting. A great deal of stone is used, but the structures seem most ambitious. Arches and columns abound. At least here in the center of town. When we passed through the outlying areas, there were grass-and-mud huts. Quite a contrast. As for our HQ, it could be a government office, bank, even a church, for all I know. I haven't been inside." He paused, seeing Shinya's expression. "If it *is* a church, there was no evidence of any . . . unnatural acts having been performed inside," he assured him. "I specifically asked."

"Well, then," Shinya said, "shall we meet this delegation? Perhaps they can explain the situation here."

More than a dozen local men were brought to what they learned was a library of some kind. There were no books, but tens of thousands of parchmentlike scrolls were inserted into thousands of square partitioned slots built into every wall. The wooden dividers were richly stained and sealed and the scrolls appeared well tended and mostly new. Long tables were arrayed about the chamber where older scrolls were apparently being copied, and it was in this way, Shinya assumed, that they prevented the loss or degradation of the knowledge stored in this place. The men who joined them were dressed strangely in heavy, brightly colored robes that touched the floor around their sandals. A few wore odd headgear, but none wore anything as large and gaudy as the "pope hats" of the Blood Cardinals. In fact, there didn't appear to be any representatives of the twisted faith in attendance at all. That was fine, because one of the first acts performed in the building was to tear down a large, gold-painted perversion of the Christian cross and throw it in the street. The Dom cross reflected the warped nature of their faith, as far as the Imperials were concerned. It was a gnarled, twisted, knotty thing festooned with spikes and sharp, thorny carvings. The locals who entered the chamber would've had to step right over it, but showed no outrage or discomfort. To the utter amazement of all present, they actually wore broad smiles on their dark faces!

"I'm not sure what the devil we've gotten into here, General," Blair murmured into Shinya's ear.

Shinya's face reflected nothing, but he answered with a sharp, curt nod. "Who speaks for you?" he asked the delegation.

"I am Suares. I shall speak for my Lord Don Ricardo del Guayak, whose city you have liberated from the vile oppression of the Dominion," said a tall man, less well dressed than the others. "I was once a trader to your, ah, *la compañia*, though I prefer to think of myself as a savior of children, and am the only one in Guayak who has your tongue." He gestured at the others. "Nor do these great men speak the Spanish well. Our city has long clung tightly to older ways," he explained, then proceeded to name those present. Shinya nodded at them all, and bowed slightly when Don Ricardo was named.

"Very well," Shinya said after introducing himself and the officers present. "You may interpret for us. How long you do so depends on your absolute honesty. We have your city in our power and will leave it in ruins if we suspect you are lying to us about anything."

"Have no concern, General Shinya!" Suares exclaimed. "You are our liberators, friends! We will do anything we can to help!"

No one knew what they'd expected when they first set foot on Dominion soil, but no one ever dreamed of a friendly greeting.

"We shall see. Tell me, why are there so few Dominion troops here? Why is the fortress abandoned?"

Suares shrugged. "They left. Six days ago there were perhaps nine thousand warriors of his evil unholiness in and around Guayak, but they marched northeast up the military road toward Manizales." Shinya glanced at Blair, suddenly concerned for the thousand troops they'd landed at Quito, and Blair waved an orderly out to relay the news by wireless.

"Why?" Shinya demanded. "And they left almost no garrison at all? You must forgive my disbelief!"

"I do not lie," Suares assured. "Virtually the entire garrison marched away with the substantial force assembled here. Our overlords are arrogant, you see, and I admit even we"—he gestured at the rest of the delegation—"never dared hope you might actually come to this land." Suares seemed almost amused. "We have long been assured that no invader could possibly set foot on our sacred soil. He would burn! Ignite! The very earth would consume his bones with fire! All the blood priests swear to this, and though I did not believe it, we feared that *you* might!"

"That wicked Don Hernan often made such assertions," Blair remarked quietly, "when he was in the Empire. None considered it more than a pathetic boast."

"Clearly that's all it was," Shinya agreed wryly, noticing the fearful reactions of the locals to the mention of Don Hernan. Obviously, they knew who he was. "But just as clearly," he continued, "the people of this land did not think so. Never underestimate the delusional power of irrationality, or the wild lie told often enough with suitable conviction!"

Blair frowned at what sounded like a slight against all religion, and Shinya smiled. "No! Regardless of what I once believed, I've become quite spiritual. But I came to my beliefs down a most rational road." He looked back at Suares. "Why did the army march away?"

"To attack you, we assumed to our sorrow. From what we gleaned, a great fleet prepares to attack Las Islas de las Galápagos, and the army that left here was but a portion of what will board transports for that purpose. The intent is to cleanse you from Las Islas forever, before you grow too strong there."

"What fleet?" Blair demanded derisively. "We've destroyed it!"

Suares regarded him gravely. "We heard that as well, that you scoured the Western Sea of every Dominion warship you could find. Unfortunately, from our point of view, you cannot have found them all, because you could not know where to look." He sighed. "My country has many secrets, some very dark and terrible, some very old. Many of our oldest secrets involve the safety of my country, and even I voluntarily kept them all my life. But Nuevo Granada has soured into a rotten stone in the breast of my country, and the old ways are not only discouraged, as they have been for so long, but now stamped upon. Precious children are again offered in sacrifice to a god not even our own! They are *no one's* gods. They go only to pleasure *los papas*, who sacrifice them to *themselves* when they tire of them! It is abomination! Darkest, deepest evil!"

"A moment, please," Shinya said, holding up a hand. "What is Nuevo Granada?"

Suares looked at him. "Of course you would not know." He paused as if fighting a lifetime of conviction, then spoke. "It is the foremost city of the Dominion, where el Templo de los Papas stands. It is from there that all evil in the world radiates."

"Not *all* evil," Shinya muttered, thinking of the Grik.

"But we thought your capital was in the Valley of Mexico!" Blair exclaimed.

"Of course you would, and once it was. Apparently you have been deceived for over a hundred years. No mean feat."

"But, then, where *is* this Nuevo Granada?" Shinya demanded.

Suares shrugged. "Here. All of this province is a part, but the *city* lies perhaps fifteen hundred miles northeast, across the great mountains and the sea of leaves."

"Is there a map in this place?" Shinya demanded. "Show us!"

One of the men brought a scroll and spread it on the table. Shinya, Blair, and the other Allied officers leaned over to peer at the priceless piece of intelligence. One thing jumped out at them immediately. It was a small feature on the map, but it had remained utterly unknown or even suspected by anyone but the Doms for centuries, and it was suddenly clear where the Doms might keep a fleet of any size secret from the Empire forever.

"My God," Blair whispered.

"Yes," Shinya agreed. He rounded on Suares. "Could this fleet have sailed already?"

"I cannot know. The army that marched from here could not have reached it yet, but I do not know any specific plans."

"Well, what will the Doms do when they learn we've taken . . . that we've landed at this place?"

"They must take it back! Your very presence mocks their most profound delusions and assails their deepest beliefs! Most corrosively, it exposes the ultimate, oft-told lie you describe so well." He considered. "There is another consideration." He seemed to fidget. "Forgive me, but I must ask: what manner of creatures accompanies your force? The furred ones with tails?"

Shinya blinked. He was so accustomed to Lemurians now that he sometimes forgot to consider what those who weren't might think of them at first glance. "They're Lemurians, Mi-Anaaka. They're fine people who come from . . ." He paused. "Lands far to the west. They fight against the Dominion with the same conviction and determination as anyone."

"No doubt," Suares hedged, "but you are sure they are all from the West? None may have come from here?"

"Not to our knowledge or theirs," Shinya answered truthfully, and Suares seemed to sigh with relief. "Why?" Shinya demanded suspiciously.

"It only occurred to us that perhaps, just perhaps, some of the old legends were true, that they were jaguar warriors come to avenge themselves against those who do not revere their God." He looked nervously at his lord. "We in Guayak persecute no one for their beliefs; we all share the displeasure of the Temple! But, though most here do not, some still revere the jaguar of the Old World we were cast from for our sins. Some feared . . ." He shook his head. "You are sure?"

Shinya suppressed a smile. "I suppose one can never be *entirely* sure about such things. Who am I to ponder the means or intent of any god?

But I assure you, ferocious as our 'Cats can be in battle, they will harm no one based solely on their beliefs." Suares looked relieved, as did the rest of the delegation when he translated Shinya's words. "Now," Shinya prodded, "how will the Doms push us out?"

"I suspect the army that marched from here will be sent back. Such a move might delay their offensive against you in Las Islas, but they can raise troops more quickly from around Manizales than from here."

"Mr. Blair," Shinya snapped. "Send this out immediately! All of it!"

"What about the troops at Quito?"

"Have them pull out, back here for now, and advise Admiral Lelaa to order that squadron of DDs back from its scout toward Costa Rica. I think it's clear what the enemy has been hiding from us now!" He glanced at Suares. "If the enemy is gathering a great fleet there, I don't want three DDs to run into it."

"At once, General!"

"You . . . *will* stay here, will you not, General Shinya?" Suares suddenly pleaded.

"I don't know if we can," Shinya admitted.

"But if you abandon us, we are doomed!" Suares almost wailed. "Our women, our children—all will be slain simply because we *saw* you! It will not even matter what we might have said!"

"We'll consider that; you have my word," Shinya replied. "In the meantime, please talk with your people; assure them they have nothing to fear from us. Our only quarrel is with the Dominion that has made war on us, not the civilian population it oppresses. Return tomorrow, after we've had time to discuss what we've learned, and I promise we'll keep you informed." He stopped and looked at every member of the delegation, meeting each gaze. "And regardless of what we decide, we won't abandon you."

"What do you think?" Blair asked after the locals were gone. "Do you believe them?"

"Yes," Shinya said simply, then gestured at the countless scrolls and pointed at the map still on the table. "They didn't know we were coming, so I can't believe they prepared that just to deceive us! And based on that map, everything else suddenly makes a great deal of sense. Does it not?"

Blair nodded, frowning. "And Suares was plainly terrified that we'd leave them. But what shall we do? What *can* we do? Even if we gather all our forces here, we'll still be badly outnumbered unless we ask for more troops from High Admiral Jenks. I've no doubt we'll drub them soundly, even with what we have, but do we *want* a major battle here?"

"Admiral Jenks will have to decide, and he'll have to weigh it against the possibility that a very large force truly is preparing to attack the Enchanted Isles. That may limit the resources he can send to our aid, but I sense an opportunity. Based on what Mr. Suares said, it can't be good for the enemy's morale simply that we're here. If we can *defeat* him on his 'holy' soil, regardless how remote from his capital, word will spread. It always does. How will he react to *that*? I, for one, would enjoy finding out." His eyebrows furrowed. "One thing is certain: Whatever Admiral Jenks decides, we can't leave these people undefended. I'm convinced Suares spoke the truth when he said they'd be slaughtered. Not only does it fit what we know of the character of our enemy, but it makes a twisted sense from his perspective—and *we* brought that fate to the people here. If we stay, we fight—and we shall enlist as many locals as we can to help. Word of rebellion will also spread, and can't hurt our cause." He shrugged. "If we leave, however, we must take as many of them with us as we can. I see no alternative if we're not to be thought as wicked as the Doms ourselves."

CHAPTER

26

///// *Near El Paso del Fuego*
New Granada Province (Costa Rica)
Holy Dominion

Captain Anson was still sitting on his horse, inserting paper-wrapped cartridges of powder and ball into the front of the cylinder of his big revolver. Each time he slid a cartridge in place, he rotated the cylinder to cram the whole thing into the chamber with a lever mounted beneath the barrel. Periodically, he glanced up and down the trail.

"Do hurry, if you please," he grumbled, lightly pinching what Fred Reynolds recognized as small versions of Allied percussion caps before pushing them onto little cones at the rear of each chamber. Finished loading, he didn't reholster the weapon, but continued to watch while Fred and Kari-Faask quickly pillaged two Dom cavalrymen. Their horses had bolted, and the riderless beasts would be just as damning as the shots if they were discovered, but Fred said nothing as he tugged the faded yellow coat off the dead man at his feet.

"Why are you stripping him?" Anson hissed. "Just take his weapons and let's be off!"

"In case you haven't noticed, I'm just about naked!" Fred countered. His robe had remained his only garment throughout their long ordeal and had deteriorated badly, leaving him covered with welts and sores. Kari wasn't much better off, but at least she had protective fur. She'd shed a lot, though, and it wasn't as thick as when they were flying. "Get that one's clothes too," Fred instructed her.

"Why?"

Fred blushed. 'Cats had no qualms about running around practically nude, but though Kari never did it just to aggravate him, like Tabby used to do to Spanky, her very feminine shape could be distracting at times. "They might come in handy," he said at last. "If more Dom cav spots us, it could help at a glance, from a distance. Maybe they'll think we're Doms too."

Kari considered. "Okay," she said, and began stripping the other man.

Fred's excuse seemed to mollify Anson as well because he quit prodding them, but he did warn that the uniforms were as likely to get them killed by the locals as the Doms.

They quickly finished and dragged the corpses into the brush bordering the track. Scavengers would eliminate any trace of them before long. Fred adjusted the cartridge box and sword belt around his waist and checked the short musket he'd retrieved to ensure it was undamaged, loaded, and the priming powder hadn't spilled when it fell. Satisfied, he climbed back on his horse, as Kari did the same. Kari looked very odd in her blood-spattered Dom coat, but he reflected again that at a distance, they might pass for the enemy. Better than they would have before! "Okay," he announced.

Anson snorted, but urged his horse back toward the narrow trail they'd emerged from just a short time before—right in the face of the enemy scouts. Anson had killed both men before they even had a chance to raise their weapons, and that had elevated Fred's estimate of their guide's usefulness even further, but he still harbored a deep suspicion of the enigmatic man. When they'd retreated a considerable distance back into the dense jungle, they paused for a while.

"This is no good," Anson suddenly announced, frustrated. He looked at Fred. "I expected them to hunt you, but not like this! We've been dodging patrols incessantly, and the closer we get to our goal, the worse it gets. They're quite clearly certain of our objective." There was no doubt about that now, and worse, they'd passed a small river village that had been utterly exterminated, apparently for no other reason than it was suspected they may have stopped there. "They're not giving up, and they're obviously willing to kill anyone who might help us or even talk to us! It's madness!" He looked hard at Fred. "Just what the devil did you learn about them that they'd go to such lengths?"

Fred shifted. "I guess I'm not really sure. I learned a lot, but I don't know how much would be secret from their own people . . . except . . ."

"Except what?" Anson demanded. Fred just looked at him. "I'll tell you every last thing I know if you promise to shoot straight with us for once! Tell me why those other guys wanted Kari so bad and why we need to make it to that particular little town you talked about. Finally, I want to know just who the hell you *are*, Captain Anson!"

Anson seemed to think long and hard, then finally nodded. "I'll tell you what I may, but our destination has changed. It's clearly impossible to take you where I wanted, so we must go somewhere they won't expect. In fact, your new wardrobe has given me a rather bold thought." He shrugged that away. "Deviating from my original plan also eliminates any possibility of reuniting young Kari-Faask with the people who wanted her, though, so their part in this is of no further consequence. I will tell you they very likely didn't mean her any harm, though."

"Very likely?" Fred demanded. "That was good enough for you?"

"Yes! Good enough for my mission to gain their trust!" Anson took a breath. "I suppose I succeeded in that, for what good it will do. Perhaps some of our party survived and word will spread that they have friends. The Christians in our party already knew that, but they put me in contact with the others. It was, in fact, the Christians who fought to allow the Jaguaristas to escape."

"Jaguaristas?"

"A cult of the old gods, opposed to the Doms. They're somewhat radical fellows, but brave enough—and pervasive enough to be of use."

"For what?"

"Why, to annoy the Doms, of course." Anson urged his horse forward.

"Where we going?" Kari asked.

"A city. A Dom city, where I hope you can steal a boat and take your news to your Second Fleet. There's no alternative now. At this point, I'd say it's just as important for your people as it is for mine to learn what intelligence you have."

"So you're *not* an Imperial!" Fred declared, almost triumphantly, and Anson smiled.

"No."

"Then who the hell are you?"

"Language, Lieutenant Reynolds! You're, what, seventeen years old?"

Fred colored. "I'm nineteen, for what difference it makes. Who are you?"

"I'll reveal that after you tell me everything you know."

"There, at last, is El Paso del Fuego," Captain Anson exclaimed, as they eased out of the jungle into the edge of a sloping meadow overlooking the sea. The sun was plunging down amid golden, vaporous clouds, but great billows of cloud streamed high in the sky above them, reflecting another, redder sun that seemed to have fallen to earth across the water to the north. It rested there, pulsing fitfully, atop the highest mountain Fred had ever seen.

"A volcano!" Fred gasped, looking up. And up. The thing was so tall, there was snow two-thirds of the way up its flanks. "And it's spectacular!"

"It is," Anson agreed, "but it has already diverted your attention from the greater marvel, which is the most important intelligence you can possibly relay to your people. Look at the sea."

Fred and Kari did. There was a city below them, large and sprawling, with many, many ships anchored near. Even as they watched, more ships swept quickly toward them from the east, beyond their view. Some were steamers, towing bare-poled juggernauts of a hundred guns or more, but they moved amazingly fast, perhaps ten knots. Fred was confused.

"The steamers are essentially tugs," Anson explained grimly, "that keep the ships of the line in the channel. They add little to the speed of their passage. Particularly against a contrary wind."

"What channel?" Fred asked quietly. He still couldn't grasp it.

"This whole area is amazingly volcanic. You've remarked on the tremors before. What you see is the result of that—or perhaps something else. Our scientific fellows can't agree. Some say it was caused by a momentous eruption some thousands, perhaps millions, of years ago. Others propose a celestial body, a great meteor perhaps, once struck here." He grimaced. "I'm skeptical of that, but it doesn't really matter. The point is, this feature did not appear on any of the maps we brought to this world, nor, I daresay, did you expect to see it."

"What feature?" Fred demanded, but things were beginning to knit.

"An equatorial passage," Anson stated simply. "A canal. A strait, if you will, between the continents. A *navigable* strait, at the proper times of day or month. The tidal surge is most impressive, as you can see. No steamer I know can move against its flood, much less a sailing ship."

"But ships . . ." Fred paused in horror. "My God! The Doms have their own damn Panama Canal—in Costa Rica! An entire *fleet* can make transit with the tide from the Atlantic to the Pacific Ocean."

"Or back the other way," Anson agreed, wondering what Fred meant about Panama. "They can't move many through at once, of course. If the tide should turn on a ship within the pass, it would almost certainly be wrecked. I've seen that." He shrugged. "There is a bay of sorts about halfway through the passage where ships may pause at need, but even there the currents are amazingly treacherous." He looked at Fred and Kari. "This is the gift I give you and your Alliance: the knowledge of this place. As you can see, whatever damage you've inflicted on the Dominion fleet is quickly dwindling to nothing."

Fred gulped.

Anson smiled. "It's not all bad. Every ship that comes through here is one less that my people must face in the East, and our Navy will take advantage of that."

"Your Navy?" Kari managed. She wasn't quite as stunned as Fred, but, then, she knew nothing of the way the world *should* be. She learned it only as it was.

Anson ignored the question, but pointed down at the sprawling city. Lights were beginning to gleam in the gathering darkness. "That," he said, "is El Corazon del Fuego. There you must steal a boat. Perhaps, in the darkness, your borrowed uniforms will help."

"What about you?" Fred asked, but Anson shook his head.

"I must make another way, to report what you told me to my own people. You're on your own from here. All I can advise is that you not be caught. Your knowledge of the true nature of the Dom faith and their ambition to eradicate all others—even among their own—certainly explains why they've spared nothing to capture you, but it gives us little military advantage other than propaganda. What *is* useful is that they know about the Grik."

Fred flushed.

"It's not your fault! No one resists the Cleansing. No one. It's a miracle you're sane. But knowing that *they* know is utterly critical information, for your people and mine, if the Grik are as terrible an enemy as you say."

"They are."

"Then there's that. There's also the fact that not only have you met the 'Emperor of the World,' but you told me exactly where he is. We suspected, of course, but couldn't know." He grimaced. "It's almost too obvious, but the Doms are nothing if not arrogant."

"Who's we?" Fred finally demanded, and Anson sighed and looked at him, frowning. "I did promise, didn't I? Well, your people will likely discover it soon enough if they have any success against the Doms— which I pray they do—so it seems only sensible that the news should not come as a complete surprise to either side. Surprises can be such awkward things." He glanced at the setting sun. "I must be brief, and there's no time to describe the adventure of my people to this point, but . . ." He looked at Fred, and a crooked smile creased his weathered face. "You and I are . . . cousins, in a sense." He turned to Kari. "And after coming to know you and learning your tale, as well as the circumstances of your Alliance, I'm personally pleased to call you cousin as well, though some of my people may hesitate at that." He stared back at Fred. "You see, you're not the only Americans to find themselves in this world."

"I knew it!" Fred exclaimed, then his eyes narrowed. "But you talk so weird!"

Anson chuckled. "As do you, my friend, but it would seem our primary difference is one of time. To be more precise, the different Americas we left behind. You're relative newcomers, arriving what, two years ago?"

Fred nodded.

"Whereas my people," Anson continued, "found ourselves in this world in the year—as I assume we both reckon such things—1847."

"But where . . . how?" Fred stammered.

"I assume the how of it was much the same as for you," Anson replied. "'Where' was during a dreadful storm off the east coast of Mexico. The United States, you may or may not recall"—he looked strangely at Fred—"was at war with Mexico at the time, and our grandfathers were preparing an invasion at Vera Cruz. Three of our ships, much like your Imperial friends', I understand, suddenly found themselves, well, somewhere else." He grimaced. "Quite traumatically 'somewhere else,' in our case, since the Yucatán Peninsula is considerably larger on this world than our old charts showed. One of our three ships found itself suddenly hard aground in the surf! I take it you know nothing of the Atlantic, or the peoples and creatures on the far side of the world from you?"

Fred shook his head, wide-eyed.

"That makes us even, since we know nothing of *your* side of the world! Perhaps if our people can be friends, we may learn much from one another."

"But . . . where are your . . . other Americans?" Fred demanded. "Obviously you're not in Yucatán. I didn't really know about this strait"—he gestured northward—"but I did get a pretty good idea what the Dominion claims and about where their frontiers are."

"I notice you understand the difference between the two." Anson grinned.

"Yeah. They *claim* everything they know about!"

"Then for now, consider us north of their frontier. I do have reason to be somewhat vague."

"Los Diablos del Norte," Fred whispered.

"That's what they call us," Anson agreed with a smile. "We've been fighting them since the day we met, and even briefly conquered their capital—their old capital—but there were always so many of them and we had so little real advantage other than training, discipline, and our artillery, of course. Eventually, we abandoned our gains and retreated north, where we could reestablish our country and extend their lines of supply. We've remained at war with the Dominion from that day to this, but as we grew stronger, they focused elsewhere."

"The Empire?"

Anson nodded. "You would expect us to be natural allies, but the Empire has always been weak on land and we didn't trust them. So corrupt!" He looked doubtfully at Fred. "They truly have changed?"

Fred nodded. "It wasn't painless either."

"Hmm. In any event, we've watched them a very long time, but I doubt they know of us. We claim nothing west of a range of mountains in what was once called the Great American Desert, but we know they claim everything east of their colonies, in the same way the British always did such things."

Fred didn't ask how Anson knew that, but assumed "his" Americans had spies in Saint Francis. It made sense, and nobody would suspect them.

"We have no quarrel with the Empire and would like to keep it that way, but conflicting territorial claims can be provocative, and our disputes with the Doms—and others—are quite enough to keep us occupied at present."

"Others?"

Anson shook his head sadly. "Let it suffice for now that our United

States are not so vast as you might remember, and we've other frontiers of our own. Our grandfathers were lucky to carve out what they did and still retain their national identity."

Why is Anson still so vague? Fred wondered. *Does he fear some of his country's other enemies might prove more attractive allies, to the Imperials, at least? Or are they even more frightening than the Doms—or Grik? Or is it just that his United States is so small and weak that he couldn't, wouldn't admit it?*

"So," Kari said, "you tell us this, knowing we will tell our people if we reach them. What made you reveal so much at last?"

Anson shrugged. "We three have become friends, I hope. Perhaps it's time that all our people did. The Dominion is genuinely evil, and I'm prepared to recommend to my people that we seize this chance, any chance, to aid in its destruction!"

"But if we split up, with no way of contacting each other, how can we ever work together?" Fred asked, but Anson smiled. "I haven't made any recent reports, but the last I sent, even before we rescued Kari, implied that I would seek this understanding—if I was comfortable about what I learned of you. And if I live for the next few days, my superiors will know my opinion quite swiftly, I assure you. Your superiors will know what mine decide somewhat longer after that, but it won't take months."

"I get it," Fred muttered. "Don't call us; we'll call you."

"Something like that." Anson stood in his stirrups. "One last thing," he warned, pointing westward. "Do you see those islands out there? Little but vague, black shapes in this light."

"I see them," Kari said.

"They're not islands," Anson told them.

"My God, they're mountain fish!" Fred exclaimed.

"Is that what you call them? Appropriate as anything, I suppose. In any event, even after you escape El Corazon, you must get past them. We believe they gather here with their young, on both sides of the strait, after giving birth somewhere else. You should be safe, since they do little here but feed off the things the strait carries into their mouths, but beware. The cows barely move, replenishing their bodies, but the young can be inquisitive. A small boat may attract their attention." He paused for a long moment, staring at them both in the gloom, while Fred and Kari absorbed this latest obstacle. Finally, he held out a hand. "God bless you both," he said. "Perhaps we'll meet again someday." He grinned. "I would dearly love a ride in one of your flying machines!" With that, he turned his horse and vanished back into the jungle.

Mar
Antillas

Puerto
Limon

Peña

Puerto
Domino

Boca Caribe

Río
Grabación

Nicoya

Puntarenas

La
Calma

Aguas
Rápidas

Abismado

El Corazón

Océano
Pacífico

Gran Mar
del
Sur

Puerto
Salvación

El Mapa
de
El Paso del Fuego

////// USS **Walker**
Andaman Sea
May 12, 1944

U SS *Walker* and her odd little squadron approached
Andaman Island from the southeast. They'd spent
two days at Aryaal, where Surabaya should've
been, refueling and "tightening bolts," as Spanky
called it, on the collection of rebuilt and refitted
ships. It was the first time Matt had been there
since it started coming back to life, and he'd been
amazed by how much had been done. B'mbaado City was alive again as
well, but most of the island across the water had reverted to the wild,
and Aryaal remained the focus of industry and restoration. It was interesting to him that it took their current, terrible war to erase the enmity
between Aryaal and B'mbaado, and with the acknowledged rulers of
both places, General Lord Muln-Rolak and General Queen Protector
Safir Maraan as devoted to one another as father and daughter, the two

city-states had practically merged. Both rulers were currently trapped within Alden's Perimeter beyond Madras, however, and the yard workers at Aryaal had surged aboard *Walker*, *Mahan*, and S-19 to perform whatever work needed to get the three ships off to relieve their beloved leaders.

Mahan needed the most care. The trip from Baalkpan had been her and S-19's "shakedown" cruise, and a lot had been shaken loose on both. *Mahan*'s new bow and hull shape were sound enough, even if she didn't like the swells as much, but her two remaining boilers were shaken up by the rough ride, and her engines acted a little unhappy. The yard workers spent all day and night putting her to rights. S-19 had performed surprisingly well considering how squat and ugly she was. Laumer had redesigned her to look something like the sleek torpedo boats of old, but he hadn't quite pulled it off, and she slammed through the waves more than riding over them. Considerably lighter even with her additions, she'd easily made the roughly eighteen knots the squadron averaged from Baalkpan, however. She leaked though, at least in her new upper works, where her enlarged crew's berthing spaces were. Those structures had been bolted on, and at Aryaal, the seams were repacked and the bolts retightened. Neither *Mahan* nor S-19 reported any other serious problems during their transit of the Malacca Strait or a somewhat tumultuous Andaman Sea, and Matt had watched with a critical eye the two strange ships steaming alongside *Walker*. They *did* look strange. *Mahan* was shorter by about forty feet and had only two boilers and two stacks. Her new bridge structure—looking just like her old one—was built directly onto the forward part of her amidships gun platform. She was several hundred tons lighter, so her speed wasn't much affected, but she couldn't carry as much fuel either. Hopefully, having only two boilers would even that out. What couldn't even out was the fact that with four 4-inch-50s, two triple-tube torpedo mounts, and a scout-plane catapult aft, just like *Walker*'s, *Mahan* still needed nearly as large a crew as she ever had, and there wasn't as much space to put them.

S-19, or, maybe more appropriately now, STB-19 really did hark back to the old turn-of-the-century torpedo boats. She had a flush deck with a spray shield forward of her four-inch-fifty gun. Behind that, a tall foremast that could supposedly support a sail if necessary ended beneath a skinny crow's nest for a lookout that resembled a bucket on top of a pole. Next was an enclosed pilothouse in the center of an elevated flying bridge, and a single, thin exhaust funnel for her diesels was just behind it. Aft was another tall mast and *Walker*'s old three-inch antiaircraft gun on a slightly elevated platform. That was it, except for a few gooseneck vents for the new berthing spaces. Laumer had done everything he could to keep his boat's profile as low and light as possible, and Matt had to admit she made a much better torpedo boat than he'd ever thought she would. He frankly doubted she'd be as effective as the purpose-built PTs Saan-Kakja had built in Maa-ni-la, but they were already headed southwest, toward Diego, aboard the SPD (self-propelled dry dock) *Respite Island*. *And S-19 does have that deck gun,* he reminded himself, *and sonar and a far greater range.* And, apparently, she could go anywhere *Walker* could. He might have to change his opinion of her.

"What are your thoughts?" asked Adar, joining him by his captain's chair in *Walker*'s pilothouse. Matt smiled. "Just pondering our little squadron, Mr. Chairman," he replied. "It's nice to be steaming with *Mahan* again, such as she is. The yard apes in Baalkpan did a swell job on her." He hesitated, glancing at the distant coast of Andaman. "I'm also worried we've got too many precious eggs in one basket again." The stampede of veteran destroyermen, 'Cat and human, who'd vied for billets on the three ships had been like a VFW reunion, and almost no one had been refused. The result was a severe shakeup in the Allied command staff, not to mention the family atmosphere aboard *Walker*.

Commander Perry Brister, Minister of Defensive and Industrial Works at Baalkpan, had gone to command his old *Mahan* again, and Chief Bosun's Mate Carl Bashear swallowed his pride and took the jump to lieutenant to be Brister's exec. Sonarman Jeff Brooks had perfected the sonar sets in use by the entire Alliance as its primary AMF-DIC (Anti-Mountain Fish Countermeasures), and stepped in as *Mahan*'s first lieutenant and quartermaster. Rolando "Ronson" Rodriguez became her CEM. Ensign Johnny Parks was engineering officer, and Paul Stites agreed to take over gunnery. Taarba-Kar—"Tabasco"—wouldn't have to suffer under Lanier's heel anymore, because he'd gone to *Mahan* as cook. He'd had Diania to help him settle in too, since Sandra had crossed as *Mahan*'s surgeon. The two of them, with Adar, would move to *Big Sal* at Andaman. A lot of *Walker*'s most experienced Lemurians went to *Mahan* too, and Matt had mixed feelings about that. He knew *Mahan* would need them, but he missed them already. He missed Sandra most of all.

Aboard *Walker*, Chief Gray seamlessly stepped back into his chief bosun's shoes, and Silva would do the same with gunnery if he made it to Andaman in time. Isak Rueben would have to get used to being chief engineer, with no buffer between him and Tabby at all. But having lost so many fine destroyermen, *Walker* got the cream of the latest draft and Matt was confident his own crew would be fine. Bernard Sandison had rejoined, responsible for *Walker*'s new torpedoes, and was still rewiring the torpedo directors on the bridgewings and mercilessly training new torpedo 'Cats—and women!—to augment the well-drilled crews he'd dispersed between the ships. Matt hadn't thought of anything for Commander Herring to do, although he seemed competent to stand a bridge watch. Herring had left his assistant, Henry Stokes, back in Baalkpan to continue his snoop work, but he'd brought Lance Corporal Ian Miles along. Miles had been helping Bernie in ordnance, so Spanky assigned him to Campeti. Courtney Bradford was delighted to be back aboard and acted like he'd never left. Matt was seriously concerned with how many critical minds were steaming back into harm's way, but his most pressing worry was the presence of Adar himself. He mentioned it again, standing next to him, as they drew closer to Andaman.

Adar waved the objection away. "Alan Letts will make an excellent interim chairman, probably better than I ever could, and he knows much more about this melding of Homes. He still has Mr. Riggs and others to help him, not to mention all the Mi-Anaaka who share the dream." He shook his head. "And honestly, I am not entirely sure how I feel about that. A true union of the Allied Homes strikes me as a necessary thing, but I do long for the old ways as well." He sighed. "No, it is time for me to go Home, to *Salissa*, and share these battles with my brother Keje." He blinked at Matt. "Besides, if you are right, these campaigns could change the face of the war we fight and I must see that done. The last I saw of this war was the Battle of Baalkpan, and it has changed so much that I do not know it anymore." He paused. "I remain Chairman of the Grand Alliance and intend to guide the policy—the overall straa-ti-gee of the war, but I learned a great lesson from Mr. Letts. He went to the war and saw it for himself. As a result, he became better at his job." He blinked firmly. "It is time I did the same."

"As long as you think Alan's up to it," Matt murmured doubtfully, not because he had reservations about Letts, but because he wasn't sure how his interim appointment would be received. "And there's still everyone else—so many irreplaceable guys. . . ."

Adar looked at him. "Cap-i-taan Reddy," he said softly, "your people—our people—have performed miracles, and, without exception, have passed on the knowledge of how to do so. The home front, as you call it, will not miss us. It runs itself now, or Mr. Letts does." He blinked amusement. "You know that most new innovations or improvements are suggested by Mi-Anaaka now? They take what you gave them and look at it from all directions, not burdened by preconceptions. It is maarvelous!"

Matt nodded. "It is," he agreed. "And though I'm sure my old crew still has stuff knocking around in their heads that it hasn't occurred to them to write down or tell anybody about, there's not really much farther we can take you technologically than we have. Even when my old guys didn't know how to do something, they told yours what they knew was possible. That's more than half the fight." He took a breath. "No, you're right. None of us are indispensable anymore. It's just . . . I've lost so many of the old guys, it breaks my heart to lose any more, especially to risk so many at once."

"We risk much on the campaign you have designed," Adar allowed, "but we risk *all* for the war, and we must win it. You are terribly wrong about one thing, however: there remains one indispensable person, without whom I cannot even imagine victory."

Matt looked at Adar, surprised, and blinked a question in the Lemurian way.

"Why, you of course, Cap-i-taan Reddy!"

* * *

Dennis Silva, Lawrence, Pam Cross, and a big Marine named Arnold Horn, whom Matt had been told to expect, were standing on the dock when *Walker* crept near with the sunset. Many others were present, but those four stood somewhat apart. Silva and Pam were separated by Lawrence and Horn, and Matt didn't know what he hoped that meant. Pam Cross would be *Walker*'s surgeon, but she and Silva had once shared—with Risa-Sab-At, apparently—an epic romance of some sort that remained amusing to some and horrifying to others. But the word now was that Pam hated Silva's guts. Matt didn't really care what their current relationship was as long as it didn't affect his ship. He and Courtney were leaning on the port bridgewing rail, and Matt raised his gaze to encompass all that "Port Blair" at Andaman Island had become. He and *Walker* had never been this far west in the war. Everything this side of Singapore was new to nearly everyone aboard, as a matter of fact, and all were amazed by what they saw. Unlike anything the Allies had yet constructed, Andaman had become one massive military installation. There were civilians, certainly, and the surrounding hills that sloped down to the bay were planted with crops. That just made sense. But every activity on Andaman Island was focused on defeating the Grik.

Pipes trilled, and sandaled feet stampeded about the deck. The steel was much too hot to stand on unprotected. "Stand by lines there," Chief Gray began, then stopped. "Oh, goddamn it!" he roared, glaring accusingly back at the pilothouse. "Fend off, you useless lubbers!" he bellowed back at the detail.

Herring had the conn and he'd botched the approach. Not badly enough to risk damage, so Matt hadn't intervened, but enough to embarrass himself. Matt shrugged mentally. Herring wanted to learn, and it was better to be embarrassed learning to handle the ship here than during combat.

"Oh, look!" Bradford exclaimed. "It's Lawrence!" He waved his trademark sombrero briskly. "Hello! Hello!"

"Heave the bowline," Gray shouted.

"I'll take the conn, Mr. Herring," Matt finally said, stepping back inside the pilothouse.

"Captain has the conn," Herring replied with apparent relief.

"Right full rudder," Matt stated.

"Right full rudder, ay," answered the 'Cat at the big brass wheel. He'd been blinking anxiously, but now he stopped.

"Starboard ahead one-third."

"One-turd, ay!"

Matt smiled, almost chuckled, but felt the ship twist and groan beneath his feet, and may have heard the churning water push them sideways toward the dock, even over the blower. "All stop," he commanded.

"All stop, ay," repeated the 'Cat. And Matt stepped back out to see. Three heavy lines arced out to the dock, caught by parties of handlers who heaved the ship closer to the dock, then whipped the lines over the cleats.

"Singled up fore and aft!" the Bosun called up at the bridge.

"You have the deck, Mr. McFarlane," Matt said to Spanky, who'd just arrived from aft. "Have the Bosun assemble his side party. The gangplank's coming aboard, and there's some fellas down there I'm anxious to see."

"I have the deck, Skipper," Spanky agreed.

Gray's side party was already waiting when Matt took the stairs two at a time, and as soon as the gangplank was secure, it rumbled with approaching visitors. Matt glanced aft where *Mahan* was nosing in, and was anxious to see Sandra too. He turned back just as Admiral Keje-Fris-Ar appeared before him. The reddish brown Lemurian still looked like a bear, but his fur was shot through with a lot more silver than Matt remembered, and even in his white Navy tunic and bright copper armor he considered his dress uniform, Matt could see he'd lost a lot of weight. Matt saluted crisply.

Keje returned the salute and saluted the Stars and Stripes standing out to leeward on the mainmast, aft. Then before Matt could object or avoid it, Keje embraced him as he'd always done.

"I have *missed* you, my brother," Keje said fervently. "We all have."

"I've missed you too," Matt acknowledged truthfully.

"How is your wound?"

Matt held out his cane. "I barely need this anymore."

"Good! By the Heavens, do we need you!"

Adar appeared behind him, and he and Keje embraced as well. Then the deck filled with many faces, all happy, and Matt found himself standing in front of Jim Ellis. Jim was a commodore now, but he'd been Matt's first exec and remained his oldest surviving friend.

"Hi, Skip!" Jim said grinning, and Matt could see the wires holding his jaw clenched shut. He'd broken it in the Battle of Madras.

Matt held up his cane. "We're falling apart," he laughed.

"Nah." It was surprising how well Jim had learned to talk without moving his jaw. His lip movement was extremely exaggerated, but he'd had plenty of practice by now.

Matt pointed at the wires. "How much longer?"

"Just another week or so," Jim assured him, looking around at the ship. "God, it's good to see the old girl!" He grinned again. "Hello, Mr. Bradford! Named any worms lately? Hiya, Campeti! Jeez, Juan, where's the rest of you?"

"I guess you saw *Mahan*?" Matt asked.

"Sure," Jim nodded, looking back at him. She'd been his first command, and he'd been at her helm during the death ride that sank her. "I never would've believed it," he added. "She looks a little weird, though."

"Yeah. Brister's got her."

"Good choice. I also saw that Laumer kid finally came up with something to do with his old S-boat. Will she be any good for anything?"

"I think so. If the new torpedoes work." Matt gestured at Sandison. "Bernie swears they will—if we can get inside two thousand yards."

Jim frowned. "That's awful close, Skipper," he warned, shaking Bernie's hand. "Those Grik battlewagons have damn big guns. They blew completely through *Dowden* at nearly that range."

Matt nodded somberly. "We'll just have to give them other things to worry about, won't we?"

Jim was looking down the dock at S-19. "*Santy Cat* sails tomorrow, to join First Fleet North," he said, using the new nickname for his flagship. "If S-Nineteen's ready to go, let me take her with us. I like the idea of having something that can shoot torpedoes, until *Walker* and *Mahan* join us. And if we mix it up, *Santy Cat*'s got the firepower to keep the Grik off her."

Matt considered. "Sure," he said. "Laumer's raring to go, and he didn't report any casualties." He scratched his chin. "Of course, he might not have either. Talk to him yourself, and if you're sure he's not hiding anything that might reflect poorly on his brainchild, take him with you. *Walker*, *Mahan*, and *Big Sal*'s battle group won't be far behind."

The elements Matt described would soon constitute the core of First Fleet South, and they'd escort a small fleet of oilers, transports, and ammunition and supply ships to Trin-con-lee a few days later, after final alterations to *Salissa* were complete. She was being modified with the complicated arresting gear that would allow her to recover Fleashooters, if she had to, and was ferrying a squadron of the planes to beef up Ben Mallory's 3rd Pursuit.

"Swell," Jim said. "I'll give him the third degree—and who knows? Maybe we'll get to find out how well the new torpedoes work before you do!"

"Cap-i-taan Reddy!" Keje boomed, so all could hear. "As always, you and *Waa-kur* arrive just in time! We have already made most of the dispositions your plan described, and much of the fleet has already sailed. Soon the rest of us will sail to do our part and relieve Gener-aal Aalden at last. But tonight there is an . . . entertainment! A party! We will have fun! We will dance and drink beer and seep to celebrate our reunion"— he grinned—"and your long-delayed mating as well, Cap-i-taan! Where is the Lady Saan-dra?"

Oh, Lord, Matt thought, *he's already calling her that too! I guess with wireless . . .* He pointed at *Mahan*, and Keje blinked. "Oh yes," he said, deeply serious. "The regulations. I suppose that if you write them, then you must surely follow them yourself. And perhaps it is best?" he speculated doubtfully. Then he laid his hands on Matt's shoulders. "Come, let us meet *Mahaan* and your mate. We will speak of killing Grik," he added with a snarl. "Soon, we shall leave to do it—together again!"

*   *   *

The Admiral's Ball ranked fairly high on Dennis Silva's "weirdest shit I've seen while sober" list, at least at first glance. But in his defense, he didn't stay entirely sober long. Everybody was in Navy whites or Marine blues, even the 'Cats, and it was a stiffly formal affair. There was no division between officers and enlisted, but a shore patrol hovered along the fresh-cut walls of the long, wide hall, prepared to quickly usher any troublemakers away. Dennis had promised Pam not to be one of those, but they'd also agreed they probably needed to keep their makeup secret if they both wanted to be on *Walker*. That made it tough; watching Pam dance with Commodore Ellis, Campeti, even Keje. Gunny Horn tried a dance with her, but it was a quick tune and he was still sore from having a ship fall on him. That was his excuse, anyway, and the story was already getting around. He wound up bowing out and going to talk with some 'Cat Marines.

Oddly, there were plenty of women, but few had a clue how to dance. Dennis tried it with the few who were willing, but nearly destroyed them. He did have a whirl with Surgeon Commander Kathy McCoy, assigned to *Santa Catalina* for the impending operation, and then started a dance with that Diania gal, who still remained somewhat suspicious of him for some reason. But to Silva's surprise, Chief Gray snatched her away with an angry glare and kept her to himself most of the night. Dennis gave up and took two mugs of beer and sat on a bench by the wall with Lawrence, pretending the beers were the two they'd been allowed—and the only two he'd had.

"The sounds are strange," Lawrence observed. "Kinda like at the Screw, just not on records."

"Yeah," Silva grumped. "There's a live band here, and I knew no good would ever come of mixin' 'Cat music with ours." Actually, though he wouldn't admit it, the sound wasn't really that bad. Lemurian music, at least what he'd heard, used strings, drums, and some kind of woodwind. 'Cats couldn't do horns at all. Traditionally, it had a slow, jazzy thing going, and the melodies rarely repeated. That was giving way to the easier to learn, catchier American tunes—swing, mostly—and the idea of repeated melodies and a chorus was catching on. The result was still weird, but tolerable, and the band played a lot of songs Silva recognized. And there *were* horns tonight, and a fiddle brought by some of the guys who'd sometimes played at the Busted Screw and helped invent this new sound, but were now back with the fleet. Dennis started stamping his foot when the band struck up "Your Feets Too Big." The old, pump organ they'd pulled out of S-19 was still back at the Screw in Baalkpan, but there was a well-tuned copy here—*And God knows where else, now,* Dennis thought. He started talk-singing a passable Fats Waller impression and realized he was enjoying himself.

Walker and *Mahan* wouldn't sail at dawn, but there was a lot of work still to do on *Salissa*, rigging the elaborate cable traps on her flight deck. *Mahan* needed a few more repairs as well, and all the crews were going to pitch in on both ships, so they'd taken their liberty by divisions. Silva hadn't—exactly—reported aboard, but everyone knew he was there. Sooner or later somebody would realize that Ordnance had already rotated back to the ship. The music stopped, and he sighed.

"C'mon, Larry. Let's go see what all they screwed up on our ship while we was off a-heeroin' again." He turned—and there was Pam. The band started a slow waltz, and Dennis suddenly realized the tune was "Marchena," one of his secret favorites. With a deep breath, he forgot Lawrence and moved toward the dark-haired nurse from Brooklyn.

"Marchena" had been a great favorite of many Asiatic Fleet and China hands, and despite the weird instruments, unusual companions, and, frankly, the musty smell, Matt suddenly felt transported back to a dim dance floor in Manila, in the old Philippines. The sensation didn't last because he'd never danced there with a woman he loved, and Sandra's thrilling, delightful form in his arms brought him straight back to the present. But even though Sandra had never been to the Philippines, she seemed to catch the mood.

"I wish they wouldn't play it so slow," she whispered against his neck. "It sounds so sad somehow." Matt didn't say anything, but held her closer. Over the top of his wife's head he saw Gray leading Diania through the steps. Beyond him, Keje was dancing very carefully, very appropriately, with a stunning Lemurian Naval aviatrix who clearly knew the steps better than he. Matt turned Sandra and gazed around some more. He didn't want to pay attention to anything but her, but the dancers, their steps, and some of the odd pairings were just so damn interesting. He almost did a double take when he saw a tall man with a black eye patch dancing very close to Pam Cross.

"That damn Silva," he muttered. "He never reported, unless he went to Spanky. Even then, he should've been aboard by now. And there he is, all over Lieutenant Cross like a peapod, after they were pretending to hate each other. He's already scamming me again! I've got half a mind to ask Jim if I can swap Pam for Kathy."

Sandra maneuvered to look. "Shush," she said. "You won't do any such thing. They've been through a lot together, and maybe Pam can straighten him out." She didn't add that they'd somehow contrived to destroy the dangerous, renegade ship that wounded her husband, but knew that thought wasn't far from Matt's mind when he nodded so quickly. She watched Pam and Dennis for a long time, then snuggled closer to Matt. "We did our best to scam everybody too, if you'll recall," she murmured. "Just leave them alone."

CHAPTER

28

////// *Mackey Field*
Trin-con-lee, Saa-lon
June 1, 1944

Colonel Ben Mallory, commanding the 3rd Pursuit Squadron, was dozing in the shade under the wing of his P-40E Warhawk, just inside the trees at the end of the grass strip constituting Mackey Field. They'd long ago burned through everything Garrett brought them, and his and Soupy's ships were the only airworthy planes left—again—and they'd been up all morning, lashing another northbound Grik convoy. A Combat Air Patrol (CAP) of Nancys was up now—not that there were many of them left either—but they'd established a good early-warning system of coast watchers and spotters who'd report via wireless if any Grik zeps came snooping. If they did, the Nancys would have to handle them. The 3rd Pursuit had shot its bolt and barely had enough fuel to get one ship in the air, for maybe an hour, and there was no ammunition left at all. Not much to do but take a nap.

Ben was dreaming about Pam Cross. She was yammering at him about something or other, and he was vaguely angry. Then he became aware that Pam had somehow vanished from his dream, gone into the jungle with that big ape Silva, and he didn't know how he felt about that. He became aware that another woman was yammering at him though, and recognized her as that pretty little ex-pat Impie gal in Sergeant Dixon's maintenance section. He hadn't thought about her in quite a while and wondered why she was pestering him now. She'd stayed at Kaufman Field in Baalkpan with Jumbo, who now commanded there. Hadn't she?

"Colonel Mallory!" the voice persisted.

"Go 'way. I'm beat."

Someone was shaking him, and his gluey eyes cracked open. He blinked.

"Um. Wow. I was just thinking about you," he croaked, recognizing the suddenly blushing girl. "Waddar you doin' here?"

"Ah, Lieutenant Soupy said I'd find ye here." The woman quickly stood. "He sent me ta get ye as soon as we arrived."

"Arrived?"

"Aye." She gestured east. "The first supply column, up from Trin-con-lee. We got fuel butts on wagons, but we gotta get 'em stowed before the next column comes."

Ben sat up, still blinking. "Fuel? Here?"

"Aye. An' Sergeant Dixon's comin' up behind me, an' if I ain't outa his way when he gets here, he'll chew me out."

Ben jumped to his feet. "Dixon's finally here?"

"Aye, he will be."

"What's he got?" Ben demanded.

"Ordnance, parts . . ."

"And you've got fuel?"

"Aye."

Ben snatched her and hugged her tight. "Gas and bullets—glory be! We're back in the war! Get with Lieutenant Diebel. He's at the head-quarters shack." He pointed. "He'll show you where to park the fuel carts. We've got a buried ordnance bunker, not that there's anything in it. He'll show you that too, and you can send those carts over when they arrive." He looked at her. "Dixon's really here?"

"He's coming very shortly."

"From Trin-con-lee?"

"Aye."

Ben released the girl, leaving her swaying, almost as disoriented as he'd been, and trotted away.

"Sergeant Cecil Dixon! It's about damn time!"

Dixon was atop a cart near the center of the next column, chewing yellowish tobacco. He'd replaced a lot of his weight since the last time Ben saw him, and seemed to have recovered—physically, at least—from his ordeal as a prisoner of the Japanese. He patted the 'Cat on the bench beside him, who pulled back on the reins, stopping the palka drawing the cart. The animal lowed mournfully.

Dixon spat a yellow-brown stream and saluted. "Yessir, it *is* about damn time."

"What've you got for us?"

"Brought a wrench," he said with a modest smile. "I might even have a little baling wire. Just a little, though."

Ben grinned. He knew Dixon had far more than that. The reason it took him so long to get here was that he'd traveled by ship—with a complete ground crew, plenty of ammunition, and all the spares he knew from experience that a squadron in the field would require. Another ship had been supposed to carry fresh—better—fuel, and a third would be full of ordnance. Ben hesitated. "Did all the ships come through?"

"Yeah," Dixon confirmed to Ben's relief. "We didn't see any of those big island fishies, but jeez, there's some whopper sharks around here!" Dixon turned serious. "Just two ships operational?"

"Yeah."

"We'll sort that out," Dixon stated confidently, "as soon as our gear arrives from the harbor. And we'll do it fast."

Many 'Cats and a few men were gathering around. Most of the "step-children" were there, but other fliers from the Army and Navy Air Corps Training Center at Kaufman Field had also arrived. Ben nodded at those he recognized. "Hey!" he said. "How about this? We've got more pilots than planes!" There was laughter, but Dixon shook his head.

"Not for long. What they're calling First Fleet South is what dropped us off, and we're gonna get Mosquito Hawks here, and at another grass strip south of town off *Big Sal* later today. We gotta jump."

"First Fleet South? What's that? And *Big Sal*'s here?"

"Right now First Fleet South is *Big Sal* and those two tin cans, *Walker* and *Mahan*," he grimaced. "Call 'em a can and a half. And some wooden sailin' steam cans. They escorted us here from Andaman double-quick—after we'd been coolin' our heels there for who knows how long. Said that with what we were carryin' we needed a proper escort." He smirked. "You know, they took most of the guns off *Big Sal*— probably to keep Admiral Keje from usin' her like a battleship anymore—and lightened her up. I swear the damn thing made fifteen knots!" He shook his head. "Anyway, they'll fuel and tool and offload planes, like I said, for a day or two, then turn around and head north to join the rest of the fleet. My bet is, soon as they get there, the big show's gonna kick off."

"That's the word?" Ben asked. One of his greatest frustrations was that the receiver at Trin-con-lee was a piece of crap—or the 'Cats in charge of maintaining and operating it were less competent than others—and the only real news he got was when he was airborne. Even the radios in the planes weren't much good on the ground because of the mountainous, jungle interference and weird, local atmospherics. Consequently, he knew less about the grand plan than he'd have liked.

"That's the word." Dixon looked sly. "Days. It has to be. Everything's stirring at Andaman and General Alden's jam keeps getting tighter."

Ben nodded. "I was starting to think we'd miss it."

"Not a chance. We're gonna *win* this one for 'em!"

Ben paused. "What did you bring me for those damn Grik battle-wagons?"

"More of what you carried to Andaman, but we didn't send 'em on because we wanted to tweak 'em a bit. I'm afraid we would'a wasted 'em all like they were. There still ain't a lot of 'em," he cautioned, "and we brought all there is, but we tacked on some tails and taped on some fins so they'll drop straighter and more consistent."

"And hit nose-first," Mallory nodded. "Thanks." He knew the improvements would be far better than tacked or taped on. "How many?"

"Just thirty-six. *Big Sal* had some, and *Santy Cat*'s got maybe a hundred, plus some HE, but that's absolutely all there was left to salvage, believe it or not. Those destroyer pukes said the Japs shot up most of 'em at *Walker*, by God!"

"It's true," Ben confirmed more softly. They'd salvaged a fair number of high explosive shells out of *Amagi*'s sunken carcass, but he'd been there when the Japanese battle cruiser shot holes in *Walker* and *Mahan* with her 10-inch armor piercing shells as effortlessly as a .22 through empty beer cans. She'd used more later, probably saving her HE back, considering it more valuable on this world. Now, with fins to stabilize the five-hundred-odd-pound AP projectiles and his planes to carry them, they'd give them back to Captain Kurokawa and his iron-plated ships.

"We brought some other stuff too, though," Dixon continued.

"Like what?"

Dixon grinned. "We put tails on some of the new, heavier projectiles for the four-inch-fifties, making 'em into fifty-pound bombs. Even the Nancys can carry a couple of those, if they don't carry anything else. Can't put more than two under each wing of the Warhawks either, but you can give 'em a helluva lot faster start!"

"What about the P-Ones?"

"We can put a single fifty-pounder on 'em, if we send 'em up without ammo for the guns in the wheel pants. Jumbo test dropped some, and we've been retrofitting hard points and attachments on all the Fleashooters, all the way from Baalkpan. They're doin' it on *Baalkpan Bay* too."

Ben rolled his eyes. "They've even got you calling 'em Fleashooters? I was afraid that name would stick." The new P-1 Mosquito Hawks looked a lot like the old P-26 Peashooter, only smaller, and Dennis Silva's penchant for bestowing irreverent names on things had struck again.

Cecil Dixon shrugged. "Can't help it." He gestured back at the rest of the column of carts, animals, women, and 'Cats, stacked up behind him. "Now, Colonel sir, if you don't mind, I'd like to spread my goodies out where I can get at 'em, and start fixing all the planes you busted!"

"Carry on, Sergeant. By all means."

CHAPTER 29

////// *The Healer's Section, near General Halik's HQ*
Grik India

Despite the best efforts of the various healers attached to General Halik's army, General Orochi Niwa was dying. Granted, Grik military medicine was ridiculously primitive—there was so little call for it, after all—and it relied primarily on appeals to the mercy of the Celestial Mother and her ancestors. The only proactive measures employed were those any Uul might use if it ever occurred to one that a wounded warrior might constitute anything more valuable than rations. Niwa's bleeding had been stopped and he'd been made comfortable. Beyond that, all the healers could do was chant loudly enough that the Celestial Mother might hear their pleas. The wonder of it all was that—for a time—Niwa seemed to improve. His wound sealed and he gained strength, but then he became feverish and began a long decline that left him wasted and near delirious, when he was conscious at all.

The head healer, normally a Chooser of meats, had approached General Halik earlier that day and abjectly apologized that the Giver of Life had clearly decided that General Niwa must die, within a few days at most. Halik went to his friend, hoping to add his own prayers to the chant, but when he arrived he knew it was no use. Niwa appeared comfortable enough, swaddled in furs and filthy blankets, but he'd clearly lost his personal battle against death. He was pale and slick with sweat, and though he could no longer fight his fate, it hadn't made him prey. He was calm and still, and though sunken, his eyes were bright and aware when Halik crouched beside him.

"Hello, my friend," Niwa said softly. "I'd hoped you would find time to come. There are things you need to know."

"I have learned a great deal from you," Halik replied. "I wanted to learn much more."

"You will—if I have the time, and"—he paused, his eyes flitting to one of the chanting healers—"if you'll get those idiots out of here. I've noticed that I'm the only patient in this . . . hospital, and suppose they have nothing better to do than pester me, but I would like to be alone with you now."

"Get out!" Halik barked at the healers.

"But, Lord General!" one protested.

"Leave us!" Halik commanded, and reluctantly the creatures scurried away.

Niwa sighed. "Thank you for that. I think they have driven me mad, but at the moment, I am myself."

"I have tried to get prisoners, to learn how enemy healers work, but without the general assault I have still not been allowed, we have taken none," Halik apologized. Their enemy must have magical medicines indeed, because so many of his slain had clearly survived dreadful wounds before.

"Yet more information we should have extracted from the prisoners we took beyond the Gap," Niwa said wistfully. "I have told you before: the enemy often has greater value than simply food."

"I know, and you are right," Halik soothed.

Niwa's eyes turned hard. "Do not humor me, General Halik! As my friend, you must hear what I say and heed my warning."

"Warning?"

"Yes." Niwa seemed to drift a moment, then his eyes cleared and he managed to grasp Halik's arm. "I am not the only one who faces doom in this place!"

Halik shifted uncomfortably. "Our situation remains grim," he conceded, "but we still outnumber the foe by a great margin. We can destroy him as soon as the final orders come."

"But why have they not?" Niwa demanded.

"General of the Sea Kurokawa has a strategy."

Niwa snorted. "Yes. Yes, he does. But I tell you again: his *real* strategy does not embrace, or even allow for, your survival or that of the Grik as they are! Kurokawa strives only to achieve victory for Kurokawa! I've told you he is mad—mind sick—and he is. But not in an Uul-turned-prey fashion. Kurokawa is vicious, dangerous, selfish mad—like those huge African predators you told me of, the radaachk'kar—that take a hundred Grik to slay."

"But he *explained* his strategy to me!" Halik objected. "And as costly as it has been in Uul, it does make sense to keep Alden's force as bait, to lure the rest of the prey to its destruction!"

"But how much more quickly would a more rapid attack have lured a weaker enemy to fight?" Niwa asked. "Or do you think the force Kurokawa now has must rely on defense to destroy the enemy fleet he faced before? All waiting has accomplished is to weaken *you*, General Halik, so the final battle will be more costly!" Niwa sighed. His forceful argument had taken its toll. "You must believe me, because I know the man's mind," he continued. "And I know a great deal more I could not tell you before. However this war began, perhaps thousands of years ago, the Lemurians are your mortal foe. They'll eventually destroy you or die trying, and the Americans have given them the means to attempt it." He gasped a moment, collecting his strength. "And I must admit, I admire them. I'm not sure your people don't *deserve* destruction for what they—we—have done," he continued. "But the greatest

short-term threat to the Grik is not the enemy you know, but Kurokawa himself!

"You and I have become friends, and I value that friendship enough
to tell you that I knew some of Kurokawa's plans before we even met. He
won't exterminate the Grik, like your"—he paused and smiled ironically—"far more honorable Lemurian enemies will try. But he does
mean to rule you, to enslave you himself."

General Halik was stunned. "But . . . how? He is but a single Hij, and
your Jaaphs a mere handful!"

Niwa's head rolled back and forth on the dingy cushions supporting
it. "You've already seen his first step," he said, "or was it his fifth or sixth?
His tenth? I don't know how deep his scheme runs. But you were there
when he proclaimed himself Regent of all India and Ceylon. *Regent!* I
have no idea how he plans to proceed, but like all the various Regents,
he is now second in authority only to the *Celestial Mother herself.* You
met your Giver of Life after your elevation. I never have, of course, but I
hear she's a formidable creature. I did meet First General Esshk, and I
fear Kurokawa may have surpassed him in cunning and ruthlessness.
What do you think? Do you believe Esshk could even imagine the au-
dacity of Kurokawa's plan? With him deceived or out of the way, do you
think your Celestial Mother would?"

"But . . . This is monstrous! How could you keep such suspicions
from me if we are truly friends?"

"We weren't friends then," Niwa reminded. "And since we became
such, I've given you hints."

Halik suddenly remembered, and the hints were proof that Niwa
was telling the truth. He and Niwa *were* friends, but it was no secret
there was much about Halik's people Niwa still despised. Yet he was
willing to betray his own—to a friend. He suddenly closed his eyes and
rocked back and forth, anticipating the pain he would feel when this,
his only friend in the world, was gone.

"What must I do?" he asked, suddenly hoarse.

"You can't wait any longer," Niwa replied weakly. "You must attack
General Alden immediately, with everything at your disposal, if you
hope to retain any strength to confront Kurokawa."

"What of the Hatchling Host?" Halik asked, oddly concerned for General Ugla, for whom he also felt a growing . . . respect. "Can I rely on it?"

"I think so, at least to hold in place," Niwa replied. "But don't forget that Kurokawa helped form it. It is his creation, to a large extent."

Halik clasped Niwa's bony hand. "I must go, my friend, and prepare. I . . . I wish I could save you."

Niwa shook his head. "Just save yourself. But before you go, there is a little more you should know. . . ."

General Halik trudged quickly through the mud back toward his dreary HQ, pondering what he was sure had been his last conversation with General Niwa. Much of what he said before slipping back into a fitful sleep was hard to understand, but it explained a lot. This thing called radio that Niwa rambled about was totally beyond Halik's comprehension, until Niwa said it was like the "ridiculous chanting" of the healers, except someone actually heard it—and could reply at once! Halik liked to believe the Giver of Life heard his words, but she hadn't ever answered, and he suddenly understood how his enemies always managed to coordinate their battles so effectively and move troops exactly where they were needed so quickly. And he also knew how Kurokawa always knew so much about events beyond his view. He was absolutely sure that everything Niwa told him was the truth, and he alone knew the terrible secret Kurokawa kept. He'd deal with that as soon as he could, but first he had to deal with Alden at last.

Alden's Perimeter, Indiaa
June 6, 1944

General Lord Muln-Rolak arrived at Alden's HQ shortly before 0100. He knew the time by the large Imperial "waatch" he kept in a pouch on his belt. He loved his waatch, and despite a period of getting used to the Amer-i-caan's concept of time, he couldn't do without the thing anymore.

"We are early after all," he told his aide, his tone surprised. The ordeal of just getting here, down the Rocky Gap, where his corps was deployed, through the maze of trenches, across a landscape he remembered as jungle but that had become a surrealistic, shattered plain of death, had taken several hours. A crescent of the Sun Brother—the moon, the Amer-i-caans called it—was visible overhead, and he was struck by how much his face resembled the battlefield he'd crossed. At no time had he felt threatened by the enemy, but the trenches were infested with vicious little scavengers, like skuggiks, that could be dangerous. Most were so fat they were easily slain or avoided, and were tolerated to a degree because they helped control the stench of the dead Grik lying heaped too close to the breastworks for their comrades to collect. The stench of excrement was at least as bad, though. . . .

The troops he passed among, B'mbaadans, Maa-ni-los, Sularans, his own Aryaalans, or those from Baalkpan, barely paid his little party any heed. He wondered at the transformation that had overcome them, so used had they become to this terrible, endless condition of constant fear, misery, filth, and deprivation. He thought he'd come to understand a little of why Gener-aal Aalden despised trench warfare so. Not only was it essentially defensive in nature, but it seemed to sap the life out of the army. The fighting had been almost constant for months, but the Allied Expeditionary Force appeared increasingly content to let the Grik come to the slaughter. Rolak had to wonder how hard it would be to get it moving at last.

For once, nearly all was quiet on both sides. The Allies never used ammunition anymore unless attacked, so the redeployments shouldn't attract undue attention from the enemy. But there was no harassing fire from the Grik this night. The word was, Grik supplies were low as well, but Rolak wondered if the Grik might also be shifting their forces? He shook his head. Hopefully, Gener-aal Aalden would have reports. He strode to the camouflaged HQ near the lake, where the trees still remained tall and thick. Only Grik zeppelins could reach so far beyond Allied lines, and those that tried had been destroyed by Leedom's dwindling Air Corps.

"Wait here," he told his escort, and entered the HQ tent with only his aide. Inside, he was met by many faces he'd come to love like family over the last two years, though far too many were absent now forever. He realized that even if he was early, nearly everyone else was there already. He wasn't the only one who'd waited anxiously for this summons.

"Morning, General Rolak," Pete Alden greeted him. General Queen Protector Safir Maraan, immaculate despite everything in a fresh black cape, embraced him. *Not quite so immaculate as in the past,* Rolak noted. *Her silver helmet and armor are brightly polished, but the brass beneath the wash is beginning to show through.*

"I am happy to see you," Safir said.

"And I you, my dear." Rolak looked at Pete. "Since we meet here in person"—he gestured around the large tent; all three corps commanders were present, as were all the surviving division commanders, acting COFO Leedom, and Alden's staff—"I assume the time has come?"

Pete grinned strangely. "In a manner of speaking. I guess you already did your part?"

Rolak nodded. There'd be no unusual wireless traffic the Grik might monitor. They still had no idea if the enemy could do that or not, but they wouldn't take the chance. The coded summons that brought him here had also meant that Rolak should deploy the bulk of his I Corps near the eastern end of the Rocky Gap, leaving only two regiments to face perhaps fifty thousand Grik beyond it to the west. He could only ever deploy a front of two regiments there anyway, and that had been enough, with the corps artillery, to keep the Grik out in the past. The regiments were rotated to keep them fresh, of course, but that wouldn't be required today. They just had to *be* there so the Grik wouldn't know the rest of the corps had gone. Fierce fighting in the craggy ridges above the Gap had long established Allied pickets that should ensure the Grik would see nothing from above.

"All right," Pete said brusquely. "We've all talked about this often enough, and planned it long enough, that everybody ought to know what to do by the numbers." He smirked. "As you know, the numbers have been known to change from time to time, but we'll just have to deal with that when it happens. I'll keep this short and sweet and just a little rough. The short part is, Follow the plan. When you run into something unexpected, kick it upstairs and you'll get what help there is to send, but in the meantime, double-clutch it, downshift if you gotta, but stick with the plan." Few present fully appreciated Pete's metaphors, but they understood what he meant. "That said, don't sit on your ass and watch a golden opportunity go down the drain. Use initiative, as always, but be cautious! This Halik Grik is a bastard. If something looks too good to be true, it just might be. I honestly think we're gonna catch him on the pot, but watch your stripey tails. Got it?"

There were definitive nods.

"Also, once the show starts, all comm silence is done. Report what you're running into and where you are." He nodded at Leedom. "Our flyboys can't support you if they don't know those things." He took a breath. There was a big map drawn directly on the tent wall, but he didn't reference it. Everyone knew their objectives by heart. "Finally, whatever you do, whatever you run into, keep pushing. It's gonna be dirty and it's gonna get bloody, but your objectives are the only things that matter once the ball gets rolling. You absolutely have to hit your marks at any cost, or it's all for nothing, and"—he paused to grimace at his new chief of logistics—"and you've only got five or six hours to do it. That's what I'm told we have the ammunition and avgas for the pace of operations we have to maintain to get the job done!" He waved a hand. "Obviously, that could change. We might have longer or shorter, depending on what we run into, but that's the timetable we're working on."

There was murmuring at that and reflective blinking. Pete scratched his beard. "Why now? you might be asking yourselves, and there's several reasons. Two that really matter. We've spent weeks making the Grik think we're running out of juice, lulling them while we hoard supplies for this stunt. Well, we're not playacting anymore. All the dino-cows are gone, and we're nearly out of food. Also, the Grik finally got wise about the barges bringing us stuff up the river, and they shut it down. They've pushed all the way up to the ford on the south side of the Tacos River, just east of the lake, and the river's too dangerous to rely on anymore. Because of that, we're starting to dip into the ammo we've been hoarding. Like I said, we've still got enough to dump about five hours of absolute savage hell on their lizardy heads, but after that, artillery and air, at least, will probably be spent.

"Now the kinda rough part, and the second reason that matters most right now." He looked around. "Rolak's pet Grik, Hij-Geerki, has been on loan to HQ for the last few weeks, and the little bastard's turned into a pretty good spy." Alden nodded at the ancient Grik, who always seemed to be relaxing on a cushion like a dog. Geerki raised his head and somehow managed a smug expression. Pete continued. "Between him and Lieutenant Leedom's air reports, I'm convinced the Grik are about to hit us, whole hog, at any time. We have to beat them to the punch!"

There was alarmed murmuring this time, but Pete held up both hands. "That's okay, because now comes the sweet part. We're only starting the show a few days earlier than I'd planned, and I'm told that *if* we hit our marks, we won't have long to wait before help arrives!" There was an expectant silence, and Pete nodded. "I don't have all the details because we're using comm discipline everywhere, but it's the traffic we're keeping down, not the content, so I can tell you some." He didn't tell them he also didn't want to take the chance someone might talk if they were taken. He forced a grin. "This Grik movement has pushed things up a bit, but *most* of our ducks were already in a row. One way or another, Kurokawa's fleet at Madras is about to get a really nasty surprise, and if all goes to plan, the city should be back in our hands directly!"

There was cheering and stamping feet. Pete grinned even bigger. "Not only that, but Captain Reddy himself and his leaky old tin can might have something to do with it." There was even more cheering, and Pete caught himself almost wishing Kurokawa could find out about that part. There was ample evidence he might behave . . . rashly if he knew he was up against his old nemesis.

"Which, ah, 'ducks' are not yet aligned?" Rolak asked wryly as he moved to stand beside his pet Grik, who almost beamed up at him.

"Well," Pete paused, then shrugged. The people around him would understand how little difference it should make to their situation. "*Walker* and *Mahan* are bringing up *Big Sal*'s battle group." He didn't say from where—again, just in case. "And they aren't exactly *here* yet, but they'll be along, and they're the only ducks we're missing. Besides, this isn't shaping up to be so much a Navy fight, and all we have to worry about is what's in front of us."

"But what about Kurokaawa and his baatleships?" Safir asked.

"There's other plans for them. The Navy shouldn't even have to get its guns dirty." He looked around again and nodded. "So, that's it. Time to go. Do or die, as they used to say, but I ain't foolin'." He paused and finally gazed at the map. "You know, I hate leaving those guys out there in the breeze," he groused, referring to the lonely pair of regiments in the Rocky Gap, "but they should be okay." He took a deep breath. "At least for a while." He turned and stared intently at the gathered faces in turn. "And that's what it boils down to. This ain't gonna be a long fight; it can't be. We either win it quick, or we're done."

Suddenly, he stiffened and saluted them all. "It's been an honor," he said. Everyone present returned the salute and held it until Pete, red faced, stepped out of the tent.

///// *The Battle of East Indiaa*
II Corps, North of Lake Flynn
0505

"Thank you, Haasa," said General Queen Protector Safir Maraan, as the old B'mbaadan warrior finished securing her customary black cape. He'd already rebuckled the shiny cuirass around her torso, and now stepped back to look at her with his one eye brimming full. He merely nodded, unable to reply. Haasa had been her personal servant all her life, and next to the great Haakar-Faask, and now her old enemy, Muln-Rolak, he was the closest she remembered to a father. He could no longer walk long distances, and a lifetime of wounds had made most types of movement painful for him, but he always attended her wherever she went and was hurt that she'd forbidden him to follow her that day. It couldn't be helped. Her corps had far to go and would face perhaps the toughest fighting. She knew, one way or another, he'd contrive to keep up; that wasn't her concern. What worried her most was what it would cost him to do so.

She prayed to the Heavens that they really had a chance in the coming fight, because if they lost, she'd have gained old Haasa—and all the rest—little time. She shook her head. *No! Defeat cannot even be considered. Only through victory can my corps and my people survive—can I survive to see my beloved Chack once more!* She shuddered. *It has been so long!* She might never know what it was about the young wing runner from *Salissa* Home that so stirred her blood when they first met. He was beautiful to her eyes, certainly, but he'd also retained a charming, tempered merriment despite the horrors he'd already seen. Perhaps it was simply that he hadn't been a warrior at all before this terrible war, and though he'd grown very good at the business of killing, he retained a different perspective, one of war as necessity, not play, unlike that which had so pervaded the cultures of B'mbaado and Aryaal. Like General Lord Muln-Rolak, Safir Maraan now knew there was nothing at all "fun" about this war, and possibly what first drew her to Chack was the realization that he, young as he was, had the wisdom to understand that no war—no *thing* that caused suffering—could, *should*, ever be fun.

She sighed and stepped from the meager light of her tent into the predawn darkness. *There is fog,* she realized. *Thick and low. It will probably thicken for a time before it burns away. Then, of course, there will be fog of a different sort. . . .*

"Good morning, my queen," said Colonel Mersaak quietly, appearing from the gloom. Mersaak commanded her own 600, the royal regiment belonging directly to her. Both battalions, Silver and Black, were composed entirely of B'mbaadans, and probably alone in all the army did such a nonintegrated force remain. *They're just as good as Marines,* she thought proudly. *They train with Marines and learn the same tactics. They also now have the same mix of weapons, which is why—along with Captain Saachic's 5th Division, consisting of the remnants of the 1st of the 2nd Marines, the 1st Sular, the 6th Maa-ni-la Cavalry, and Flynn's Rangers, of course—would lead the breakout north, to cut the Madraas road behind the enemy.* Saachic's "division" had only about 140 effectives, not even two companies, but they'd requested the honor and she'd granted it. Supporting their thrust would be everything else she had, in echelon. Most of Rolak's I Corps would attack north as well, then east. Hopefully, *hopefully*, the Grik in front of Safir's corps would rout in the confusion, in the old way they once had, then Rolak's flank attack would scatter them to the north. It was all they had. The battle would soon commence around the entire perimeter and everyone had a job, but I and II Corps would have the farthest to go and would have to keep what they took or all was lost.

"Colonel Mersaak," Safir greeted. "What news?"

"All appears in readiness. This fog could be a problem," he hedged.

"As great or greater for the enemy."

Mersaak paused. "That may be. There are . . . noises to our front. That vile pet of Lord Rolak's . . ."

"Hij-Geerki?"

"Indeed. I believe he may have been right. It is said he overheard shouted orders from the enemy lines that when pieced together indicate the Grik plan their final attack against *us* at first light!" He blinked.

"Vile he may be," Safir agreed, "but his information has been amazingly accurate. Lord Rolak says he sneaks back and forth between the lines! His only fear, apparently, is that, old as he is, the Grik Choosers will catch him and send him to the cookpots!"

They snorted dry chuckles.

"Still, the timing for their attack is most interesting," Mersaak observed.

Safir considered. "But fortuitous. We've been in our starting positions for some time. If we catch them moving into theirs, with this fog, they will already be confused, strung out, afraid . . ." She blinked predatorily in the darkness, and her tail swished in anticipation. "We await only the signal, Colonel Mersaak! Where is Captain Saachic?"

"His company—I cannot call it a division, in good conscience—guards the right flank of the Six Hundred. I will try to shield it as best I can."

"Do nothing extraordinary, Colonel. I'm sure we will all have to look to ourselves before the day is done. There are few reserves beyond what we leave within our defenses. Captain Saachic and his troops know what they have asked for."

To the south, across Lake Flynn, a sharp, pounding rumble began. Safir had no doubt that the rightmost battery in III Corps had commenced firing at exactly 0515. The thunder continued as the next battery to the east fired as well, by the piece from the right, at predesignated targets, fuses carefully set. On and on it went, battery after battery, with a growing, accelerating, unending *whump, whump, whump, whump, whump!*

"I wish *we* had a wall of fire to advance beneath!" Mersaak muttered.

"As do I," Safir agreed, "but General Aalden says if we advance without a preparatory barrage, the enemy will be even more surprised; hearing the guns to the south, he will think the main attack falls there and will not expect us! It does make a kind of sense." She grinned. "Fear not; we have all the mobile artillery and will employ it soon enough!" She paused, listening a moment longer. "I believe the signal for us to advance has been sounded, Colonel! Lieutenant!" she said to a comm officer behind her. "Signal 'Second Corps is advancing!' Drummers, if you please."

General Halik's HQ
South of Lake Flynn

Halik was awakening slowly to oversee the final preparations for his dawn attack. The confusion following his orders had been profound, and he'd visited nearly every part of his southern line before going to his bed just a short time before. He was exhausted and had no choice but to rely on the judgment of his more promising officers to complete the plans he'd laid if he hoped to greet the day with the slightest semblance of a clear head. Groggy and still half-asleep, he was lapping from a bowl of water beside his bedding when a stupendous thunderclap sounded, seemingly just over his head.

His first thought was that it *was* thunder—until the next blast, and the next. Lanterns swayed in the command post, and dust filtered down from the bombproof ceiling as the concussions rolled over him, receding, then returning to jar him from the very ground. The prey—the *enemy*—had been silent so long, except in response to his own attacks, it hadn't dawned on him they remained capable of such a barrage, yet clearly they were. There had to be a reason they'd unleashed it now.

"My weapons! My armor!" He roared as he leaped, swaying, to his feet. An attendant rushed in, already burdened with his kit, and began dressing him as fast as he could. Halik saw the attendant's eyes and noted the first gleam of panic reflected there. *This creature is not far from turning prey already,* he realized, and wondered what the attendant saw in his own eyes. Forcing a calm, steady voice, he soothed the creature as he soothed himself and prepared for what he'd see outside.

Sword in hand, cape flowing behind him, he slashed through the entrance to his quarters and viewed the world. A fog lay heavy, almost impenetrable, and his vision could pierce only a short distance in any direction, but what he saw was enough. Dull strobes of fire pulsed to the north, from the direction of the lake, and flashes of exploding shells popped in the darkness overhead. Hot iron and copper fragments whirred all around, or sizzled on the damp ground as he strode among them. Bodies were already heaping up, some moaning in agony, others still. A column of warriors shifting positions had been caught in the open by an unlucky stroke, and some lay sprawled, still in marching order. The pounding continued unabated, and the sound was enough to deafen him. Worse, the dense white smoke of the cannon bombs was joining the fog and making it even more difficult to see.

"Sound the horns!" he bellowed, referring to the note he'd added that meant, essentially, "stand-to in place." Too many shapes were already dashing past him to the south, and he hoped he'd have the strength to stop the assault he knew was coming. Somehow, the enemy had divined his plans. Most of his preparations hadn't begun until after dark, but the enemy still controlled the skies, albeit more feebly than in the past, and they *must* have seen something! And the enemy's air mapping had to be responsible for the precision of the preparatory bombardment! Alden's terrible mortar bombs had long possessed the range to his forward positions, and his viciously efficient artillery could reach farther still. But this barrage was methodically pounding the marshaling areas and reserve encampments, as well as Halik's head-quarters section! It must also be focusing on his sadly limited artillery emplacements, since he didn't think many of his own cannon were adding to the general din. Ultimately, Alden couldn't have struck at a better time—for him—with Halik's army still deploying for its own attack.

To the cookpots with him! Halik raged. *How? How did he know?* He must have observed something, and with his cursed radio that General Niwa told him of, had been able to coordinate his forces in a way Halik could only envy.

Or did he know, indeed? Halik suddenly wondered. General Niwa had only recently explained the meaning of "coincidence," and though Halik wasn't sure he believed in the phenomenon, something about Alden's attack here now just didn't make sense. Even if he smashed through, he'd still be trapped between the escarpment and the sea. Perhaps his army had chosen to die like the small force on the hill west of the Gap—selling their lives in exchange for the cream of his army? If one considered it from a position of strength, that would seem all they could achieve. But with radio . . . *How far can radio speak?* Halik pondered. *They may NOT have seen me massing,* he decided, *and even Alden couldn't have prepared an attack such as this in the short time since they had, in any case.* Could the *timing* of the attack be coincidence after all? Possibly coordinated with something else, even larger? With radio, they might know something he—or General of the Sea Kurokawa—didn't.

An eerie roar muffled by the fog and his own damaged hearing reached him from the trench lines to the north. It was a yell from thousands of throats, unlike anything the voices of his own people could manage. Another whip crack of primal terror jolted his spine. "They are coming!" he roared. "SOUND OUR CURSED HORNS!" He paused, listening, as the roar built to a crescendo that overwhelmed the guns. Then he heard his horns at last, braying in the smoke and fog along the seven-mile front between the crags to the west and the low-water ford across the river to the east.

"I need runners!" he yelled over the thunder of war. "Fast ones. At least two tens! Send two along the pathways to General Ugla, and six to try to cross the river and contact General Shlook!"

"The rest, Lord?" cried a commander of ten hundreds.

"To Madras, to General of the Sea Kurokawa. We must report what is happening here and warn them to . . . beware."

"At once, Lord General!"

A staccato crackle of musketry erupted in the gloom, the flashes still blanketed. The clatter of volleys and independent fire quickly grew to a sustained, throbbing rumble. The duller pop of Halik's own musketeers joined them, but he knew his fire weapons would be next to useless in this thrice-cursed damp. There was more yelling, closer now, and the sharp, metallic clamor of shields and edged weapons joined the tumult. Then, just as his own horns began to fade, he heard another sound that stunned him to his marrow and convinced him that the fight, south of the lake at least, was lost before it truly began. The horns blared again, but this time with the signal to withdraw.

"Who ordered that call?" he shrieked. "*I* did not order that call!"

"I . . . I do not know, Lord General!" another officer cried in a tone that made Halik's heart sink even lower. The officer, a good one, was near the edge. If his senior officers turned prey . . .

"Destroy yourself immediately!" Halik commanded sadly.

"Of course, Lord General," the officer replied, his voice steadied by the order to release himself from the conflicting imperatives surging in his breast. He drew his sword. Halik was already pacing away, ordering other officers to stem the rush of warriors streaming to the rear—possibly never to be recovered.

"To the fire with Kurokawa!" Halik seethed. He immediately suspected that the enemy must have learned the secret of the horns and captured or made enough to give his army the one command it yearned to follow at that precise moment! They *couldn't* have prepared for this long, but Kurokawa had delayed the final assault long enough for this latest trick, at least. He ordered his own horns sounded again, but it was no use; it was too late, and too many had probably already been abandoned. Nothing could stop the rout—but what could the enemy do? Alden *had* to know this attack, regardless of its gains, couldn't hope to churn so far south as to combine with the troops guarding the Ceylon tongue. They'd face another entire army before they reached it.

And the horn trick would *not* work again, Halik swore. *So what does that leave?*

This is a diversion! he suddenly realized. *The greater mass of the enemy lies to the north of the lake, astride the western end of the Madras road!* He'd seen no bombardment flare across the lake, but that might be the point. *General Shlook could be caught unaware, thinking the whole battle was in the south!* He peered north through the choking smoke and fog. It seemed a little lighter, the sky a bit grayer, but he also now saw sheets of musket fire plodding closer by the moment, and as far as he could tell, nothing of his own force remained to oppose it.

"Lords of the Celestial Mother!" he roared. "Pass my command: all officers to me! Quickly gather what troops you can. This fight is lost. We must make east and force the river crossing and hope it is not too swollen. All that remains is to join General Shlook and stop the enemy from breaking through to Madras—that *must* be his design!"

One of the healers hurried to join the group gathering around Halik. He was cringing against the onslaught of sound, and the growing *vip!* of bullets in the air. "What of General Niwa, Master?" the creature asked anxiously.

"He still lives?"

"He does. Should I end his suffering?"

Halik shook his head. "No. Bring him."

"Just moving him might kill him, Lord."

"Or it might not. Bring him."

General Alden's mobile CP
North of Lake Flynn

"They run like hell in south, Gen-er-aal!" cried a comm 'Cat, hurrying forward with a message form. "They was scared outa shit, an' then them horns skedaaddled 'em!"

Pete nodded. They'd been preparing those horns for a long time, ever since Alan Letts realized their significance before the invasion of Ceylon. Pete had been tempted to use them before, but knew they'd get only one shot, and he wanted it to count. Now seemed as good a time as any, and the ploy had worked better than he'd ever dreamed. At least in the south.

"Not much Grik aartillery down there. Flyboys was right about that. They must not get many guns over them mountains in west, and they not get *nothin'* from Madraas. Nine an' Eleven Divisions overrun some guns right off, though, before they even shoot! They kickin' aass hard!"

"That is good news," replied General Grisa, commanding 5th Division, with which Alden's HQ was advancing.

"Yeah, swell," Alden said, "but tell General Faan not to get too strung out. I want him to beat the shit out of what's in front of him, and no mistake, but he's got to keep a handle on things and stay ready to pull back to his trenches." Pete rubbed his eyes. It was growing lighter, but the fog and gunsmoke had reduced visibility even more, if that was possible. II Corps had swept through the first Grik positions north of the lake quickly enough as well, even without an artillery barrage, but the Grik hadn't run as far, as fast, as those in the south, and the opposition was firming up. The Grik here also apparently had a deeper artillery reserve, and if it wasn't causing much trouble yet, it might when visibility cleared. The horns had kind of worked here as well, but the Grik honcho began a "gathering" call and *kept* his own horns blowing from the very beginning, and the results were more mixed. "How's Rolak doing?"

"The part of First Corps not holdin' the stopper in the Gap still rushes quick north-northeast, and finds few Grik except on their right flank," the comm 'Cat replied. "There's fighting, but so long as Gen-er-aal Lord Rolak don't direct attack them, they seem happy to let him pass."

"Fine. Weird, but fine. Make sure the guys we left in the western trenches know there's a big wad of Grik that *didn't* get pushed back and might jump on 'em from out of the blue."

"Ay, ay, Gener-aal Aalden!"

Pete was starting to fidget. He couldn't bloody *see* anything, and the reports were too sporadic to give him a good mental image. He had no "feel" for the battle. "Where's General Maraan?" he asked. One of

Grisa's staff unfolded a map. It was just light enough for Pete to recognize the expanding battlefield pictured there.

"She here," said the comm 'Cat firmly, pointing at a spot just short of the Madras road. "She report they reach this corral for dino-cows. It's in a big clearing, an' the Griks is use it to raally. They put at least two baatteries o' guns there. So far, they just knockin' down trees with roundshot, but Gener-aal Queen Maraan can't go round 'em cause o' these cracks—gullies—on her west, I mean left. She bringin' up her own guns to blow 'em outa there, soon as she see 'em better."

Pete felt a pang of concern. He always worried about Safir Maraan. She had more guts than any ten men or 'Cats he knew, but could be impulsive. He was glad she was showing restraint now, but wasn't sure they had time for it. They were ahead of schedule, true, but that could change at any moment—and, if anything, they were running through their ammunition faster than anticipated. They were killing a *lot* of Grik, but even if everyone in his army killed two of the enemy, they could still wind up at the end of the day surrounded by three times their number and nothing but bayonets and swords to fight with. Pete shifted his ever-present 1903 Springfield on his shoulder. "I'm goin' up there," he said. "I'll be back on the net as soon as I link up with General Maraan." He looked at Grisa. "In the meantime, you continue due north. Maybe you can take some heat off Safir if you cut the road behind whatever's gathering in front of her. Take that road and hold it! That remains the primary objective. Dig in from here"—he pointed at the northeasternmost point of the road shown on the map—"southeast to the Tacos River. And as soon as you can see to kill 'em, I don't want a live Grik running loose between there and the lake. Clear?"

"Clear, Gener-aal Aalden," Grisa agreed.

"You can take more reserves out of the trench line to help with that, then throw 'em into your new line."

"Lieutenant Leedom begs can his squadrons lift off now?" Another comm 'Cat asked, hurrying up.

"No, dammit!" Pete retorted. "He's patched up nearly fifty airworthy aircraft, but half of 'em'll run into each other taking off in this soup!"

"And the fog will linger longer on the water," Grisa observed.

"Right." Pete looked at the comm 'Cat. "Tell Leedom he's on the loose as soon as he can by God *see* to take off, and not before. Anybody who wipes out due to visibility's on his head! Send that. Then send that once he's in the air, I know he'll make me proud as hell." He looked at Grisa. "So long, General."

"You should not go," Grisa objected. "If anything happens to you . . ."

"It could've happened anywhere, as mixed-up as this day is turning out. Don't worry. I'll have most of the Third Maa-ni-la Cav, and all their scary meanies to watch my ass!"

///// *Port of Madras*
Grik Indiaa

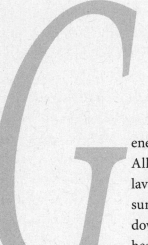

eneral of the Sea and Lord Regent-Consort of
All India Hisashi Kurokawa awoke amid soft,
lavish cushions and blinked resentfully at the
sunlight washing through the "waking window" of the palace he'd commandeered as his
headquarters. The place once belonged to the
former Regent-Consort, Tsalka, and was much
nicer than anything he'd enjoyed since arriving on this terrible world. It
was cleaner, prettier, and airier than Tsalka's palace at Colombo, which
the creature had apparently preferred, and the high view it afforded of
the city and port of Madras was actually quite beautiful. *It must be the
breeze,* he thought, standing and wrapping a luxurious robe around
himself. A fine breeze swirled through the stone passageways, keeping
the place cool even here. *That could be one reason,* he decided. *That hid-*

eous reptile Tsalka was always going on about cold places and how dread-
ful they were. Ancient ruins of some sort had been incorporated into the
construction, as in various other structures around India, he'd heard.
He'd studied them but could make no sense of them. Ultimately, he
couldn't have cared less about the ruins, but perhaps there was something about them that Tsalka disliked? He no longer cared about that
either, but remained mystified why the Americans hadn't used the palace while they were there.

He stepped out on a broad porch with a stunning view of the rising
sun and sleepy harbor below. He couldn't help a feeling of pride, looking
down on the mighty fleet he'd not only assembled here, but essentially
built from scratch. Nineteen mighty battleships of the ArataAmagi
class now rode at anchor on the calm water, smoke wafting gently from
their funnels. Tons of plate iron had been discovered, hidden around
the city. He knew the Americans and their apes had taken some, but
he'd found more than enough, hidden for (or from) him, to repair all his
damaged ships and even augment their armor. He'd lost too many to his
own *Amagi*'s salvaged secondaries, and refused to lose more to such
comparatively light weapons. The new armor would slow his ships and
make them even more top-heavy than he already considered them, but
he hadn't added armor to the peaks of their casemates. The risk shouldn't
be too great in anything but a very rough sea. His massive dreadnaughts
could bull through anything less, unaffected and unconcerned, as long
as they had power. If their engines failed—something they were prone
to do—a battleship might be lost even in a moderate sea. That didn't
concern him personally beyond the potential loss of combat power. If he
found himself on any ship with a powerplant casualty, he'd simply shift
to another.

A small Japanese orderly approached, carrying a tray of cups, and
Kurokawa impatiently motioned him closer. He rather liked the small
young man—little more than a boy, really—and never berated him like
the others, so he couldn't understand why the youngster seemed so
afraid of him. The fact that he was feared made him happy, but he
would've preferred this boy in particular just show him due defer-
ence. . . . He shook his head, mildly revolted at himself. The utter lack of

female company for him—for all his people—was starting to take a strange toll. He now knew the Americans had found women among their British allies in the East, and that was one more reason to conquer them quickly at last. He took a cup of nectar from the tray and began to dismiss the boy, who was clearly uncomfortable.

"General of the Sea!" called one of his Grik aides.

"Yes?" Kurokawa replied, stifling anger at the intrusion.

"Signals Lieutenant Fukui begs an audience!" the creature rasped.

"Very well. Show him in, then excuse us." Kurokawa looked at the boy. "Leave the tray and go."

Fukui entered, glancing about to ensure they were alone.

"You have a report?" Kurokawa demanded.

"Yes . . . Lord. Another transmission of the sort you instructed me to listen for has been received. I did not hear it, with my limited capability here, but it was picked up by our people at Zanzibar," he hesitated, "directed *at* them, by name, for the very first time."

"Most interesting," Kurokawa mumbled, but in his heart, he was terrified. "Did these people identify themselves?"

"N-no, sir. But they called themselves our *friends*, and said only that they would contact us again."

"Most interesting," Kurokawa repeated. He took a calming breath. "So. Somehow, they—whoever they are—have discovered the location of our most secret place, and there are only so many possible ways they could have managed it."

"Y-yes, Lord. Either they have sophisticated transmission direction-finding capabilities, or they triangulated our location with multiple receivers. It is also possible they have somehow actually observed our presence at Zanzibar . . ."

"Or the Grik told them," Kurokawa finished coldly. He shook his head. "I find *that* difficult to believe."

"What? That the Grik may have told them, or they may have been in contact with others such as ourselves and never told *you*?"

"Either. Both!" Kurokawa snapped. "It is not possible, Lieutenant! I would have known!"

"Are . . . are you *sure*, Lord?"

Suddenly, Kurokawa wasn't sure at all. The Grik controlled vast territories and could certainly have come in contact with other beings. He knew they *had* in the past, and unless they *decided* to tell him, he'd never know. His fear turned to a mounting rage but he managed to control it. *If* the Grik had met more . . . others, they'd done so recently, since he led the Grand Fleet against Madras. The Celestial Mother was capable of guile, but the Chooser would've told him, and First General Esshk would have contrived to use the knowledge against him somehow. Kurokawa's rage diminished as quickly as it built, and he considered. "These . . . beings say they are our friends?"

"Yes, Lord."

"Then we can assume, if they know of the Grik at all, they find them just as vile as we do. If you hear any more, report to me at once!"

"Of course, Lord." Fuqui paused. "Lord, I *do* hear something."

So did Kurokawa. A growing, roaring drone was building, seemingly just above his head. He stepped out from under the porch and looked up. "No!" he whispered.

He'd never personally seen a P-40 before. Most of the frontline American fighters in his old theater of war had been destroyed in the Philippines. He'd seen Hurricanes and a few Spitfires mobbed out of the sky over Singapore, but there'd been few, if any, American fighters over Sumatra and Java when his old task force moved south. He recognized them, though, from identifications cards distributed throughout the Japanese fleet. He'd also heard they'd proven very difficult for the army flyers in China, so they were far more capable than their quick annihilation in the Philippines implied. But where did they *come* from? How could they *be* here? And what terrible stroke of destiny could allow *eight* of them to come barreling out of the south like vengeful ghosts of another war on a different world, aiming directly for his precious, helplessly anchored battleships?

No alarm he could sound from here would be of any possible use. Even if it was heard, the planes were impossibly fast, and whatever they planned to do to his ships with those large bombs beneath their center lines would be done before anyone in the harbor could react. For just an instant, he was tempted to flee, to hide, to send to the aerodrome and have Lieutenant Iguri fly over and take him away because he knew, *knew* that the Americans and their apes wouldn't have sent these precious planes now unless they were but the tip of a bigger, broader spear. But he'd be helpless in a zeppelin. Those terrible planes would blot him from the sky in a tumbling ball of fire as effortlessly as swatting a fly. As it so often did, Hisashi Kurokawa's terror turned to rage, and he tore the robe from his back.

"Bring my uniform!" he roared in the halls that still echoed with the thunder of passing engines.

Flashy Lead
Over Port of Madras 0748

They're big mothers, all right, Colonel Ben Mallory thought as the anchored ironclads came in view. *Nearly as big as Lemurian Homes, and mostly gathered together in a nice, tidy square in the middle of the harbor like a buncha ducks!*

"Flashy Flight, Flashy Flight, this is Flashy Lead," he spoke into his mic. "Snuffy and I will go in first and take the far-left wagon. Soupy, Conrad, Shirley, you lead your guys in an orbit back around and observe the effect of our attack." They'd planned as best they could, based on recon gained by Nancys, but they hadn't known exactly where the Grik battleships would be because the enemy moved them around the harbor from time to time, completing repairs and practicing maneuvers. But the word had been they were always bunched up somewhere like this at dawn. Based on that, they *planned* to use two planes for each ship, at least for the first attack. They didn't have a lot of bombs, but they wanted their first strike to make an impression. That agreed, Ben wanted to evaluate how well their weapons and tactics performed before they went all in. If just one bomb would do the trick, they could potentially double the damage before retiring to rearm and refuel. It was a thousand-mile round-trip from Mackey Field to Madras, and would take several hours before they could return and hit them again. That was a long time for the Grik to do something different. Besides, even with better gas, that was a long flight with nowhere to set down if an engine crapped out or something. Fortunately, the 3rd Pursuit Squadron wasn't the only punch the Allies had today. *Too bad they couldn't have built us a strip at Lake Flynn,* he thought, *and flown us in some bombs. But if things kicked off there like they were supposed to this morning, it would probably be like setting down in a meat grinder!*

"I wish we'd had a chance to practice this more," Ben continued. "But just remember what we figured: treat it like a strafing run. Use your sights, and keep your airspeed up. We need our bombs to hit their armor square to punch through. I'll try to make corrections if me and Snuffy screw it up, so abort your runs if we don't blow that first bastard sky high!"

A series of "Rogers" answered, and he keyed the mic once more. "C'mon, Snuffy. On my wing," he said to the tall 'Cat who reminded him of a Lemurian version of Sergeant Dixon. He'd arrived from Baalk-pan with his nickname, and Ben hadn't asked what inspired it. "Let's show these Jap-Grik bastards what Pearl Harbor felt like!"

"You bet, Col-nol," came the terse reply.

Already in a gradual descent, Ben Mallory pushed the stick forward at 2,900 feet and advanced his throttle. With his airspeed indicator creeping toward 350 mph, he found his target in his gunsight. They'd carefully calculated the airspeed, dive angle, point of aim, and release point that *should* put their five-hundred-pound bombs somewhere on the armored casemate of the Grik battleships. The flat fo'c'sle and poop decks were tempting targets, but were much smaller and would require a steeper dive to hit. If the target was moving, they'd be almost impossible to hit. Besides, the engines, boilers, guns, and ammunition were all behind the casemate. Punch through that, and blooey! At least that was the theory.

"Damn, that thing's big!" Ben muttered again, centering his sight on the top of the second funnel aft, engine roaring, airspeed creeping toward 370. His fingers touched the auxiliary fuel-tank release that would drop his ten-inch, five-hundred-pound armor-piercing, high-explosive shell with the tail tacked on. He glanced to his left and there was Snuffy's ship, maybe ninety feet off his port wing. He grinned. The dark gray, nearly black ironclad loomed ever larger in his sights. He saw the weird Japanese-like flags streaming from the two tall masts, and noted the dozens of Grik racing for cover all over the ship. Some were even trying to climb the forward casemate. All the gunports were open, probably for ventilation, and he supposed even Nancy firebombs might've done some good today, so complete was the surprise. *They'll have their chance soon, he thought to himself. This one's mine! Just a moment more, just . . . NOW!* He shifted the lever and pulled back on the stick. He was gratified to feel the plane leap upward as the weight of the bomb fell cleanly away and he roared through the smoke hazing the top of the funnel he'd been concentrating on. Another quick glance revealed that Snuffy was still with him, climbing away, and before he could look back through the small windows on either side of the narrow armor behind the headrest, his earphones exploded with whoops of glee.

"Looky dat!" Shirley squealed.

"Oh, *magnifiek*!" came Conrad Diebel's voice.

Snuffy was banking left, and Ben crawled up beside him. "Holy shit!" Ben breathed. Below them, the first target had opened like a great, jagged iron flower. Shards of shattered timbers and twisted iron plates were still tumbling into the sea in all directions, but except for a monstrous toadstool of smoke, there was no more gushing from within the wreck because water was already pouring in to douse the flames and quench the hot iron. Only steam remained, spurting fitfully as the sea choked it out. "One bomb! One bomb!" Ben shouted, trying to stamp on the jabbering that filled his ears. "Silence!" he roared. "Flashy Flight, this is Flashy Lead! All Flashies confirm receipt! Use one bomb only on each target! One bomb only! Misses can be retargeted, but not hits! Assume any noncatastrophic hit has caused *some* damage! We don't have to sink 'em all, just put as many as we can on the bench, understood?" He waited while the replies tumbled in. "Good! Soupy, Shirley, Conrad, designate targets for your wingmen. Take 'em by sections in the order I called your names so there's no doubling up! You can shoot up their armored cruisers after you drop your bombs, but we gotta clear the airspace before the Navy air arrives! Snuffy and I will fly top cover and keep our guns loaded in case any zeps show up or we run into anything on the way home. Tally ho, kids, and give 'em hell!"

Port of Madras

Kurokawa was stunned by the sight he beheld when he reached the waterfront. Without a word to the pair of Grik pulling his rickshaw, he leaped from it as it slowed and stumbled slightly before gaining his balance. *Six* of his mighty dreadnaughts were either sunk at their moorings or streaming tall columns of dark, acrid smoke! Even as he watched, one of his burning ships, already listing, suddenly rolled on its side and rapidly filled. Grik in their hundreds squirmed out through open gunports and raced about in panic as the deadly sea approached. They were doomed. The fleet was anchored in the main channel, the deepest part of the harbor, and that ship, at least, would disappear entirely. They'd long known the waters around India were some of the most dangerous ever encountered, and voracious tuna-size predators swarmed in the shallows. The port of Madras was no exception, and all who went in the water would be shredded in moments. One of the ships had gone down a little shallower, where its crew had managed to move it after a near miss opened great seams below the waterline, and the horde of Grik clinging to the funnels and apex of the casemate would've struck Kurokawa as amusing under other circumstances.

More smoke rose in the distance from his squadrons of protected cruisers. They were lovely if somewhat disappointing ships, designed to destroy the powerful American frigates, but sadly vulnerable to air attack. He had no idea how many of those he'd lost to the strafing P-40s. *P-40s!* His mind still reeled over that.

"My lord!" came a cry. It was his Grik aide again, breathing hard after running all the way from the palace.

"What are you doing here?" Kurokawa roared. "I want my fleet underway this instant! Do you want *every* ship destroyed at anchor?"

The aide gestured at the sky. "But the flying predator has gone, Lord!"

"They will be back, fool! Can you really be such an imbecile?" He paused, listening. "You see? They are back already!" He pointed. A large flight of planes was approaching from the sea, out of the still-rising sun.

"They are just more water planes!" the aide objected. "They cannot harm the Grand Fleet!"

"Idiot!" Kurokawa shrieked. "They couldn't before, and they knew it. But would they send them now if they thought that still? Regardless, they're dangerous to all our other ships, and the harbor facilities as well!" He squinted. "And look, fool. Those are not the patchwork planes from the lake! They're new, brightly painted—from an enemy carrier, no doubt! The enemy is here. His fleet is *here*!" He gasped to control the fit threatening to overwhelm him. "Everything he *has* is here!" He straightened, his hand straying to his sword. He was *so* tempted to slay this hideous, ridiculous creature! "Get word to General Halik immediately! I don't care how you do it or what it costs. Run the messengers to death! Tell him to attack General Alden's perimeter at once with everything he has! I want no survivors from that place. Kill everyone!"

"Lord," the aide said nervously, as though finally realizing his danger. "A runner arrived from General Halik just moments ago! He is being carried here now to report! Another runner just told me, while I was on my way to join you, and I ordered the creature fetched here as well. It is nearly destroyed," he added.

The flying boats began swooping at the ships, and bombs fell on and around them. *Real* bombs, Kurokawa thought sickly. Amid the booming on the water and the buzzing of small engines, Commodore Fuji arrived, trailing some of his staff. He looked just as stunned as Kurokawa felt.

"Fuji! Good! You must get the Grand Fleet underway immediately! I will board *Kongo* as quickly as I can, but do not wait for me!"

"A-at once, General of the Sea . . . but what is our objective?"

"To save the fleet, of course! And destroy the enemy!" Kurokawa pointed east. "He is out there now, Commodore, and I assure you he's coming this way!" He turned at the arrival of several Grik bearing a litter. "Is this the runner from Halik?" he demanded.

"It is, Lord."

Kurokawa looked at the wasted creature. It had clearly run its life out. "Ask its message."

The aide spoke, and the runner gabbled weakly in reply. Kurokawa understood most of what it said, and his face went hard.

"It says Alden is attacking all around his perimeter and has made significant gains. General Halik is trying to contain him now—or was a few hours ago."

"I heard him," Kurokawa seethed. He looked at Fuji. "You have your orders." The harbor had become a maelstrom of explosions, smoke, and flitting aircraft. "All signals are now acceptable. I'll have my communications officer transmit the sortie command. All ships will engage the enemy as closely as they can and leave nothing alive upon the sea!" A plane roared by, low, like nothing he'd seen before. It was painted like the floatplanes, but smaller, with a radial engine and fixed landing gear! For just an instant, he thought Muriname had returned with one of the planes his people were working on back at Zanzibar—it *did* look similar—but the American roundel and single small bomb tumbling from its belly quickly convinced him otherwise. *Muriname promised me an advantage, but already the apes have real fighters! Besides the ones they showed us earlier!* The bomb exploded in a storehouse by the dock, and a massive secondary detonation obliterated it and nearly knocked Kurokawa flat. Dusting debris from his uniform—his new white one—he jumped back in the rickshaw and glared back at his aide. "Destroy yourself!" he commanded, "this instant! And be glad I do not give you the traitor's death for your stupidity!" Without another glance, he ordered those shackled to the vehicle to take him back to the palace.

At a distance from the devastation still roiling in the harbor, he shouted for Lieutenant Fukui as soon as he left the rickshaw. He ordered every single Grik he met, regardless of purpose, to destroy itself, and had to admit, amid all the turmoil, it was amusing watching them instantly slash their own throats.

"Fukui! There you are at last!" he cried, seeing the radioman peek from his alcove, where no Grik was ever allowed. Fukui looked beyond Kurokawa at the abattoir the palace was becoming and gulped.

"Yes, Lord?" he asked shakily.

"Send this at once: 'Lieutenant Iguri is to launch every airship he has. The enemy fleet is to the east. Find it and destroy it!'"

"But, Lord! The enemy has new planes with machine guns!"

"Yes, but not many! They *can't* have many of those P-Forties!"

"Not them, sir!" Fukui pleaded. "The smaller ones have machine guns too! They have strafed the palace!"

"Indeed? I had not seen them use guns . . ." He shook his head. "It is no matter." He paused, thinking. "Tell Iguri he must send everything—except his personal craft, of course. But tell him to wait until sunset. I want as much confusion as possible among the enemy just after dark. Is that understood?"

"Yes, Lord. Lord? We are leaving?"

Kurokawa barked a bitter laugh. "We have no choice! The enemy is coming *here*. Don't you understand? We were preparing to go after him, but he is here! Don't you know what that means?"

"Forgive me, Lord, but I thought you *hoped* the enemy would come to us?"

Kurokawa sputtered, but though his face went dark, he didn't explode. "Of course! But not like this!" He waved vaguely at the sky. That's when Fukui realized how badly the enemy aircraft—and how effortlessly they'd savaged his fleet—had rattled his lord. Kurokawa came from the old school of big guns over aircraft, and though he appreciated air power when it was on his side, this was the first time he'd been on the receiving end of decisive, effective air superiority. He couldn't fight it and couldn't endure it, so he had to get away from it.

"*He*, their Captain Reddy, no doubt, knows exactly what we have at this place," Kurokawa continued. "His creatures have been counting each ship they did not sink as it steamed up the east coast of Ceylon! He wouldn't be coming now if he wasn't sure he could beat me. . . ." Kurokawa wiped his brow with shaking fingers. "By all my ancestors, I do despise that man, and I will kill him someday." He raised his round chin. "Perhaps today. But this attack was too well planned—did you know Halik has been pushed back? No? He has, which means everything is part of a bigger scheme—a scheme to destroy *me*!" He stared hard at Fukui. "That will not happen. Reddy thinks he can destroy me and is resourceful enough that, this once, I will trust his judgment. But I will beat *him*, Fuqui! *We* will beat him by making sure he doesn't get me!"

If Kurokawa was trying to encourage Fuqui, it didn't work. All he managed was to finally convince the young radioman that he was utterly, wildly insane.

"Now send to all fleet elements in the port of Madras: 'Sortie immediately and destroy the enemy! The battleships *Kongo*, *Akagi*, and *Kuso*'—I want no ships with revolting Grik names!—'will remain until I can join the fleet, along with six cruisers!'" His face hardened when Fukui just stood there, confused.

"Send it!"

////// *The Corral north of Lake Flynn*

he fog was beginning to burn away at last, but the visibility in the smoke-choked forest hadn't much improved. General Pete Alden and his cavalry escort were pounding down a convoluted pathway, constantly halted by confused clots of Lemurian troops separated from their divisions, regiments, companies, even platoons, and there was no way Pete could sort them out. Some he told to follow behind him, and others he simply ordered toward the sound of the guns. He vaguely remembered a story he'd read about the Civil War Battle of the Wilderness and thought it must've been a lot like this. The damp woods wouldn't catch fire, thank God, so at least the wounded wouldn't burn alive. He had to ensure they wouldn't be eaten, though, and the only way to do that was to win. A volley of rifle fire suddenly slashed into them from a gap ahead, and two of his 3rd Maa-ni-la Cav pitched from their mounts. Pete urged his me-naak forward, before the cluster of Lemurian infantry—their volley identifying them easily enough—could reload.

"What the hell's the matter with you?" he roared. "You hit some of our own guys!" He yanked back on the reins of his savage animal, delivering its own volley of snot at the suddenly chastened troops. "Who's in command here?"

A skinny, dark-furred 'Cat stepped forward. "I teenk I am," he said nervously, "Lieuten-aant Taalat, Comp'ny Dee, Nint' Aryaal, Third Division . . . sir. I sorry. We tought you was Griks!"

Alden yanked his reins again. "Do the goddamn Grik ride meanies?" He shook his head, his anger fading. Taalat was just a kid, maybe in his very first battle, and what a mess it was. Mistakes were inevitable. He had more than thirty scared troops with him, and they'd need all they could get. Further shouting would only torture their souls even more than they were already starting to do themselves. "You're part of Second Corps. Why are you lollygaggin' in the woods?"

"We get lost in dark fog!" Taalat almost wailed. "I can't see sky! Don't know which way to go!"

"Son," Pete said, almost gently, "we're bound for Second Corps HQ now. Where it was, anyway. You guys can follow us." He took a breath, staring around at the dense wall of trees. "If you get lost again, just remember one thing: most of the shooting you hear is ours—at least until the air dries out. Any map o' this fight'll probably look like a damn amoeba germ, so you can't go far wrong just heading toward the guns and killing any Grik you meet. I'll guarantee that's the best the enemy can do today!" With that, he plunged forward down the pathway, with his escort hurrying to catch up.

"General Queen Maraan!" he cried, when his squadron of cavalry and the near regiment of stragglers he'd picked up emerged into the clearing south of the Grik corral. He'd seen the distinctive silver-washed helmet and black cape surrounded by officers standing on a little rise facing north. Two batteries of twelve-pounders were nearby, silent at the moment, but the fighting across the unusually wide clearing was growing to a roar. Safir turned to face him as Pete dismounted. A trooper immediately took his reins.

"Gener-aal Aalden," Safir greeted. "I'm glad you found us!" She gestured around. "A most confusing battlefield. Is it not?"

"You can say that again!"

"Consider it repeated. Orderly! Send a message that Gener-aal Aalden has joined us at last!" She looked at Pete. "Some were growing concerned for you."

"Yeah. Look, we picked up some stragglers. You better detail somebody to sort 'em out—and maybe send scouts back along your lines of advance and see what else they can scare up. God knows how many guys are lost out there—and Grik too. There might be *dozens* of little battles going on in that damn forest!"

Safir turned to another 'Cat. "See to it," she commanded, then looked back at Pete. "We have our own 'little' battle here, as you can see." She paused. "As you might also hear, this Grik commander has *continued* blowing his rally call all morning, and I suspect he's drawing more and more warriors to him from across the battlefield! Quite a large number have already assumed a defensive position on the far side of this clearing. *Defensive*, mind you," she stressed. "Hij-Geerki said all the defense-trained Grik were west of the Gap." Her tone was accusatory.

"Yeah, well he also said some other Grik were starting to get wise, and this Splook or Sklook, whatever the hell, is one of Halik's and his pet Jap's golden boys. Face it. Even a goat couldn't send as many warriors against our trenches as these creeps have over the last weeks without getting some clue how to hold a position."

Safir gestured at the growing fight to the front. "More than a clue, I'm afraid. This is our third assault, and Gener-aal Daanis has committed much of his division! The Third Baalkpan, Third B'mbaado, and Tenth Aryaal are engaged just now, and I am about to send the Black Battalion of the Six Hundred and the Fifth Sular to join them. The Six Hundred has a more innovative mix of weapons, as you know, and I hope to . . . confuse the enemy directly." She bobbed impatiently on her toes, trying to see across the field. "Oh, I wish I knew how we fare!"

"No eyes in the sky?"

"Leedom's squadrons have finally taken flight, and punish them between attacks, but most of the enemy masses in the trees beyond the clearing and cannot be seen. We have sent many mortar bombs in there, but I honestly don't know what I face beyond what the enemy chooses to show me."

"But it must've been air that told you more is coming."

"That much our planes have confirmed," Safir agreed. "The Grik come in groups and clumps from all directions."

"Where's Saachic and his . . ." He'd started to say "division," but didn't want to start thinking of 140 troops in those terms. "His special force," he finished.

"They probe forward on the right flank, together with the Silver Battalion of the Six Hundred." She blinked at Pete, guessing his thoughts, "So though perhaps not a division, Saachic has a formidable regiment at his disposal." She turned east-northeast and pointed. "When he reaches the end of the enemy line he will pounce with nearly five hundred of our most vengeful troops and their new weapons. They are few," she added wistfully, "but with the enemy focused on Daanis, they should prove a rude surprise, and their fire will be our signal to advance the rest of our modern weapons." She waved at the Black Battalion of the 600.

"Daanis knows a good chunk of his division's getting chopped up out there as a diversion?" Pete demanded.

Safir blinked at him. "Not a mere diversion. They fight to kill Grik—and gain his attention. But they will also cover our greater advance."

"Shit." Pete turned back to watch the fighting. He was a lot taller than Safir and was tempted to offer to hold her up so she could see better, but decided that might not make the most dignified impression on the troops around them. About four hundred yards away, across a lattice of scattered deadfall, was the closest thing he'd seen to linear combat since Ceylon. Daanis's engaged regiments were scattered, using cover as best they could, but were right on top of the enemy line, pouring in fire with rifle muskets as fast as they could ram the hollow-based bullets down their barrels. Alden's army had many more breechloaders now, the Allin-Silva conversions to .50-80 caliber, flown in or smuggled up the river before the Grik shut it down, and over a thousand Blitzer Bugs were in the hands of more specialized troops, but those currently engaged still had only muzzleloaders. Even those were better than what the Grik had; about half used crossbows and half the unwieldy, unreliable matchlock smoothbores, but Daanis was in a terribly unequal fight and even the primitive Grik weapons were taking a ghastly toll. Some of their heavy lead balls were even reaching the troops arrayed on this side of the field, and though they were nearly spent, they caused a steady trickle of cries of pain and wounded 'Cats being carried or escorted to the rear. Worse, as the morning wore on, the air was drying out and a lot more Grik matchlocks were joining the fight.

Pete removed his helmet and scratched his head thoughtfully. "Just so we're clear, your whole plan is to slug it out, nose to nose with what's growing into the whole Grik army on this side of the lake, then blitz his flank with Saachic's . . . regiment. As soon as that hits, you'll punch 'em in the nose again with everything you've got left?"

Safir blinked hesitantly. "Essentially, yes."

"What about his right flank—our left?"

"As I reported, it is blocked—and anchored—by ravines that cannot be quickly developed by us or the enemy. He is safe from us there, but so are we safe from him. You forget, however, and hopefully the Grik have not discovered, the approach of my Lord Rolak toward their right rear!"

"I hadn't forgotten Rolak," Pete assured. He didn't say he wasn't as sure as Safir that the old warrior's I Corps would just serendipitously be in the right spot at the right time to exploit the opportunity Safir described. Rolak had a lot of jungle to slam through, even if the Grik kept ignoring him as they'd been at last report. Safir seemed certain, though, and the two former enemies were so in tune with each other now, it was almost spooky. He sighed. Ultimately, if the Grik truly were massing everything in front of them, there wasn't much else they could do—and if anyone could sense the right time and place to jump in the fight, it was Rolak.

"I like it," Pete said, throwing caution to the wind for the first time since the near disaster at Raan-goon. He realized he hadn't just trusted to luck since—but look where that got them. He still didn't *depend* on luck anymore, but he trusted his gut—and believed in Safir Maraan and Muln-Rolak even more.

Safir blinked surprise and Pete grinned. "We're in the fight, General Maraan, so we might as well fight! We've busted 'em south of the lake, and if you're right, their horns are suckin' everything they've got left into one big wad in front of us. That'd make long odds in a numbers game, but their numbers are at least as confused and disorganized as ours." He jerked a thumb behind them. "Notwithstanding what I saw back in the woods, our people can deal with confusion a hell of a lot better than theirs." He patted Safir's shoulder affectionately. "What the hell? Let's go for broke!"

The firing to their front intensified and, his mind made up, Pete was growing antsy again. Faded, patched-up Nancys swooped over the distant trees, dropping firebombs that ignited with rushing roars and roiling black smoke. The trees crackled and steamed, but didn't catch fire. One plane dove in trailing blue smoke. It dropped its bomb, but couldn't pull up and crunched into the treetops. Pete frowned, shaking his head. The Nancy hadn't been shot down, as best he could tell. Even if the Grik had any of their antiaircraft mortars here, they wouldn't be much good in the trees. The plane's long-abused engine must've simply given up. He took a breath. "Daanis and his kids have guts, that's for sure," he murmured. "What the hell's taking Saachic so long?"

"He will be in position as quickly as he can," Safir assured. Two great puffs of smoke heralded the delayed thunder of a pair of guns on Daanis's left, right in front of the Grik, then another pair opened up on the right.

"I had already sent aar-tillery to support Gener-aal Daanis," Safir explained. She motioned at a six-gun battery clattering up, with gasping, moose-shaped palkas in the traces running as fast as they could. Gunners rode atop each animal or clung to ammunition chests on the limbers for all they were worth, certain that if they fell they'd be ground to paste by the heavy guns towing behind. "More are coming to support our advance."

A staccato of thunderclaps shuddered down the enemy line, and solid shot sent dead trees cartwheeling like Tinkertoys. A couple of balls bounded on, striking gaps in Safir's reserve amid harsh shrieks.

"I am surprised the Grik have any cannon left," Safir observed. "I am told we overran more than fifty when we pushed through before dawn."

"More like eighty, just north of the lake," Pete confirmed. "And General Faan claimed a lot in the south. If nothing else, we've put a big kink in their artillery train today."

A runner scampered up, holding a wooden canteen with a gaping hole shot through it like a talisman.

"Cap-i-taan Saachic say he in position!" the Lemurian yelled over another splintering impact that hurled more trees in the air.

"Very well. He may proceed!" Safir cried back. With an air of satisfaction, she drew her gleaming sword. "Second Corps!" she roared in that peculiar Lemurian tone that seemed to carry to the horizon. Her shout was echoed down the line, with the addition of division, regimental, and battalion designations. "Forward!" she trilled, stepping off amid the rattle of a hundred drums.

"Wait just a damn minute," Pete said, grabbing her arm, as the remainder of II Corps flowed to join the fight. "You ain't goin' into *that!*"

Safir smiled at him. "Of course I am!" She pointed her sword. "We have decided that everything the enemy has left on this side of the river must be there by now. All I command is here as well. If my corps is destroyed, I have nothing left to do. So why not share its fate?"

"Goddamn it, that's not how it's supposed to work!"

"Is any of this how it is supposed to be?"

"Well . . . just wait a second, okay?" Pete ran to the comm cart, still attached to its aerial. This model was capable of wireless transmission but could also be connected to the landline network they'd established around the perimeter. "Send: 'Continue general advance toward assigned objectives. Objectives must, repeat must, be achieved! All air will concentrate on assisting ground elements. Out.' Got that? And send out the gist of what we're doing here, attention Rolak specifically. Oh, and try to stay close with that thing, wilya? I don't want to come lookin' for you if something else occurs to me." The comm 'Cats nodded briskly, wide-eyed.

"Okay," Pete said, rejoining Safir Maraan. "Not another damn thing I can think of to influence this brawl. You said if your corps is destroyed, you're out of a job." He shrugged. "Well, if Second Corps goes down, so does the whole damn army, so where does that leave me?" General Pete Alden unslung his M1903 Springfield rifle, rechecked the safety at the rear of the bolt, and affixed his bayonet. "We got plenty of generals running around. What we need is more riflemen. Maybe I'll get a look at this General Shlook, and I can knock his damn head off."

Over the growing rumble of battle, the distinctive ripping sound of .45 ACP–caliber Blitzer Bugs joined the surging storm, and Pete looked at Safir. "Music to my ears," he said.

The unengaged regiments of 3rd Division, under Colonel Mersaak, and all of General Grisa's 6th Division had practically ground to a halt when General Queen Maraan stopped to wait on Pete—even while the fighting to their front rose to a fever pitch. Irritably, Pete waved them on and the thundering drums resumed. "See?" he grumbled, "that's why we don't belong in the front ranks. Sure, it makes us feel better, and might even stir up the guys and gals, but everybody's *conscious* of us, see? We're a distraction!"

"You may be a distraction, with your great, huge body tramping along," Safir said lightly, grinning, "but I mean to be an inspiration to my troops! My sword has been dry too long, while others fight in my stead. I am a gen-er-aal now, a corps commander, but I remain the queen *protector* of my people!" She laid her ornately chased sword blade on her shoulder, and it was then that Pete realized it was the only weapon she had.

"Jesus!" he exclaimed. "I sent you one of the new Blitzer Bugs!"

"It was heavy," Safir complained, "and I could not get the hang of it. I assure you, it is in better hands."

"Well . . . just stay with me, okay?"

"It is my pleasure."

Even Daanis's troops were moving forward now, chasing Grik that had finally broken under the combined flank attack and frontal advance. More guns rattled forward, their lathered palkas weaving through the fallen trees or straining to drag their burdens over them. A six-gun battery to the right fired, one after the other, sending exploding case into the trees. Then they quickly limbered up and advanced alongside the fresh regiments.

"On! On!" Safir urged loudly. "They are breaking! They flee! Drive them!" Regimental commanders repeated her cries, but added their own admonitions to maintain formation. No one was foolish enough to scramble pell-mell after running Grik anymore. One-on-one, hand-to-hand, a single Grik was more than a match for most Lemurians, no matter how panicked it was, and mutual protection remained a fundamental part of every Allied infantry tactic. The Grik before them had vanished into the trees by the time the corps absorbed the remnants of Daanis's force and pushed on.

"Where is General Daanis?" Safir demanded of an exhausted lieutenant, suddenly trying to keep up.

"Dead," the 'Cat gasped. "A crossbow bolt."

Safir was stung. As an officer in the 600, Daanis had been part of her life since she could remember, and talent had made him its commander, then commander of the entire 3rd Division. Now he was gone. There was no time for grief, however. "You have done well," was all she could say. The first ranks of II Corps entered the trees on the far side of the clearing at last and found nothing but Grik bodies heaped in all directions. The guns couldn't proceed any further, and Safir ordered their crews to arrange breastworks, load with canister, and wait. Hopefully, their part in the fighting was over. The *buuuurp!* of Blitzer Bugs still continued ahead and on the right, accompanied by the deep crackling of Allin-Silvas and the thump of grenades. Pete was just beginning to wonder how they'd keep any semblance of order in the dense trees when a great roar erupted far to the left, accompanied by heavy volleys of musketry.

"Rolak's here!" he exulted. "They'll really be on the run now! We have to keep pushing," he told Safir. "It can't be more than a mile to our part of the road. Once we take it and dig in, there won't be a damn thing the Grik can do to stop us! Have your troops keep their alignment as best they can, but we've got to push them now!"

"Exactly my sentiments!" Safir grinned.

It was tough going and any real alignment was impossible to maintain, but as long as they all emerged at the Madras road cut at about the same time, all should be well. There were still a lot of Grik in the woods, though, and few seemed panicked, in spite of everything. If Pete hadn't known better, he'd have suspected they were facing a fighting withdrawal! Crossbow bolts still sheeted through the woods and festooned the trees, and Lemurian troops were falling at an alarming rate, but their blood was up and they sensed an end to their months-long suffering and exile was finally within their grasp.

"Advance by ranks, firing as you go!" Safir commanded. "Kill them! Smash them!" The advance slowed just a bit, but the fire that preceded it was withering. Occasionally, Grik lunged up from where they'd been lying on the ground and tried to take cover behind a tree—only to be killed as the entire tree was shredded by the density of fire.

"You're gonna run out of ammo fast at this rate," Pete warned.

"We need only enough to reach the road!" Safir countered. "We retain a small reserve at our starting point and can bring that up when the road is secure. It will be more than enough to hold the position!"

The trees began to thin. "Almost there!" Safir roared. Just then, Captain Saachic scrambled up to join them. He looked terrible—exhausted, bloody, and maybe a little afraid, judging by his blinking. Pete realized it was the first time he'd ever seen the Maa-ni-lo dismounted in battle.

"Gener-aals!" he cried, "I beg to report!"

"You have succeeded magnificently!" Safir gushed at him. "The day is ours!"

Saachic shook his head. "No, Gener-aal Maraan! It is not! You must halt your advance at once. The Grik have fortified the road!"

"What?" Pete demanded, incredulous.

"Just so!" Saachic pleaded. "We thought we were herding the enemy into Gener-aal Rolak's arms, but the Grik were *drawing* us here!" He pointed.

The first ranks of II Corps had emerged into the Madras road clearing, and just as they did, six or seven thousand of the crude, heavy Grik muskets vomited fire, smoke, and lead right in their faces. It must've been every firearm in the entire Grik army, and wild as it was, the volley was still devastating. The Allied advance shuddered to a halt, and scores, hundreds of Lemurians fell when the big, nearly one-inch balls savaged them. There was only the slightest, stunned pause before companies and regiments started shooting back, but they were standing in the open, almost shoulder to shoulder, and couldn't trade fire like that for long. Besides, even while the Grik musketeers reloaded, swarms of crossbow bolts, more accurate than the muskets, kept flying.

For an instant, Pete considered calling for a charge. They wouldn't be expecting that, and most of Safir's corps would be on top of the Grik before they had a chance to shoot again—but a glance was all it took to convince him a charge couldn't succeed. *These* Grik had been charged before and they'd held, or at least stopped their flight to gather here. And he could tell this force alone still outnumbered II Corps rather badly. If he could get Rolak to charge at the same time . . . but there was no communication at all just then, and no way to coordinate anything. "Take cover!" he finally yelled. "Take cover behind anything you can find! Keep firing!"

The word spread down the line, and II Corps did its best to hunker down. Some even dug shallow trenches in the wet, sandy soil with their musket butts and helmets before rejoining the fight.

"Get down here!" Pete yelled at Safir Maraan, who still stood looking about as though calmly observing a mild curiosity. "Down! Now!" he repeated. When she still made no acknowledgement, Pete finally lunged up and grabbed her black cape and yanked her to the ground. He could've sworn that half a dozen bullets and bolts impacted the tree she'd just been standing by.

"I must insist on an apology!" she huffed.

"No apology necessary," Pete grunted. Lying prone, he'd brought his '03 Springfield to his shoulder and was scanning the Grik position. Safir looked at him and blinked annoyance. "Dug in!" he said in wonder. "Dug in an' *waitin'* for us! I'll be damned." He shook his head. "Actually, I *should* apologize. I had three choices and picked the wrong one. We gotta get out of here."

"That . . . is what I was about to say," Safir said sharply. She'd just noticed the tree herself. "Cap-i-taan Saachic?"

"Gener-aal?" came a reply from a short distance away.

"Please pass the word that we will retire by ranks. Has your command any ammunition for its special weapons remaining?"

Saachic held up his Blitzer Bug. "I have one maag-azine beyond the one inserted. I tried to enforce fire discipline, but it was not easy even for me. The Silver Bataallion, with its breechloaders, is better off, I think."

"I understand. You will support the withdrawal of the final rank. Only be prepared to duck as you approach the corral clearing, back the way we came!"

Pete's rifle barked, sweeping leaves and dirt away from the muzzle on the ground. "I swear," he said ironically, "I don't know if that was an officer or not, but he was sure standin' around like one." He worked the bolt and aimed again.

"Come, Gener-aal Aalden, we must retire."

"Just waitin' on you, sister." He fired again.

Safir stood, as if intent on defying Pete's desire to protect her. Before Pete realized what she'd done, there was a metallic *thunk*, and she sat down heavily.

"What the hell?"

"I suppose I'm shot," Safir replied angrily, fingering a large hole in her polished breastplate.

"Goddammit!" Pete swore, and crawled to her. There was a slight depression just beyond, and he shoved her in. She tried to protest, but he was already sawing at the leather straps along her side.

"You could have unbuckled them, you know!"

He removed her shapely cuirass, then looked at her wound. It was low on her side, bleeding profusely, but looked like a deep gouge instead of a hole. He grabbed the cuirass again and saw a fist-size exit hole in the metal back. He flung it away. "Lucky girl," he said, tearing open a field dressing and pressing it to the wound. "Hold that there while I tie it around you." She did as instructed, and while he worked Pete suddenly realized this was the first time he'd ever seen Safir Maraan without the cuirass. He'd grown accustomed to topless 'Cats, but Safir wasn't *supposed* to be topless! He felt a little awkward.

"What?" Safir asked, sensing his discomfort.

"Oh, nothin'. Just that the turtle shell you wear all the time doesn't do you justice—and old Chackie'll be a lucky boy someday too, if you don't both die of stupid bravery first!"

The withdrawal wasn't easy, and as Safir foresaw, the Grik charged out of their trenches when the final rank drew back. Saachic managed to stall the pursuit momentarily, but then it came hot and heavy on *his* tail. Pete had sent Safir with the first withdrawal and stayed with Saachic, his Springfield a potent weapon. But when the Grik pushed forward, followed by further swarms vomiting from the woods beyond the road, they were inexorable. All Pete and Saachic's troops could do was run for their lives. Grik were faster sprinters than Lemurians, and in the open they would've caught their prey. Escaping through the trees, however, the 'Cat's greater agility was a tremendous asset. Finally emerging in the bright sun of the corral cut, Pete turned and skewered a Grik he'd heard panting up behind him with his bayonet. Others did the same, stabbing or shooting. The pursuing Grik paused just long enough for the ranks that had already pulled back to rush forward again and fall in around them, still gasping from their run.

"First rank: fire!" Colonel Mersaak roared. A ragged, rushed volley of perhaps 1,500 rifle muskets momentarily stunned the leading Grik pursuers. "First rank to the rear!" Mersaak called. "Second rank: fire! Second rank to the rear! Third rank: fire!"

By the time the third rank backed through the files, the first rank, armed now with an assortment of rifle muskets and .50–80 breechloaders as the various units became hopelessly mixed, had already reloaded. At Mersaak's command, they delivered yet another stunning volley that scythed through the mass of Grik still trying to advance. Pete had remained in the front rank with each evolution, firing his Springfield with every volley. He placed another stripper clip in the guide at the rear of his weapon's receiver and shoved five more rounds into the magazine with his thumb. Looking up through sweat-bleary eyes, he saw they'd *carpeted* the ground with Grik, but the horde still emerging from the woods was a solid, determined mass. Some were still firing matchlocks and crossbows, but the vast majority carried only swords and spears.

What surprised him most was their almost utter silence. Always in the past, the Grik came roaring, beating weapons against their shields, but these were very quiet, very businesslike. *Veterans,* he realized.

"These are like some we faced on North Hill," Saachic gasped beside him. His Blitzer Bug empty, the Lemurian cav 'Cat had gotten hold of an Allin-Silva and remained with Pete in the front rank. "They will not stop."

Pete looked at him, then glared back at Mersaak. "*All* riflemen to the rear!" he bellowed. Mersaak nodded and repeated the command down the line. Perhaps spurred by what looked like a general retreat, the Grik horde swarmed forward, a yell finally mounting. But the shattered regiments of II Corps weren't retreating. They were withdrawing behind the artillery that had continued to deploy ever since the infantry went in the forest. What had been four or five batteries when Pete last saw them—twenty-five or thirty guns—had grown to more than *sixty*, and there were even some captured Grik guns mixed in. All were loaded with at least one round of canister, turning them into giant shotguns. Doubtless under the circumstances, most gunners had ordered a second canister filled with musket balls rammed on top of the first.

As soon as Pete was behind the guns, he looked back to the front. The Grik were still coming. If he and Saachic were right, and these truly were veterans that knew what they were doing, they had to know what they were running into, but still they came, roaring defiantly now. For the slightest instant, he almost admired them.

General Queen Protector Safir Maraan's voice rose high and clear a short distance away. "Corps aar-tillery! At my command . . . fire!"

With a staccato thunderclap that lasted half a minute and left Pete feeling like he was being clamped in a vise and tossed around like a leaf at the same time, the space between the gun line and the forest was consumed by an enormous, roiling cloud of smoke. *It's always a little yellowish when you shoot canister,* he observed absently. It puzzled him. He tried to pop his ears. *Time to get back to work*, he realized. Clapping Saachic on the arm, he started shoving his way through the troops toward where he'd heard Safir. He found her standing, wrapped in her cloak as if hiding her wound, peering intently into the smoke.

"You okay?" Pete demanded.

"Yes. Fine."

"We need to get ahold of Rolak," Pete insisted, gesturing at the comm cart a short distance to the rear. He suddenly remembered refusing a few of the new field telephones he'd been offered, preferring the space they'd take on supply flights be devoted to ammunition. He'd considered his communications sufficient, but now realized how wrong he'd been. If he could've just called Rolak *then* . . . He was struck by the irony that, having gotten used to not having all the conveniences he'd taken for granted on his old world, he had trouble adapting to having some available again.

"I ordered such as soon as I got here," Safir replied. "Thus far, he has not responded."

"Maybe his line's been cut or he's on the move and can't rig an aerial," Pete speculated. He looked to the front. 'Cat infantry had advanced back between the guns and were firing into the smoke, while the gun 'Cats reloaded their artillery. Some guns were already blindly spewing more canister into the space before them. As far as Pete could tell, not a single Grik warrior had emerged from the carnage of that first great barrage. They couldn't have gotten them all, but the Grik couldn't have halted such a charge themselves . . . Could they? He'd never seen such a thing before, but like everyone kept saying, the Grik were changing. He shook his head. No matter. Even if the Grik stopped, they couldn't have backed out of range yet, and the canister would keep killing them. He turned back to Safir.

"You got this?" he demanded.

"I do!" she said defiantly.

"Swell. Keep firing until you're sure your front is clear, then pull back to the other side of the corral cut—back where we started. It'll give you a broader killing field, and maybe they won't cross it in the face of all these guns. . . ."

"Which we cannot feed much longer!"

"No. But they don't know that, and we'll have air again."

"Where are you going?"

"To find Rolak!"

CHAPTER 33

////// *2nd Battle of Madras*
USS Santa Catalina

Commodore Jim Ellis stood with Commander Russ Chapelle on the bridge of the converted "protected cruiser" *Santa Catalina*, sharing binoculars and staring at the distant shore of India. A smudge of dark smoke lingered high in the unseasonably clear, early-afternoon sky above their objective. Constant wireless reports kept them apprised of the situation at Madras, as well as that of General Alden's embattled force. Ellis was in overall command of the event-hastened effort to retake Madras and relieve General Alden until Matt and Keje returned from their escort mission south. It hadn't been planned that way, but when Alden reported it was essential he go *today*, everything had to be moved up, and neither Captain Reddy nor Keje would second-guess the imperative or try to insinuate themselves into the decision-making process from a distance. At the moment, *Walker*, *Mahan*, and *Salissa*'s battle group, including oilers and the frigates (DDs), of Des-Ron 6—were still just northeast of Trin-con-lee, having turned back to deal with more heavy Grik ships reportedly approaching from the south. Half of what remained of Ben Mallory's 3rd Pursuit was back over Madras now, and the other half, under Lieutenant Diebel, was hunting the Grik reinforcements with a much more rapid sortie rate.

USS *Santa Catalina* (CA-P-1), was currently flagship of First Fleet (North), composed of USNRS *Arracca* (CV-3), and USS *Baalkpan Bay* (CV-6). Most of the DDs of Des-Ron 9 constituted their screen, and they were accompanied by oilers, tenders, and sufficient transports for the four divisions of the newly minted VII Corps. Those troops included not only two regiments of Imperials—about to face the Grik for the first time—but a full division from the Great South Island, recruited by (now Commander) Saaran-Gaani. They'd land just south of Madras as soon as it was safe to do so. About half of VI Corps, under General Linnaa was aboard *Baalkpan Bay* and yet more transports.

S-19 was also attached. Ellis had managed to get Laumer to admit the voyage from Baalkpan to Andaman had demonstrated that his submarine-turned–torpedo boat had some unfortunate tendencies in heavy seas. She was relatively fast but didn't ride the waves very well. To Laumer's intense disappointment, Jim had to recommend that Matt not take S-19 on his ambitious raid. It *was* hoped she'd be useful to Jim Ellis, and being a smaller target and faster than *Santa Catalina*, maybe Laumer would get a chance to test the new torpedoes against the enemy.

Chief Bosun's Mate Stanley "Dobbin" Dobson appeared on the bridge. "Commodore," he said respectfully to Jim, then looked at Russ. "Skipper. The comm shack's about to catch fire, with all the hot traffic."

"What's the latest?"

"We're not getting much outa Alden right now, but COFO Leedom says his air is burning Grik around the perimeter like ants with a blowtorch. He has to be careful, though; the positions are shiftin' around like water on the wardroom deck. He hasn't heard directly from Alden either, but the word is that crazy gyrene's gone amok and thinks he's just a rifleman again!"

"All Marines are riflemen, Dobbin," Ellis chuckled. "First, last, and always. He may've gone 'amok,' but he did pretty well like that on B'mbaado, if you'll recall."

"With respect, sir, it ain't the same. It's like if you took off in a whale-boat with a pistol in the middle of a fleet action!"

"Which I guess I would—if it came to that," Ellis stated in a tone that implied Dobson should get on with it.

"Yessir. Anyway, Colonel Mallory sank two more Jap-Grik battle-wagons, but lost two of the four P-Forties he took on the second strike. One knocked a wing off on its bomb run when it smacked a smokestack. It spiraled into the bay, and there's no chance for the pilot." He shook his head. "Another one's engine quit and the pilot bailed out—not far from Fifth Corps's forward position guarding the crossing to Ceylon. Colonel Mallory asks that scouts be sent to find his flyer. Fifth Corps CO says he'll do what he can."

"Okay," said Russ. "That accounts for eight of the battlewagons. What are the rest doing?"

"Actually, ten, sir. *Arracca*'s and *Baalkpan Bay*'s Nancys and Flea-shooters claim they at least disabled two more of 'em. The new fifty-pound bombs made outa four-inch shells apparently punch through the thinner armor covering the enemy fo'c'sles. It's a smaller target, harder to hit, and they dropped a helluva lot of bombs! It cost us, though. The latest tally is eleven Nancys and nine Fleashooters lost. I'm sure the Grik got some of 'em, but most were probably collisions."

Russ frowned. "Okay, but I repeat: what are the Grik doing now?"

"Aye, sir. Sorry. Last report is they're underway. Six of those left anyway, along with most of their cruiserlike things. Looks like they're comin' out with everything they have."

"According to recon, if we got as many as claimed, there should be nine battleships left," Ellis reminded.

"Yessir, but three were moved over to the dock, and they're just sittin' there. *Baalkpan Bay*'s COFO says they must be broke. His guys dropped a few bombs on 'em until smoke started comin' out their gun-ports, an' he left 'em alone to go after the others."

Jim nodded. "Okay. Six is plenty, anyway." He looked at Russ. "All air from *Arracca* and *Baalkpan Bay* will stay after the ones coming out, but the ships—and all elements of First Fleet North—will stay out of their way, except us and S-19."

"What about the DDs?" Russ asked.

"We hung a little armor on them, but not enough to matter against hundred-pounders. We know how that matchup worked last time." Jim still talked a little funny, even though his jaw was no longer wired shut. "Des-Ron 9 will stay with the carriers and transports—and as soon as we tangle with the big boys, they'll scoot in behind them and land their troops south of the harbor. Tell Captain Tassana she'll have complete discretion with her landing force, but stay the hell out of the harbor! Those three wagons at the dock may be broke, they may not, but even if they are, they've got damn big guns!" He paused, considering the huge responsibility he'd just handed the young captain and High Chief of *Arracca*. The kid had guts and a big grudge against the Grik. She'd *ram* a battleship with her massive Home-turned carrier if she had to, and that's part of what worried him. He consoled himself that she'd never do such a thing except as a last resort, however, and *as* a last resort . . . why not?

"One last thing," Jim said, "I want air eyes on the Grik battleline, even if it means those watching have to stay out of the fight. I also want all the Fleashooters recovered and prepped for antiair, with their guns loaded. We haven't seen any Grik zeps, and I want a CAP of Fleashooters on the prowl for them. It looks like the Grik—and Kurokawa himself, most likely—understand this is the big day, so we can expect every airship and suicider bomb they've got at some point." He paused. "Send all that via wireless so everybody knows the score, then repeat it on the TBS." He smiled slightly. "Tell Mr. Laumer it'll just be him and us, and he's about to get a chance to show us what that pork-bellied, silk purse of a pigboat of his can do after all."

It wasn't long before the handset on the aft bulkhead warbled and a 'Cat talker picked it up. "Mr. Monk," she said, handing the receiver to *Santa Catalina*'s exec. Russ had left the bridge for a quick tour of the ship.

"Exec speaking," Michael Monk said. "Okay, I'll pass the word." He handed the set back and spoke to Jim Ellis. "Air reports the enemy bat-tleline has cleared the harbor mouth. Our lookouts in the crow's nest would probably see their smoke by now, if not for all the smoke from the harbor."

"Very well. Call the captain to the bridge and have S-19 proceed to her position." It had been decided that the hybrid torpedo boat should place herself on the flank of the enemy's projected line of advance, as-suming they'd make for *Santa Catalina* as soon as they saw her—or as soon as she opened fire, declaring herself their most immediate threat. "Remind Laumer to keep a bows-on aspect to the enemy. His boat's small enough they might not see her, and give all their attention to us."

"Captain on the bridge!" cried a 'Cat, and Jim briefed Russ Cha-pelle.

"Yes, sir," Russ said. "I hope we made the right call putting S-Nineteen out there all alone. It's an awful clear day. Bernie Sandison figures the maximum range for his fish to have an even chance of hit-ting is about two thousand yards." He frowned. "That's inside ham-merin' distance for those Grik monsters, and one good whack is all it'll take to crack S-Nineteen's egg!"

"I know," Ellis replied, "and I thought about keeping her tucked un-der our skirt, but three things nixed it. First, I hope we don't have to *get* that close to the bastards!" There were nervous chuckles on the bridge. "Second, if we do, we're liable to draw more fire down on S-Nineteen whether they see her or not." He shrugged. "Finally, Mr. Laumer'd never forgive me. He and his guys have worked so hard and so long to save that old pigboat and turn her into something useful, they've earned a chance to throw some punches—and we need to know how well her torps work!"

"I guess," Russ nodded. "I just hope Laumer remembers he's fighting above his weight. He still strikes me as a kid who thinks he's got some-thing to prove."

"Maybe," Ellis allowed, rubbing his sore jaw and remembering a time he'd felt the same way. "Maybe we've all been there at one time or other," he added quietly.

Russ said nothing. Jim Ellis's confession explained a lot. There'd been a couple of times when Russ wondered about him, but he figured the commodore had outgrown such things. His performance at the first Battle of Madras had been courageous, but not crazy—or wastefully—brave. But who knew? Career officers often mystified Russ Chapelle. He'd achieved command of one of the most powerful warships in the Alliance, but never forgot he was "just" a jumped-up torpedoman. He knew what it was like to feel pressure to perform, to accomplish whatever task he'd been given to the best of his ability—but he also retained a strong sailor's sense of what those under his command were capable of, and that their desire to prove themselves to someone was limited to each other, and maybe him, to some degree. He'd figured out a long time ago that despite being a "born" officer, that was why Captain Reddy inspired such loyalty. He fought for a cause he was willing to sacrifice everything for, but except for his hatred of their enemies, it wasn't personal, wasn't *about* him. He didn't have anything to prove. And if he ever asked the unsurvivable from those under his command, everyone knew it was because there wasn't any choice—and it wouldn't be for nothing.

Russ was pretty sure Jim Ellis understood that as well. He was less sure Laumer did. His crew was certainly devoted to him and their strange little ship—but they *all* probably felt they had something to prove. He sighed.

"Sound general quarters, if you please," he instructed his quartermaster, a Lemurian Sky Priest, or "salig maastir." Those in that position weren't always execs anymore, but they usually made excellent navigators.

"Ay, ay, sur," the 'Cat replied. "Sound gener-aal quarters!" he repeated to a 'Cat signalman, who opened the shipwide comm circuit and commenced whacking a bronze-pipe gong on the port bridgewing.

"Black smoke an' mastheads on horizon, bearing two eight seero!" exclaimed the talker. "No course, no speed, no range yet!"

"Very well. Helm, make your course two eight zero, engine ahead two-thirds."

"Ay, ay! Makin' my course two eight seero, ahead two-thirds!"

Russ turned to Monk. "This might take a while to develop, but you might as well get started for the auxiliary conn, Mikey."

"Aye, aye, sir," Monk replied. "Good luck."

"You too."

Russ and Jim stepped out on the port bridgewing and watched S-19 speed away to the southwest. The weird little craft was already a thousand yards out and her silhouette really wasn't much. What betrayed her most right then was the white wake her near twenty knots kicked up.

"They shouldn't see her," Jim said hopefully. "Not if she's sitting still, bows-on. And Grik can't see as good as 'Cats," he added.

"No, sir," Russ agreed, equally hopeful. "All the same, I wish we could've fixed her back up as a sub after all, right about now."

"Don't be ridiculous," Jim replied, forcing a laugh. "They'd've been working on her until the damn war was over, and she never would've been safe. Even Spanky said she only had one dive left in her—all the way to the bottom!"

"Yeah," Russ agreed, but he couldn't help wonder if, omniscient as Spanky undoubtedly was, he might've been influenced by his natural destroyerman's aversion to submarines.

"Speaking of engineers," Jim said, changing the subject, "what's that damn Laney been up to? I haven't seen him since Andaman. Is he living in the engineering spaces?"

Russ blinked consternation in the Lemurian way and nodded. "He's got a rack chained up in the engine room, if you'd believe it."

Dean Laney was, quite simply, an asshole. He'd been Dennis Silva's chief enemy and rival on *Walker* since before anyone could remember, though a strange rumor now had it that they'd once been friends. In spite of his personality, though, Laney was a good engineer, and they'd tried to find something constructive for him to do ever since their arrival on this world. The problem was, he apparently did everything in his considerable power to make everyone hate his guts as a matter of principle. Whenever he'd been placed in a position of authority, those beneath him, 'Cats or humans, eventually rebelled against his petty tyranny. Only now, as *Santa Catalina*'s engineering officer, did it seem he'd finally found a place. That was good, because they'd just about run out of options, short of banishment. He must've known *Santy Cat* was his last chance, because even though his snipes still claimed to hate him, he knew more about the ship's powerplant than anyone on the planet and they respected his knowledge. In his little realm encompassing *Santa Catalina*'s engineering spaces, he'd finally found a home where he could contribute something besides discontent to the cause.

"A rack? He *sleeps* down there?" Jim asked, amazed.

"Yeah. Even has his chow brought down. Nobody minds but the snipes trying to work around him, and it keeps him from pestering the deck apes."

"He does *report* to you, doesn't he?"

"Sure," Russ grinned. "But he prefers it if I go down there to take his report. He's gone even squirrellier than *Walker*'s Mice used to be."

"But he does his job?"

"Oh yeah. And he's good at it. Remember, he did more than anybody to get this heap off the beach in that swamp. He got her engine restarted and took on the overhaul when we got her in dry dock. I think he's grown attached to the old girl. What's more, much as his division bitches and rants about him, I think they're kinda . . . well, proud of him too. It's hard to explain."

"The pride of communal misery endured?" Jim asked with a smirk.

"Maybe some," Russ conceded wryly, "but that can't be all. There haven't been any requests for transfers in a while. Who knows? Maybe he's remaking them all into a bunch of Mice. But the screw keeps turning, and that's good enough for me."

"Lookout confirms six Grik battlewagons, an' a dozen-plus cruisers!" the talker announced. "They seen us, an' it looks like the wagons is headin' straight for us."

"What about the cruisers?"

"They line up a bit north, like they screenin' the wagons from the rest o' the fleet."

"Speed?"

"Eight to ten knots."

"Very well," Jim said. "Have *Arracca*'s wing concentrate on the cruisers, while *Baalkpan Bay*'s Fleashooters maintain the CAP. As soon as we're engaged, Tassana may release the transports and *Baalkpan Bay* to land their troops. Just keep an eye on those battleships that didn't come out!" Jim looked at Russ. "*Santa Catalina*'s your ship. Fight her as you see fit, Captain Chapelle."

"Thank you, Commodore Ellis," Russ answered formally. He turned and spoke to the bridge watch at large: "The main battery and all secondaries will commence firing at five thousand yards. Sparks," he added to the wiry Lemurian signal 'Cat. "Get on the TBS and confirm with *Arracca* that we'll have spotting planes to correct our fire and report any damage we inflict on the enemy!"

S-19

Lieutenant Irvin Laumer watched the growing behemoths through his Imperial telescope, hat tucked under his arm, longish, tow-colored hair streaming back. The wind was out of the west and there wasn't much of a sea, but S-19 was laboring against cross-grained swells that *Santa Catalina*—maybe any other ship ever built—would hardly notice. The boat had a small enclosed pilothouse atop her flying bridge, but the only people in it now were the Lemurian helmsmen and talker.

Newly minted Ensign Nathaniel Hardee tramped up the stairs aft and handed Irvin a cup of monkey joe. The ersatz coffee on the boat was far better than that Irvin remembered from *Walker*.

"Thanks, Nat," Irvin said, taking a sip. Hardee was little more than a kid, barely sixteen. The son of a British diplomat on Java, he'd been one of the youngsters S-19 evacuated from Surabaya, and like Abel Cook, he'd grown up fast and jumped into the cause. Even before they crossed to this world, Hardee had been fascinated by the old submarine and now knew her as well as Laumer himself. Most considered him part of the boat's original crew, and he was her acting exec. There weren't many original S-19s left, and only four were aboard, counting Irvin and Nat. Danny Porter was chief of the boat, and "Motor Mac" Sandy Whitcomb was engineering officer. There were five ex-pat Impie gals too, but the rest of the crew was Lemurian. Some of the 'Cats had been with the boat ever since they rescued her from the now obliterated Talaud Island.

"Those things *are* pretty big," Nat observed quietly over the rumble of the boat's NELSECO diesels.

Irvin snorted. "You know it. Sound general quarters."

"Aye, aye, sir." Nat moved to the pilothouse. Inside, he twisted the switch that activated the old diving alarm. 'Cats burst from below and uncovered and unplugged the 4"-50 on the fo'c'sle, while others scampered to prepare the three-inch gun aft.

"Torpedo room report maanned an' ready," the talker cried. "Main baattery . . . all stations maanned an' ready!"

"Very well," Irvin said. "All ahead slow. We're close to our assigned position. Let's see if we can cut down on the wake." He smiled nervously at Nat. "No sense waving a white flag! I sure wish we could make this attack submerged," he murmured. "Those devils have an awful lot of big guns on 'em!"

"*Saanty Caat* commence firin'!" the talker echoed the lookout, high above the wallowing deck. Irvin looked through his glass in time to see the white smoke sweep away from the big gun on the old freighter's fo'c'sle. All *Santa Catalina*'s guns, her twenty-foot breech section of one of *Amagi*'s ten-inch rifles, and the four, 5.5-inchers in the superstructure casemate were bag guns. They hadn't received the same priority for modern propellants as the 4"-50s and 4.7-inch dual-purpose guns, partly because so few of even the humans had much experience with them. Most had trained on them, aboard other ships, before coming to *Walker*, *Mahan*, or even S-19, and they had the manuals but almost no idea about acceptable pressures—and how to keep them that way in a bag. Therefore, all of *Santa Catalina*'s guns still relied on black powder. *Big Sal* had done fine under that constraint, but recon reported the Grik had up-armored their dreadnaughts. They'd soon know how much difference that would make.

"Five thousand yards," Irvin stated, just as a monstrous waterspout erupted in front of the leading Grik battleship. "We're not far from that ourselves," he continued. "I hope Mr. Chapelle and Commodore Ellis can keep their attention while we creep closer!"

For the next ten minutes or so, those aboard S-19 could do nothing but watch the battle develop on the vast purple sea. The Grik heavies went from column into line, just as they had against Des-Ron 6 in the previous battle. Again, they clearly meant to close the range as quickly as possible before turning to present their heavy broadsides. *Santa Catalina* was barely half as big as the enemy ships, and seemed pathetically vulnerable confronting them all alone. But Laumer knew looks were deceiving. In addition to her powerful guns, they'd lavished considerable armor on her—maybe more than her skeleton could bear, some feared. Her frames had been reinforced, of course, and she'd made it here through some heavy seas that should've tested her structural integrity. Still, she wasn't *really* a warship; she was a freighter. Laumer had to admit she looked tough, though, as Silva once described her. On an experimental whim, hoping to confuse Grik gunners, she'd been painted in the old-style "dazzle" camouflage pattern of sharp angles and contrasting shades of gray. At a distance, it made her look shorter, squatter, and farther away. Irvin smiled. The giant Stars and Stripes battle flag she now streamed also added to the illusion that she was smaller than she was.

Her big gun continued firing once every two or three minutes. Irvin knew the effort it took to raise the heavy shells from the magazine with a hoist, place them on a removable feed ramp, then seat them in the breech with a hydraulic ram. The same process was repeated for the powder bags. The most time-consuming and frustrating part was that each time it was loaded, the gun had to be traversed back to a centerline position, then aimed all over again. It was a tedious, backbreaking process, and they'd discovered that big as *Santa Catalina* was, she was nowhere near as stable as *Big Sal*—and therefore more liable to miss. She needed to get closer.

After a succession of heavy geysers—near misses, mostly—one of the Grik battleships suddenly fired its three forward guns. Almost simultaneously, soot and steam rocketed from two of its funnels, and a gaping exit hole opened in her starboard casemate, also gushing steam. There was smoke too, and a series of yellow-orange flashes lit the inside of the great ship. Seconds later, a mammoth internal explosion practically bulged the roughly five hundred feet of her armored casemate, and as quickly as that, the whole ship seemed to *drop* beneath the sea.

Nothing remained but a dirty gray cloud and the slowly dissipating streams of her own coal smoke.

"Silence there!" Laumer shouted down at the gun crew on the fo'c'sle, hopping happily on deck and trilling with glee. "You want 'em to hear you?"

There wasn't much chance of that. The distance and thunderous boom of the explosion that rolled across them would drown their celebration, but S-19 had crept within three thousand yards of the closest Grik ship, and Irvin was growing more concerned by the moment that they'd be discovered. That remained unlikely. The old boat couldn't look like much from that distance; she made almost no smoke, very little wake, and her dark paint closely matched the surrounding sea. But S-19 was cruising directly toward the enemy's open gunports, the giant weapons pointed directly at her. *Santa Catalina* had, most likely, just concentrated the enemy's attention amazingly, however. Irvin contented himself with scolding his crew and continued his advance.

"The Grik shots all missed," Nat Hardee said, gazing through his own glass. "*Santa Catalina* has opened with her secondaries!"

Two tall splashes towered over another Grik ship, and two explosions snapped against the forward casemate. Chunks of iron spiraled away, splashing into the sea, but the dreadnaught surged on.

"Damn. They can't penetrate!" Irvin said.

"Not yet," Hardee agreed, "but they peeled off a layer. The next rounds might punch through."

One did. The others missed entirely, but one was enough. There was no massive explosion this time, no catastrophic damage at all that they could see, but the Grik monstrosity careened sharply to starboard—with surprising agility for its size—and smashed hard into the stern of the ship alongside. The collision was audible aboard S-19 a mile and a half away.

"Looks like they got her right in the eyes!" Danny Porter chortled, joining them on the bridge platform. Both ships closest to their boat had slowed to a crawl, turning into each other until they crashed together again, beam on. Through Laumer's telescope, he saw a smoldering gap where the bridge or conning slits should be on the one now pointing at them, and the thing seemed already low by the head. The other ship wasn't flooding, but white water churned from the starboard side aft, and it continued turning into the ship that rammed it.

"I guess we can now definitively say they've got twin screws," Irvin observed absently.

More splashes rose among the three battleships still steaming toward *Santa Catalina*, but even as he watched, their aspect began to change. "They're turning to fire!" he stated. Three great puffs of smoke erupted from the stern of the closest Grik ship, now pointed at S-19! "They've seen us," he said unnecessarily, steeling himself for the fall of shot. Splashes rose, widely scattered, far to port. They'd clearly been rushed, but the next ones might come closer. There was no doubt they were in range.

"All ahead flank!" Irvin shouted. "Come left to course three two zero. We'll do an end around and try to come up on the unengaged sides of the ones still in the fight!"

"Can we shoot now?" shouted the Lemurian captain of the 4"-50.

"Yeah, but only at the one that shot at us," Irvin cried back. "You'll have to quit when we clear those two wrecks. If the others haven't seen us, there's no sense poking them in the nose if we can tear out their guts! Danny, get on the TBS and tell Mr. Ellis what we're doing—and warn him there's an awful lot of iron about to come his way!"

"I bet he already knows," Danny said, racing for the pilothouse.

The three undamaged Grik ships steadied on a north-northeasterly course, and almost as one fired their broadsides of heavy guns at *Santa Catalina*.

Santa Catalina

"What the hell?" Dean Laney roared when something—maybe a flying rivet—shot his coffee mug out of his hand. He'd been happily watching *Santa Catalina*'s powerful, immaculate, lovingly tended triple expansion engine turn the ship's great shaft while the massive rods made their eccentric way—down, around, up! Down, around, up!—with a staggered, rhythmic thumping like the beat of a giant heart. He knew they were in action, and he'd responded to bells. He even felt the ringing concussion of the ship's guns in her fibers as she pounded the enemy. But something had just slapped the hell out of *them*! That was bullshit! A 'Cat scurried down the stairs from the catwalk above, and Laney grabbed him by the arm. "What the hell was that? Sounded like a hailstorm of goddamn *moons*!"

"They ain't moons, but they nearly as big!" the Lemurian gasped, looking around. "Our five-fives not doin' so hot, so we get closer, an' they hammer us! I sent down to see for leaks!"

"Why not just call?"

"Elec-tricksy out, for-ard, an' nobody get you on voice tube!"

Laney grunted. He hated the wail of the voice tube, and he'd taken the whistle out and put it in his pocket. He fished it out. "I, uh, guess this got knocked out. I found it . . ."

"But there no floodin' in here?" the 'Cat interrupted his excuse, and Laney's face darkened. "No, there ain't no goddamn floodin' here! Check the firerooms an' work your way forward! I'll send a party aft."

The hull shuddered under another, sustained series of terrible blows that sent 'Cats sprawling on the deckplates. Laney grabbed a support and saw—*saw*—great dents appear as if by magic in the portside hull plating between the frames. More rivets flew—and so did a high-pressure jet of water. Whatever was hitting them was big. *Santa Catalina*'s plates were half an inch thick, and they'd armored certain areas—like *here*—with another two inches of *Amagi*'s steel! Laney yanked the 'Cat up and yelled in his blinking face. "We got floodin' *now*, by God! Tell those idiots on the bridge to get my engine the hell away from whatever's knockin' holes in us!" He flung the 'Cat back at the ladder. "Go! I'll check the firerooms myself!" He grabbed the voice tube and blew in it. "Damage-control parties to the engineerin' spaces, right damn now! What the hell're you lazy bastards waitin' for? We got water comin' in!"

Another series of blows racked the hull, not as many but just as hard, and another seam opened. Lemurian sailors poured down from above and Laney berated them as they arrived, directing them to shore up the sprung plates.

"They's water in for'ard fireroom!" one harried 'Cat informed him.

"I don't doubt it! There's gonna be more water *in* the ship than out-side if we keep takin' this thumpin'!" He paused. "You're a fireman. Get forward and stop up your own damn holes! I'm goin' to the Skipper!"

Laney thundered up the stairway, shoving 'Cats aside. "Make a hole!" he bellowed, bowling through the press. Emerging aft of the case-mate for the 5.5s on what had once been a kind of promenade for the few adventurous passengers *Santa Catalina* once carried, he stopped, gasping, and looked to port. "Beezle-bub in a penny-sundae cup!" he breathed. Dean Laney hadn't seen action in a while, and had never seen anything like this. In the distance were great columns of smoke and ris-ing mushrooms of fire where *Arracca*'s air wing was stomping all over a division of fairly smart-looking ships that bore no resemblance to the Grik "Indiamen" he remembered. Closer—much too close, in his opin-ion—were three momentous shapes that immediately reminded him of perversely overgrown versions of that old Confederate ironclad he'd seen in the history books he'd been forced to wag around as a kid. Two more of the things were in a bad way, one obviously sinking, but the three up front . . . *Shit! They just fired!*

Laney darted to the starboard side of the casemate just as the whole ship shuddered again. Splinters from one of the lifeboats above lanced down and swept his hat over the side. More splinters, pieces of steel or iron, peppered him as well, and one of the funnel support cables parted and whipped past, nearly cutting him in half. *Couldn't've done doodly if it did,* he realized. The thing was gone before he knew it was coming. For an instant, he stood there, hurting and stunned, then the 5.5s opened up again, the pressure of the salvo pushing him along. He raced forward and scampered up the ladder to the starboard bridgewing. A single Lemurian lookout stood there, blinking furiously, his tail whip-ping back and forth. All the action was to port, but he was supposed to be keeping watch to starboard. *Hard to ask of a fella,* Laney realized with an uncharacteristic burst of sympathy. Then he remembered his engine was getting wet and charged into the pilothouse wearing a more customary scowl. It vanished.

The port side of the pilothouse was battered in, the heavy plates designed to drop down over the windows shot away. The engine-room telegraph was bent over at a right angle, and the big brass wheel looked like a bicycle rim that hit a curb going way too fast. Conduit and bundles of wire dangled and swayed, and the bowling ball–size roundshot rolling slowly across the deck to port gave Laney the impression this all just happened right then, while he was hiding behind the casemate. There was blood too, lots of it, and the dented roundshot left a little red trail until it thumped against one of several bodies lying on the deck. Two of them, 'Cats, were obviously dead. One was particularly, horribly shredded. The other two were men Laney knew well. Before he could move, a pair of Lemurians knelt beside them, while another took the warped wheel in hand. To Laney's amazement, the blood-covered man the cannonball bumped suddenly opened his eyes and looked at him.

"What're you doin' here?" Russ Chapelle demanded, sitting up, reaching to explore his face with his hand.

"Careful, Skipper!" one of the 'Cats warned. "You got busted glass in you face! I think you okay, though. You wearin' lots o' blood, but not bleedin' bad that I see."

"Swell. Help me up. Where's the commodore?"

"He *not* okay!" cried the 'Cat talker, kneeling beside Jim Ellis. His ears were back and his tail was almost rigid. "He not dead, though!"

Russ grimaced at the sight of his commander, friend, and one of the highest-ranking and best-respected officers in the Grand Alliance. He'd just been talking to him! Hadn't even finished what he was saying! "He doesn't look good," was all he could manage, and it was a serious understatement. Most of Jim's left arm and the associated muscles across his chest looked like they'd been peeled away. Russ lurched to the bank of speaking tubes. "Corps 'Cats to the bridge, on the double! Bring stretchers!" He looked back at the 'Cat at the wheel. "Does she steer?"

"Ay, Cap-i-taan! came the stiff, controlled reply.

Russ looked at the engine-room telegraph. "But the lee helm's shot away." He turned back to Laney, just as the first corps 'Cats arrived on the bridge. "Which is okay, if somebody in engineering'll keep an ear close to the voice tube." He looked at the talker, who'd returned to his station. "Damage report!"

"More o' the same so far; we takin' damage, but still holdin' up better than we was afraid." He paused. "The number one gun reports a caash-ulty."

"Can they fix it?"

"Not now. They *can* fix it, but it take longer than *this* fight lasts, one way or other."

Russ frowned. "Very well. Have its crew secure what they can and join the crews in the casemate." He suddenly noticed Laney again. "What *are* you doin' here, Laney?" he demanded, his temper brittle.

"Why, uh, there's water comin' in," Dean replied, suddenly realizing how lame his complaint sounded under the circumstances.

"We sinkin'?" Chapelle snapped.

"Not when I headed up here, but it was gettin' worse, and who knows now. . . ."

"*You* should know, you puffed-up, self-centered boar's tit!" Russ roared, his temper cracking. It wasn't the response of a "born" officer, but if Russ Chapelle ever cared about such things, he certainly didn't then. "You came up here to bitch that things ain't exactly like you wish they were below—that's exactly why you're here! Well, listen up!" He waved at the wreckage and blood around them. "We're in a fight, and bad shit happens! Your *job*, mister, is to keep my engine running, fix what breaks, and plug the holes the enemy shoots in us. As far as I'm concerned, you've abandoned your post in the face of the enemy. Do you know what that means? If I see you above decks again before this fight's done, it better be *after* the last roach and rat have fled the rising water! Am I absolutely clear?"

"A-aye, aye, sir," Laney sputtered.

"I better be." Russ looked down as Jim Ellis was hoisted off the deck and carried from the bridge. "Just . . . get out of my sight," he said, his voice subdued.

The 5.5s were still hammering, and a few more shots jolted the ship amid plumes of water that cascaded across the decks. Laney, utterly ashamed of himself, happened to glance out the shattered pilothouse as he turned away. He stopped, eyes bulging. "Captain Chapelle . . . look!"

"Secure from flank. All ahead two-thirds. Flood tubes one through four!" Irvin Laumer shouted at the 'Cats on the torpedo director, amid the spray raining down on the flying bridge. S-19 had come around to a course of 080, and the three Grik ships were dead ahead, bow to stern, smoke streaming from broadsides still punishing *Santa Catalina*. S-19 hadn't done much damage to the ship they'd shot at as she passed, and it was disconcerting that the "new" 4"-50 shells had so little apparent effect at such close range, but after only a few halfhearted return shots, neither collision victim paid them much attention. Both had more pressing problems. The first was going fast, her bow dipping deep, her screws—yes, she *did* have two—rising above the water. Grik were swarming all over her flooding carcass like ants flushed from their bed, and their shrieks of terror mingled in a shrill, steady drone. There were no lifeboats in the water. The second ship was noticeably low by the stern now, but steaming away in a wide turn to port—toward the cruiser squadron coming up from the northwest. The cruisers were preoccupied as well. *Arracca*'s Nancys flocked around them like lethal blue-and-white gulls, dropping firebombs, and the new fifty-pound bombs.

"Target course remains unchanged at three four five. Range!" Irvin yelled.

One of the 'Cats called "One t'ousand four hundreds!" and another Lemurian turned a dial on the torpedo data computer, or TDC, sheltered inside the pilothouse. "Set!" the 'Cat called back, blinking rapidly. They'd already input the course, speed, and bearing of the target—the last ship in the line.

"Open outer doors!" Irvin commanded. "Standby tubes one and two!"

"Tubes one and two ready in all respects, Skipper," Hardee shouted back after what seemed a lifetime. The headset was held to his ear, and he was staring at the ready lights that had been moved to the aft bulkhead of the pilothouse.

"Fire one!" Laumer shouted.

"Fire one!" Hardee repeated, and the racing boat shuddered as a column of air exploded to the surface at the bow. Laumer counted to five. "Fire two!"

A second Mk-3 hot-air torpedo, proudly marked "Baalkpan Naval Arsenal," plunged forward out of its tube, joining the first war-shot torpedo made on this world to be fired in anger.

"Both fish running hot, straight, and normal, Skipper!" Hardee repeated the report from the sound room excitedly. "Mr. Sandison's done us proud!"

"We'll see," Laumer hedged. "New target is the center ship in the line!" he shouted, the excitement raising his voice.

"Ay, ay!" cried the 'Cat behind the director. "Bearing . . . mark!"

"Bearing seero seven eight!" shouted his mate.

"Recommend course seero four two!"

"Make your course zero four two!" Irvin shouted at the helm.

Theoretically, they could program the torpedoes themselves to intersect the target at a given point, but for this first effort, Irvin decided to set all his fish for straight runs at a depth of ten feet. To simplify things for the new torpedoes, he'd aim S-19 where the target should be when his torpedoes reached it. In a way, this seemed almost a betrayal of all the hard work and hard-won technical expertise that went into making the new Mk-3s just as capable and versatile as their old fish had been—except for speed and range, of course. But simpler was always better, and they knew the fish would go off if they hit. That was a confidence they'd never had with the modern torpedoes they'd started their Old War with. Still, for this type of shooting, *Walker* should have it easier, since she could traverse her torpedo mounts on deck.

"My course seero four two!" cried the 'Cat at the wheel.

"Ten seconds!" came the shout from the torpedo director.

Irvin Laumer looked at his watch. "Fire three!" he yelled. "Fire four!"

Two more gouts of air burped at the bow, and the old sub bounced.

"Three and four are running hot, straight, and normal, sir!" Hardee exulted.

"Very well. Close the outer doors and reload all tubes!"

S-19 had started with twelve torpedoes. Enough of her complicated pumps, pipes, and internal tanks remained to trim the ship as the weight of each weapon left her, but manually cranking the doors closed, reloading, and retrimming took time. It was necessary, though, since S-19 was essentially the gun that aimed the torpedo "bullet," and she had to be as steady as possible when she fired. Irvin Laumer judged the angle of the final dreadnaught forward, and gauged the distance to the harried, dwindling cruisers to the north.

"We'll never reach that first one from here," he said simply. "Helm, come to three five five. All ahead full. We'll try to throw all four fish at that last sucker before we get too close to the cruisers."

"We may not have to worry about them," Danny said, glancing up from his watch and pointing aft at the frothy wake they were making. "And, besides, I hope—I *bet*—those Jap-Griks are about to start looking in our direction pretty quick. Our first torps ought to be there . . . well, now."

For a terrible moment, nothing happened. Apparently they *had* been seen, though, because a few of the Grik battleship's dozen-odd broadside guns fired on them, the heavy roundshot rumbling mostly overhead to splash some distance to port. One came dangerously close, deluging the fantail and the crew of the three-inch gun aft.

"Yes!" Nat Hardee practically squeaked, raising both hands in the air and nearly dropping his headset. Maybe ten seconds later than expected, a tight, high plume of water jetted skyward, aft of amidships on their first target. The geyser rose and rose, higher than the ship's funnels, before collapsing back on the ship and into the sea. A monstrous jet of coal dust and black smoke belched from the third funnel as well, joined an instant later by a dirty gout of steam. There was no second hit—they'd likely missed with their first torpedo—but one was more than enough. Even at this range they could see they'd opened a massive hole in the side of the enemy leviathan that extended even a short distance up the armored casemate. From what they'd heard from previous actions and observed that day, the Grik ships had no real watertight compartmentalization belowdecks. It had probably never been considered necessary during their design. Their heavy armor and armaments must've been thought sufficient to protect them from a distance, and Kurokawa—or whoever dreamed them up—likely never worried about how vulnerable they'd be to an honest-to-God torpedo!

The gaping hole quickly vanished as the great ship rolled toward them, spewing more steam from her gunports as water rushed against hot boilers. It was stunning how fast the ship turned turtle once she got started, and soon she lay belly-up in the bright sun. Even before she quit wallowing back and forth, her wooden keel pointing at the sky, she was already slipping. Irvin was staring through his glass at the few Grik that had managed to squirm through gunports into the sea, but that wouldn't save them. The flashies—or flashylike fish—teeming in these seas were already gathering to the flailing, shrieking buffet laid before them. Irvin had just lowered his glass, grimacing, when *both* torpedoes they'd fired at the second ship impacted—aft again, but close together—and virtually demolished the entire stern of the massive, iron-plated monster.

"Glory be!" Dean Laney shouted. "Glory BE! Wouldja look at that!"

The second Grik battleship had wallowed to a halt, trailing smoke and debris that was still falling in the water. "Damn things are tough as hell—till you take a real switch to 'em!" he chortled. "Who'd've ever thought we'd have to come to a whole new world to get torpedoes that actually work?"

"It is amazing," Russ conceded, his tone still sharp, "but you'll be even more amazed what I do to you if you don't get your worthless, fat ass off my bridge and back to work where you belong!"

Laney finally bolted, and Russ took a deep breath, still wiping blood from his face with his sleeve.

"Lookout says the last Grik wagon turnin' away," the talker cried, "but S-Nineteen's streakin' straight in her teeth!"

Russ started to tell the talker to order Laumer to break off—he was charging directly at a full, fresh broadside in what amounted to a Dixie cup, by comparison—but what was the point? He raised his binoculars. S-19 must be at flank, racing right in with her 4"-50 booming away. The new torpedoes worked swell, there was no doubt now, and Laumer had a perfect target. He'd sink that ship if he lived long enough. He was already well in range of the enemy guns, and calling him off would only make him a bigger target when he turned. Right now he had a few things going for him: S-19 was small and pretty fast, both of which would make her hard to hit. The Grik would know what had happened behind them by now and had to be scared to death. Maybe they'd rush their fire? Finally no longer taking a pounding of her own, *Santa Catalina* and her 5.5s were getting good hits on the enemy. Maybe that would distract them too?

"Come left to two eight zero!" Russ commanded. "Drop a grenade down the voice tube to the engine room if you have to, to get their attention. If Laney ain't there yet, he's relieved—and whoever answers and gets me full ahead will have his job! Let's get close enough to that damn thing that our five-fives'll shoot right through her, if S-Nineteen doesn't make it!"

"Ay, ay, Skipper!" the Lemurian at the helm replied.

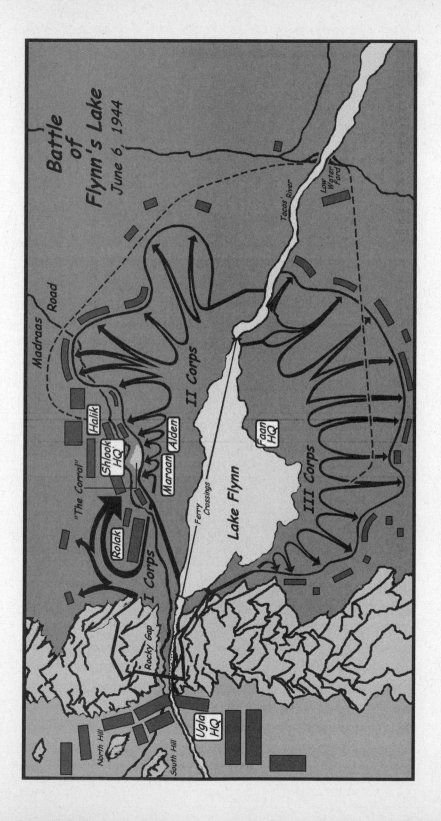

Battle
of
Flynn's Lake
June 6, 1944

Madraas Road

Tacos River

Low Water Ford

II Corps

Halik

Shlook HQ.

Maraan Alden

Faan HQ.

III Corps

"The Corral"

Rolak

Ferry Crossings

Lake Flynn

I Corps

Rocky Gap

Ugla HQ.

North Hill

South Hill

///// *The Corral*
I Corps

"We're fighting on borrowed time," General Pete Alden stated sourly to General Lord Muln-Rolak, when he and his cavalry escort finally found the old warrior a little before 1600 in the afternoon. Pete didn't dismount from the grumpy me-naak he rode. First, to prevent the irritable creature from slapping him to the ground with its muzzled head full of teeth, and second, he didn't mean to be there long. He needed to get back to Safir. Rolak stepped from within a cluster of his staff, where they'd been consulting a map held by an aide. Hij-Geerki followed, kind of hop-limping along. Rolak nodded at Pete's words, blinking thoughtfully. He didn't appear wounded, Pete noted with relief, but there was plenty of blood on his armor and matting his fur. There was blood on Hij-Geerki too, Pete realized with surprise, and then he saw the old Grik was actually wearing one of the Baalkpan Armory copies of a 1917 Navy cutlass!

"You speak truly," Rolak agreed. Despite his appearance, his tone remained urbane as always. "We fought little to reach this place, so we brought plenty of ammunition to the battle." He blinked wryly. "We have used much of it since."

"What happened to your comm?" Pete asked.

Rolak blinked irritation. "The cart was destroyed by Grik round-shot. I get occasional reports dropped from aircraft, but I know little of how the greater battle progresses."

"I've picked up some stuff here and there; kept runners going between us and Safir while we looked for you. The big picture's not so bad. Most of the army's objectives were achieved by, or a little after, twelve hundred. Even the Madras road's been cut about five miles northeast of us and there should be enough troops there with enough ammunition to hold. Especially with most of the Grik still pounding on us. What's more, General Linnaa's Sixth Corps has landed, and as of fourteen thirty, some elements were already advancing down the road to reinforce that strongpoint. Seventh Corps is ashore too, moving to block any Grik approach from Madras itself. There hasn't been a ground assault on the city yet, but nothing's getting in or out except in the north or by sea. It *sounds* like the sea route's been locked up, though, and nothing that gets out to the north can get here today, that's for sure." He paused, grimacing, because nothing he'd said really mattered much to them right then. Like a surging, living storm, the real battle for Grik India had turned into a knockdown slugfest in the vicinity of the abandoned corral.

"General Maraan's attack shook the Grik up pretty bad," Pete continued. "And the new weapons—the Blitzer Bugs in particular—mowed 'em down and scared the shit outa the rest."

"No doubt you observed that firsthand," Rolak said dryly.

Pete shrugged. "Yeah, and it was a sight to see. I figured it was all over, that Courtney Bradford's 'Grik Rout' would kick in and they'd keep runnin' till they dropped dead." He nodded at Rolak. "Especially after your First Corps slammed into their right flank—that was great timing, by the way!" He stopped.

"But they did not rout," Rolak said as softly as could be heard over the fighting now raging in a vast semicircle, with the sparse, spread-out Allied forces somewhat wrapped around the concentrated Grik. The mental image forming in Pete's mind was a soap bubble surrounding a grenade. "They did not run themselves to death," Rolak continued. "They were stunned and dispirited, I think. At least at first. But then they . . . gathered themselves. I have not seen this before. Once, the initial shock of my dear queen's attack would have been sufficient to end the battle. All would have been over but the chasing and slaying. If that were not enough, my corps's attack *would* have induced Grik Rout if anything possibly could anymore." He shook his head and his tail swished irritably. "They recoiled and contracted away from our mighty assaults," he mused, "but did not flee."

"No," Pete agreed, "they *dug in and held*, then counterattacked!"

"I feared as much," Rolak confessed. "I heard the renewed fighting— and then they did much the same to me!" He looked intently at Pete. "Something has happened. Something profound has occurred to stop the Grik retreat in its tracks."

"Halik?" Pete guessed, looking at Hij-Geerki, who seemed to tremble. "I thought he was in the south."

"Is! Is at start!" Geerki pleaded.

"He could have escaped and crossed the river to Shlook's aid. There *was* time," Rolak countered.

Pete nodded reluctantly. "I'm afraid you're right, and that ain't the worst of it. We've kicked their asses everywhere but here, and more Grik keep flocking to those damn horns that've been brayin' all day long. Grik that must've already been beaten somewhere else," he added significantly. "Which suddenly makes more sense if Halik's leading them. He's one scary, dangerous lizard." He took a deep breath, then smirked and pointed up. "Message streamers dropped by Nancys say we're 'surrounding' the biggest concentration of Grik ever seen in so small an area."

Rolak couldn't help but chuckle at the irony.

"It ain't all bad," Pete assured. "We *are* killin' the hell out of 'em. We've got constant air strikes hammerin' 'em from the lake. Lieutenant Leedom says he's just about out of gas, though, and I told him to start rearming and refueling at *Arracca* and *Baalkpan Bay* if he can—but we've got air from the fleet now too. We're absolutely slaughtering the bastards."

Rolak nodded. Aircraft were overhead almost constantly, and the jungle forest occupied by the enemy seethed and pulsed with so many explosions, so much fire and choking smoke, it was difficult to imagine anything surviving within it—but air power could only do so much.

Pete saw his doubtful blinking. "Yeah," he said. "I know. I wish we could kick off a firestorm like they did on New Ireland, but it's different here. Even though it hasn't rained today, the ground, trees, hell, even the damn air is wet. We ain't gonna be burnin' the vermin out."

"So what can we do?" Rolak asked. "We have stretched our ammunition as far as we can, farther than we thought possible. We still have bayonets and swords, and our hearts remain eager to kill the enemy, but I do not think that will be enough."

"I've called up all reserves not guarding the Rocky Gap, even started ferrying the troops over from the south side of the lake. They can't bring much artillery, but their fight was so short, they should still have plenty of ammo. Every spare round will be distributed among what's left of First and Second Corps."

"What if the Grik counterattack in the south?" Rolak asked.

"Then they'll capture the empty bank of a lake. Honestly, though, I figure any Grik left down there with any fight still in them have already gone downriver, crossed, and joined up with this bunch in front of us."

Rolak blinked grudging agreement. "With Halik," he said.

"I guess probably so."

"So, what is your plan?"

Pete hesitated. He'd actually contemplated breaking off and pulling everything back to the Rocky Gap—he was still convinced they needed to keep it at all costs—and let VI and VII Corps come get them. But then those two new green corps would have to face this veteran Grik force and its wily commander, first rattle out of the box. That didn't just smell like a lot of unnecessary casualties but a possible disaster that might leave him and all his people in the same fix they'd started with.

"We wait a little longer until we've been replenished as much as possible, then at dusk we'll go at Halik and Sklook—whatever—hammer and tongs. We kick their asses the old-fashioned way, with guts and steel if it comes to it, and take and hold our part of the Madras road until relieved." He forced a smile. "Our guys can see better in the dark than theirs can, remember?" It wasn't much of an advantage, but at that point, it was about all they had.

Rolak blinked philosophically, then grinned. His old teeth were worn and yellowed but still sharp.

A squad of Maa-ni-lo cavalry thundered out of the trees, carbines and accoutrements jangling and clattering. "Where Gen-raal Aalden? Gen-raal Rolak?" a disheveled cav 'Cat demanded.

"Here!" Pete and Rolak chorused. The mounted Lemurian urged his meanie closer, and Pete's animal snarled at the newcomer.

"Gen-raals," the 'Cat continued, nervous, almost shouting, "Gen-raal Queen Maraan sends her dearest love an' begs you both to join her!"

"What the hell? Have the Grik beat us to the punch after all?"

"They no attaack harder," the 'Cat replied, blinking something like utter confusion. "They *stoppeen* attaack! An' Gen-raal Queen says you two is only ones who ever talk to Griks under . . . troose flag!"

Pete and Rolak stared at each other. "A *truce*? Bullshit!" Pete growled. "They'll get us all together and hit us for sure!"

"I agree," Rolak stated emphatically. "We must not gather our entire high command in one place the enemy can strike." He looked at the cav 'Cat suspiciously. "And such my dear Queen Maraan would never counsel!"

"She do!" the trooper insisted. "The whole Grik commaand is mustered before her with their Haalik! It's him that ask to talk!"

Pete and Rolak exchanged another stunned look. "Then why didn't she just blast 'em?"

"You aask her, Gen-raal," the messenger pleaded. "I just folloween' orders."

Rolak flicked his tail in the equivalent of a shrug. "You will have to loan me a mount . . . Lieuten-aant, isn't it? We brought none with us." He looked at his pet Grik. "Come along, Hij-Geerki! We may have need of your tongue—and at last you will ride upon a me-naak!"

Pete Alden had hoped to launch his final attack at dusk, but instead he was picking his way through the shattered trees in front of II Corps's position toward a bright fire set to illuminate the large white flag erected on a charred sapling trunk. He wasn't alone. Forty of Saachic's troops with Blitzer Bugs and some of the last ammunition they'd scraped up for them escorted him, Rolak, Hij-Geerki, Colonel Mersaak, and Saachic out to what appeared to be less than a dozen Grik. Pete had flatly refused to let Safir Maraan accompany them. "What if they eat us?" he'd demanded. "You want me to hear what they have to say—all right. But somebody's got to stay in charge if I buy it, see?"

Pete felt fairly safe. A screen of me-naak-mounted cavalry patrolled ahead on the flanks as well, to make sure this was no trick, no ploy to assassinate the Allied leaders, and everybody in the little group was armed to the teeth. The Grik were armed too, Pete noted as they drew closer. It probably never even occurred to them that they shouldn't be.

"Let us try to talk to them *before* you shoot one this time, my friend," Rolak whispered as they stepped into the firelight, and Pete couldn't stop a snort.

"I tell that?" Geerki asked anxiously.

"No! Just tell 'em what we *tell* you to tell 'em, savvy?" Pete said, exasperated.

One of the Grik stepped forward and spoke. *That's got to be Halik,* Pete realized, without any doubt. He didn't know what he expected, or why he came so quickly to that conclusion, but savage and frightening as all Grik were, this one just . . . carried himself differently. He wasn't any taller than many Grik he'd seen, though he was far more muscular and wore the scars of many years. *Maybe that's it? He's not old, exactly, not like Geerki, but he's older than most of the others.* The creature spoke again, looking right at Pete, its yellow eyes intent in the firelight.

"General Alden," it said with some difficulty, and Pete felt his skin crawl. *So he guessed who I am too,* he thought. *No big deal, I'm the only human here, and we know they know stuff about us.*

"That's General Halik," Geerki confirmed, "and he hears English good. You talk; I tell you his talk."

Pete nodded, surprised, then wondered why he was. It was known that the Grik considered English the "scientific" tongue, and their Hij wrote in it. Halik had probably learned to understand it from Niwa, who likely understood spoken Grik.

"Okay. What's he want to talk about? We've got a perfectly good battle goin' here and he's wasting time."

Halik spoke, his voice harsh.

"He say this is not a good . . . 'attle, to neither side," Geerki translated.

Pete could only blink in the Lemurian way and he looked at Rolak, who'd leaned forward.

"I am General Lord Muln-Rolak, Protector of Aryaal—a city you slew and occupied and devoured! Any battle, any opportunity to kill Grik, is a great pleasure to *me!*"

"I have slain no city," Halik replied through Geerki. "I came late to this war and fight only as my Giver of Life commands. Why we fight is not my concern, only how, and . . . perhaps when and where." He gestured around. "This battle cannot be won by either of us. We can only both lose."

Pete listened while Geerki repeated Halik's words, and was more surprised than ever. When he spoke again, he was more careful. This really was no ordinary Grik! "You've already lost," he said. "We've retaken Madras, and a great army moves to join us as we speak. Your army south of the lake is shattered, and the Gap remains blocked. You'll get no help from that direction. Our flying machines tell us our numbers here are about even," he lied, "and our weapons are better than yours. You have no place to go." Pete shrugged. "If you surrender, you'll live." He pointed at Geerki. "We don't *eat* our prisoners!"

Geerki shrank back at Halik's gurgling sound. "He laugh at you," Geerki said in a small voice, then translated as Halik spoke again:

"I too have reports of how the wider battle proceeds, and you have some information correct. You hear news from ray-dee-o, I have no doubt. Much of the Grand Fleet has been destroyed, Madras teeters as you say, and the traitor Kurokawa prepares to flee. When he is gone, the city will fall. But your relief is not so vast as you claim, nor are our numbers so nearly matched!"

Pete shrugged when he heard this, although the fact that Halik knew about radio surprised him. According to the Japanese sailor they'd found on Diego Garcia, Kurokawa was keeping it secret from the Grik. *But what does he mean about Kurokawa? Is he still in the city? How does he intend to get out?*

"Kurokawa's a nasty bastard," he probed, "out for nobody but himself. I'm surprised you didn't eat him a long time ago. As for our little fight here, you gotta know that even if we both lose, as you say, we still win. We may go down, but so will you—and with Madras in our hands and your navy licked, that leaves us on top."

"I thought you were more concerned for the lives of your warriors than that," Halik said.

"We are!" Rolak almost exploded when Geerki finished. "We care about all our troops, all our people, whom yours have tried to exterminate since before our history began! It is *you* who cares nothing for life, who lives only to conquer and kill! *You who even eat your own!*"

Halik was silent a long moment while Rolak seethed. Finally, he replied, "Again, I know nothing of what has gone before my . . . life as a general, but I have come to care for my army *as* my people. I really have no other. I expend them in battle, and we consume our slain, as you say, but I would not see them all destroyed any more than you would enjoy the consequences of the final battle you contemplate." He gestured at the officers around him. "These other generals and I live to serve our creator, but we have agreed that this campaign, designed by Kurokawa, serves only him. We would gladly die for the Celestial Mother or First General Esshk, but we would not gladly do so for General of the Sea Kurokawa!"

"What the hell does he mean by that?" Pete demanded after he got the gist of Geerki's convoluted translation.

"Kuroka'a took the regency here," Geerki explained. "He say all India is his, and all Grik here is his. I thought you knew. I tole you!"

Pete frowned. Maybe Geerki had told them, but it never occurred to anyone that the Grik might not like it. "So," he said slowly, "what you're saying is that we have a common enemy!"

"We do NOT!" Rolak protested hotly. "The *Grik* are the enemy, and Kurokawa is merely their tool! There can never be cooperation between us! All Grik must be destroyed if we are to survive!"

Pete held up his hand. "Just hold your horses, Rolak. Nobody's talking about spoonin' with 'em." He looked squarely at Halik. "That's never going to happen," he said simply. "But we already know not all Grik *are* Grik, if you know what I mean. Some are even friends of ours, like Lawrence. That's not because of what he is, but *who* he is. Let's hear what Halik has to say." He looked at the Grik general. "I know you understood that, so what's on your mind?"

"Simply this: Kurokawa claimed all India as his regency, but only ever controlled the part that even I will admit you seem capable of wresting away. But you will have conquered it from *him*, not the Grik."

"And he'll be blamed!" Saachic said, a note of genuine delight in his voice.

"He will be blamed," Halik confirmed coldly.

"So what will *you* do?" Pete asked.

"Kurokawa has failed to rule all India, and with victory impossible, my army will cease fighting for him and move to defend that part of India he did not control," Halik said simply.

"What part will you leave?"

"From here to Madras."

"No. We've got three corps moving virtually unopposed across the low-tide crossing from Ceylon. All southern India to the escarpment, and north to the end of the world will be our cease-fire line." He gestured at the craggy ridge to the west where the Rocky Gap was. "Those mountains are the boundary—for now. Take it or leave it."

Halik began talking to his generals, and Pete felt a chill. He may've demanded too much, right when he was beginning to think his army might just survive the night.

"Very well," Halik said at last. "I agree—for now. My army will disengage and move through the river gap to our side of the escarpment immediately."

"No!" Rolak growled, looking at Pete. "He cannot go through the Rocky Gap! He could change his mind and decide to attack our troops within from east and west! He still has the army beyond. Why else would he desire to join it there?"

Pete held out his hands. "General Rolak has a point. Our forces in the Gap must remain in place as our defense against *you*, and I won't have them pull out to let you through—where you can get at 'em in the open, or maybe decide to fortify *this* side of the Gap!"

"Then how will we pass across?" Halik demanded.

"March back south, across the river, then down and around. I know you can reach the escarpment from Madurai, maybe closer. You know better than I do."

Halik discussed this with his generals again, once glancing at what looked like a pile of dingy blankets. Finally, he jerked his head in a nod. "On one condition." He gestured for the blankets to be brought, and personally knelt beside them and raised a corner. "This is General Orochi Niwa. He . . . he is my friend. He is near death, as you can see, so I do not demand that you heal him, only that you try." He paused. "And if he should live," he said quietly, "I would speak to him again someday."

"Okay," Pete said, a little flustered, but recognizing an opportunity. "On *our* condition that any of our people, any prisoners or wounded you might've captured, be returned as well—alive. We don't have any Grik prisoners I know of, but we'll have Geeky here tell any isolated groups we run across that they're free to follow you south."

For a very long moment, Halik looked into Pete's eyes, then finally jerked a diagonal nod. "It will be so," he barked, and turning away, he paced into the dark with his officers.

Pete could only stand staring after them for quite a while, and no one around him spoke. Finally, he shook his head as if clearing it. "Did that just happen?" he asked Rolak.

As carefully as they could, members of the escort carried Niwa back to the Allied line, while Pete and his companions walked slowly, talking, within the safety of the rest of their cavalry.

"Do you think he will live?" Mersaak asked. He hadn't spoken at all during the parlay.

"The Jap? Who knows. Who *cares*?" Pete asked. "We just won the battle I was pretty sure would kill us, and got a big chunk of India in the bargain."

"For a while," Rolak reminded.

"Yeah. But Captain Reddy's little expedition might just sort it all out."

"That would be pleasant," Rolak agreed. "We must do our best to save this Jaap, though."

"To interrogate? Sure. And we will."

"Not only for that," Rolak said, looking back. "But because it is the honorable thing to do—and this deed of honor was asked of us by a Grik."

"Whoa, Rolak! I thought you hated the whole idea of this cease-fire! What about all you said?"

"I meant every word," Rolak replied. "We can never have peace with the Grik—as long as they are Grik. But I played the . . . skeptic? The unpleasable? For purposes of the negotiation. I am personally thrilled that the killing will end," he smiled, blinking sadly, "for a while. I am also, oh, I do not know . . . 'Encouraged' is not the right word. Less heart weary, perhaps, to learn at last that our enemy is capable of understanding honor. Not only that, but he expects it of us! Halik must have learned that from General Niwa, and for that the man must be saved."

"Hmm," Pete grunted. "If he knows what honor is, that means he—Halik at least—ain't just a damn animal anymore. I don't know how I like that."

////// *USS* **Santa Catalina**

R uss Chapelle descended wearily down the companionway to the gun deck within the ship's armored casemate. The area had once been devoted to a dining salon, quarters for the ship's officers, and staterooms for higher-paying passengers. All that was gone now, leaving only an open space filled with 5.5-inch guns and support structures for the deck above. Residual smoke from the long fight still blurred Russ's vision, but he also saw the Lemurian guns' crews cleaning their heavy weapons with a practiced diligence that made him proud. There'd been no serious casualties inside the casemate, beyond some likely permanent hearing loss, and the 'Cats seemed if not happy—all knew there'd been hefty casualties elsewhere on the ship—then certainly satisfied with their work that day. *Satisfied but tired,* Russ reflected. Some of the 'Cats, youngling shell handlers mostly, were tucked away in little alcoves, fast asleep, despite the loud, ongoing work. There was noise everywhere. Repair parties were shoring sprung plates all over the ship, and the general uproar was profound. But they weren't sinking and they'd helped destroy nearly every enemy ship that steamed out of the port of Madras. A few may have gotten away, there'd been no word from the Air Corps about one of the damaged battleships and a couple of cruisers, but everyone knew they'd scored a great victory and taken a step toward avenging the Allied losses at the first Battle of Madras, not to mention their own shipmates—and one in particular. *The scuttlebutt is the fastest means of communication ever devised by any creature,* Russ supposed grimly.

"Caap'n on deck!" several 'Cats called at once, but he waved at them. "As you were! You've got work. I just wanted to tell you all well done and thanks. Otherwise, I'm only passing through." There were tired cheers, but the gunners quickly returned to their duties. They knew where he was going. Suddenly reluctant to proceed, he paused a moment longer to look around before shaking his head and continuing down the companionway. There'd once been more staterooms on this level and were again, in a sense, for officers and POs. There was also a pharmacy, a real sick bay, and the wardroom that had once been a lounge. Just then, the sick bay and wardroom were crammed with wounded, and Surgeon Commander Kathy McCoy and her mates, corps 'Cats and SBAs (sick-berth attendants) were very busy treating what seemed to be mostly broken bones caused by the concussion of heavy shot hitting the ship, and lots of moderate to severe cuts and gashes made by iron and wooden splinters and flying fragments of enemy shot.

Commander McCoy saw Russ enter the noisy bustle and frowned as he approached.

"He's been asking for you," she accused.

"I know. I had to finish the fight. There were still some cruisers . . ." He stopped and removed his hat, running fingers through sweaty hair. They'd destroyed the last cruiser they could catch two hours before. "And it's hard, you know?"

Kathy nodded understanding. "Yeah."

Russ looked at her hopefully. "Is there any chance at all?"

"None," she replied almost defiantly, then lowered her voice. "He's torn wide-open, Captain. Even if I *could* save him . . ." Her tone turned scolding again. "But he wouldn't let me seep him up, to ease his pain, before he talked to you."

Russ nodded, squaring his shoulders. "Where is he?"

Kathy led him to Jim Ellis's own stateroom. It was larger than the others, as befitted a commodore, but remained sparse compared to such accommodations Russ had seen on real Navy cruisers. Jim was lying on his rack, swaddled in bandages. Bright blood showed against the tan gauze and absorbent padding covering his chest and the short stump of his arm.

"Hiya, Russ," Jim managed huskily. "I was afraid I'd miss you."

"Not a chance, Commodore. Just had a few details to tend."

"Like finishing a battle," Jim said, forcing a grin. "And leave off the 'Commodore' crap. Tell me everything."

Russ sat on the chair beside the boxed-in rack. "You did it, sir," he said simply. "You won. The troops from the transports and *Baalkpan Bay* are all ashore, and several divisions are already on the Madras road, moving to link up with Pete Alden. Pete's okay, sir! And so's ol' Rolak and Safir Maraan! The orphan queen's wounded, they say, but not bad, and the biggest chunk of all three Corps that were in Alden's Perimeter are safe!" He paused. "The Grik have pulled back from every point of contact except across the west side of that Rocky Gap. Nobody seems to know what that's all about, and Pete's been too busy to make a full report. He says it's the real deal, though. The battle's over, for now." Russ scratched his head. "The funny thing is, according to TBS chatter— some of Alden's planes have been out to the carriers, bringing wounded and carting ammo back—Pete's not too happy about that, even though his army was just about down to throwing rocks."

Russ stopped. Jim had closed his eyes, but now opened them again. "Go on," he ordered.

"Aye, sir. However it wound up, Pete had a god-awful confusing fight, spread over a hell of a lot of jungle. It could be a while before we get a casualty count, but most of 'em made it, and I guess my point is, that's your doing. They couldn't have hung on much longer if we hadn't come when we did."

"Bullshit," Jim coughed with a wince, but smiled. There was blood on his lips. "Thanks, though," he added more carefully. "It's . . . nice of you to say."

"Only the truth," Russ persisted.

Jim shook his head slightly. "It wound up being your fight, though, at least out here. How's your ship? And S-Nineteen?"

"We're at anchor, sir, south of the Madras harbor mouth, inshore of the rest of First fleet. All's quiet." It was anything *but* quiet aboard the wounded ship, but Jim knew what he meant. Russ forced a grin. "Laumer and his goofy S-Nineteen sank *three* Grik battlewagons with our new torpedoes!" he announced proudly. "One of 'em while it was blasting away right at him! The boat took a couple hits," he confessed, "but nothing too bad, and they slammed four fish in the side of that wagon at eight hundred yards! Blooey! I never saw anything sink so fast. We wondered before, but now we know those Grik wagons are top-heavy as hell and the armor only extends a little way below the waterline. Open up that wooden hull, and they flop over like a dying duck!" He shook his head. "I started as a torpedoman myself, if you'll recall, but I honestly never believed our new fish would work. Too many bad experiences, I guess. Now I wish we had a set of tubes here aboard the ol' *Santy Cat!*"

Jim was nodding, a slight smile on his lips, but his eyes were closed again. His breathing was more difficult too, and a bright orange bubble suddenly popped at his mouth. Russ's vision blurred.

"Where's Matt?" Jim managed. "I wish he were here."

"He would've been, if he could," Russ assured him. "*Walker* and *Mahan* left *Big Sal* and all her DDs and they're hauling ass back up here to pick up any leakers from this fight. The Third Pursuit hammered the Grik relief, and it wasn't as big as the scouts reported. Some of it must've already turned back. Captain Reddy'll stop anything we might've missed, and wrap everything up in a nice, tidy bow."

"Sure. And then it won't be long before he heads for Diego, and eventually Madagascar. Maybe that'll finally end this damn war," Jim Ellis gasped.

Russ doubted that, but didn't say so. "I wish I could go with him," Russ agreed instead, "but *Santy Cat*'s gonna need a refit before she takes such a jaunt." He peered down at Jim's slacking face. "Maybe *you* can go," he suggested softly. Jim stirred and coughed orange blood through clenched teeth, in what might've been a laugh.

"No way. Don't b'shit," he wheezed. For a moment, Commodore Jim Ellis stared hard at Russ Chapelle. Finally, as distinctly as he could, he spoke. "Tell Captain Reddy that, weird as it's been, it's been an honor and a privilege to serve with him . . . and be his friend. Tell him I wouldn't have missed it for the world—this one or the last, and I hope to serve with him again wherever we wind up next."

S-19

The tired former submarine was wallowing at anchor not far from where *Santa Catalina* rode more gently at hers. The night was pitch-black and the smoke from Madras added an opacity that hid even the stars. The city was bright, however, with flames and swirling sparks rising high in the sky. The Grik had evidently torched the place again, because as far as Irvin knew, there'd been no fighting there. There'd been bombing, though, he reminded himself. Maybe the air raids started all the fires? It was possible. The raids had gone on all day.

"That's a heck of a sight, Captain Laumer," Nat Hardee said.

"Yeah. I've heard how Aryaal and B'mbaado looked when we had to abandon them at the beginning of the war, and I guess that must've been worse. But this," he gestured at the city. "Well, it looks like hell."

Danny Porter was with them on the somewhat disheveled flying bridge. A big Grik ball had knocked away several of the supports and it was sagging a little to starboard. Sandy Whitcomb was below, completing temporary repairs to the top of the pressure hull in the old forward berthing space. There were fuel bunkers in there now, and until earlier that day when they shifted them forward, two torpedo reloads. No water was coming in, but the outer hull encompassing the *new* berthing space had a big hole in it, and some recently laid deckplates had been torn up. If enough water slopped in, the pressure hull would leak eventually. That would've been undesirable in any case, but even though S-19 wasn't a sub anymore, the integrity of her pressure hull remained sacred to her crew.

"I hope we can avoid any heavy seas until that hole's patched," Irvin said, proving he and Danny were thinking along similar lines.

"Our damage is awful light considering the sheer weight of metal those Griks threw at us during the charge," Danny pointed out. "And even more amazing is how few got hurt—and nobody got killed at all."

"Yeah," Irvin agreed, but his tone was somber. They all knew it was a different story on *Santa Catalina*, but they remained relieved. They were also proud of S-19. Their long insistence that she be returned to service instead of scrapped had been justified at last, and Irvin personally felt a happy sense of vindication. He thought he'd just been coasting for far too long, and though he'd faced other dangers, even the Doms, this was his first action against the hated Grik. He hadn't shirked his duty, as he'd always secretly feared he might; hadn't even hesitated. He was proud of his ship and himself, and he had a new confidence that he could handle any assignment. Ben Mallory's Air Corps had whittled the enemy down to a bite-size chunk, and *Santa Catalina* had certainly done her part, but S-19 administered a stunningly spectacular coup de grace to the Grik fleet at Madras, and the show-stopping finale would be remembered, Irvin was sure.

"The fellas did real fine," Danny said, a benevolent smile splitting his sun-bleached beard. The "fellas" included a number of women; one a shell handler on the four-inch-fifty, just then helping its otherwise Lemurian crew clean and secure the weapon. She and a 'Cat were pulling on a long wooden pole, dragging a bristle brush down the bore from the breech to remove fouling and copper from the rifling grooves. Danny couldn't help but watch the girl closely. Like most ex-pat Impie gals who made it as far west as Baalkpan or joined the Navy, she was young, adventurous, and very pretty. Danny frowned. But he was chief of the boat. Showing favorites, let alone sparking up a member of the crew, simply wasn't acceptable for him. He sighed and concentrated on the big gun.

"I'm still disappointed with the new shells against armored targets," he said. "Our guys did swell and landed some shrewd, damaging licks at close range—I mean, once we got inside fifteen hundred yards. But that's *too* damn close!"

"We'll do better when we get armor-piercing shells. The ones they sent out from Baalkpan were dropped as bombs by the Naval Air Corps, and apparently did fairly well. We'll get them soon enough."

"It's always a matter of priorities," Danny mused. "Sure, we'll get AP shells eventually, like everything else that can use 'em, but after today, the Air Corps'll be screaming for something that can drop torpedoes!"

"That'll take longer," Irvin chuckled. "Those big, four-engine 'Clippers' could carry a torpedo, but nothing else we have yet can—and 'Clippers' are stretched thin, with lots of other jobs."

A bright blue-orange flash lit the sky over Madras, blooming, then falling earthward like the petals of a dying flower.

"What the hell?" Danny grunted.

"Grik zeps is inbound!" cried the talker. "Lots o' Grik zeps!"

"How many?" Irvin demanded, then bit his lip. He couldn't see the 'Cat well enough in the dark, but didn't doubt he was blinking something like "Are you kidding me?"

"I don't know. 'Lots' is all they say. Maybe *all*. It jus' come over TBS! Nancys spot 'em—an' get one, I bet—but they ain't enough Nancys armed for air fight!"

"Sound general quarters!" Irvin ordered. "The three-inch gun crew will stand by for air action." He looked at Danny. "Call the anchor detail and get ready to pull the hook, Chief. Better tell Whitcomb to fire up the other diesel too. Let me know as soon as we're ready to maneuver!"

"Aye, aye, Skipper!" Danny replied, and bolted down the crooked stairway aft, raising his whistle to his lips.

"Should I flash *Santa Catalina* to make sure they copied?" Hardee asked.

"No! No lights! Those damn Grik'll have had spies to tell 'em about where the fleet was relative to Madras, but they can't see anything down here. We won't give 'em any targets! Confirm that *Santy Cat* got the word with the TBS."

"Aye, Skipper."

For a few moments, Irvin was alone with his thoughts. There were 'Cats on the flying bridge, but nobody spoke. All were focused on the fiery light show developing in the sky above. After that first explosion, more zeppelins quickly started burning in rapid succession, giving the impression that fire was pouring from the heavens. Irvin was amazed by how comforted he was by the sound of the starboard diesel starting up, adding to the oddly muffled exhaust escaping from the tall, slim funnel behind the bridge.

"There *are* a lot of them," Hardee said grimly, returning to Irvin's side.

"Our flyboys must see 'em better up there, because I still can't see squat—until one lights up. And they're chewing hell out of them! Did General Alden have more air-to-air capable Nancys at Lake Flynn that came to help?"

"No, sir," Hardee replied. "Tassana-Ay-Arracca sent that *Baalkpan Bay* scrambled her Fleashooter wing."

Irvin's skin crawled. "Jesus! Those poor guys are still learning to land on a carrier, and they already crack up half the time! No way they can land in the dark. And they don't have fuel to last till daylight!"

"No, sir," Nat agreed, "but there's a clearing west of the city. A regiment of Impie troops with Seventh Corps overran it earlier, but now they'll try to secure the environs and light it up with bonfires."

"My God. Those guys haven't been ashore eight hours! They're green as grass. And now they're going to fight a battle in the dark so they can light up a grass strip?"

"Maybe not," Nat said. There are still Grik in the city, but the word is those outside have quit fighting. Pulled back."

"Huh." Laumer shook his head. "It'll still be a bloody mess."

"Yes, sir."

They watched in silence again as the air battle crept east-southeast. Not toward them so much, but definitely toward the bulk of First Fleet. It *was* getting closer, though, and they could see it in greater detail, particularly through a telescope. Occasionally they caught the flitting, tracer-spitting shapes of the P-1 Mosquito Hawks swarming through the mass of zeppelins. Twice they saw pairs of the little planes apparently collide and fall like tumbling meteors into the sea. It was impossible to say how many of the big gasbags there were—perhaps thirty had already fallen—but every now and then they saw clusters of them illuminated by one of their flaming, falling herd. Laumer was stunned by the sheer wastefulness of the attack. Each zep represented a tremendous expenditure of labor and material, not to mention the time it took to train its crew, and they were just throwing them away! No doubt this massed night attack had a better chance of success than a similar attack in daylight, but the profligacy of the effort, of the *strategy*, struck Laumer as insane. Of course, the Grik had never been concerned about losses, but even if the Allies had developed aircraft that could keep zeppelins away from the front, they were still useful, could still carry more passengers and supplies than a "Clipper," and could deliver them just about anywhere. Laumer wished the *Allies* had a few of the damn things.

"The Grik aren't stupid, not anymore," Irvin murmured. "At least not all of them. There's got to be a reason they're doing this now. Is there something else up their sleeve, or do they really have enough zeps to bull all the way to the fleet?"

"Maybe," Nat said, a little nervously. Big, scattered explosions started flinging illuminated geysers up from the sea. Clearly, some of the suicider bombs had begun to fall. Those things were dangerous as hell—if they could see their targets. Essentially big bombs with stubby wings, a tail, and a Grik pilot lying on his belly with a one-way ticket, they'd almost destroyed *Big Sal* at the first Battle of Madras. But they couldn't see anything now, and were being wasted too. Or were they? One of the ships in the fleet—it was impossible to tell which—suddenly lit up the sea a couple of miles away. It was probably just luck, or maybe a Grik suicider—how the *hell* did they get them to *do* that?—saw a target in the light of a near miss. Suddenly, they got a little better idea just how many zeps must be up there, because maybe six or seven more suiciders immediately slammed into the burning ship, one after the other. The last few probably hit only floating debris.

"God almighty!" Irvin breathed. He spun and paced aft. "You will *not* fire that weapon for any reason. Is that clear?" he ordered the crew on the three-inch gun. The 'Cats just stared at him, again probably blinking something that meant "Do we look nuts?"

Irvin turned to the front, looking up. Tracers arced lazily just above, and a small flash, like a little cannon shot, replied. What was clearly a Fleashooter burst into flames and began a long spiral toward the sea. Other tracers converged and sparkled against what looked like a growing, dull orange moon.

"Heads up!" a 'Cat trilled on the fo'c'sle. "Iss gonna fall on us!"

That wasn't going to happen. Already, the great dirigible was edging northward, still a few thousand feet up, its forward section engulfed in flames that surged greedily aft. Somewhat unusually, it was falling in one piece, the glowing embers on the rigid frame growing larger as it accelerated downward. Engines fell away and drifting fragments of burning fabric fluttered like giant fireflies.

"It ain't gonna hit, but it's gonna be close!" Danny yelled from forward. "I sure hope it doesn't draw any damn glider bombs!"

The flaming, glowing skeleton of the Grik zeppelin fell less than two hundred yards off the starboard beam, but for a moment everyone stood and stared, confused. Much of the wreckage never quite made it to the water, but with a great, towering swirl of sparks, it impacted something else and collapsed across it like a massive, glowing web. Laumer's first horrified thought was that it had fallen on *Santa Catalina* . . . *But that can't be!* he realized. *She's over* there, *northeast!* He confirmed it with a quick glance that revealed her dark shape off S-19's starboard quarter. *Whatever that is* . . . He jerked his glass to his eye just as the lookout screeched from above.

"On deck! Grik baatle-waagons is comin' right at us, starboard side!"

That's impossible! Irvin screamed at himself. *There* are *no other enemy ships around! The Air Corps would've told us, and they'd been scouting the whole area until the sun went down!* Then his heart ran away like high-speed screws leaving the water in heavy seas. *But there* are *more! There'd been at least three 'wagons still in Madras! Just because they hadn't come out before, didn't mean they couldn't!*

"All ahead, emergency flank!" he screamed at the 'Cat in the dark pilothouse, but knew it was already too late. All the effort they'd expended to refloat and refit S-19, all the hell they'd endured then and since, the proud little ship she'd become that turned the tables that day, and the devoted crew who'd made it possible—it was all over, about to be snuffed out like a bug on a railroad track! "Close all internal compartments. Sound the collision alarm!" he added, his soul dying inside him as the monstrous, still-glowing silhouette churned inexorably closer, its armored bow aiming at him like a giant ax. *Maybe that glowing zep carcass'll at least bring some of their own bombs down on that thing,* he thought bleakly.

The twin NELSECO diesels roared and the old boat began to move, but it was too little, too late. Laumer and Hardee were knocked off their feet when the knife-edge bow of the Grik dreadnaught slashed straight through S-19's engine room, toppling the little funnel, and driving the three-inch gun and all its crew over the side. For a moment, S-19 was pushed along, jackknifed, the sea curling over her port beam and surging across the deck. Then, with a terrible screeching moan like a dying palka, she finally broke. More of Irvin's precious crew was tossed into the savage sea when the forward half of S-19 lurched upward, buoyed by internal compartments. Irvin looked up and saw the monstrous Grik battleship rumble past, a mere dozen yards from his stricken vessel, the machinery noises inside almost deafening. It was huge and black, except where burning debris from the zeppelin still flickered, and it looked for all the world like a great moving island covered with the lights of little villages. High above, a few sparks rose amid the coal smoke from the funnels, but otherwise all the gunports were shut and it was completely blacked out. They never would've seen it in this dreary night at all if the zep hadn't crashed on it, and it occurred to Laumer that it probably never saw S-19 either. With all the noise and accompanying vibration of the ships crude, monstrous engines, the Grik might still be unaware they'd just, accidentally, avenged three of their sister ships!

What was left of S-19 had achieved an almost even keel, but was extremely low aft—and getting lower fast.

"Control room bulkhead's sprung, an' water comin' in fast!" the talker cried.

"Tell 'em to evacuate forward!" Irvin yelled, struggling to his feet.

He looked around, quickly taking in the hopelessness of the situation. S-19 had small boats, of course, but they'd been mounted on either side of the funnel. Even if they hadn't been smashed in the collision, water was already past there. It was suicide to jump in the water, and there was no other way to get off the sinking ship. The Grik battleship finally passed them by, rocking them ruthlessly with its wake and churning screws. *Surely Santa Catalina saw the damn thing, lit up like a Christmas tree!* Irvin thought. *Yes!* Two of the protected cruiser's 5.5-inchers flared and detonated against the aft port side of the battleship's casemate. They were close enough that that had to hurt! Just north, from the direction the Grik came, the sea lit under the rolling broadside of another Grik battleship, then *another*! Phosphorescent splashes erupted around *Santa Catalina* amid terrible, metallic crashes. Even from this distance, Irvin heard the clattering rush of what could only be *Santy Cat's* heavy anchor chain, and he wondered if it had been shot away or Mr. Chapelle had it released. Either way, whether *Santa Catalina* was about to join the fight in earnest or run away, S-19 was on her own and there remained only one, desperate possibility.

"Danny!" Irvin screamed down to the chief of the boat, clinging to the 4"-50. "Get everybody below!"

"Below? Are you nuts? The boat's goin' *down*!"

"And we can't get off, so we gotta get *in*. Remember S-Forty-Eight?"

Danny blinked, then nodded. It really was the only choice, and he started yelling for everyone to "get down the hatch into the old forward berthing space!" The 'Cats must've thought he was nuts too, but every S-boat sailor remembered S-48. She'd been considered jinxed because of the string of accidents she'd endured, but the pertinent one was how she'd sunk in sixty feet of water back in '21, but her crew managed to bring her bow to the surface and escape, every one, through a torpedo tube! She'd later been salvaged and recommissioned—only to be sort of "lost," and returned to duty yet again. The last they heard, she was still afloat and probably fighting their Old War on that other earth. Irvin heard Danny yelling a condensed version of this tale to the scared 'Cats he was cramming down the hatch.

Another thunderous broadside shattered the night, and *Santa Cata-*

lina returned fire—but she was moving now, angling away. The second Grik battleship plowed toward them, but, mercifully, it would miss. Irvin scanned the sky for a moment, wishing the damn suiciders would swoop down and slam into the enemy, even if they got S-19 too, but by now there were quite a few explosions on the water near First Fleet— and not as many zeppelins were falling anymore. He prayed it was because they'd been swept from the skies, and not because the Fleashooters were out of ammo.

"C'mon!" Irvin shouted at the 'Cats in the pilothouse. "She's going, and we have to get to that hatch before the water does. We don't have the weight of the stern to drag us down, and the more air we keep in the pressure hull, the higher she'll ride!" The Lemurians didn't need any more encouragement and bolted down the stairs forward, all but the talker, who remained by Irvin and Hardee's side.

"I . . . I think my arm is broken," said Nat Hardee through clenched teeth. He sounded like he was going into shock.

"That's okay. We've got you, Nat," Irvin said as he and the talker helped the kid down the ladder. It was crowded by the hatch, but 'Cats were almost diving in the hole now as water crept closer and the angle grew more pronounced. There was still light below, and Laumer remembered they'd kept some of the boat's batteries. Somebody must've rerouted the power since the main switchboard was probably on the bottom with the stern by now, but he feared the specter of chlorine gas if water made it into the berthing space.

"Hurry up, damn it," Danny said to the last five or six waiting 'Cats. "Mr. Hardee's hurt. Stand by to grab him when you get below!"

The water was coming faster as the bow rose, and suddenly there was only Irvin, Nat, Danny, and the talker.

"Get your stripey tail down that hole, sailor!" Danny yelled at the 'Cat. "Take Mr. Hardee's legs with you. I'll lower the rest of him down."

"You go first," Nat objected. "I'm perfectly able . . ."

"We'll be right along, Nat," Irvin said softly, as boy and 'Cat disappeared down the hatch.

"After you, Chief," Irvin then said to Danny. He looked at the rushing water and shrugged. "I've gotta be last, you know."

Danny nodded reluctantly and started down. Just then, the boat groaned and the bow pitched farther up. Irvin's feet fell out from under him and he started sliding backward, towards the deadly sea.

"Shit!" Danny screamed, and launched himself back on deck.

"Get below!" Irvin cried, voice high with terror. "That's an order!" Danny ignored him and caught Laumer's scrabbling arm.

"Orders ain't no good at times like this," Danny gasped, slinging Irvin up the sloping deck. He'd always been wiry, but Irvin never thought he had the strength for something like that. He landed beside the hatch and turned with his hand outstretched for Danny to grab, but the chief slammed to the deck beside him and literally shoved him down the hatch headfirst. Danny started to jump in after him, but realized that at this angle, there was no way they could pull the hatch cover shut from below. Somebody had to *lift* the damn thing!

"Oh, shit," he murmured again. Squatting behind the heavy cover, he lifted it up until it balanced on the hinge, then tried to get around, still holding it, and put his leg inside. He groped desperately for the ladder rung with his foot and could hear the shouts of encouragement below, but there was just no possible way he could hold the hatch cover and squeeze through the narrowing gap at the same time!

The first surge of water sloshed down the hole.

With a terrible sense of dread, Danny Porter knew he was finished, but just then, to him, the most important thing in the world became that his shipmates never know how terrified he was. "So long, fellas!" he roared down into the berthing space as cheerfully as he could manage, then he slammed the hatch cover down and dogged it shut.

Immediately, he tried to scurry forward, to get as far up the bow as possible in case it did stay afloat, but the angle was too great and the wet deck too slick. It was no use. He crouched by the hatch, water washing around his waist, watching as the bow rose ever higher. *It's gonna be hell down there,* he realized, *with all that stuff breaking loose and falling all over the place. People too. There'll probably be gas. Maybe they can climb into the torpedo room and get away from it, but the boat may not even stay above water, and they'll all suffocate anyway.* He looked east. *Santy Cat's still poundin' 'em, but the last Grik ships are scooting past now, some of those cruiser things. Huh. Santy doesn't look like she's goin' after 'em. I hope she's not too chewed!* In the distance, the attack was definitely tapering off. Several ships were burning, but no more glide bombs were hitting anymore. He hated not knowing how it would all turn out, but his certainty was growing that, of all S-19's surviving crew, he was going to get off the easiest. At least that's what he thought until the first flasher fish tore a baseball-size hunk out of his side. Another hit his left leg. Even as he flailed, screaming in the water, the hits became continuous and the water frothed around him. Oddly, he never really felt any pain; the attack was too fast, too traumatic. Flasher fish are greedy things, and very good at what they do.

////// *USS* **Walker**

"Skipper!" Ed Palmer cried, scrambling up the stairs aft and dashing into the pilothouse. Spanky glared at him for his breach of propriety, but Ed didn't notice. Instead, he rushed to where Matt was sitting in his Captain's chair, bolted to the forward bridge bulkhead on the starboard side. Matt saw that Ed held a message form in his trembling hand, something Matt had learned to dread. He took it calmly enough, but his heart felt like lead. There'd been a lot of message forms that day, and the news was mostly good. He'd been frustrated that *Walker* and *Mahan*, two of the most formidable combatants in the Navy, had been on what turned out to be a wild-goose chase while a major battle was underway, but all early reports indicated First Fleet North had done well enough without them. But Ed's behavior implied *this* message form contained seriously bad news. Reluctantly, Matt squinted at the dark page.

"What the hell?" demanded Spanky.

Matt looked up. "Yes, please, Mr. Palmer. Just spill it."

Ed hesitated, but Courtney Bradford stepped forward and put a soothing hand on the communications officer's arm. "Indeed," he urged. "I think Captain Reddy believes your distress indicates you bear news we all should hear."

Palmer gulped and looked at Matt, who nodded gravely. "Skipper," he said, then glanced around. "Everybody." He paused. "Commodore Ellis is dead."

There was only the dimmest lighting in the pilothouse, so no one saw Matt's green eyes turn that frightening, icy shade, but there was no hiding the telltale stiffening of his spine and hardening of his features that signified a mounting rage. From an earlier report they'd known Jim was wounded, but the extent of his injuries hadn't been disclosed. Maybe they just assumed however bad it might be, he'd heal eventually. The curative Lemurian polta paste they relied on so had instilled a sub-conscious conviction that if someone wasn't killed outright, chances were they'd be okay. After all, nearly every living human destroyerman had been wounded at some point by now, often badly. Jim himself had just recovered from a serious injury. If he'd died from wounds he suffered that day, they must have been terrible indeed.

A profound silence lingered on the bridge as Ed's words sank in, the only sounds from the ship herself; the rumbling blower, and the rush of the beam sea leaning her slightly starboard as she pitched. But the rhythmic, vibrating groan of the steel transmitting the motion of machinery and turning shafts made it seem like USS *Walker* herself was reminding them that Jim Ellis once belonged to her as much as the rest of them, and she wanted her own say in how they'd avenge his loss.

"What else?" Matt asked, his voice as brittle and hard and black as obsidian. He held up the message form in the gloom. "There's more here."

"Yessir," Ed acknowledged. "Apparently, the fighting's mostly done ashore, but those last three Grik wagons, the ones everybody thought were knocked out or broke, steamed out of Madras in the dark with a covey of cruisers." He shook his head. "Swarms of zeps attacked at the same time, so maybe that's why nobody noticed. *Baalkpan Bay*'s pursuit planes slaughtered 'em, but the fleet got hurt. Two DDs, a transport, and an oiler are just gone. No survivors." He let that sink in, then continued. "*Arracca* and *Baalkpan Bay* both took hits from suiciders, but they came out okay. Neither had planes on deck, and the new damage-control procedures worked pretty well. *Baalkpan Bay* should be back fully operational by morning. *Arracca*'ll take a little longer, but all her damage was aft. She can launch and recover Nancys already."

"What's the worst?" Spanky demanded, knowing the comm officer was holding back.

"Well." Ed gestured outside the pilothouse windows. "It's really dark, overcast, and there won't be a moon for another hour or so. Add in all the smoke . . ."

"What happened?" Matt insisted.

Ed looked at him. "The Grik came out in line, pretty much invisible, and steamed straight through where *Santa Catalina* and S-19 were anchored. *Santy Cat* got hammered pretty bad by successive broadsides at close range. A round punched through and knocked out her main steam line. Her forward fireroom's flooded and she's got no power, even for her pumps. She's dead in the water. DDs from the fleet rushed over when they saw the fight flare up and they're standing by to do whatever they can to keep her afloat or take her people off."

"Shit!" Spanky breathed.

"Yessir," Ed agreed.

"What about S-Nineteen?" Matt asked.

Ed winced. "Nobody's real sure yet, but there's no sign of her except an oil slick and floating junk. Some 'Cats on *Santy* hollered across to the DDs that they think the lead Grik wagon rammed her amidships."

"Good God!" Courtney exclaimed.

Matt sat silent for several moments, staring forward, then he looked at Ed. "Signal to Commander Brister on *Mahan*: 'Maintain course three six zero.' Ask him what's the highest speed he can sustain." He turned to Spanky. "Post extra lookouts when the watch changes, and have Bernie prep his torpedoes however he needs to. Sprinkle holy water on 'em, if that's what it takes." He stood and glared out at the darkness, his hands holding his cane behind his back. "Those ships—that's *got* to be Kuro-kawa coming at us, trying to bail out of Madras and save his crazy, evil ass." He shook his head. "Not this time, by God." He stepped slowly out on the bridgewing and savagely flung the cane into *Walker*'s churning wake. When he returned to face the bridge watch, the meager light in the pilothouse finally glittered off the ice in his eyes. "*This* time we kill him."

Through the remainder of the first dog watch, the last dog watch, and into the first watch, *Walker* and *Mahan* steamed north-northwest, making turns for twenty-five knots. How *Mahan* did it, slowing *Walker* only slightly, Matt had no idea. But he accepted that if Perry Brister thought his ship was about to come unwrapped, he'd let him know. *Or maybe he wouldn't?* Perry had to be equally convinced that Kurokawa was, if not Jim's, then certainly S-19's murderer. He'd cost them—and the whole Alliance—an awful lot of lives ever since they first met the bastard, and he'd prolonged and immeasurably raised the price of the ongoing war by *aiding* the Grik. Kurokawa was a legitimate military target, but killing him would fetch the Alliance in general, and Matt's old destroyermen in particular, a tremendous measure of satisfaction. Matt was determined that that night would see the end of their chief collective nemesis, embodied by Hisashi Kurokawa, once and for all.

The wind was rising and so was the sea, still hitting *Walker* on the port beam, but now sending sheets of water over the fo'c'sle. The sky had cleared to reveal a rising crescent moon, however. There seemed no way Kurokawa's squadron could escape the keen-eyed Lemurian lookouts who changed every hour, but anxiously hoped they'd be the ones to spot the dark silhouettes of massive ships and telltale sparks of coal-fired boilers. There was little talk on the bridge throughout the grim sprint and Matt remained in his chair or paced the bridgewings the entire time, drinking cup after cup of Juan's monkey joe. Occasionally he peered at the chart spread on the table, beneath the scuffed sheet of Plexiglas, and consulted his watch.

He'd calculated their quarry had two choices: a straight shot, hugging the coastline and making all possible speed, or a southeasterly course that would give them a bigger ocean to hide in. The first would take them the farthest, but leave them vulnerable to air attack from Trin-con-lee with the morning. It would also, incidentally, land them in *Walker*'s and *Mahan*'s laps before much longer. The second might seem more attractive, but wouldn't do them any good because *Big Sal* was still plodding up from astern. Her planes would find the big Grik ships quickly enough, and would call Matt's little squadron to the fight.

Personally, Matt figured he was on the right trail, and Kurokawa would try to bull straight through. *Those Grik BB's will eat a lot of coal,* he thought, *and Kurokawa can't have enough to throw too wide a loop in his course. He'll have figured out what we used to sink his wagons at Madras, and knows we don't have many more, if any. He'll come straight on.* Matt was sure. *He'll expect to lose his cruisers to our air, but there's not much air, particularly our planes at Trin-con-lee, can do against underway battleships. Ben's P-40s'll shoot their fifty cal dry, and the Nancys and Fleashooters'll rain fifty-pound bombs all over him—but they had a hard enough time hitting the few vulnerable spots on stationary targets at Madras. Otherwise, all they have is incendiaries—which don't do squat—and he knows it.* Matt nodded, satisfied. *Kurokawa will come straight on, thinking he's got all the aces—but he doesn't—can't—know* Walker *and* Mahan *will be waiting for him!* He glanced at his watch again, considering the closure rate based on his ships' speed and what he thought the Grik dreadnaughts could make. "Soon," he whispered.

"Scuttlebutt says we're goin' for Kuri-kawi hisself," Chief Isak Rueben announced flatly to the aft fireroom at large in what, for him, was an almost giddy tone. There were hoots of tired appreciation in the dank, sweltering space. It had probably achieved 130 degrees in the firerooms that day, and though the heat had moderated with the night, it was still over 90. Lieutenant Tab-At slid down the ladder from the escape trunk above, her bare feet splatting in the grimy muck on the deckplates. She glared at Isak. "You happy now it's nasty down here again?"

"We're goin' after Kuri-kawi!" Isak told her, ignoring her jab.

"You don't say," Tabby replied with a trace of sarcasm. She didn't point out that she'd just spoken with Spanky and probably knew a lot more than Isak. That would be mean. She thought Isak had finally gotten over her being his superior and they got along about as well as ever, but she didn't like to remind him of the official gulf between them. As far as she was concerned, Isak was more like a partner, a backup engineering officer, and they both did essentially the same job. She was better at organization and paperwork, even considering her limited letters, and was infinitely better at translating Isak's admitted genius concerning the powerplant to the rest of the snipes—not to mention other officers and divisions.

"Yah," Isak said. "We'll sink those iron-plated Grik-Japs' asses like . . . somethin' easy! Like turtle heads in a stock tank!"

"They handled *Saanty Caat* pretty rough," Tabby reminded, a little confused by Isak's reference.

"So? She's a damn log, just wallowin' there. All she could do was creep along like a slug an' take it." He tapped a hot boiler with a wrench affectionately. "We can outrun their shot!"

Tabby blinked annoyance. "No, we can't," she said. "We're fast enough to spoil their aim, maybe, but we got no armor at all. The *rest* of the word is, *Saanty Caat* had to get close to do any damage with her guns, an' S-Nineteen had to get just as close for torpedoes. Don't get cocky down here! When we fight, be ready to patch holes an' shore up plates on the double! If they shoot holes in us, they gonna be damn big ones!"

Isak peered at her. "You sure have turned grumpy in yer old age— an' since you officered up!"

Tabby blinked surprised irritation. "Well . . . when did you change to such a 'all's swell' kinda guy?"

Isak shrugged. "Never did. You want I should carry on an' spew woe ever'where—like okra seeds?"

Tabby chuckled. She and Isak—and Gilbert—once spent most of a day discussing okra. In that one respect, the two half brothers deeply disagreed. Isak hated it, Gilbert loved it, and even never having tasted it, Tabby came down on Isak's side, based solely on his description of the stuff. "No," she conceded.

"Then lemme be, an' quit trompin' on my genu-ine pleasure at goin' up against that Jap booger in my very own fireroom, aboard my own ship! I been toilin' away at so many stinky jobs lately, even puttin' up with that beetle-brain Laney!" He paused. "Say, I don't s'pose he bought it?" he asked hopefully.

"No word on that."

"Too bad. It's a cryin' shame good fellas like Mr. Ellis always get it, but the Laneys o' the world thrive like roaches."

Tabby shook her head, but couldn't argue. "I'm headin' to the aft engine room. Screwy noises comin' from the port shaft. Might just be this beam sea shovin' us around. Come look when you get a chance. Otherwise, I'll be at the throttle station."

"So what does a sore, beat-up Marine do in a surface action on a destroyer?" Gunny Horn asked Dennis Silva. They were on the amidships gun platform, over the galley, and they weren't alone. Most of the crews of both 4"-50s, port and starboard, not on watch somewhere else were there already. Everyone had their own opinion about when they'd meet the enemy but they'd all concluded it must be soon. Too anxious to sleep, those without other duties had gravitated to their battle stations as the night wore on.

"You wouldn't have to ask if you'd come to drill instead o' lollygaggin' around, m'lingerin' an' hidin' from honest work," Silva scolded piously.

"Should'a drilled," Lawrence agreed emphatically, arms crossed over his chest. It was awkward for him to put his hands on his hips like Spanky often did—he just wasn't built right—but his stance implied a saltiness that Gunny Horn didn't have.

Horn goggled at the . . . *lizard* scolding him, but held his tongue. He liked Lawrence and he'd already heard Silva's fuzzy, reptilian buddy knew his way around *Walker*'s main battery. "I've been on limited duty," he protested, taking a drag off one of the vile cigarettes starting to show up in cartons marked "Pepper, Isak, and Gilbert Smoking Tobacco Co." at Andaman. The nasty-smelling things weren't very popular yet and they'd already earned the nickname PIG cigs, but Isak—who owned the process for making them back in Baalkpan, was pushing them as hard as his personality allowed. Many of the humans who'd kicked the habit left them alone or kept chewing the Lemurian tobacco they'd gotten used to, but a few gladly resumed. Even a few 'Cats had tried them. Now the gathered Lemurians cackled at Horn with nervous amusement, or pretended to gag on his smoke.

"'Limited' don't mean 'pro-hibited' from doin' anything harder than smolderin', stuffin' yer face, an' wallowin' in yer rack," Silva insisted. "It means 'no jumpin' overboard an' tryin' to outswim the ship—while whuppin' flashies with a stick.'" There were laughs, and Silva continued. "It means 'no climbin' the foremast by a backstay an' standin' on yer stupid head on top of the crow's nest!'" More laughter exploded, and the 'Cats stamped the deck.

"Knock off that shit!" roared Earl Lanier, waddling out from the galley beneath them. "I been building a mountain o' sammiches, an' you nearly tumped it over!"

"You're just makin' excuses for havin' ate half of 'em!" Silva roared down, and Lanier shook his pudgy fist, eliciting more hilarity.

"Being on limited duty only means you don't have to carry Lanier's fat ass to his battle station in the aft crew's head when they sound GQ," Chief Gray said dryly. The Super Bosun had suddenly appeared among them. Silva guffawed, but most of the 'Cats only chuckled politely. Enjoying themselves somehow felt too much like shirking when the Bosun was looking. Gray slapped the nearest 'Cat on the back. "C'mon," he said, "that was funny!" A few more Lemurians dutifully laughed and Gray shook his head. He hadn't meant to be a wet blanket, and he'd known exactly what Silva was trying to do. He even thought he could help. But his status as the terrible Chief Bosun of the Navy prevented him from enjoying the same familiarity with the crew that Silva had grown into. Silva's ability to do that actually perplexed him. Before they came to this world, the maniac always had his clique—other troublemakers, mostly—but he'd finally harnessed and directed his destructive powers; learned to focus them on the enemy instead of everyone around him. He liked people now, at least those on his side, and his exploits had achieved an almost mythical status. Ultimately, even if he was still alarming in a "don't play with the rattlesnake" sort of way, his ship-mates weren't actively *afraid* of him anymore. Gray thought that was a good thing, particularly since Silva seemed to like it that way too.

Gray glared at Horn. "You've had field artillery training. Didn't you guys use those old French seventy-fives in the Philippines?"

"Some guys called 'em that," Horn grumbled.

Gray shrugged. "So what? Same gun." He pointed at the portside 4"-50. "The Welin breech on these is different, but you still gotta slam a shell in it, and you can do that." He gestured around. "That'll free up one of these guys to do something that takes more experience."

Horn hesitated.

"Hey," said Silva, grinning. "He's doin' you a favor. I was gonna have you humpin' ammo up from the magazine. As first shellman, you'll get to be up here with *me*, watchin' the show!"

"Sea action at night is . . . 'rettier than running through the jungle, shooting at Jaaphs!" Lawrence confirmed. He looked at the breech of the number two gun. "Just look out. She kicks to the rear around thirty inches!" He beamed at Silva, who'd taught him, but snarled when Den-nis ruffled his crest.

The general-quarters alarm sounded. The thing had been so abused by age, use, and even submergence, it was commonly called the dying-duck call, even by 'Cats who'd never heard a duck. They'd learned what ducks were, and there were plenty of creatures that made similar sounds on this world. The alarm was joined by Minnie's childlike voice on the new loudspeakers: "All haands—maan you baattle stations!"

Chief Gray moved to the middle of the platform and blew "Clear ship for action" on his bosun's pipe, and when he heard the call re-peated, he looked back at Silva and waved. "So long, fellas. Good hun-tin'!"

Silva punched Horn on a particularly sore shoulder muscle. "Here we go, ol' buddy. Put your tin hat on!"

"Lookout confirms three Grik baattleships, bearing two seero five!" Minnie informed the bridge over the tumult of thundering feet and clattering gear. 'Cats and men raced up the ladder to the fire-control platform above, some carrying extra boxes of ammunition for the Browning .30s already mounted there. "Range is maybe six t'ousand tails—I mean, yaards!" Minnie still got those mixed up, but the measurements were virtually identical and it made little difference. Commander Simon Herring chose that moment to arrive on the bridge, ushered up the stairs by the clanging peg in place of Juan Marcos's left leg. Matt noted that Herring was dressed in whites, something he and the rest of his officers never did in action anymore.

"Here, Cap-tan," Juan said, snatching Matt's hat and reaching up to drop a helmet on his head. Matt tried to stare through his binoculars while Juan struggled to fasten a pistol belt around his waist, complete with his battered academy sword. There was no point complaining, and Juan would sulk. He concentrated on the view while the rest of those on the bridge exchanged hats for helmets, even Courtney. *Walker* had Pam Cross and a good 'Cat surgeon now, so Courtney was free to do whatever he wanted unless really needed in the wardroom. It had brightened considerably with the moon creeping higher, and Matt distinguished the black coast of India against the scattered stars, but that was it. "I can't see them yet," he said. "Any word on the cruisers?"

"Lookout sees only waagons. They is hugging the coast," Minnie reported. "Prob'ly tryin' to hide against it." She snorted. "Maybe they all run aground!"

"That's a pleasant thought," Courtney Bradford agreed, "but, sadly, they doubtless know the depths here far better than we. The charts captured on Ceylon and during Keje's previous, brief stay at Madras are strikingly precise."

"I see exhaust sparks!" confirmed Bernie Sandison on the port bridgewing. He'd joined the lookouts there with his binoculars while his torpedo 'Cats readied the director. "Definitely coal burners ahead!"

"Have the crow's nest watch for the cruisers," Matt cautioned. "They might be up to something. Maybe screening more to seaward."

"Ay, ay, Cap-i-taan!" Minnie said. After a short pause, she reported: "All stations maaned an' ready. Mister Palmer says *Mahaan* aack— *hears* our warning an' also maanning baattle stations!"

"Very well. Have Mr. Palmer ask her to watch for the cruisers as well." He looked at Spanky. "Better take your station aft," he said. "Let's hope you don't have anything to do this time," he added wryly.

"You said it, Skipper! I'd just as soon sit in a rockin' chair and watch the show if it's all the same to you! See you when we're done." With that, Spanky nodded at Courtney and the others, stepped quickly to the ladder aft, and clattered down to the weather deck on his way to the auxiliary conn.

"Do you really think those . . . cruisers could be a threat, Captain

Reddy?" Herring asked. "They've contributed little to the fighting so far."

"They're fairly helpless against air attack," Matt allowed, "but Jim . . ." He frowned and cleared his throat. "Jim said they're good ships and might be trouble in a slugging match." He sighed. "I don't ever want to take anything for granted on this goofed-up world again, so, yeah, if they're out there, armed, and full of Grik, they're a threat. I believe we can handle them: they've got nowhere near the armor of those BBs, but we have to *see* them to kill them. Much as I hate Kurokawa, he's a real naval officer and he's not stupid. He's crazy as hell, but I can't put anything past him. I don't like surprises unless they're ours."

"Lookout sees cruisers!" Minnie cried triumphantly. "They *is* to seaward, in line, bearing seero two seero!"

"All of them?" Matt asked doubtfully.

"He thinks four."

"That may be all, Captain Reddy," suggested Herring. "No one knows how many sortied."

Matt grunted. "No, but something you may not've picked up is that Grik naval—and air formations, I guess—generally come in multiples of three, and that's something Kurokawa seems to have embraced. He hasn't discouraged it, anyway."

"Maybe the other two, if they exist, broke down between Madras and here," Courtney suggested. He looked at Herring. "It *has* been reported that their engines appear somewhat unreliable."

"That's possible," Matt nodded, "but we still need to keep our eyes peeled for at least two more." He looked at Minnie. "Have Mr. Palmer signal *Mahan* to take station aft. We'll proceed between the two forces in line of battle. Stand by for surface action, port and starboard, but we'll reserve the starboard torpedoes and use the port tubes on the BBs." He considered. "Have Mr. Campeti concentrate his fire control on the cruisers to starboard. We don't have any of the new AP shells yet and, by all reports, our common shells won't have much effect on the BBs. We'll have a better chance against the cruisers with the main battery. Silva can direct the number two gun against the wagons in local control if he likes."

"Ay, ay, sur."

"Won't that alert them and cause them to maneuver?" Herring asked. "They may prove more difficult targets for the torpedoes."

Matt looked at him, reminding himself that for all his occasional bluster, Herring wasn't an experienced line officer. This would be the man's first naval action and he had to be nervous. Matt still didn't know what he thought of Herring, but he was obviously trying to learn. He chose to be tactful. "Against the Jap Navy, I'd agree. But the Grik don't—*didn't*—have integrated fire control yet, and had to aim each gun individually. I hope that's still the case. If so, they'll have to steam straight and steady to hit us, and if that *is* Kurokawa over there, he'll *damn* sure want to hit us. That said, I know Silva can whack the big bastards, even in local control. I doubt he'll do much but ring their bell, but that's liable to encourage the enemy to maintain their line of battle— especially when we start clobbering their cruisers." He nodded out at the bridgewing. "That's when Mr. Sandison's new toys'll have their best chance."

"I see," Herring murmured. "But surely surprise would still benefit us?"

Matt nodded. "Of course, and we'll sure take it if we get it. Squeezing right between the BBs and cruisers undetected before we launch torpedoes would be ideal. We might sink all the big boys, then stand off and hammer the cruisers at our leisure. We can't count on that, however. Grik don't see as well as 'Cats in the dark, and they might just miss us, but you can bet they're on the lookout, and we're going to pass awful close." He waved aft. "We're kicking up a mighty bright wake, and the one thing we don't dare do is slow down. They've got a lot of big guns!"

Herring was silent a moment. "I confess," he finally said, "I'm unaccustomed to making such elaborate plans—considering so many contingencies—on the fly. There *should* be a way, through careful planning and preparation, to eliminate more of the variables you described. Perhaps . . . Perhaps we shouldn't attack tonight. We've found the enemy and should be able to shadow him until daylight and make a more considered attack, in conjunction with our air power."

Matt frowned. "We don't have any more ship-killing bombs, Mr.

Herring, so our air is limited. Since we have to get close for Bernie's fish to have a good chance, a night action is to our advantage." He snorted angrily. "Besides, we're here, the enemy's there, and we're going to fight him. You can analyze everything later and point out all the ways I screw this up, but one thing you need to learn is that long, careful plans are great—until the first gun goes off. The whole point of command is the ability to make, revise, and reject a dozen plans all at once, on the fly, as you said, because if your enemy isn't a complete idiot, that's what he's doing!"

"Range is twenty-eight hundreds to wagons, thirty-five hundreds to cruisers," Minnie reported.

"Very well," Matt said. Staring hard through his binoculars, he could see the Grik dreadnaughts now. He'd read the descriptions and talked to others who'd seen them, but this was his first personal glimpse. "They *are* pretty big," he said grudgingly. Sweeping his glasses right, he barely saw the dark shapes of the cruisers as well. On a calmer sea, they'd have been clearer, but all he noted was their bare-poled masts moving against the moon-hazed night. A bright flash lit the left lens of his Bausch & Lombs and he quickly redirected them. "So much for surprise," he muttered.

"Lookout says first Grik waagon opens fire!" Minnie cried. A big, phosphorescent geyser erupted three hundred yards short. "Caam-peeti asks to commence firing!"

"Wait," Matt said. "The cruisers may not see us yet, but once we shoot, everybody'll know where we are. I don't want the cruisers cutting in front of us. Tell Campeti to stand by." He didn't need to send word to *Mahan*. Perry Brister wouldn't shoot until *Walker* did. He looked at Bernie still fussing with the torpedo director. "You ready for this?" he called.

"I sure hope so, Skipper," Bernie replied nervously. A lot was riding on his torpedoes, and though S-19 had proved they actually worked in combat, he was still anxious.

At a closing speed of more than thirty knots, the range was winding down fast. Two flashes lit the forward casemate of the Grik dreadnaught at fifteen hundred yards as the angle on the bow neared forty-five degrees. Both shots went long, but they were well in range now. The cruisers hadn't closed the gap, but the first two opened fire with their forward guns.

"They all see us *now*," quipped Chief Quartermaster Paddy Rosen at the helm.

"I don't want to seem a worrywart," Courtney said, watching the flashes, "but might we close the metal lids over these windows and perhaps begin shooting back?" Everyone in the pilothouse, even Herring, laughed.

"I suppose we might as well," Matt said wryly. "Close and latch the splinter shutters," he ordered. "The main battery may commence firing."

Guns one, three, and four flared, and the odd-colored tracers arced away, converging toward the closest cruiser. All three were short, throwing up a wall of bright water that doubtless drenched the ship.

"Goddamn!" Silva roared, picking at his ear. "They might warn a fella!"

"You no hear saalvo bell?" cried Gunner's Mate Pak-Ras-Ar, or "Pack Rat." He was sitting on the trainer's seat, staring at the lead Grik dreadnaught through his telescopic sight and slowly turning the wheel that traversed the big gun. The bell he was referring to had been salvaged from *Amagi* to replace *Walker*'s old salvo buzzer.

Lawrence was the gun's pointer, and was moving his wheel back and forth to keep the proper elevation. He wasn't built for the seat and had to stand awkwardly, peering through his own sight. "I heard it!" he said.

"What bell?"

"You're already half-blind," Horn accused. "Now you've gone deaf too. What the hell good are you?"

"Shut up, you." Silva spun to his own talker. "Campeti said we can shoot if we want, right?"

"Right," the 'Cat confirmed.

"Then let's shoot! I've sunk bigger than those stupid Grik tubs with just one gun before." He yanked open the breech. "Load!"

Three more muffled booms came from aft, and *Mahan*'s tracers lashed past. *Walker*'s own guns spat another salvo, and Silva cursed again. "Hey, one o' you apes warn me next time, wilya? Somebody gimme somethin' to stick in my ears!"

A 'Cat passed a shell to Horn, and the China Marine slammed it in the breech creditably enough. Dennis closed the breech and yelled, "Ready!"

"Ready," echoed Pack Rat, still turning his wheel.

"Ready!" cried Lawrence, still making the muzzle bob slightly up and down.

"Fire!" Silva roared.

Matt saw an explosion light the lead Grik battleship, but couldn't tell if any damage was done. The salvos were flying furiously to starboard, and the cruiser line was starting to straggle. One of the ships was afire, and it looked like there'd been good hits on another. Matt was focused to port, however. To prevent confusion and maximize the possibility of hits, he'd ordered that *Walker* and *Mahan* each fire one torpedo at each battleship. It was unorthodox, but since both ships had a triple mount rigged out, that gave their torpedomen—and torpedoes—six separate tries to get it right. As soon as the fish were in the water, the two destroyers would come about and fire six *more* torpedoes from the starboard side.

Ragged broadsides roared from the first and second battleships, kicking up massive, silver-gray waterspouts in a broad pattern around them, but Matt felt no slamming impact. "They're all yours, Bernie," he almost whispered to the intently concentrating torpedo officer, personally standing behind the director, constantly calling corrections.

"Stand by!" Bernie cried, his voice rising. "Fire two!"

"Fire!" Minnie repeated in her microphone, not to the torpedo mount but to Ed Palmer, who'd relay the command to *Mahan* by TBS so she could launch just a few seconds later.

There was a flash aft as the impulse charge flung a long, glistening cylinder from the number two tube. With a smoky trail of hot air, it vanished in the swells dashing by. Immediately, Bernie swung the director toward the second target. The third battleship fired and there were more splashes, but a terrible crash also jarred the ship forward. Bernie ignored it and suddenly cried, "Stand by. Fire four!"

"Fire!" Minnie said loudly, then immediately demanded a damage report. Matt looked out the window just in front of Rosen; it was the only one not covered. The crew of the number one gun had been thrown off their stride and missed the last salvo at the cruisers, but quickly recovered themselves. Matt didn't see any damage.

"We got a big damn hole forward in the chain locker, Skipper!" Minnie reported. "The chain stop the ball from punchin' out the other side, though, an' we only takin' a little water."

Matt nodded. Two more impacts, less sharp but still heavy, jarred the ship.

"Lucky hits from those cruisers," Commander Herring shouted from the starboard bridgewing. "Though I can't imagine how they managed it. Their formation is quite disheveled!" Matt's eyebrows rose. Herring actually seemed to be *enjoying* himself!

"Damage report!" Matt demanded.

"Stand by. Fire six!" Bernie yelled.

"Fire!" Minnie squeaked, then listened. "Those two not punch through; they maybe skate in. Leave big leaky dents, though!"

The first dreadnaught thundered again, quickly followed by a few rounds from the second. The enemy had gone to independent fire, but there was no coordination and any gun might be shooting at *Walker* or *Mahan*. There was no denying that Grik gunnery had improved, but more concentrated fire would've been more dangerous.

"*Mahan* reports hit on her port torpedo mount—but she already shoot fish. She also hit on aft deckhouse, an' takin' water in her steering engine room!"

"Tell Captain Brister to hold her together and follow our turn. Right full rudder, Paddy! Bring us about to course two zero zero!"

Rosen spun the big brass wheel. "Right full rudder, aye! Making my course two zero zero!" A moment later, *Walker* shuddered under a double hammer blow inflicted by the third dreadnaught.

Matt heard Minnie demanding a report while Bernie and his assistants scampered toward the starboard torpedo director. "How much longer?" he asked Bernie as he passed.

"Any second . . . I hope!" Bernie shot back.

"Well, our shootin's done," Silva grumped as the ship heeled sharply and began her turn.

"No, it ain't!" Pack Rat denied. "We still shoot at cruisers!"

"Yeah, but now we'll be shootin' at what Mr. Campeti tells us to." He glared at the battleships. "I sure wanted to cut me a notch for one of those bastards!"

Silva's feet left the deck and he landed on his face near the port-side ready locker. He jumped up like a shot, but he was stunned. "There's fire!" he yelled, seeing a blossom of flame aft, and the sight of it associated with the ready locker alarmed him. He shook his head. *Fire's aft. No immediate danger o' these rounds cookin' off.* He shook his head again and took another look. The ship's Nancy seaplane was shredded and burning, its wings drooping down on either side of the catapult. Jeek, *Walker*'s air-division crew chief, was leading a charge toward the flames with a hose, and Silva saw Spanky on the aft deckhouse, pointing and yelling. Other 'Cats were bailing out of the 25-millimeter tubs on either side of the burning plane, some lugging ammo boxes. *Should've flown the damn plane off,* he thought, *or pitched it over the side like they did last time, but nooo. It wasn't runnin' right, an' Jeek didn't want to lose another one like that. Skipper's too soft on the flyboys sometimes,* he decided, neglecting to remind himself that *he'd* agreed the plane didn't pose much of a fire hazard in action against ships armed only with solid shot.

There was yelling below him from the galley, and he realized one of the big Grik balls must've hit there, to toss them around so. The most recognizable voice was Earl Lanier's, roaring like a gored bull, and Silva wondered briefly if the filthy, bloated cook had taken another one in the gut. He turned and scanned his gun crew. Lawrence was helping a semiconscious Pack Rat off his seat. The 'Cat's helmet was gone and his forehead wet with blood where he must've conked it on something. Gunny

Horn was up, looking aft. A few 'Cats were sitting on deck, but seemed okay.

"Larry! You an' Poot get the 'Rat down to the wardroom. Might as well put Earl outa our mis'ry on the way. At least check his mates." He looked at his talker. "Any more business for us?"

"Caam-peeti say 'secure, an' check on number t'ree gun.' It drop off the fire-control circuit!"

Silva glanced to starboard, but couldn't tell what was going on over there. "What's with you guys?" he yelled to starboard. When there was no response, he shouted at his crew. "Whichever o' you mugs that ain't dyin' better come with me to see if those guys're okay or need a hand."

The Grik dreadnaughts continued their rumbling fire, and tall splashes rose all around the ship. *Walker*'s number one gun sent a tracer toward the cruisers—which Silva could see now, as the ship's turn continued; they'd become scattered, flaming wrecks, like burning brush piles in the night. He nodded satisfaction and looked aft again, but the bright flames and smoke kept him from seeing the first torpedo slam into the lead Grik ship.

"We get hit! *Two* hits on lead Grik waagon!" Minnie cried, just as a cheer exploded on the starboard bridgewing. "Spanky say, 'They beat-i-ful!'"

"We saw them, Minnie!" Matt said, as *Walker*'s bow came around, "And they were!" *Walker* had been taking a beating from the big Grik guns, and Matt was growing increasingly frustrated. So far, there'd been no crippling damage and his ship still responded with the nearly new vitality she'd exhibited since her overhaul, but she was getting hurt. The towering waterspouts that rocked the first enemy dreadnaught relieved Matt as much as Bernie, who was practically giddy with excitement. All his hard work had been vindicated, and perhaps what he considered a long-ago failing had been purged at last.

"Well done, Mr. Sandison!" Courtney complimented grandly. "Oh, well done indeed!"

"Congratulations, Mr. Sandison," Commander Herring said sincerely.

The ironclad slowed immediately, and was already listing heavily to port. Suddenly, a *third* phosphorescent waterspout rose beside her, aft, raining debris in the sea around her and accelerating her roll.

Matt sobered. "Okay, back to work. That one would've missed 'em all if the first one didn't slow."

"Silence!" Bernie shouted at his torpedomen. "Sorry, Skipper," he added.

"Don't be sorry. That's already more hits than we ever got against the Japs! It's kind of weird having a torpedo you can count on."

"My course is two zero zero!" shouted Paddy Rosen at the helm.

"Very well," Matt replied. "Stand by starboard torpedoes, but let's wait a minute more to see if we get any more hits with the first salvo."

"Aye, aye, Captain," Bernie replied, his voice determined.

"Campeti says number three gun is back up, and asks can he engage the waagons?" Minnie reported.

"By all means," Matt answered, and the salvo bell immediately rang.

Most of the Grik guns had gone silent for a moment, as word about what happened to their lead must've spread through their remaining ships. The range had opened during the turn as well, and for the last few minutes they'd just been pounding water. Now they resumed firing as first *Walker*, then *Mahan* steadied to make another run. Plumes of spray erupted around the old destroyers amid the tearing-sheet sound of incoming shot. *Walker*'s bow lanced through a tremendous splash just as a hundred-pound ball skated off the fo'c'sle; tore a leg off the number three shellman, sending the poor 'Cat spinning into the sea; and clanged off the newly reinforced plating on the front of the bridge structure. Matt was grateful and relieved to hear Chief Bosun Gray's distinctive roar: "Get that gun back on target, damn your useless tails! You don't like gettin' shot at? Shoot back! Goddamn. Do I have to *show* you how to do it after all this time? I thought you were real *destroyermen*, not a buncha pansy-ass, mouse-chasin' housecats!" He'd missed Gray in the pilothouse during this fight—he usually stopped in now and then—but it was unusually crowded and he was needed where he was.

A final waterspout jetted up alongside the third ironclad, the one that had, frankly, given them the most trouble. Steam and sparks vomited into the sky from the aft funnels, and almost immediately a tremendous, bright blast blew away a quarter of the armored casemate, sending funnels, guns, bodies, and hundreds of tons of shredded timbers and shattered plating spinning away in the dark.

"Killed it, by God!" Commander Herring exulted. Matt nodded amid the cheers that thundered aboard his ship. He raised his binoculars to watch the huge ship dip low by the stern while more, smaller explosions crackled inside the remainder of the casemate. *I hope you're in there, you bastard,* Matt thought, meaning Kurokawa. *And I hope every ghost you've helped to make is in there with you, watching you burn.* He shifted his glasses to the first ship in line in time to watch it lay on its side and begin to fill. That left only the middle ironclad, and he looked at it.

"Second target turns to port," Minnie relayed the word from the crow's nest.

"I see it," Matt acknowledged. "They're going to try to close the distance and hammer us." He looked at the 'Cat stationed at the lee helm. "All ahead flank! However much they've been taught to lead us, let's throw 'em a curve. Signal *Mahan* to match our speed if she can, or fire her torpedoes as soon as Perry likes the range. Once she does, she's to make smoke and zigzag the hell out of the line of fire. I don't want anybody else hurt killing this last one, if we can help it."

"I . . . I don't know what the torpedoes'll do if we launch them going that fast, Skipper." Bernie warned apprehensively.

"Between us and *Mahan,* we'll be pointing six fish at that damn thing. I bet at least one'll hit, and since it doesn't look like they spent much time worrying about compartmentalization, that should do the trick."

Bernie took a deep breath. "Aye, aye, Captain." He moved back to the director. "Stand by for torpedo action, starboard."

Walker and *Mahan* lanced forward, closing the range on the last Grik dreadnaught. If Kurokawa hadn't been on one of the others, he was certainly aboard this one, and it seemed like everyone on both destroyers knew this was more than just an attack to avenge the loss of friends and ice the cake on the Allied victory at the second Battle of

Madras; it was a remorseless execution of a rabid beast. The Grik fired furiously, but just couldn't cope with the near thirty knots *Walker* suddenly achieved, and the twenty-seven that *Mahan* somehow managed. At the same time, both destroyers punished the massive ironclad with rapid, accurate salvos that had to be doing damage at this range. Three yellow flashes pulsed at *Mahan*'s side, one after another, and she turned sharply away to starboard as soon as the torpedoes were clear. Brister probably hoped this would particularly confound the Grik gunners.

"Tubes one through five, in salvo!" Bernie cried. "Fire one . . . Fire three . . . Fire five!" He took a deep breath and stepped back from the director. "All torpedoes expended, Captain Reddy," he said formally, as a near miss threw water on the bridgewing.

"Very well. Left full rudder, Mr. Rosen. Make smoke!"

"Left full rudder, aye!"

"Make smoke!" Minnie said in her mouthpiece. It was dark enough that they'd soon be invisible to the enemy, but the smoke should hide their wake. Matt also thought it could have the added psychological effect of making the enemy think they'd just vanished. At least for a few moments—long enough to get out of range and turn to see what happened. They didn't quite make it.

"Hit! Hit!" Minnie screeched. "Lookout says two *Mahan* fishes is hits!"

"Secure from making smoke!" Matt ordered. "Rudder amidships. Slow to two-thirds!"

Walker had described a surprisingly tight circle for her hull shape, and the enemy was back off her port side, about three thousand yards away.

"Look at her blow!" Gray reveled. The Chief Bosun had finally appeared on the bridge. "We'll never know if *we* hit her or not!"

It was true. Massive explosions racked the wreck, and any of *Walker*'s torpedo impacts would've been lost in the violence of the cataclysm. Everyone in the pilothouse was watching with binoculars or Imperial telescopes, and so many of the crew had raced to port to see, the ship was heeling slightly.

"We did it," Matt whispered, his words lost in the tumult. He hadn't doubted they could, and unlike so many before, this action had been largely voluntary. But he felt tremendous relief that they'd succeeded so well, with such small loss compared to what the rest of the fleet had suffered, and he was deeply satisfied that they had—most likely, he cautioned himself—finally destroyed that madman Kurokawa. He smiled as his ship and her people continued celebrating.

"Cap-i-taan Brister on *Mahaan* sends 'Bless us all!'" Minnie shouted over the din.

Matt grinned wider and raised his glasses to find *Walker*'s truncated sister. There she was! Just north of the burning hulk, she was turning back toward them. Matt was watching her fondly when something—it had to have been one of *Walker*'s own torpedoes, thrown horribly off course—suddenly exploded without warning against *Mahan*'s thin steel and blew her bow completely off.

Hisashi Kurokawa slowly lowered his binoculars and stared at the distant, dying flares on the dark, moon-dappled sea, his heart surging with a rage like he'd never known before. It dwarfed the puny piques that once would've left him ranting homicidally. He'd tamed those comparatively whimsical things to the point that they barely changed his expression unless he just wanted to vent. But *this*! This fury was so profound that it vaulted him beyond the ability to rant, and actually struck him speechless.

He'd known his escaping squadron would have to fight its way past Trin-con-lee, at least, but didn't think there could be much of anything there that might harm his remaining battleships. He had, in fact, intended to transfer aboard one before dawn so he could lead his force from a more powerful (and protected) platform. Doubtless, part of what stoked his rage to such a height was the realization that if he'd already been "safely" aboard one of his precious capital ships, he'd be dead. Only fate—or was it destiny?—had led him to board the cruiser *Nachi* during the breakout from Madras. He'd expected a fight then too, but the armor-piercing bombs didn't worry him. He knew where the enemy got them, and they couldn't have many. No doubt they'd make more, but if they already had, they'd have used more at Madras instead of reverting to the smaller weapons. Besides, even if they had all the big AP bombs in the world, their planes would have difficulty hitting his ships in the dark. No, what guided his decision most was the prospect of facing whatever enemy weapon had destroyed his battle line earlier that day, and he'd considered it only prudent to place himself aboard a less tempting target until he knew what that weapon was. Now he did.

What enraged him most, however, was that the torpedoes that demolished his squadron were delivered by none other than *both* the hated American destroyers that had plagued him from the very start of his odyssey! He already knew *Walker* still swam, but had believed her far to the east. He'd *seen Mahan* destroyed, though, at Baalkpan! How could they have possibly restored her? *Ultimately,* he realized with blinding clarity, *all that had passed has boiled down to a test between me and Captain Reddy! Like chess masters, he has his pieces and I have mine, and if I am ever to be free to pursue my true destiny on this world, I must sweep him entirely from the board!*

Destiny had not abandoned him, though. Why else had he decided to hug the coast aboard *Nachi*, in company with her sister *Maya*, remaining inshore of the rest of his squadron? He would've called any other commander who hid behind his fleet a coward—but he wasn't just any other man, was he? Destiny had ruled his choice and would continue to guide him he was sure. Slowly, his fury waned and he raised his glasses again. All but one of the pyres of his distant cruisers had flickered out, and only burning debris marked where his final battleship had gone to the bottom. He focused more carefully. *Yes!* He rejoiced. *One of the American destroyers has been badly damaged somehow! Perhaps it will even sink! Regardless, the other will stand by to aid it, and will give no further thought to me!*

"My lord," Signals Lieutenant Fukui said quietly, drawing near him on *Nachi*'s quarterdeck.

"Yes? What is it?"

"Lieutenant of the Sky Iguri has reached Bombay, and asks if he should remain there until we arrive to coal. He does not expect a re-sponse under the circumstances," Fukui hastened to add, hoping Kuro-kawa would take the hint not to transmit, "but will linger a few days until you feel less constrained to send instructions."

"We will coal at Cochin," Kurokawa snapped, "and I will summon Iguri." He caught Fukui's surprised intake of breath. "We are not run-ning away," he growled sarcastically. "We still hold most of India, and it remains my regency! The enemy had Madras before, and we took it from him. We will take it back! Our better warriors, *my* warriors that I designed, are just beginning to arrive in numbers, and we will soon have enough to annihilate the Americans and their apes."

"But . . ." Fukui paused, gathering his nerve. "But what if the Grik—General Esshk—decides India is not your regency anymore?"

Kurokawa didn't lash out as Fukui expected, but brooded in silence for a moment. Finally, he spoke. "The Grik here are mine," he said. "As are those already in transit. Without our communications advantage, General Esshk cannot change that, and with such a force even he will hesitate to challenge me. In the meantime, our own projects on Zanzi-bar should soon be far enough along to establish our proper dominance over all the Grik!" He saw that Fukui wasn't convinced, and forced a conciliatory tone. He still needed the man. "The crew, and perhaps even you, are not persuaded we will even reach Cochin?" he asked. "Never fear. There are several rivers nearby. We will enter one and conceal the ships against the shore throughout the day so any enemy aircraft pass-ing overhead cannot see us. Then we will proceed again by night." He stopped and looked back out to sea. The destroyers were still there, still motionless.

"There is one other thing, my lord," Fukui added hesitantly. "The, well, listeners that contacted us before with overtures of friendship have apparently continued to monitor a great deal of the radio traffic and have deduced that our battle did not proceed favorably." He took a breath. "They have asked if they might be of assistance," he added.

Kurokawa regarded him with distaste. He still knew nothing about the source of the offer, and frankly feared it. If those behind it considered themselves strong enough to help him, he might deeply regret that help one day.

"Indeed?" he considered. "Then perhaps once we reach Cochin we might endeavor to learn more about these strange folk. You will consider a dialogue that will discover as much about them as possible, without giving away too much about us."

/////// *June 9, 1944*

I t was early afternoon, two days after the Second Battle of
Madras, when USS *Walker* slowly towed USS *Mahan*'s shattered hulk into the port of Madras. USNRS *Salissa* and her
battle group had joined them the morning before, and they
all came in together. They were just in time. The sea outside
the harbor was rising and the sky was dark with heavy
clouds. *Mahan* was actually a little low by the stern, having
more trouble pumping water from her steering engine room than keeping it out forward. Jagged, twisted plates and frame fragments were all
that remained of her bow forward of the bridge structure, but the heavily reinforced and improved Lemurian-inspired bracing of her bulk-
heads—particularly near where her new bow had been grafted on—had
prevented serious flooding past the lost section. She had steam up and
might've even made port on her own, but if that forward bulkhead did

let go . . . Either way, she wouldn't have survived a storm, and it was with great relief that she was delivered and received.

"There's *Santy Cat*, over there," Gray said, pointing past the helmsman, and Matt nodded. His eyes were red and he'd begun to wonder if Juan's monkey joe might kill him after all, slowly, like arsenic poisoning. *Santa Catalina* looked almost as bad as *Mahan*, lashed to a dock that recently accommodated Grik battleships.

"I'm glad they saved her," Matt said, "and most of her crew. S-Nineteen's too." The bow of the former submarine had been discovered at dawn, bobbing there like a finger pointing at the sky. The current had carried her dangerously close to *Santa Catalina* in the night, and it was amazing she hadn't been rammed again by a rescue vessel. More than half her crew had been saved, crawling out her torpedo tubes, but two of her original crew—Danny Porter and Sandy Whitcomb—were lost. Opening the tubes had also let water in faster, and an hour after Irvin Laumer, the last out, emerged, blinking in the sunshine, the old S-19 finally slipped gracefully to the bottom forever.

"Yeah," Gray agreed. "I hope Mr. Laumer doesn't go into a funk. He's been so obsessed with that damn boat so long, he's liable to pine away." He didn't add *like you did when* Walker *was sunk at Baalkpan*, but didn't have to.

"Get him back on a horse," Courtney suggested. "Any horse—figuratively speaking, of course. That's what he'll need." He chuckled. "The irony is, he was right all along. That ridiculous submarine came in quite handy, after all."

"Yes, she did," Matt agreed softly. "And she'll be missed." He was looking at the harbor and surrounding city. Smoke still towered over sections that had burned, blowing in the gust front of the storm, and portions of Grik ships protruded from the water where they had sunk at their moorings. Buoys already marked many hazards to navigation. It was a hard, dreary sight. *Arracca* and *Baalkpan Bay* were both tied at the docks as well, undergoing feverish repairs alongside other ships damaged by suiciders. *God knows how many people we lost,* Matt thought, *and then there's Alden's casualties to consider. II Corps is shattered, and I Corps isn't much better. And Jim Ellis . . .*

Sensing his mood, Gray wanted to pat him on the shoulder, but that would never do. Instead he slapped Courtney on the back. "Well," he said, cheerfully gruff. "It may not feel like it or even look like it right now, but this is the biggest win since Baalkpan Bay—and we did it in *their* livin' room this time."

Matt shook himself and managed a smile. "That's right, Boats. It was a home run. Let's put *Mahan* to bed, then we'll go alongside *Big Sal* for fuel. After that, we'll get with everybody and iron things out for the grand slam!"

Walker already reverberated with the racket of repair parties banging on warped and dented plates, and torch sparks spattered brightly and hissed on the damp deck as the first line of thunderstorms eased a bit. Sandra and Keje came aboard while Matt, Spanky, and Gray were itemizing repair priorities and assembling details. With that complete, Matt, Sandra, Courtney, Keje, Commander Herring—and Silva and Lawrence, "in case there's lizards hidin' in the ruins"—trooped through the dockside debris back to *Big Sal*, where a command-staff meeting was gathering.

Once in Keje's "ahd-mi-raal's" quarters, there was a reunion of sorts, and many present hadn't seen each other in a very long time. Pete Alden and Rolak were there, looking thin and haggard. Safir had remained behind, but would come to Madras after Pete returned to the army. Captain Jis-Tikkar, COFO of *Big Sal*'s First Air Wing, fussed over Lieutenant Leedom, who looked like a cadaver raised from the dead. Irvin Laumer and Russ Chapelle sat side by side with haunted looks, discussing their shared battle in quiet tones. Ben Mallory had arrived from Trin-con-lee on a Clipper flight with Soupy, and they looked pretty ragged too. Beside Keje and Adar sat Tassana, *Arracca*'s young commander, and next to her was *Baalkpan Bay*'s exec. Finally arriving, drenched by renewed rain, were Commander Perry Brister and Chief Bashear from *Mahan*, looking even worse than the rest. Gray and Silva maneuvered them to a punch bowl of seep-laced nectar.

Perhaps more notable than those attending were the absent, either tending wounds to their commands or being tended themselves. Most conspicuous of all were those who'd never join them again. Matt and Sandra sat closely together on one of the lounging cushions that served as a sofa. They held hands and touched often, and, as usual, Matt seemed to regain lost strength with Sandra's proximity, but his wife's expression was guarded when he wasn't looking at her. She knew Jim had been Matt's best friend and worried how the loss would affect him. More refreshments came, and after brief, heartfelt greetings, they all tried to relax. There'd be plenty of time later for everyone to become intimately acquainted with every aspect of the battle. What they wanted to know just then was, what next?

"I have a few things to say," spoke Adar, then he paused as if searching for the right words. "But I don't quite know how," he confessed. Finally, he merely blinked his deepest appreciation. "Thank you," he murmured. "Thank you all. This was the greatest battle in the history of our people, in terms of sacrifice, duration, and perhaps even straa-tee-jic significance. There can be no question in any mind, ours or the Grik, that we achieved the victory, painful as it was. But we must consider how the Grik will react." He looked at Pete. "You made no vow of a lasting truce with this Halik creature, I am sure?"

Pete shook his head. "Nope. We agreed to quit killin' each other long enough to get both our asses out of the jam we were in. That's it. I might've *implied* we wouldn't come after him if he stayed on his side of the cease-fire line, but I didn't promise anything past the cease-fire itself—oh, except we'd swap prisoners. You could've knocked me over with a willow switch when he agreed. That's a promise I'll keep if he does no matter what." His face turned thoughtful. "Halik could've wiped us out, but he knew he'd be screwed. I even sort of suggested we finish it, knowing he'd be easy meat for Sixth and Seventh Corps, but he didn't take the bait. Can't say I'm sorry. My boys an' girls were in constant combat for months, and there ain't any tougher *veteran* troops in the world. In my opinion, sacrificing 'em wouldn't have been balanced by rubbin' Halik out." He frowned. "Besides, there's somethin' odd about the bastard. Maybe bein' around that Jap so long did it to him. He's smart and dangerous as hell, but I'm kind'a curious to see what pops with him. I'm not sure *he* even knows which way he'll jump just yet."

"What about the Jap?" Herring asked. "Will he live? I'd like to interrogate him."

Pete held out his hand and waggled it. "Touch and go. Who knows?" He looked back at Adar. "Yeah, that was another promise, to try to save the guy, but that's absolutely all."

"You did right and well," Adar assured. "We can ponder this Halik and his motives later."

"One thing you need to sort out pretty quick is that, uh, weird cavalry force that showed up yesterday morning," Pete told Adar, and Matt and Sandra leaned forward, curious. They hadn't heard anything about that. "They nearly queered the whole deal, pitchin' into the Grik that were gatherin' up in the north, getting ready to march around us and cross the Tacos River."

"What're you talking about? What cavalry?" Matt demanded.

"Do you remember the report of riders that showed Captain Saachic the way through the mountains?" Pete asked, and Matt nodded. "Well, they showed up again, maybe two thousand of 'em this time. Really weird ducks, ridin' somethin' like meanies—with horns! And they were a mix of humans and, well, a kind of continental Lemurian, I guess, for lack of a better description." He snorted. "There's some *Czech* guy in charge, if you can believe it! I can't remember his name right off. They were happy as hell to be killin' Grik, though. I had to send Saachic to *stop* 'em!"

Matt looked around and blinked. "They want to join us?"

"As long as we're serious about killin' Grik," Pete confirmed. "I promised 'em we ain't done by a long shot; just need a breathing spell. They were okay with that." He gestured vaguely. "I told Saachic to deal with 'em for now."

"How extraordinary!" Courtney gushed. "A Czech! I wonder how *he* got here? And another race of Lemurians! I cannot wait to meet them! They must abide primarily beyond the range of the Grik. Perhaps they can tell us about Asia proper—even Europe!"

Adar blinked quizzically at Courtney. "Indeed." He turned back to

Alden, clearly preferring to focus on what he considered more pressing matters. These strange people were not a threat, or they would've proven to be one already—or conquered the Grik on their own. "I gather that you intend for Sixth and Seventh Corps to replace the First and Second in their forward positions? And Tenth Corps should replace the Third as soon as it arrives?" Pete nodded. "In that case, Fifth and Eighth Corps will proceed to the cease-fire line you arranged in the south." He looked at Rolak. "You and my dear General Queen Protector will march your noble troops back here to Madras for a well-deserved rest."

"And perhaps redeployment?" Rolak asked, looking at Matt.

"We will see," Adar said, glancing at Commander Herring. "I remain as keen, perhaps more so than anyone, to take the war to the very heart of the Grik empire—our own ancient, sacred shores—but our losses have been severe, and not only has one of the key ships we intended to take on our raid been hideously damaged"—he blinked apology at Brister—"but with *Saanta Caatalina* also ravaged, and S-Nineteen destroyed, we have nothing to send in its stead. It will be some time before the iron steamers we are building will be complete. I fear . . ." He sighed. "I fear we should postpone Cap-i-taan Reddy's raid until we are better recovered from this campaign."

"With respect, Mr. Chairman," Commander Herring said softly, "I believe that would be a mistake."

Matt had suspected Adar would urge caution. He always took heavy losses like blows to his own body. He'd need time to recover himself before ordering more people to their deaths. Matt wasn't even sure he disagreed this time. But Herring's turnaround caught him completely by surprise.

Herring looked at him. "I've been wrong about a great many things, Captain Reddy, but most of all I've been wrong about you." He snorted. "When you took *Walker* and *Mahan* against three Grik battleships and at least four cruisers, I was sure we were dead. It was most exciting," he confessed, "but I really didn't think we'd make it. Your . . . instinctive command style is so alien to me, I just assumed it was reckless, at best, and I've believed that ever since we met. But then I saw it in action and knew—*knew*—there's no way I could do what you did. You *mauled* those Grik, and you did it so fast, by *feel* . . ." He blinked and cleared his throat. "Some people are born horsemen, I suppose. Others can learn to be very good through practice, but it's never quite as natural to them." He grimaced. "Some people never learn to even stay on a horse, and I hope I'm not one of those. My point is, though, that you fought your ship by *instinct*, while I would have still been analyzing everything to death even as my ship sank under me." He turned to Adar. "The other night I learned to trust Captain Reddy's instincts, and if he still thinks now is the right time to punch the Grik in the gut, I have to agree." He smiled. "And it even makes sense from an analytical, strategic standpoint. The Grik are on their heels and will probably scramble to send reinforcements here. I say that, combined with our new allies in southern Africa, we should do more than simply raid Madagascar; we should send enough troops to open a whole new front!"

"Yeah!" Silva barked, surprised to agree with Herring. "Th'ow *their* asses back on the ropes for a change!"

Adar blinked sadly at Matt, but managed a smile. "Do you agree with Commander Herring?"

Matt looked at Sandra, then nodded. "At least raid Madagascar—*hard*. We've no idea what they have there, so actually taking it would depend on what we find. We definitely need to get troops on the ground in southern Africa, though. If we're going to ask the people there to join this fight for keeps—which it seems they're ready to do—then we need to help them."

"Wait just a minute," Sandra said. "I agree that a raid is just the thing, but trying to *stay* anywhere that far away . . . supply will be a nightmare!"

"Sure," Matt grinned, "but that's what Mr. Letts is for. Besides, we have two major advantages. With active sonar on all our big ships and starting to be installed on the smaller ones, we can cross the open ocean, and the Grik can't. Supply runs don't have to come all the way here or even to Andaman, but can scoot straight west from Baalkpan through the Sunda Strait. We'll also have Diego as a base of supply, which isn't any farther on a straight shot than Andaman, and there's—there *should* be—a bunch of other islands east of Madagascar that the Grik might've never found."

Sandra frowned. "You make it sound so easy."

Matt shook his head. "It won't be. But it's a big step in the right direction." He nodded for her to look at Courtney's expectant, beaming face. "And who knows? Whatever we run into along the way'll be new to everybody, not just us. One way or another, I expect an . . . *interesting* trip!"

////// *Diego Garcia (Laa-laanti)*

Chack-Sab-At strolled the sandy, shady beach of Diego Garcia (called Laa-laanti by the natives) with Greg Garrett, Becker Lange, Lieutenant (jg) Winston "Winny" Rominger, and Lieutenant Miyata. They were looking at the veritable fleet gathered near the little island. Rominger's PT squadron zooted about, making mock torpedo runs on *Respite Island*, the great floating dry dock supporting SMS *Amerika*. *Donaghey* was moored inside the bay itself and only her tall masts were visible, but taken as a whole, the motley collection of warships in the vicinity was a very odd sight. That wasn't why Chack found it difficult to concentrate on the conversation flowing around him, though. Word had just arrived that the raid was a go, and not only would it be larger than originally envisioned, but his beloved Safir Maraan was coming to participate as well! He hadn't seen her in so long, his chest felt fluttery at the very thought.

"So, you've actually been to Madagascar?" Garrett asked Miyata, for maybe the tenth time.

"I am—I have," the young Japanese officer confirmed. "I have not seen it all, but I well know the environs of the Celestial Palace and the harbor that serves it." His brows furrowed. "It is a desolate place, devoid of any life not Grik, but the land beyond the city seemed . . . wild, almost as if deliberately preserved as a zoo or park." He took a deep, scouring breath. "The jungle was not enough to cover the stench of the city, however."

"But we will not be going in blind, at least," Lange said thoughtfully. Obviously, he trusted the Jap completely. Winny Rominger didn't, and he snorted to emphasize it.

"I won't be going in at all," Greg grumped. "I'm supposed to scout the islands east of Madagascar for signs of Grik, then proceed with my mission of exploration!"

"I fear you will never round the cape," Lange warned again. "No sailing ship ever has, not from the east."

"*Donaghey* can do it," Greg stated confidently. "Besides, I'm also supposed to stop at Alex-aandra—that's how you say it, right?"

"Close enough," Lange chuckled. "The Kaiser will be most interested to meet you and hear your news."

"I'd rather be in the Skipper's show," Greg persisted. Chack stirred.

"But you will be. Yours is an essential part. Once the baal-loon goes up, we will have free communications, but until then you will be our only contact with the Republic of Real People." He blinked at Becker. "Mr. Lange says his people prepare for war, but they do not even know if his mission to contact us was successful. You must assure them it was, and we will fight by their side." Chack stopped walking and paused, staring back at the jungle. "I wish we could raise some regiments here, but these people . . ." He sighed. "They have regressed too far; they are too primitive." He smiled wistfully. "I envy them that, you know? To them, the Grik are mythical monsters—and they *would* fight if asked— but I cannot condone it. They allow us here and that is help enough. We have not yet reached the point of arming younglings, not since Baalk-pan, and recruiting these people to fight the war we have come to know would be no different, and more cruel than I can imagine." He blinked sad determination and his tail swished emphatically. "Let us try to leave one bastion of innocence on this world."

Elizabeth Bay, the Enchanted Isles

High Admiral Harvey Jenks was discussing the ramifications of General Shinya's latest report on the situation at Guayak with Admiral Le-laa-Tal-Cleraan, Orrin Reddy, and Surgeon Commander Selass-Fris-Ar. An urgent knock on the ornate wooden door to *Maaka-Kakja*'s admiral's stateroom suddenly interrupted them.

"Excuse me, High Ahd-mi-raal," Lelaa said, then raised her voice. "Enter."

A Marine sentry opened the door and stepped inside, escorting two amazingly bedraggled forms, wearing ragged remnants of *Dom* uniforms! One was human, and they immediately suspected a prisoner or spy, but the other was Lemurian—and Lelaa could only stare as realization dawned. Both visitors managed sharp salutes and Lelaa's suspicions were confirmed when the human spoke. "Lieutenant Fred Reynolds and Ensign Kari-Faask, Special Air Division, USS *Walker*, DD-163, reporting!" The young man's voice was firm, but there were tears in his eyes.

"My God!" proclaimed Jenks. "I remember you two! You were *Walker*'s pilots who went missing near Monterrey! How in God's name did you survive—and wind up here!"

"It's a long story, Commodore," Fred said, using the rank he remembered. "We were captured by Doms, but escaped"—he paused, considering—"a few weeks ago?" He looked at Kari as if for confirmation, but Kari could only stare at Lelaa and the spotless tablecloth between them. "The short version," Fred continued, "is that we swiped a fishing boat and made our way southwest until a Nancy spotted us and sent a seaplane tender-frigate to check us out. That's a great idea, by the way. Anyhow, they flew us here in two Nancys, and here we are."

"You should be in sick bay!" Selass exclaimed.

"They should have at least allowed you to freshen up!" Jenks agreed, annoyed.

"No, sir. We had to see you right away. We were afraid we'd be too late."

"Too late for what?" Jenks demanded.

"Too late to warn you, sir. We met some interesting folks and learned a lot of weird stuff—but we also picked up an awful lot of intel on the Doms. I guess that's why they chased us so hard." He glanced at Kari and took a breath. "But a bunch of what we found out, well, you're not going to like at all."

SPECIFICATIONS

American-Lemurian Ships and Equipment

USS *Walker* (DD-163)—(Initially under repair in Maa-ni-la). Wickes (Little) Class four-stack, or flush-deck, destroyer. Twin screw, steam turbines, 1,200 tons, 314' x 30'. Top speed (as designed): 35 knots. 112 officers and enlisted (current) including Lemurians (L). Armament: Main—3 x 4"-50 + 1 x 4.7" dual purpose. Secondary—4 x 25mm Type-96 AA, 4 x .50cal MG, 2 x .30 cal MG. 40-60 Mk-6 (or equivalent) depth charges for 2 stern racks, and 2 Y guns (with adapters). Proposed upgrades: Replacement of 4.7" dual purpose with 4"-50 dp, reinstallation of numbers one and two 21" triple-tube torpedo mounts, installation of impulse-activated catapult for PB-1B scout seaplane.

USS *Mahan*, (DD-102)—(Initially completing reconstruction at Baalkpan). Wickes Class four-stack, or flush-deck, destroyer. Twin screw, steam turbines. 960 tons, 264' x 30' (as rebuilt). Top speed estimated at about 25 knots. Rebuild has resulted in shortening, and removal of 2 funnels and 2 boilers. Otherwise, her armament and upgrades are the same as USS *Walker*.

USS *Santa Catalina* (CA-P-1)—(Protected cruiser). Formerly general cargo. 8,000 tons, 420' x 53', triple-expansion steam, oil fired, 10 knots (as reconstructed). Retains significant cargo/troop capacity, and has a seaplane catapult with recovery booms aft. 240 officers and enlisted. Armament: 4 x 5.5" mounted in armored casemate. 2 x 4.7" DP in armored tubs. 1 x 10" breech-loading rifle (20' length) mounted on spring-assisted pneumatic recoil pivot.

S-19—Former S Class submarine, rebuilt as a long-range MTB. 220' x 22', 780 tons. Twin 8-cylinder NELSECO direct-drive diesels, about 18 knots. Armament: 4 x 21" torpedo tubes (forward), 1 x 4"-50, 1 x 3"-23.

Carriers

USNRS (US Navy Reserve Ship) *Salissa "Big Sal"* **(CV-1)**—Aircraft carrier/tender, converted from seagoing Lemurian Home. Single screw, triple expansion steam, 13,000 tons, 1,009' x 200'. Armament: 2 x 5.5", 2 x 4.7" DP, 4 x twin-mount 25mm AA, 20 x 50 pdrs (as reduced), 50 aircraft.

USNRS *Arracca* **(CV-3)**—Aircraft carrier/tender converted from seagoing Lemurian Home. Single screw, triple expansion steam, 14,670 tons, 1,009' x 210'. Armament: 2 x 4.7" DP, 50 x 50 pdrs. 50 aircraft.

USS *Maaka-Kakja* **(CV-4)**—(Purpose-built aircraft carrier/tender). Specifications are similar to *Arracca*, but is capable of carrying upwards of 80 aircraft—with some stowed in crates.

USS *Baalkpan Bay* **(CV-5)**—(Purpose-built aircraft carrier/tender). First of a new class of smaller (850' x 150', 9,000 tons), faster (up to 15 knots), lightly armed (4 x Baalkpan Arsenal 4"-50 DP guns—2 amidships, 1 each forward and aft) fleet carriers that can carry as many aircraft as *Maaka-Kakja*.

"Small Boys"

Frigates (DDs):

USS *Donaghey* **(DD-2)**—Square rig sail only, 1,200 tons, 168' x 33' 200 officers and enlisted. Sole survivor of first new construction. Armament: 24 x 18 pdrs, Y gun and depth charges.

*Dowden Class—Square rig steamer, 1,500 tons, 12–15 knots, 185' x 34', 20 x 32 pdrs, Y gun and depth charges, 218 officers and enlisted. ****Haakar-Faask** Class—Square rig steamer, 15 knots, 1,600 tons, 200' x 36', 20 x 32 pdrs, Y gun and depth charges, 226 officers and enlisted. *****Scott Class**—Square rig steamer, 17 knots, 1,800 tons, 210' x 40', 20 x 50 pdrs, Y gun and depth charges, 260 officers and enlisted.

Corvettes (DEs): Captured Grik "Indiamen," primarily of the earlier (lighter) design. Razed to the gundeck, these are swift, agile, dedicated sailors with three masts and a square rig. 120–160' x 30–36', about 900 tons (tonnage varies depending largely on armament, which also varies from 10 to 24 guns that range in weight and bore diameter from 12–18 pdrs). Y gun and depth charges.

Auxiliaries: Still largely composed of purpose-altered Grik "Indiamen," small and large, and used as transports, oilers, tenders, and general cargo. A growing number of steam auxiliaries have joined the fleet, with dimensions and appearance similar to Dowden and Haakar-Faask Class DDs, but with lighter armament. Some fast clipper-shaped vessels are employed as long-range oilers. Fore and aft rigged feluccas remain in service as fast transports and scouts. *Respite Island* Class SPDs (self-propelled dry dock) are designed along similar lines to the new, purpose-built carriers—inspired by the massive seagoing Lemurian Homes. They are intended as rapid deployment, heavy-lift dry docks and for bulky transport.

USNRS—*Salaama-Na* Home—(Unaltered—other than by emplacement of 50 x 50 pdrs). 1,014' x 150', 8,600 tons. 3 tripod masts support semirigid "junklike" sails or "wings." Top speed about 6 knots, but capable of short sprints up to 10 knots using 100 long sweeps. In addition to living space in the hull, there are 3 tall pagodalike structures within the tripods that cumulatively accommodate up to 6,000 people. **Commodore (High Chief) Sor-Lomaak** (L)—Commanding.

Woor-Na **Home**—Lightly armed (ten 32 pdrs) heavy transport, specifications as above.

462 *Fristar* **Home**—Nominally, if reluctantly, Allied Home. Same basic specifications as *Salaama-Na*—as are all seagoing Lemurian Homes— but mounts only ten 32 pdrs.

Aircraft: P-40E Warhawk—AllisonV1710, V12, 1,150 hp. Max speed 360 mph, ceiling 29,000 ft. Crew: 1. Armament: up to 6 x .50-cal Browning machine guns, and up to 1,000-lb bomb. **PB-1B "Nancy"**—W/G type, in-line 4 cyl, 150 hp. Max speed 110 mph, max weight 1,900 lbs. Crew: 2. Armament: 400-lb bombs. **PB-2 "Buzzard"**—3 x W/G type, in-line 4 cyl, 150 hp. Max speed 80 mph, max weight 3,000 lbs. Crew: 2, and up to 6 passengers. Armament: 600-lb bombs. **PB-5 "Clipper"**—4 x W/G type, in-line 4 cyl, 150 hp. Max speed 90 mph, max weight 4,800 lbs. Crew: 3, and up to 8 passengers. Armament: 1,500-lb bombs. **PB-5B**—As above, but powered by 4 x MB 5 cyl, 254-hp radials. Max speed 125 mph, max weight 6,200 lbs. Crew: 3, and up to 10 passengers. Armament: 2,000-lb bombs. **P-1 Mosquito Hawk, or "Fleashooter"**—MB 5-cyl radial, 254 hp. Max speed 220 mph, max weight 1,220 lbs. Crew: 1. Armament: 2 x .45-cal Blitzer Bug machine guns. **P-1B**—As above, but configured for carrier ops.

Field Artillery: 6 pdr on split-trail "galloper" carriage—effective to about 1,500 yds, or 300 yds w/canister. **12 pdr** on stock-trail carriage— effective to about 1,800 yds, or 300 yds w/ canister. **3" mortar**—effective to about 800 yds. **4" mortar**—effective to about 1,500 yds.

Primary Small Arms: Sword, spear, crossbow, longbow, grenades, bayonet, smoothbore musket (.60 cal), rifled musket (.50 cal), Allin-Silva breech-loading rifled conversion (.50-80 cal), Allin-Silva breech-loading smoothbore conversion (20 gauge), 1911 Colt and copies (.45 ACP), Blitzer Bug SMG (.45 ACP).

Secondary Small Arms: 1903 Springfield (.30-06), 1898 Krag-Jorgensen (.30 US), 1918 BAR (.30-06), Thompson SMG (.45 ACP). A small number of other firearms are available.

Imperial Ships and Equipment

These fall in a number of categories, and though few share enough specifics to be described as classes, they can be grouped by basic sizes and capabilities. Most do share the fundamental similarity of being powered by steam-driven paddlewheels and a complete suit of sails.

Ships of the Line—About 180'–200' x 52'–58', 1,900–2,200 tons. 50–80 x 30 pdrs, 20 pdrs, 10 pdrs, 8 pdrs (8 pdrs are more commonly used as field guns by the Empire). Speed, about 8–10 knots. 400–475 officers and enlisted.

Frigates—About 160'–180' x 38'–44', 1,200–1,400 tons. 24–40 x 20–30 pdrs. Speed, about 13–15 knots. 275–350 officers and enlisted. Example—**HIMS** *Achilles,* 160' x 38', 1,300 tons, 26 x 20 pdrs.

Field Artillery—8 pdr on split-trail carriage—effective to about 1,500 yds, or 600 yds with grapeshot.

Primary Small Arms—Sword, smoothbore flintlock musket (.75 cal), bayonet, pistol (Imperial service pistols are of two varieties: cheaply made but robust Field and Sea Service weapons in .62 cal, and privately purchased officer's pistols that may be any caliber from about .40 to the service standard.

Republic Ships and Equipment

SMS *Amerika*—German ocean liner converted to a commerce raider in WWI. 669' x 74', 22,000 tons. Twin screw, 18 knots, 215 officers and enlisted, with space for 2,500 passengers or troops. Armament: 2 x 10.5 cm (4.1") SK L/40, 6 x MG08 (Maxim) machine guns, 8 x 57 mm.

Coastal and harbor defense vessels—specifications unknown. **Aircraft? Field artillery**—specifications unknown. **Primary small arms:** Sword; revolver; breech-loading, bolt-action, single-shot rifle (11.15 x 60R—.43 Mauser cal). **Secondary small arms:** M-1898 Mauser (8 x 57 cal.), Mauser and Luger pistols, mostly in 7.65 cal.

Enemy Warships and Equipment

Grik

ArataAmagi Class BBs (ironclad battleships)—800' x 100', 26,000 tons. Twin screw, double expansion steam, max speed 10 knots. Crew: 1,300. Armament: 32 x 100 pdrs, 30 x 3" AA mortars.

Azuma Class CAs (ironclad cruisers)—300' x 37', about 3,800 tons. Twin screw, double expansion steam, sail auxiliary, max speed 12 knots. Crew: 320. Armament: 20 x 40 or 14 x 100 pdrs. 4 x firebomb catapults.

Heavy "Indiaman" Class—Multipurpose transport/warships. 3 masts, square rig, sail only. 180' x 38', about 1,100 tons (tonnage varies depending largely on armament, which also varies from 0 to 40 guns of various weights and bore diameters). The somewhat crude standard for Grik artillery is 2, 4, 9, 16, 40, 60, and now up to 100 pdrs, although the largest "Indiaman" guns are 40s. These ships have been seen to achieve about 14 knots in favorable winds. Light "Indiamen" (about 900 tons) are apparently no longer being made.

Hidoiame **(Kagero Class)**—Japanese Imperial Navy Destroyer, 2,500 tons, 388' x 35', 35 knots, 240 officers and men. Armament: 6 x Type 3, 127-mm guns. 28 x Type 96 25-mm AA guns, 4 x 24" torpedo tubes.

Giorsh—Flagship of the Celestial Realm, now armed with 90 guns, from 16–40 pdrs.

Tatsuta—Kurokawa's double-ended paddle/steam yacht.

Aircraft: Hydrogen-filled rigid dirigibles or zeppelins. 300' x 48'; 5 x 2 cyl, 80-hp engines; max speed 60 mph. Useful lift 3,600 lbs. Crew: 16. Armament: 6 x 2 pdr swivel guns, bombs.

Field artillery: The standard Grik field piece is a 9 pdr, but 4s and 16s are also used, with effective ranges of 1,200, 800, and 1,600 yds, respectively. Powder is satisfactory, but windage is often excessive, resulting in poor accuracy. Grik "field" firebomb throwers fling 10- and 25-lb bombs, depending on the size, for a range of 200 and 325 yds, respectively.

Primary small arms: Teeth, claws, swords, spears, Japanese-style matchlock (tanegashima) muskets (roughly .80 cal).

Holy Dominion

Like Imperial vessels, Dominion warships fall in a number of categories that are difficult to describe as classes, but, again, can be grouped by size and capability. Almost all known Dom warships remain dedicated sailors, but their steam-powered transports indicate they have taken steps forward. Despite their generally more primitive design, Dom warships run larger and more heavily armed than their Imperial counterparts. **Ships of the Line**—About 200' x 60', 3,400–3,800 tons. 64–98 x 24 pdrs, 16 pdrs, 9 pdrs. Speed, about 7–10 knots. 470–525 officers and enlisted. **Heavy Frigates (Cruisers)—About** 170' x 50', 1,400–1,600 tons. 34–50 x 24 pdrs, 9 pdrs. Speed, about 14 knots. 290–370 officers and enlisted.

Aircraft: The Doms have no aircraft yet, but employ "dragons," or Grikbirds, for aerial attack.

Field Artillery: 9 pdrs on split-rail carriages—effective to about 1,500 yds, or 600 yds with grapeshot.

Primary small arms: Sword, pike, plug bayonet, flintlock (patilla style) musket (.69 cal). Only officers and cavalry use pistols, which are often quite ornate and of various calibers.